THE

JOHN WOOD CASE

Ruth Suckow

THE

JOHN WOOD

CASE

A novel

NEW YORK: THE VIKING PRESS

FIRST PUBLISHED IN 1959 BY
THE VIKING PRESS, INC.
625 MADISON AVENUE, NEW YORK 22, N. Y.

M B G

PRINTED IN THE U.S.A.

TO

FERNER NUHN

I wish to express thanks to
Maud Hart Lovelace
for her helpful reading of this manuscript.

PART

ONE

CHAPTER

I

PHILIP SIDNEY WOOD got up on a bright May morning. The house seemed filled with sunlight. In the Fairview high school, in which he was a senior, Philip had much the standing of a youthful king; but he looked forward with exultant joy to graduation in June, after which he would "go out into the great world." This whole springtime was glorified by the coming Commencement.

Fairview had been in existence since before the days of the Civil War, but at first was not much more than the trading center of a Midwestern farming section. Now in the opening years of the twentieth century it had become a thriving town of more than two thousand people. Some of its streets and buildings had begun to look old. But in other ways the town still showed its newness. There was no city sewer system as yet—only the best houses had bathrooms and indoor toilets, the owners having put in their own plumbing and cesspools. The John Wood house—a medium-sized white-painted house, standing last on a short street that ended in a bushy ravine—was not among the few considered the best houses, but John Wood had gone to the expense of putting in a nice bathroom because "Minnie needed it." Philip tiptoed in stocking feet into this bathroom. With scarcely conscious self-satisfaction he looked at his fresh face in the mirror, enjoying every moment of the recently begun shaving process. Clean, bright, with pleasantly stinging cheeks and damply combed hair, he returned to his room.

Philip's room was a boy's room, plainly furnished, but with things he himself particularly cherished: the framed photographs of the first-grade pupils on the steps of the old Central School; of his high-school class, the boys with parted hair and stiff collars, the girls with varying heights and kinds of pompadours; his debating team; the summer baseball team; his class of boys at the Congregational church; the Meserve family shown against a cloudy background; and his own family group taken when Philip was twelve. The red and gold FAIRVIEW H. S. felt pennant he had fastened up with gold-headed tacks above the kitchen table which he used as a study table. The shelves which he had made from nice pieces of board given him by Mr. Meserve at the lumber yard held his own books; the family books were in the large, stately combination desk and bookcase—a legacy from Philip's grandparents—in the front room downstairs, and a few others were in his mother's little set of bookshelves in her room. Philip's narrow walnut bed, an heirloom, was covered with a dark blue and white spread handwoven in her girlhood by Philip's great-grandmother, old Grandma Terrill, and was probably the only thing of intrinsic value among Philip's possessions. But Philip did not know that. He loved his room.

After Commencement he would have to leave it. That time was not here—although it was coming. Standing before his dresser, with his face uptilted because the mirror was small and hung rather high, Philip felt throughout his nerves a singing expectation. Confident in his family life, which was closely knit and yet allowed him freedom, Philip felt his happiness made sharper, even poignant, by the fact of his mother's frail health. This put an edge of precariousness upon what was otherwise unalloyed security. But even in this precariousness Philip found a challenge. He was a boy raised in the church, and he often thought, quite naturally, in scriptural terms. One phrase came to him now—"Not to destroy but to fulfill." He—the only son born of a wonderful love between two wonderful people, a love which had overcome difficult obstacles—was to fulfill that love by what he did and became in the world.

The marriage of John Wood and Minnie Terrill was one of Fairview's renowned romances. Gertrude Schilling, who taught the eighth grade (her father, Ferdinand Schilling, an old-style German intellectual and free-thinker, kept the shoe-repair shop), compared it to the love story of the Brownings—"and it took place right here in our town." Minnie had been ill with what was then called "consumption," when John Wood, a newcomer, had married her; she had not been expected to live another year. But after twenty years she was still living, and the couple had this eminently satisfactory son.

Philip got the breakfast on Sunday mornings. He tiptoed downstairs, opened doors, put up shades, then went on through the dining room and out into the kitchen. The light rain of early morning sparkled on the grass of the neat back yard and on the fresh early lettuce in the garden.

Philip always took his mother's Sunday breakfast up to her bedroom; she was the only matron in town who had the privilege of breakfasting in bed. Later on Minnie might come downstairs in her soft challis wrapper, the white cashmere shawl that had been a gift from Mrs. Merriam about her frail shoulders. But she stayed in bed on Sunday mornings until she felt entirely ready to get up—on orders from her two men. Philip and his father ate their breakfast at the kitchen table.

But why not eat out on the porch this morning? There would be time. They kept an old table on the back porch, covered with a blue and white oilcloth which Philip now washed off with a damp cloth, whistling just above his breath and thinking the words to himself: ". . . oh, what a foretaste . . . glory divine . . ."

John Wood received a moderately good salary as assistant to

Colonel Merriam in the Merriam Title, Insurance, and Farm
Loan Company; but following Minnie's inheritance of the
Terrill farm, he had managed to add various comforts, besides
the bathroom, to the house. The sale of the Terrill place did
not bring in such a sum as the sale of Iowa land would have
done in later years. But "it was a help." In the kitchen there
was a good easy-to-light three-burner oil stove as well as the
range. But Philip, when he had time—as he did this morning
—liked to start the fire in the range with the crisp kindling
sticks and curly, clean-smelling shavings he had brought home
from the lumber yard the day before. Philip's closest friend
was Lyle Meserve, whose father, Henry Meserve, owned the
Fairview Lumber Company. Both boys worked for Mr.
Meserve on Saturday mornings. Then Mr. Meserve let them
take home odd-sized chunks of wood and all sorts of kindling
material for their respective kitchens in a big wheelbarrow.
Things tasted better cooked over the wood fire; a slight flavor
of wood smoke from around the rim of the stove lids seemed
to get into the food and even the coffee.

Philip, still humming, prepared a dainty breakfast for his
mother but put out a man-sized meal for his father and himself,
with bacon and fresh eggs, thick slices of Mrs. Dissendorfer's
good bread, wild-grape jelly, cream from Tommy and Phoebe
Hardcastle's Guernsey cow, and coffee. The smell of the coffee—always the best brand, because Minnie couldn't start the
day without good coffee—come to a boil in the granite coffee
pot of mottled blue and white, was the call to breakfast.

John Wood came into the kitchen, well scrubbed, like
Philip, dressed for Sunday school with the exception of collar,
necktie, and shoes. The starched narrow white shirtband was
fastened around his strong neck with a gold collar button; he
had on brown felt slippers. But John Wood's appearance could
stand even this particular kind of Sunday-morning disarray—
or lack of array.

"Good morning, son." He spoke in a dignified, grave tone,
but pleasant.

"Oh, hello, Papa." Philip then asked the customary question, but with real concern. "How's Mama?"

"She had quite a fair night's rest. She was awake off and on, though, coughed quite a little. We must try to give her all the time upstairs we can."

John usually said that. Philip nodded.

"Look here! Table set out on the porch, eh?"

"It's such a swell morning, I thought we might as well make the most of it."

"Fine idea," John Wood said with approval.

Yet as he drew out the heavy kitchen chair and sat down, Philip heard him sigh. Philip turned to glance at him, wondering if his mother's night might have been less restful than his father had said. But John Wood's face seen in profile kept its usual grave calm. A certain stony look of the drooped eyelid caught Philip's attention for a moment—but only a moment. Philip was aware of his father's need for patience, and deeply respected his constant exercise of it and his apparently boundless capacity. Did love make people long-suffering, as St. Paul said in Corinthians I, 13—their minister's favorite reading in the Sunday morning service? Would he himself ever achieve it? Philip thought, but would not have spoken, these words. He turned his eyes away from his father's unselfconscious profile. He accepted and held in a kind of reverence his father's habitual reticence. He never tried to penetrate it.

John Wood was an exceptionally handsome man—the best-looking man in town, many people said. The young Hungarian-born photographer, Mr. Rakosi, had more flash; with his black curly hair, brilliant eyes, twisted mustachios, he was cutting a swathe in Fairview. The unattached young women were, most of them, competing for his attentions. But had a community vote been taken, John Wood, even though married and in his forties, with little doubt would have come out first as to looks. He was of good height, strongly built, with almost perfectly regular features, thick brown hair and mustache, the hair having just enough wave, and large blue-gray eyes. Then, too, John bore that look of quiet fortitude. Women all liked him—he was "so good to his wife." But men liked him also. Although a man who kept his own counsel among others as well as at home, he had a pleasant quality about him. People liked to come into Colonel Merriam's office because of John Wood.

There were women in Fairview who pitied "poor John"— and "poor Philip"—because Minnie Wood didn't do what they considered real housekeeping. Of course she was sickly, but didn't they too have their troubles? "She has things pretty easy."

The pity was more than thrown away. John and Philip enjoyed their home. They got things done, too. Philip didn't in the least object to helping, had done so since he was a small boy, and it was impossible to call Philip Wood sissy. He had always been large and strong, excelled in games, was the crack player on the summer baseball team, didn't go out strenuously for basketball only because he himself had decided he couldn't give the time. "Not that I couldn't make the team—I think!" Philip said with disarming confidence, and he was probably right! But he preferred debating. Other boys accepted Philip's firm, easy "I'll have to leave you now, fellows, got some dusting and stuff to do at home." Most boys would have been embarrassed, but not Philip!

The Woods kept no regular help. The tall, dark, aristocratic-featured Mrs. Lavina Randolph, the only colored woman in Fairview, came in to wash, iron and clean, and do the heavier part of putting up fruit and vegetables and making preserves. Minnie excelled in jams and jellies, unusual kinds such as rose-geranium and green-grape jam. With her delicacy and her feminine accomplishments, Minnie Wood was more like the ladies in the South for whom Lavina Randolph had worked as a girl, and who—although Lavina said she "had it better" in Fairview and never wanted to leave—were still her models. Bertha Bisbee came spring and fall to do the main part of the sewing. Minnie herself did exquisite hand sewing and darning,

and made point lace; the little handkerchiefs which she gave
her friends for Christmas were marvels of daintiness. Mrs.
Dissendorfer, who had the bakery and home delicatessen shop
downtown, made extra pies and "fried cakes" for the Woods,
as well as bread and biscuits; she would do anything for Mr.
Wood, who was so nice to her and looked after her little property. Minnie's own rose-flavored white cake was famous. John
and Philip cooked the meat, and Philip got the vegetables
ready. All in all, the Wood family lived well.

The house had something few others in Fairview possessed
at that time in any such degree; and if any did have a touch of
it, it was because of young daughters, soon to marry and leave
home. Minnie Wood added to that basically small-town house,
in structure little different from others, an element of elusive
charm—going lightly about in her ruffled or lace-trimmed
wrappers and her soft little slippers, with her trailing shawls
or scarfs. She could coax difficult plants to bloom, lilies and
gloxinias. People liked to give Minnie pretty things. Her handwoven work basket came from the Philippines—a missionary
friend had brought it—and her darning egg of pale, hard ash
wood had been made for her by an itinerant laborer, an Eng-
lishman, who for a few months had been her father's hired
man. The silver thimble, with its encrusted garland of tiny
roses, had come from Italy, a long-ago Christmas present from
one of the Merriam girls. There were gifts from Mrs. Merriam
too, antiques of real beauty and value, which in the ordinary
course would have gone to the Merriam daughters, or to the
daughter-in-law "if things had been different."

Philip took up the tray. He had set it with the dishes his
mother cared for most, the fragile plate, gold-rimmed, which
had been one of Mrs. Merriam's heirlooms; the cup painted
with colored pansies, a souvenir of Vera Meserve's period of
fierce devotion to china painting; the little spoon with the
twisted gold handle tipped with a calla lily, from Miss Gertrude Schilling; the small damask napkin which Mae Meserve

had embroidered with an artistically formed "W." Minnie
loved these things both for what they were and for their associations. Philip had also picked two of the morning-glory blossoms, a rose and a blue, and put them in a tiny, crusty white
vase that looked as if it had been sugared over.

"Don't wait for me, Papa. I'll warm up my stuff when I get
back. Don't let yours get cold."

Philip carried the tray carefully but easily up the narrow
carpeted stairs with the rail at the side, and over to the doorway into his mother's room.

This bedroom was the largest in the house, which did not
mean very large: the massive old bedroom set of black walnut
—bed, dresser, commode, and table—filled up considerable of
the space. The set had belonged to Minnie's family and, although out of fashion at the moment, had its own dignity. The
low cane rocker, with its ornate pattern of curlicues, its silky
ecru cushions tied on seat and back with ribbons, was Minnie's
own. The side windows looked out across the trimly kept lawn
with its bushes and flowers, to the rim of the ravine; the curtains were of sheer dimity.

Philip thought it a fine room, even at this morning hour,
with the slept-in bed and a few of his parents' belongings scattered about (not many, however, for John Wood was a very
orderly man). For Philip there was a special aura about this
room because of its place in the love of his parents. But the
attractiveness was centered in the small person of his mother
in the wide, old-fashioned bed. Her long-sleeved white nain-
sook nightgown with embroidered ruffles had been put on
fresh last night after her bath. Her straight black hair, parted
in the middle, was brushed back from her ears and left hanging like a girl's. She did not have much of it; when it was done
up it made only a small coil at the back of her neck. Some people considered Minnie Wood "a homely woman." (They also
thought she put on airs and wasn't so delicate as she pretended,
that she got John and Philip to wait on her.) No one could say
that she was pretty. Yet with her fragile figure and girl's waist,

her little head with the parted and smoothly drawn hair, the broad brow, snub nose, wide expressive mouth, chin small but firm—most of all her black-lashed, bright gray eyes—there was "something about her." There were other people who admired her extravagantly. Gertrude Schilling did, and all four of the Meserve girls. They said she wasn't "just like everybody else." "*Spirituelle*," Mr. Rakosi had once called her—and then had spent fifteen animated minutes trying to explain to some highly interested women precisely what he thought the word implied. "No, no, not *spiritual*. You sink so, but she is not sat." Minnie's husband and son, who were so much with her, knew all her physical troubles with intimate realism, yet felt this hard-to-define quality of delicate yet intensely individual charm in her. She seemed at the same time a little girl, almost doll-like, and a plain, worn New England woman who had endured suffering and again and again had risen above it.

Minnie was already sitting up in bed when Philip stopped a moment at the door to be sure his mother was ready for him. Her nicely brushed hair was black against the white pillows, and her eyes, in their dark sockets, seemed just as black. She smiled and made a little welcoming gesture with one hand as Philip crossed the room. Minnie held her face to be kissed, lifting her small chin with a gallant air—but then she noticed the flowers on the tray.

"Oh, Philip! Our morning glories!" she said in her slightly husky, not strong, yet strangely vibrant voice, with a lower timbre than one expected from her small body. Her eyes grew big, and she lifted both hands eagerly.

"They were suddenly out this morning."

"They *are* so bright and fresh—even if they don't last long."

Philip held the tray and looked down at his mother's expressive face as she just touched one of the blooms. He was gratified at the success of his little offering. Then he set the tray on the walnut bedside table and stooped to kiss his mother's cheek as she lay back once more with a sigh. In the deeply sculptured sockets of her eyes the skin had a worn look, with fine wrinkles and discoloration in the hollows below the black eyelashes. Yet, expert as he was at judging her condition, Philip thought that her face had a more rested look than it often did, as if she had had one of her better nights.

Philip put his hands under his mother's thin shoulders and drew her back against the support of the high, carved headboard. He straightened the two big pillows at her back, which were still silky smooth from the beautiful laundering Mrs. Randolph had given them.

"I do give you so much trouble, Philip!"

"You can pay me back by cleaning up everything on this tray."

"I'll try, I'll try!" Minnie said, with the note of vibrancy in her husky voice. "It won't be your fault if I don't; everything looks so lovely."

Philip was about to tell her that she needn't eat the morning glories. But she sighed again, then looked up, not so much at as past Philip, to the window where the light struck the sheer curtains. Another light, which Philip had sometimes seen before, played on his mother's face, shining in her large gray eyes and bringing a little, almost secret lift to the corners of her wide mouth.

"You know," Minnie said, "it isn't *this* food I live on, lovely as it is, Philip! It's another kind of food in which I'm so blessed. I needn't tell you what it is, or the strength I get from it. That's what I thank my Heavenly Father for, every night and every morning, and my husband and son too, if the truth were known."

If Mr. Rakosi had been present now, he could have pointed triumphantly to an example of what he meant by the word *spirituelle*, for Minnie's oddly beautiful face held this quality just now. To Philip it seemed to answer his own feelings this morning and to give an added glow to the sunlight that lit the bedroom.

But Minnie's expression quickly changed, and she said, "Oh,

Philip, your own breakfast is getting cold! Do run down and eat it with your father."

"You're sure everything's all right?"

"Look, I'm eating!" his mother said playfully.

Philip grinned and turned with a sense of lightheartedness. He ran, boyishly clumping, down the carpeted stairs to the kitchen. Soon he was out again in the May morning.

CHAPTER

2

AT ABOUT a quarter past nine John and Philip Wood set off for Sunday school. Later Mrs. Merriam would stop by with her small surrey to take Minnie with her to church.

The two Woods were a fine-looking pair as they walked along side by side. In the last year Philip had grown to be nearly as tall as his father. Strongly built as he was, however, his shoulders and his whole figure still looked boyishly unfledged when seen beside John's; and his face (so much admired by the high-school girls!) did not have his father's regularity of features. His eyes were gray and rounder in shape, more like his mother's; they glanced about with a clear, shining confidence different from John Wood's calm, inscrutable gaze; and his nose, while not Minnie's snub, did not repeat that line of almost perfect straightness which made John Wood's profile classic. But he had his own youthful brightness, boldness, and fine coloring.

The trees were freshly leafed out this morning, the planted elms and maples of the prairie town. The heavy timber near Fairview lay mostly around the river banks about a half-mile or so away. Some of the farms had good stands of trees, native and planted—notably Deacon Kruse's wood—but the finest timber was in Merriam's Grove. The early-morning rain had brought down a few shining buds which still lay untrodden on the damp sidewalk. Small sky-colored pools were left near the crossings, and there was a fresh, cool, earth-leaf-and-air smell everywhere.

"There should be a good attendance today," John Wood observed.

The bell to be heard ringing was that of the Methodist church—the largest and newest in town, a brick building—and it had to do for all Fairview's five churches. The Lutherans were engaged in raising money for a bell. The Congregational church (of which the Woods were members), although of frame, was substantial and well kept, painted last summer a shining white with black trim. Tommy Hardcastle, who two years ago had moved in from the country, made a scrupulous janitor, and besides, had his wife Phoebe to look the place over every week and help with the dusting and polishing. Phoebe's meticulousness led her to do this even though she didn't get paid for it. However, it saved the Hardcastles from having to "give"—that is, give money.

The Woods went up the six front steps and entered the cool, bare vestibule together. John Wood took off his Sunday hard Cady hat and Philip his best gray cloth cap; they hadn't got out their straw hats yet.

John Wood went at once to the front of the auditorium, and Philip stayed at the back of the room to sit with his class. He was the only one there at first. But a few moments later he slid over to make room for his friend Lyle Meserve. The two boys liked to get in some talk together before the others came and the Sunday school opened. Lyle was slighter, so fair as to seem almost colorless—a nice-looking boy but not strikingly good-looking as was Philip Wood. When the two boys took out girls, the girl asked by Philip was considered to have a little the better of it—this in spite of the fact that the Meserves were "worth more" than the Woods. Their big new house, all rounded porches and balconies outside and light-colored

highly polished hardwood inside, occupied a lot and a half on
the best of the newer streets and, partly because of the vigorous hospitality of Mrs. Meserve and partly because of the general attractiveness of the four girls and the candy they made,
was highly popular. Philip rather than Lyle was the young
monarch of the high school; but Lyle could go into his father's
thriving business if he cared to, while Philip would have to
make his own way. Each of the boys in himself was aware of
his own advantages; that may have been one thing that helped
them to get on so well together. Will Cowie also came from a
leading family, and was quite good-looking, got good grades,
but somehow he didn't rank with the other two.

Philip and Lyle had only a minute or so to themselves before
the others began coming, which kept them sliding along in the
pew. The class of boys their age was unusually large and active—considered outstanding, in fact, and all the more so since
Mr. Storm, the young minister, had undertaken to act as
teacher. Philip, Lyle, Will Cowie, Howard Rechtner, Mort
Hungerford—a wonderful group of boys, but Mr. Storm
counted most of all on Philip. The boys talked with loud ani-
mation until they heard the tap of the superintendent's bell;
then they quickly got settled in the long back pew and were
quiet—much quieter than they might otherwise have been,
because Philip's father was the superintendent. Philip and Lyle
felt themselves bound to help keep control. During these few
minutes the room had pretty much filled up.

"The Sunday school will please come to order." John Wood
spoke in his usual quiet tone and waited gravely for the little
ones to get seated. He needed no help; as someone had once
said, his presence was enough. Jerry Storm, the minister (his
name was actually Jeremiah, but he had let no one know that
—except that Vera Meserve had somehow found it out), by
comparison appeared a nervous, overactive youth, with his
thin, freckled face and unruly hair, his intense light eyes.
Strangers coming into the church might well have mistaken

John Wood for the pastor—and in fact that had happened. ("I suppose that gentleman is your pastor," a visitor had once said in a tone of approval.) Although John's clothes were not ministerial, there was a correctness about them and about John himself with his well-brushed hair and trim mustache; while Mrs. Latham and her sister, Almeda Blanchard, from whom the young minister was at present renting a room, often were in distress, wondering if they shouldn't tell Mr. Storm they had the iron right at hand and would be *so* glad to press his suit before Sunday or the Wednesday-night prayer meeting if he would just allow them—but they were shy. There were men in the congregation who dressed better than John Wood. Austin Cowie wore a tailor-made Prince Albert to church. John had worn this dark best suit a long time; he seldom bought much of anything for himself. His shoes had been twice resoled by Ferdinand Schilling, yet the black tips shone faultlessly. His white shirt and Sunday collar seemed to have an extra-immaculate luster. (Of course, having a superior laundress like Mrs. Randolph helped. She could pick and choose what families she would work for.) The slate-blue corded-silk necktie, John had worn for three years on Sundays; it had been a Christmas present from Minnie. But John Wood took extremely good care of everything of which he had charge. Colonel Merriam, at the office, stuck his papers into odd boxes and pigeonholes where only he would think of looking for them; but all that John handled there was in apple-pie order.

Philip kept his eyes on his father, looking with open, artless satisfaction at that dignified figure. But when John Wood turned aside to speak to Mr. Storm, a kind of stony sadness showed again in the droop of the eyelid. No lines were discernible around his large, fine eyes. Perhaps the slight oddness consisted in there being no marks of time, and yet the eyelids—the blue eyes themselves—did not seem young. But John Wood had a load to carry. His strength and control and steadiness were the wonderful part. The impression—fleeting and ambig-

uous—that had troubled Philip just now as it had earlier in the
morning was gone when his father turned to the school and
showed his full front face.

John Wood tapped the bell again, said some few pleasant
words about being glad to see this large Sunday-school attendance on this beautiful May morning, along with the flowers
"some of you" must have been finding in the woods—nodding
at the tall glass vases filled with red columbines and bluebells,
one at each side of the pulpit.

Then: "We will open our morning exercises by singing
Number Twenty-four, 'Bringing in the Sheaves.' Mae will
play through the stanza first for us on the piano, and then let
us all join heartily in the singing. This is a hymn you all know.
'Bringing in the Sheaves.' Number Twenty-four in the green
book."

Mae Meserve, the oldest of Lyle's four sisters—a very pretty
girl of twenty-three with curling golden-brown hair—struck
up brightly on the upright piano used for the Sunday-school
music; the organ was reserved for the church service. She
played the stanza through with vigor, with a better touch than
the piano itself merited. Then, bending her head so that the
flowers bobbed on her new hat of lacy straw, in the effort to
convey some of her own musical enthusiasm and sense of tim-
ing to the Sunday school at large, she began the hymn again,
and after a preliminary dragging and uncertainty, which Mae
wouldn't allow to continue, the school sang "heartily." Mae
Meserve, home only two years from the four-year course at
Willard College School of Music, had full charge of the music
in both church and Sunday school. Vera Meserve, the red-
gold-haired sister next younger, taught the Primary Department. Mr. Meserve was the church treasurer. Mrs. Meserve
taught the Young Ladies' Class and was president of the Missionary Society. Only John Wood did as much in the church
as the Meserves. To the Reverend Jerry Storm, a family such
as the Meserves seemed an unhoped-for joy and marvel to find
in his congregation.

The minister stood a little aside during the singing, not wanting to look at Mae too obviously—thinking also of his Sunday-school lesson, which dealt today with the Book of Job, with which he himself had had much trouble when he was the age of the boys in his class. He was not afraid of sharp questioning, believed in giving his Sunday-school class his "best thinking," and could not have answered in the rigid and sonorous stereotypes with which his father and grandfather had often silenced him. Yet he had been raised in the iron grip of those stereotypes and could not help feeling himself to be a sinner even though he did not believe that he *was* sinning when he spoke the truth as he saw it; quite otherwise. His own rebellion against his father's and grandfather's rock-ribbed Calvinism was scored so painfully into his memory that he had to brace himself against his class hour. Yet why expect trouble from boys like Philip Wood, Lyle Meserve, Mort Hungerford? —boys so intelligent and decent and so well brought up that Jerry Storm, used to the rough conditions of his own boyhood in a scarcely settled Western region, was always astonished, when he stood up to teach them, at his own present good fortune.

He was astonished at his whole situation: a few short years out of seminary, through which he had worked his own way —and then he had been called to be pastor of a well-established church of more than two hundred members in a town like Fairview. The town had been settled largely by New England people and still kept what was spoken of as "an atmosphere of culture." This whole Sunday school was wonderful to Jerry Storm; he looked forward to every phase of it after his good Sunday-morning breakfast, which he was served solicitously by Mrs. Latham and Miss Blanchard. Having a talented girl like Mae Meserve willing and even eager to take in hand all the music, a man like John Wood to act as superintendent! If he hadn't had his class of boys, it seemed to Jerry that he would scarcely have been needed at the Sunday school.

To be sure, there were a few difficulties: two or three of the boys and girls reported to be "getting a little wild"; in the church itself, a little fussing about the way Tommy Hardcastle manipulated the furnace, occasional tearful outbursts from women who had been lacerated by Caddie Rathbun's ungovernable tongue. ("It must be good for a boy to have a mother always on the point of death!" had been one of Mrs. Rathbun's more amusing remarks, directed, in this case, at Minnie Wood.) Deacon Kruse—once both a pillar of strength and a dreaded monster of oversight, at least to the young people—was old now, a mere attender, and, sitting with his blue eyes fixed on the preacher, his aged hand held to his ear, an interesting and stimulating one. So far, Jerry had not had a run-in with Caddie Rathbun; somehow, he did not know why, he was in her good graces, perhaps because he was too inexperienced to be afraid of her. His own nervous fears that his sermons would not be lofty enough, or that he himself would prove not well read enough to come up to Mrs. Merriam's expectation, had fizzled out: Mrs. Merriam had been exceptionally kind, had listened to him, counseled with him, lent him all of Emerson's *Essays*. He had fine men in his church: Deacon Kruse, Henry Meserve, J. T. Rechtner; above all, John Wood. Austin Cowie was a strong member. But Jerry Storm had never before met such women! They were a revelation to him. Mrs. Merriam would have been enough by herself to elevate any congregation. But there were also Mrs. Meserve and the girls; his landlady and her sister, both devout and kindly; Miss Caroline Kruse, whom he regarded as a saint; Mrs. Wood, whose health did not allow her to do much church work but who was a woman of a type new to Jerry, so delicate and unusual. When he called on Mrs. Wood as pastor he always felt with humility that he had received far more than he had given. The young man was in love with Minnie Wood in an ethereal way quite different from the glowing human desire he had grown to feel for Mae Meserve.

Jerry knew that neither the church nor the town, unusual as each seemed to him, was perfect. Curly Meems—was he really

"getting that Blaney girl into trouble," as the minister had
heard by chance? How closely did he know Austin Cowie,
whom he relied on as one of his trustees and a heavy supporter
of the church? Jerry realized he felt little intimacy with
Austin, and did not really care to have very much, to tell the
truth! Austin, successful businessman that he was, was not a
type that interested Jerry especially. A few people spoke dryly
of Austin Cowie, suggesting that he "wasn't quite all that he
seemed." But Jerry could not inquire into all the gossip that
came to him, and there were always those who envied a successful man. He remembered too well the harsh old dictatorial
pastor of his youth, who had respected no privacy and had
helped drive some of the young people into sheer rebellion.
Jerry had an aversion to prying, and many of these things
were never stated directly to the minister, but came as innu-
endo, with blank looks and expressive silences.

He came back from the far drift of his thought to hear the
singing, led by the graceful but eager movements of Mae's
pretty person seen from the back, her flying hands, the charming hat bobbing slightly as did its flowers, so that Mae kept trying to put up one hand and push in her hatpins. . . .

> *"We shall come re-*joi-*cing*
> *Bringing in the sheaves."*

The song ended in a glow. Then, after more of the familiar
little opening ritual, which all went off well on this fine morning, the younger pupils and those of the Primary Department,
in their freshly starched Sunday clothes and efficiently shep-
herded by Vera Meserve, marched out to the additional room
known as "the Sunday-school room," although the older pupils
settled into their various places in the main auditorium.

Jerry Storm, all his faculties sharply alert now, hurried up
the aisle to his class, which was waiting for him and filling up
one section of the long back pew. He met Philip Wood's shining attentiveness and the nice, light, completely untroubled
eyes of Lyle Meserve; Howard Rechtner's brown eyes, misted

over with sensuous dreaming (he had just pulled his gaze away from Ione Meserve); all seeming fully confident that their young pastor could make Job's troubles credible and comprehensible to their so-little-experienced youth. To be sure, Curly's audacious eyes stared with satiric defiance, and Boysie Wheeler looked ahead with a kind of emptiness. The vigorous discussion developed none of the particular difficulties that Jerry—it seemed—would never stop expecting. The individual traits and circumstances of the boys came out interestingly in their comments. Lyle thought that Job had "done a good job" in building up his prosperity, which enabled him to benefit everybody around him, and couldn't see any point in God's testing him with all those trials, but was glad Job came through; while Philip maintained that a certain personal knowledge of suffering "brought out more." Will Cowie stated that nobody, even Job, ought to question God's reasons. (Here Curly idly winked, but Jerry thought it better not to take notice.) Jerry got so absorbed in his talk with the boys that he felt almost ready to throw aside his sermon and preach on "The Lesson of Job: What Is It?" But he was too inexperienced a preacher to dare to speak wholly extemporaneously.

As he went up to the leather-upholstered pastor's chair on the slightly raised pulpit platform (he still felt bashful about occupying that, to him, imposing chair) and sat listening to Mae's beautiful prelude on the small pipe organ (Bach's "Jesu, Joy of Man's Desiring"), as he thought of how Mae's musical training was due to her father's being well able to pay for it, Jerry was half ready to side with her young brother Lyle and consider it questionable that Job had not been left undisturbed with his family and flocks in his fruitful abundance. The cleanly sunlit room, with its well-polished pews and its (in his modest eyes) fine, well-to-do people, spoke eloquently of the virtue of pleasant places. Jerry Storm liked the town and the church so much, both had already taken such hold on his affections, that he almost feared in himself the restless spirit and probing, prodding conscience, which at times made him feel that he ought to seek a harder kind of pastorate in which he would be "more closely tested" and "more needed." The few things which pricked him with shame at this moment were that he had not yet succeeded in "waking up" Boysie Wheeler and had not made any impression on Curly Meems, with that cynical little smile just twisting his lip. But Jerry still hoped to "reach Curly through other means," rather than confront him directly with the stories that would first have to be verified— that Curly got liquor with a vaguely defined "pool-hall bunch," and about "girls' being mixed up in it." Then, too, Jerry and the church had done little as yet for Fairview's one open drinker, Dan Postel. (Fairview was a "dry town," through the use of local option.) Last night Dan had again been heard roaring and singing along the street and this morning had been picked up in a sodden sleep on the walk leading to the Rechtners' front porch. Dan's son, Dell, merely shifted his gaze when Jerry invited him to join some of the activities of "our young people," although Jerry had hinted that if "clothes or anything of that kind stand in the way, we can take care of that for you." He had not been able to persuade the darkly dignified Mrs. Randolph to attend a church service, or even a church supper, or get her boy Jason into the Primary. Jerry knew that Mrs. Randolph would be welcome, since Mrs. Merriam set the tone, and she believed that all people were alike children of God. But—"Thank you, sir, I guess I won't be there."

Philip and Lyle had much left to talk about when Sunday school was over, but tore themselves apart. Philip was one of the two ushers. He had tried to get Lyle to be the other, but Lyle wouldn't promise to be regular, so Philip's partner instead was Will Cowie. Lyle thought it a particularly good joke, when he did stay for church with his family, to follow Philip with immense solemnity to the pew where the Meserves always sat.

Philip took his place at one side of the door opening into the vestibule, Will at the other; Philip with just a little consciousness that the girls coming in had their devices for getting him as usher—not that they didn't like Will.

His father came up to him, said, "I'll wait outside for Mama."

Philip nodded. But he wondered why his mother and Mrs. Merriam should not yet have come. Mrs. Merriam was in the habit of being on time. Mae was well through the prelude when the Merriam carriage drove up, the two-seated surrey drawn by the two brown horses known all over town as Bro and Sis. Philip was escorting old Mr. and Mrs. Sayles to a seat well forward. It was not until he turned to come back that he saw the Merriams enter the auditorium. He had known, of course, that Mrs. Merriam was expecting her son Bradford and his daughter Elaine as usual, but not before summer, since Bradford Merriam taught at a college in New York City. The fresh color in Philip's cheeks suddenly became a flush, and his eyes shone more brightly as he courteously led the Merriams to their pew—still maintained by Mrs. Merriam as a family pew, although most of the time she sat there alone. The Colonel was not a church-goer.

When Philip went on up the aisle again his father and mother were just settling into one of the pews at the back of the room, chosen because of Philip, so that he could keep an eye on the door for late comers. His mother had spread her skirts to take up all the room she could, so that there would be less danger of any other person's making it impolite for the Woods not to give up the place they were trying to hold for Philip. After the close of the first hymn—"Crown Him with Many Crowns," which rang out strongly on this bright morning—Philip considered it safe to slip in beside his father, next to the aisle, but he was alert to get up at any minute.

Philip scarcely heard the responsive reading, even the prayer. Only now and then he caught a sentence. He realized for the first time that—as his mother had been saying—he had not many Sundays left at home. He would not be in Fairview even during the summer. Philip too, as he glanced about, felt keenly the qualities of this well-known room—its simplicity and substantiality, the shine of the woodwork which Phoebe Hardcastle had no doubt spent most of yesterday afternoon going over. The Wood family was so firmly entrenched in the Congregational church that Philip felt as if it were theirs in almost the same degree as their own home. He could remember when the building was put up, when he and Will (then "Willie") and Lyle and Mort had gone all over town to back doors, selling kindling wood picked up in the lumber yard, so that they could contribute—little boys in short pants. . . . The Gothic-pointed windows were open from top and bottom, showing a stretch of yard in which the grass had taken strong hold by now, as well as the healthy-looking maple trees along the sidewalk. The bluebells and columbines, mingled with maidenhair ferns in the two glass vases, made Philip think of the woods, of the muddy smell and flow of the Upper Wahkonsa River, on which he skated in winter and in which he had gone swimming in summer, always with the promise to his mother to watch out for mud holes. . . . He remembered the little boy, Tracy Pendleton, who had got drowned in a mud hole. . . . Merriam's Grove—but he kept his dreams from the Elysium of Merriam's Grove. . . .

Again like the minister, he thought mostly about the people in the congregation, with whom his own life and that of his family were so intimately bound up: he was seeing them with new vision now that he was aware that he would soon leave them. The Meserves, of course; Lyle, sitting with his parents and three of his sisters, brought to Philip the image of their large frame house which he knew almost as well as he did his own—the big third-story room that was entirely given over to the young people—and the resin and fresh-wood smells of the lumber yard, too, in the hot sunshine.

Across the aisle, in another of the back pews (because of what they regarded as their humble station), sat Tommy and Phoebe Hardcastle, known throughout Fairview as "Tommy and Phoebe." An English couple, they had come to the Middle West years ago to take up farming, but were now living in town. Tommy filled his time with the church janitor job and with work for the Merriams. Tommy, bow-legged and bulky-shouldered, with a rosy face fringed with a white beard, giving him the look of a sailor although he had "niver followed the sea," and Phoebe in her neatly ageless black dress and little "decent" flat hat, were ineradicably English. Dissenters—so they still thought of themselves, as fixed in their doctrines as in their ways, eating the same kind of meals throughout the year, heavy on bread and cheese, drinking strong tea instead of coffee—they were so scrupulously loyal and dependable that the ladies forgave Tommy "that stinking old pipe," although Mrs. Rathbun and Mrs. Cowie and one or two others were sure they detected the smell in the church after Tommy had been at work there. But "Where would the church ever find another janitor?"—*pair* of janitors, really. . . . Philip recalled an incident from last winter, when Phoebe had set out to bring the Woods "a bit o' cake for yer supper"; Minnie had been in bed with one of her bronchial colds. But the old lady had slipped on the ice at the crossing, fallen, and broken her wrist. Tommy had told John Wood about it the next morning. When Minnie had sent Philip, before he went back to school at noon, to stop in and inquire, he had found Phoebe resolutely sitting upright in her chair, her hair screwed up into an even funnier little tight topknot than usual because she had to use her left hand; her right forearm was in splints. But she had refused sympathy, telling Philip, "No, it was the Lord rightfully punishing me for taking but two pieces o' cake when I knew there were three in the family." Philip hadn't felt how much he cared for Tommy and Phoebe until this moment.

His eyes searched for and found Miss Schilling, a woman so ugly that she was grotesque, but the ugliness was so familiar to Philip that he took it for granted. Today with heightened acuteness he saw every detail of that face in profile: the great nose and tiny chin, the long goose neck, the greasily grayish-

brown hair combed up into a coil hidden now by the weathered tan straw hat which Gertrude wore every summer. The
perception of his old eighth-grade teacher's ugliness gave
Philip a pang of chivalrous sympathy, as he thought of how
good she was. Gertrude Schilling was a stand-by in the school
and in the church. "Ask Gertrude Schilling; she may be willing to do it." She had unbounded admiration, almost worship,
for the whole Wood family. Her father, old Ferdinand Schilling, was so strong an agnostic and beer drinker that there had
been discussion among a few of the ladies as to whether they
ought to patronize him. "But who else is there? Except Dob
Peters, and he ruins shoes." Philip had always heard Gertrude
pitied. But this morning it gave him a brief pang of sadness to
realize that Mr. Schilling was very old and before long might
not be found in his stifling shop between the old restaurant and
the Racket Store, his steel-rimmed dirty glasses pushed up
above a nose which was even bigger than Gertrude's; pausing
with a shoe held in one hand while in his atrocious English he
loudly sounded off on "de system." "Why do you listen to
him?" Lyle would ask. But Philip, as a student of government,
said he wanted to hear all sides.

And others might soon be gone, people who to Philip were
among life's fixtures: the Sayleses, Mrs. Sayles, the only old
lady who still wore a bonnet trimmed with a quivering, glit-
tering jet butterfly, always so appreciative when as usher he
pulled the little carpet-covered stool under her feet and helped
her put the hymn book behind her back; Deacon Kruse, able
now to get to his front seat only with Miss Caroline's aid, but
who even last fall had sat at the back of the church to interfere
if any of the young people passed around notes scrawled in
hymn books. Philip felt that he was going to miss everybody,
even Mrs. Rathbun.

But some day he would make them all proud of him, and
through him proud of the church and of the town itself. He
saw his path leading into the golden future.

But all this while the Merriam pew was the one of which

Philip was acutely aware. He didn't want to be caught staring
at it. But he saw Mrs. Merriam's firmly held shoulders in her
well-fitted gray silk dress, Professor Merriam's urban-looking
back, and, between the two, Elaine, the light gold shimmer of
her hair showing under her straw hat.

Philip quickly withdrew his eyes. The whole scene became
even brighter; the wild flowers on each side of the pulpit were
fresh and living, the young leaves outside the windows more
tenderly green.

Philip's attention returned; he followed and felt every word
in the minister's short prayer of thanks. Mae's playing in the
response was soft and true in tone, and indefinably moving.
Philip realized that Jerry and Mae were in love, and experienced a glow of sympathetic happiness. When the congregation rose for the second hymn, Philip, standing beside his
father and next to the aisle, joined in with clear, strong voice,
quite true in its notes. His mother glanced at her husband with
a secret look of pride. Minnie had studied singing in her early
youth. The song also was as if new to Philip; again he seemed
never to have realized the promise in the last two lines he was
singing now, he felt, from his very heart:

> *"And in that light of life I'll walk*
> *Till traveling days are done."*

Then, following the announcements, there came the statement for which Philip was waiting.

"Will the ushers please come forward so that we may present
our morning offering to the Lord."

Philip, confident and bright, from one side of the church,
Will, trim and well set up, from the other, went down the two
red-carpeted aisles to meet in front of the Communion table
and receive from the minister the polished brown wooden
plates with red velvet linings on which the coins fell muffled.
As Philip went back up the aisle, passing in and out of the May
sunlight from the windows (which briefly illumined to the
congregation his boyish profile), he was living to reach that

one special pew. . . . He reached it, stood waiting while the plate was handed on from person to person, his head lifted but his eyes seeing the small envelope placed quietly by Mrs. Merriam's gray-gloved fingers, the coin by slim fingers smoothly gloved in fawn-colored kid, the dollar bill casually laid on envelopes and coins by the professor's well-kept hand. He had one look at the side view of Elaine's beautiful little nose, then stepped on to the next pew to receive his plate. He seemed to lose track of everything else again until he and Will were walking back down the aisles to give their well-filled plates to the minister and wait with bowed heads for his brief blessing.

A moment later Philip was back in his own pew. He had nothing more to do now but listen to the sermon. He liked to hear the Reverend Jerry Storm. But his listening this morning stopped with the giving out of the text; it was one which the Reverend Jerry might have chosen for Philip himself: "I will sing unto the Lord a new song."

The words brought to Philip the sense of what was now and what was to be. He became lost in a vision of himself, grown up, noble, and in fact perfect in every respect, coming back to Fairview from—somewhere, Washington, D. C., all the capitals of the world; he felt the joy of the welcome, the pride, the love of old friends . . . and saw somewhere a shimmer of gold hair. . . .

A slight cough and movement made him conscious of his mother, his father turning toward her, she shaking her head with her dainty handkerchief held to her lips, his father putting her light spring coat around her shoulders and then sitting back again with arms folded and face almost expressionless in its gravity.

Philip's emotions were a mixture now; the marvel of God's goodness shown him by giving him such parents—that almost, not quite, perfect handsomeness of his father, and still more John's fortitude; and his mother, her delicately but distinctly marked individuality as she sat in her best foulard dress of the odd shade of slightly faded blue that became her, the little

straight-brimmed spring hat that would have been prim on
any woman but herself, with her small, thin hands in their
light kid gloves, not particularly smooth like the scarcely
glimpsed fawn-colored glove of the young Elaine, but expressive even in their wrinkles. The plump engraved gold watch
given her on her graduation from high school, worn on a long,
fine gold chain, was thrust into the velvet ribbon around her
slight waist. Her face, worn by ill health, was not less fascinating—a face so known to her son in all its peculiarly individual
characteristics that it made Elaine's pretty little pale face, blue-
eyed and light-golden-haired, almost fade out of memory except for that beautiful patrician outline of the nose.

The Woods did not go home directly after the morning
church service but ate their Sunday dinner in Mrs. Dissendorfer's dining room, which was only three blocks from the
church building, not too far for Minnie to walk; so that Minnie did not drive back with the Merriams in the surrey. Stopping at Mrs. Dissendorfer's neatly split the distance home.
Ordinarily John and Minnie went on immediately, so that they
would not need to hurry or to wait for places at table. The dining room had become very popular; people from the other
churches, and from no church, ate there. The no-church people were able to be the first on hand.

Today, however, Minnie put her hand restrainingly on
John's arm as she said, "You'll want to wait a moment and
speak to Bradford Merriam, won't you, dear?"

John said, "Oh, yes, we must do that."

Philip waited with his parents until some of the boys called
him out to the sidewalk. "Hey! Post!" (The initials of his two
given names, Philip Sidney, had been translated into "Post
Script," which in turn had become "Post," now Philip's official,
if quite meaningless, nickname.) He felt so impatient as he
stood just beyond the steps that he scarcely heard what the
boys were saying, except that Howard, who was to lead the
Christian Endeavor meeting that evening, wanted to make sure

that Philip would be there. Philip said he hoped to, but even while Howard was talking he turned and went back up the steps, his young face with bright eyes looking straight at Professor Merriam.

"Well, good morning, young Philip! I suppose this *is* Philip. My word, what a big fellow! I can't keep track of you, Philip, from summer to summer; you outpace me."

"You should come back more often, sir," Philip said warmly as he shook the professor's hand.

"Oh, I should!" Bradford Merriam replied in amusement. "You remember Elaine, don't you?"

"I should say I do!" Philip blushed, but laughed at the same time.

That was a foolish question on Professor Merriam's part, since Philip had played with Elaine since they were both small children—ever since she had begun spending the summers with her grandparents, at the time she was about four years old and he seven. Elaine had taken off her fawn-colored glove, and Philip shook hands with her, holding the satin slimness of her hand for an instant in his, although she scarcely looked at him. He saw, too, how she had grown since last summer.

"We hadn't expected you quite so soon, but I'm awfully glad you came!" Philip said. He was thinking of his graduation; perhaps Professor Merriam and Elaine would be there when this great event came off.

Smiling urbanely, Bradford Merriam replied, "No, we got away a trifle earlier this year." Elaine had moved aside a little —Evvie Evans was talking with her—and Professor Merriam flatteringly came close to Philip and added, "To tell the truth, we came partly because of Elaine's health; the school year has been a bit hard on her." He looked at Philip thoughtfully. "She's a little on the fine-drawn side, as no doubt you know, the Woods and the Merriams have been so close together. She needs, ah"—now the amused look came back in Bradford's eyes—"the wholesome air and restful quiet of this solid, homespun part of our country."

Philip never knew just how to take Professor Merriam when
he talked in this way, but was flattered by the confidence.
And of course he did know about Elaine's "delicate constitution," as they used to speak of it. He had always been warned,
when they played together as children, to watch out that Elaine
didn't get overtired or nervous. There had even been occasions when Elaine, quite distressingly, had burst into tears for
no reason that anyone could see; and Philip had always been
the one to watch out for these times and to take her to her
grandmother. Philip, looking at Elaine now, could not see that
she looked ill. On the contrary.

"I'm sorry to hear that, Professor Merriam. We'll certainly
do all we can to be of help to her," Philip added eagerly.

"Well said, well said!" the professor answered, but rather
carelessly.

Other Fairview acquaintances of Bradford came up to greet
him—acquaintances rather than friends, for Bradford had not
made friends. Philip started to leave, but Professor Merriam
turned to him and asked, "Why don't you drop over this afternoon, Philip, and see us? I'm going back at midnight. How'll
that be, Elaine?"

Elaine returned to her father's side. She slightly nodded her
head in its perfectly chosen, expensively simple straw hat with
moderately wide ribbon around the crown—hat and ribbon
fawn-colored, like her jacket, dress and gloves, and the small
leather handbag she carried. Her blue eyes gave Philip just one
cool side glance that held some indefinable, exhilarating promise.

He said, "Thanks, I'll be there."

He went away so elated that, although he soon caught up
with his father and mother, he could not fit his steps to their
slow pace. Calling back to them, "I'll go on up ahead and try to
save chairs," he sped along the three town blocks to Mrs. Dissendorfer's and up the inside wooden staircase to the room in
which she served her Sunday dinners with the help of her two
older children, Karl and Charlotte.

It was a barny room above those on the ground floor which served as bakery, bakeshop, and home for the Dissendorfers— the shop being also a kind of local delicatessen in which, on specified days, Fairview patrons could buy Mrs. Dissendorfer's white and rye bread (not only "like homemade" but better), her own baked beans, and German potato salad. They could feel justified in buying ready-cooked food because they would be helping out Mrs. Dissendorfer, a little, hard-working woman whose husband had gone off and left her with four children to support. Two years ago, when the older ones were big enough to help her, she had instituted these family-style Sunday dinners, charging first twenty-five cents, and now (with a sense of great daring, but with the backing of John Wood) having put her price up to thirty-five.

The room was barely large enough, at that, to hold the long table (actually two tables pushed together, one a trifle higher than the other, making the setting down of gravy bowls and such precarious) and allow Charlotte and Karl to squeeze behind the chairs.

Three places were reserved for the Woods, indicated by their rolled napkins in wooden holders on which their names had been burned by Vera Meserve with her pyrography set. Charlotte gave Philip a look which said that she was responsible for keeping the places, and he in turn gave her a laughing glance which told her, Thanks. Charlotte liked Philip, but so many girls did that he more or less took his popularity for granted, had no realization that this Sunday hour was, for Charlotte, the one great hour of the week. She had glimpses of Philip at high school, where she was a freshman, but they were apt to be brief; she was not in Philip's crowd. Her fair German skin was flushed pink as she waited on the table after Philip had sat down. When she brushed against his shoulder, and he turned and asked courteously, "Can you get past, Charlotte?" the pink color flamed painfully, as bright as if she were sunburned.

Philip himself enjoyed eating with this different crowd from those his parents usually referred to as "our own church people." He enjoyed the feeling that here he was in the world at large. The crowd usually included several of the teachers; a few other unattached persons; an elderly couple, the Babsons (he silent because his teeth fell out if he tried to talk much, although he could use the set for chewing); the recently widowed Mr. Spear and his daughter Genevieve, a shy, fat girl of twelve (they had no one at home now to cook for them); and the popular Mr. Rakosi, with his black hair curled, and wearing a brilliantly flowered necktie. Mr. Rakosi was vaguely believed to be a Catholic but in Fairview "went nowhere" as far as church attendance was concerned. He had a teacher this noon seated on each side of him, the two prettiest, Miss Janeway and Miss Gale, so that he was gaily triumphant. He called to Philip, through the good steamy aromas from the big platters of roast veal cut in chunks, peeled boiled potatoes, green beans, boiled cabbage with caraway seeds, coffee hot and strong in thick white cups.

"Hello! Phee-leep looks more bright than May in Fairview on se banks of se Opper Wah-kah-kah-kahn-sah." All the teachers giggled. "Sat so? Somet'in nice happen? Sat so?"

"Oh, Philip looks that way all the time," Miss Janeway, the high-school English teacher, said in a flattering tone and with a glance from her hazel eyes.

Mr. Rakosi sighed. But his own black eyes flashed. "Oh, how eet is fine to be all happy and young, look on ahead. Sat so, Phee-leep?"

"I guess that's so," Philip agreed. To him Mr. Rakosi, in his thirties, was not at all young, even if the teachers did admire him. It was rather shocking that such an old fellow should be so admired.

Charlotte's prominent blue eyes misted over and she blushed that painful pink again as she poured Philip's water, standing just behind his shoulder, so that she saw the light brown gloss of his hair. Her eyes were china-blue, not like Elaine's with their pure lake color, deceptive in its apparent transparency.

Mr. Rakosi looked at Philip with wonder. He could not

make out some of the Fairview American boys, Philip Wood
especially. Were they as good as they acted? Why was not
Philip a spoiled and precious youth, only acting goodness before his proud parents? Yet he seemed healthy, ingenuous, real.
Could life be as this boy saw it? Philip Wood summed up to
Anton Rakosi a certain unbelievable—and yet, he hoped, be-
lievable—aspect of Fairview.

Footsteps were heard on the creaking stairs—the steps, slow,
yet somehow light-sounding, of Minnie Wood, and John's steps
timed to hers. Here was another unbelievable thing, the devotion of this abnormally handsome man to his faded semi-invalid
wife (fascinating as Mr. Rakosi called Minnie, and really
thought her to be). Not that the devotion was strange, exactly,
but was it possible that John Wood went to no other woman
anywhere? That would be—oh, marvelous! That would be a
phenomenon. But could the perfection of the Wood marriage
be possible, even though people in this little so-young town,
with its five churches and its dry laws, all took it for granted?
The delightfully gay Miss Janeway, for instance—even she
never gave a flirtatious look at John Wood. . . . No, this I
cannot— Somewhere there must be—Mr. Rakosi thought.

The steps approached the doorway. Mr. Rakosi tossed back
his crest of jet-black curling hair and, rolling his brilliant eyes,
declaimed, "Ah, here come se wooman in Fairview I might luf
—except her heart it ees taken! So what to do, do you say, Miss
Janeway, but eat this excellent cabbage?"

Philip did not know whether to laugh or be affronted to
hear his mother and father spoken of in this queer way—nor
whether to think that Miss Janeway and Miss Gale in their
mirth were impudent or subtly flattering. However, it was the
accepted view in Fairview that Mr. Rakosi, a foreigner, something as outlandish as a Hungarian rather than the better-
known English, Germans, and Scandinavians, should be
laughed at indulgently for his dramatic exaggerations, and generally liked, even admired. In his photograph gallery, which he
had made over from an old frame house left standing down-

town, he was courteous to the point of gallantry, but never "took advantage."

Besides, what he said Philip thought was true, funny as his way of saying it might be.

Mr. Rakosi regarded the whole Wood family, indeed, with puzzlement, admiration, zestful delight, and skepticism. He sprang up, bowing and holding his napkin to his chest, when Minnie's slight form appeared in the doorway. Philip thought, Yes, he must have meant to compliment the folks—and was proud.

3

T H E Wood house was very quiet. Philip almost imagined that he could hear the springtime ripple of the stream through the ravine below the house. His mother was upstairs, sleeping, and his father sat in the front room at the combination desk and bookcase, with ledgers and records around him, while he studied the financial page of the Chicago Sunday paper. It disturbed Minnie that John should have to spend Sunday afternoon in what ought to be a weekday occupation. But what other time did he have? As assistant to Colonel Merriam in the loan company, he must follow land values and farm prices, especially now that Colonel Merriam was aging and leaving more and more of the business to him. The Colonel, in fact, did little nowadays but take care of the congenial parts— talking with old farmers to whom he had sold land years ago, studying the population growths and trends of the nearby townships, while in the back room of his house, which he called his "home office," he devoted increasing time to his interest in local pioneer history. He seldom drove out into the country any more on active business; when he did go, it was to pass Helmar Cullom's place to see how the oats were doing this season; to stop in to see his companion of early days, Deacon Kruse; or to drive slowly through the narrow, rough roadways of his beautiful patch of virgin timberland, Merriam's Grove. He no longer dug a few wildflower plants as he used to do for his old handy-man-gardener, Jake Patch, to set out near the house. He said this was because Tommy Hardcastle, who now worked around the place, was no good with transplanting; but his wife feared that it was also because his own knees were too stiff for him to climb easily in and out of the buggy.

Philip hesitated, reluctant to disturb his father—both Philip and Minnie greatly respected John's ability to work in silence —but he finally said, "Good-by. I'm going to the Merriams' now, Papa. I'll be back before supper."

John answered, "What's that? Oh, all right, son"—but did not take his eyes off the column he was studying. Philip himself was "bright in his studies," but he sometimes wondered if he had his father's power to work continuously and drudgingly, and silently, if necessary. John was often up until midnight with his accounts. Minnie would have protested at that too, if John himself had not insisted that work never hurt him. And in fact it had never seemed to do so. He could carry his own load and everybody else's too. Minnie could rest with grateful security in the big bed upstairs until John came, climbing the stairs very softly with his even footsteps, and not turning on the light in their room.

If Colonel Merriam ever *did* decide to retire and take his hands completely off his beloved business, it was felt throughout the town and section that John Wood was well prepared to take over—even though the Merriam Company was a title built into the very structure and existence of Wahkonsa County. Certainly John was qualified in so far as knowledge and experience went; he might not be so shrewd and astute a bargainer as the Colonel, but his other good qualities would make up for that. Whether John himself was hoping to get into the business, no one could quite make out. He had never uttered a word about it even to Henry Meserve (another close-mouthed man). But his loyalty to his employer could account for his silence. With a wife in frail health, a son to be educated,

the years of work behind him, John must hope for it! Some
of the men in town had naturally talked the matter over and
asked, If not John Wood, who else? Certainly Brad Merriam
was not the person. But these men had agreed that the Colonel
and the Missus both thought a great deal of family and might
prefer to keep the business nominally under family control.
John might become merely full manager, with an increased
salary. George Merriam, although strictly honest, had a hard
streak in him. He might not be willing to give over his business
on easy terms, in spite of the years John had been with him;
and John himself couldn't have more than a very moderate
amount to put into it (if that, was Henry Meserve's opinion).
Then, too, John might prefer to work as somebody else's right-
hand man.

Philip had such trust in his father that these questions
scarcely came into his mind.

He stepped now out into the afternoon, which was still sunlit and bright. He wore his best cap again and had kept on his
best suit, the one which he would wear for his graduation.
With his quick, youthful pace, the few blocks he had to walk
scarcely gave him time for his thoughts. The walks had dried
off by now, although patches of the ground, the rich, dark
soil, were refreshingly moist.

The Merriam house had formerly been the principal resi-
dence in Fairview. In a way, it was still. There had been no decline in fortune or standing on the part of the Merriams. But
several newer and more pretentious houses had been put up as
Fairview kept on growing—the Meserve house was one—and
now the Merriam house, with its long, narrow porches and
ornamental porch posts wound with vines, its shuttered windows arched over at the tops, had become old-fashioned. The
family was mostly gone; the two daughters had died abroad,
and the only son, the Professor Bradford Merriam who had
been with his mother at church that morning, lived in New
York, where he taught English literature and was said to be
doing writing "of a scholarly nature." Except for summers,

when this son brought his daughter to stay with her grandparents, Colonel and Mrs. Merriam were the only members of
the family at home. The one other person in the house was Lola
Carpenter, the hired girl, successor (so far as anyone could be)
to old Aggie, whom so many people in Fairview remembered.
Mrs. Merriam's influence was still strong in the Congregational
church, but after the death of her daughters she had gradually
withdrawn from most of her activities. The day when Mrs.
Merriam had "given up her class"—the Adult Bible Study Class
—was looked back upon as a sort of melancholy landmark by
all but the new people. The period when the Merriam house
had been the cultural center of Fairview, the meeting place of
all worthy organizations such as the Tuesday Evening Reading Circle, had faded, no one knew just when or how, and the
town had passed into a new era. Yet, as many people said, it
was remarkable how Mrs. Merriam kept up—considering
everything.

The thriving, fresh, still youthful Fairview of today was
the one in which Philip lived. But he had a kind of vision of
the earlier time as he came up to the white-painted looped-wire
fence which enclosed the Merriams' big lot spreading over half
the block in which the house stood near the farther corner.
Philip had heard of those days from his mother. She—then
Minnie Terrill—had been a special friend of the Merriam girls,
Florence and Cora. That was the period of Minnie's life when
she had not been expected to live much longer; old Dr. Bushnell had with sorrowful conscientiousness prepared her parents
for the loss. Flo and Codie had taken an interest in Minnie, and
a liking for her, as "unusual." They used to drive over to the
Terrills' with the pony carriage and the safe, although brisk-
stepping, pony, and bring Minnie to the Merriam place; in the
warm spring and summer days she would lie out in the hammock which Jake Patch had put up for her away back among
the flowering bushes and the fruit trees out of sight from the
street. She had told Philip of how she used to lie looking up at
the sky through the branches and watching the apple blossoms

drift past—feeling unattached to earth, like those floating petals. She was so hidden and secure that she could be dressed as an invalid and yet be out "in nature."

There in the netted fringed hammock, clad in a white dotted-swiss wrapper, and with her hair in two black braids, she had first met John Wood. He had recently come to Fairview from "some town in Upper New York State," by way of Cleveland, Ohio, and had begun to work for Colonel Merriam. Minnie had kept hearing about John Wood from the two girls, who had told her that he was "the handsomest man you ever beheld." People talked about "Greek gods"; he actually *was* a Greek god—although Minnie was not to repeat this to their mother, who held that no person should be judged according to outward appearance. ("He has a *good* face"—Codie had mimicked her mother's tone of austere reproof.) The girls themselves might have fallin in love with John if he had not worked for their father and so seemed just a little beneath them! But to Minnie Terrill, lying half helpless in the unsteady hammock, fever beginning to mount through her frail body so that she had seen the world, the trees and flowers and grass with their springtime beauty, heightened and wavering as in a dream, the young man with his brown hair and blue eyes had seemed more than human. His sudden appearance, as if from nowhere, with no human background that any one knew about, added to the Greek-god impression. Minnie, to him, appeared as an ethereal wraith. And yet her little face with black eyebrows was so definite, so individual! The volume of Matthew Arnold's *Essays* which Mrs. Merriam had given her for her edification had slipped out of the hammock and down upon the grass. The young man had stopped to pick the book up for Minnie. He was wandering through the big lot in search of Jake Patch, to whom the Colonel wanted him to give a message, and had not known that Minnie was there. Their eyes had met for the first time. Then . . . "before very long John was insisting that we were to be married. He would keep me with him just as long as he could. If it should be only a few days, then we would have those days. But God has been good. Oh, He has been *so* good!" Minnie's large round eyes, brilliant with unshed tears in their setting of black lashes, had looked into her son's eyes as she breathed, "It was like a miracle." . . .

That scene was in Philip's mind as he walked on past the fence of vertical loops of wire with the tender young sprays of bridal wreath pushing through here and there. The whole lot had begun to give out the sweetness of the bridal-wreath odor mingled with the fresh grass scent that belonged to both spring and summer. The place must have been different in those earlier days—the lilac and syringa and snowball bushes not so lofty, nor the ferns beside the cool foundation stones of the north house wall so thick and tall and deep green. The girls, as well as Colonel Merriam, had brought ferns and wildflowers for transplanting from Merriam's Grove, where only they and their few chosen companions were permitted to do any digging or picking. . . . In later summers, when Elaine and Philip were children, Mrs. Merriam had sometimes driven out with them to the Grove, taking along a picnic basket packed by old Aggie, and a volume of Thoreau for reading aloud (Philip had liked it, but Elaine had seemed politely bored). . . . Philip knew that Colonel Merriam had set out most of these plants and bushes himself; Mrs. Merriam did not "take to gardening." For years Colonel Merriam had been the only man in Fairview who employed a man regularly to cut his grass and tend his grounds. (And Fairview had not even yet reached the stage when people called in landscape gardeners to make over their yards.) Nowadays the place was kept in good shape by Tommy Hardcastle, a diligent worker if not a professional gardener; the grass was well trimmed even though it was getting heavy and hard to cut. By way of doing odd jobs for the Merriams, besides carrying on his church janitor work and selling milk and cream, Tommy and Phoebe did not have to "pay out" what they had saved—for whom, except themselves and their cat Malty, nobody knew.

To Philip, the Merriam place as it was now had a historic

air, reaching back into that half-legendary time of his parents'
youth. He had never seen the two Merriam girls, but he knew
them from the photographs his mother cherished: a picture of
the two young girls together hung, framed in gilt, above Minnie's little desk in the front room. Codie and Flo were in
a queer way real to Philip; although they belonged to that same
earlier era, they were part of his life. He did not know their
full history. But who did? or ever would? The fate of the Merriam girls had been such a blow to Minnie that she could
scarcely bear to have it touched upon even now. When Minnie and Mrs. Merriam were together, they seldom spoke of
Florence and Cora: Mrs. Merriam's reserve was too deep, and
Minnie's sensitiveness too tender.

Yet Philip did know that there had been conflict between
the girls and their mother. Both girls had been gifted: Florence
had played the violin, and Cora had painted in oils. But Mrs.
Merriam had kept inbred the old Puritan aversion to the arts,
even though she was known as "advanced" in her thinking.
She did admit literature to some degree, but only on what she
thought of as the highest plane and having ethical content—
Milton, Browning, Emerson; she did not even "care for"
Shakespeare. Not music, because that "aroused the passions";
so that when Flo was a little girl she had not been permitted
to take music lessons. The violin had seemed to her mother
even more "emotional" than the piano. Mrs. Merriam might
have consented to lessons on the organ if there had been anyone in Fairview whom she had thought really capable of giving them; the organ was of use in the church. Painting Mrs.
Merriam had regarded as less harmful than music, although
frivolous, mere decoration. But later on, when Florence had
begun to develop something that ran from ecstasy to melan-
cholia (Flo, Minnie had said, was "never out of her mind"),
old Dr. Bushnell cautiously urged that she be allowed to take
up music as "an outlet." On the Colonel's stepping in, as he
seldom did in disputes between his wife and daughters, Mrs.
Merriam had agreed. And if Florence was to study music, she

must have the best instruction. The two girls were sent to Europe, and their mother's cherished plan of having them follow her to Mount Holyoke was dropped, although their names had been entered when they were babies.

All this had taken place at about the time when John Wood and Minnie Terrill were getting married, and before Bradford Merriam went to Oxford, while he was at home for summer vacation from Harvard.

As to the girls, there might have been a man in the picture. Or it could have been that Dr. Bushnell's surmise was right, that Florence herself was partly in a state of revulsion against the development of her own gift. Florence had "a religious side." It was true that the Merriam girls—Bradford too—had rather looked down upon the small Congregational church in Fairview, and of course had rebelled against their mother's views. During one of her periods of depression Florence had "swung toward" the Catholic Church—had kept a rosary, crucifix, and shrine in her bedroom—and Dr. Bushnell believed that in Europe she might have felt this pull again and at the same time have felt that for her to "turn Catholic" could have been more of a grief to her then-Puritan mother than her having chosen to take up the violin instead of going to college.

At any rate—as Minnie had once told Philip when he had kept on questioning her, speaking in a whisper, and her great round eyes again brilliant with tears—"She took her own life."

He had dared ask nothing further. In Fairview generally, the story was only vaguely known. According to Caddie Rathbun, "they"—the Merriams—had "kept things from getting out." Some even among the older settlers knew only that the Merriam girls had died and been buried abroad. "I suppose it seemed too far to have them brought back." The Merriams had expected Cora to give them "particulars" regarding Florence. But Cora herself had been ill when "it" happened. Her illness had developed into pneumonia, and within a few days she too was gone. Her death had been almost more of a shock to the

Merriams than that of Florence, because they had always thought of Cora as the more stable one.

"It doesn't seem as if we could be the ones," Philip remembered his mother saying, "who had such wonderful times in the Merriam yard that summer."

But for at least two of that partly vanished group of young people the wonderful times had continued—for his own father and mother, Philip thought with a sense of gratification as he glanced into the overgrown lot through the Maytime intermingling of sunlight and shadow. The ideal character of their marriage struck even a European like Mr. Rakosi. Other wives all pointed to John Wood as the ideal husband. And Philip could not summon up any great unhappiness about the others of the earlier group. The Merriam girls were not quite real to him, after all, and "Brad," the brilliant poetry-reading youth of that faraway summer, was "Professor Merriam," the incarnation of intellectual and metropolitan sophistication in Philip's eyes.

But the Merriam yard itself was vitally real on this Sunday afternoon, even though the vision of the long past summer hovered somewhere in and about it and, like the ever-present sense of his mother's frail hold on life, made more vivid its fresh scents and blooming flowers. Philip's clear, alertly gazing youthful eyes were not trying to conjure up an image of his mother before her marriage; he was looking to see if he could find Elaine.

All of a sudden he did see her out in the flower garden, caught that same shimmer of light gold hair. Philip stopped. Elaine saw him too and, somewhat to his surprise, came over to the fence. She was carrying an armful of the long-stemmed iris which she had been cutting, lavender and cream-colored (Colonel Merriam had been the first person to introduce into Fairview gardens the more highly evolved forms of iris, although he himself still preferred the simple purple "flags," and as she spoke to Philip she kept looking down at the great blossoms and with her slim forefinger touching the ruffled edges of the elaborately beautiful petals.

Philip spoke to her—"Hello, Elaine"—and she answered in a small, sweet, indifferent voice.

"Hello. Are you going in to see Grandma?"

"Your father asked me to stop in this afternoon."

"Oh, did he?"

"When I was talking to him after church. Don't you remember?"

"Oh, yes," Elaine replied again with courteous indifference. She glanced away.

Philip was not much troubled. He had played with Elaine since they were both small children, and he was acquainted with her ways. She always met him at first with this cool indifference which seemed to have hostility in it somewhere beneath its fine polish of correct, sweet-toned politeness; but Philip accepted this and rather enjoyed it—enjoyed melting the coldness and mollifying the hostility. He realized that this feeling was not directed at him especially, that it was something deep in her. He believed that he knew how to get along with Elaine, to himself even went so far as to say "how to handle her." Philip took proud pleasure in the knowledge of his being the only boy in Fairview who was really acquainted with Elaine Merriam and not in any awe of her. Even Lyle Meserve said that he never knew how to talk to Elaine. The girls—the few whom Mrs. Merriam asked to come and see Elaine—admired Elaine's fine-spun elegance but never felt acquainted with her. But although she did live in the East and attend a private school reported to be "very exclusive" as well as expensive, and although her father had got a degree from Oxford, Philip believed that he himself had too much of his own to stand in any real awe of Elaine's "advantages."

"Can I help you with your flowers?" he asked her. "That's a swell bouquet."

Elaine replied with her sweet coolness, "No, thank you."

Then she added, speaking in quite a different tone, shyly confiding, "I'm going to take them in to Lola first in the kitchen. She wants to see them."

"Well, I could take them for you."

Elaine stood with eyes averted, an enigmatic small smile on her lips. Philip studied the fine sweep of her eyelashes, dark against her very fair skin. Her eyebrows, too, were slightly darker than her pale gold hair.

"No, thank you, I'll take them," she decided. Again she added confidentially, "Grandmother doesn't like cut flowers in the house. One shouldn't cut flowers, *she* thinks. Lola and I like them."

Elaine still stood there, but with her eyes now raised. She looked straight at Philip. It was seldom that anyone got the chance to look into those eyes; they were either averted or glacially unresponsive, or Elaine glanced down, and her eyelids—white and purely cut, but tilted upward at the corners— obscured the eyes themselves. Now, when Philip did have the opportunity, he found himself looking not into shallow, cold, pale blue but into depths that kept and yet seemed to be asking to confide their secret, to have it known and comprehended. Philip forgot what he was going to say. He too simply stood there. He had the sensation that he had heard about but never experienced—that of having his heart "turn over." He had never in his life before found himself actually at a loss for words; he was always ready to give or return greetings, recite in classes, speak up to anybody, even strangers.

He was aware again, as he had been at church, of how much Elaine had changed since last summer. She had not suddenly shot up, the way many boys and girls do at the start of adolescence. Her figure seemed slender and light as ever, but somehow more graceful. Her face had become less childishly rounded, and her nose was no longer a little girl's nose. Elaine's nose had always been pretty. But it had become beautiful. Philip's fascinated eyes kept tracing its line, as Elaine stood with face half averted. He tried to look away, for the first time

fearful of offending Elaine. She still wore her pale golden hair
down her back, but the curls and half-curls were brushed together into one loose, longer curl hanging almost to her waist
—so smoothly brushed that the fair hair might have seemed
prim if Elaine herself had not possessed such intrinsic elegance.

It was Elaine's patrician look that seemed to come out today
and to disconcert even Philip—except that it attracted him
more. The dress she had put on for afternoon looked simple,
but even Philip knew better; it was honey-colored, almost the
shade of her finely drawn eyebrows, with a shimmering cotton
texture over her silken slip. But more than the dress and the
bronze kid slippers, it was something about the way she carried herself that gave Elaine the slight, straight elegance
which was both the admiration and the despair of pretty, am-
bitious Evvie Evans—and yet held a suggestion of something solitary which Philip saw and wondered if anyone else
saw, even her grandparents. Not in the same way, he thought.

"I'll meet you in the house," Elaine said, again in her ladylike tone, with capricious suddenness. Philip watched her step
delicately along the little trodden path beside the flower beds
to enter by the back door, which was at the other side of the
house.

The sensation of the stopped heart was gone now, but Philip
felt that he had passed through some experience which later
might show as momentous. Although Elaine had refused to
let him carry her flowers for her, he knew that it was not from
dislike or disdain—that the hostile air, at least where he was
concerned, was shallow and meant nothing. Somehow or other
Philip knew that, knew too that it was an inner loneliness that
caused Elaine's first inclination to refuse any invitation and
walk aloof. And it was a loneliness that Philip felt perhaps he,
and he alone, could reach and answer. He realized too that
much of Elaine's solitariness and strangeness, which offended
Fairview people, might be due to her "delicate constitution,"
her tendency to "nervousness." This, after all, was not her
fault, and it represented another challenge to Philip. He re-

fused to accept this malady, whatever it was, as something final or fixed. Surely it could be changed, bettered, perhaps removed altogether!

Yet every summer when Philip again saw Elaine he had to break through that glacial reserve. But before he left her she had always become friendly—even, in her own way, intimate: in the big yard, or the old nursery playroom, or under an oak tree in Merriam's Grove as they sat together, above the partly sluggish, partly swirling, river, Elaine would be chattering easily to Philip, in her small, highly cultivated voice, so unusually sweet and clear in tone, and every word precisely enunciated.

Philip walked on slowly. He felt his heart beating faster again, but from expectancy, not from dread. Going up the wide steps of the narrow front porch, he caught the smell of the vines and of the wood of the aging house. The impressively heavy front door stood open. Philip pushed the bell and looked through the screen into the entrance hall with its carved staircase and square landing. Colonel Merriam had had all the lumber for his house here in Fairview hauled from some of his own outlying timber; he still kept large holdings, although he had allowed John Wood to sell several fine stands. Black walnut had been the fashionable wood used in most of the local mansions of the period. But Colonel George Merriam had cherished a preference for oak and had used it throughout his house. In the shaded interior, Philip could just see the large framed colored reproduction of "Washington Crossing the Delaware," above the heavy oak table on which stood a fine old Bradford pewter plate, used now to hold notes and calling cards. Although Philip had no doubt of his being welcome—and felt himself fully competent to meet and converse with Professor Bradford Merriam, or anybody else, for that matter—he was affected by the sense of dignity and distinction which he always felt in this house—pleasantly affected; the Merriams' was the only house in town (besides his own!) which held romance for Philip. He enjoyed the Meserve place, with its well-managed abundance and the many things going on among that large, active family. But here at the Merriams' there was, as in the marriage of his parents, just that little something extra, an atmosphere palpably present but never wholly to be defined. Elaine possessed that special quality, and no other girl (at least, so Philip thought) living in Fairview.

Professor Merriam came to the door, wearing an old professorial tweed coat and house slippers, and carrying a cold pipe in his hand, his gray-threaded hair slightly rumpled. But even so, he had, in Philip's ingenuous eyes, the Merriam patrician look—an air of Oxford, so far away to Philip that it seemed a storybook, or textbook, place rather than one in actual earthly existence.

"Oh, come in, Philip," Bradford said with easy cordiality. "We're all in the library."

The Merriams were the only family in Fairview to have a room that could be called a "library." Actually the big room served as a general living room. However, it held the tall bookcases filled with books, most of them well read, many in musty but interesting bindings from Mrs. Merriam's girlhood home, the old Bradford mansion in Massachusetts; and was the room in which the Fairview cultural organizations had been accustomed to meet. A select group from the Adult Bible Class had gathered for special study on Thursday evenings. With its polished oak floor and fine rugs, the long shuttered windows hung inside with sober brown damask, the furniture of oak and mahogany and leather, the Merriam library still represented the highest standard of elegance in Fairview. Even the Cowie parlor, often spoken of as "richly furnished," did not have the same air.

The room reflected interestingly the tastes of both Colonel and Mrs. Merriam. To the Colonel were due its comfort and solidity, the massiveness of some of its furnishings which offset the chaste delicacy of the old New England pieces, the warmth and interest of the large gold-framed pictures representing patriotic occasions (like the reproduction in the front hall) or scenes from wild nature; and to her, the books, the heirlooms, the atmosphere of elegance and austerity commingled. The grandfather's clock standing near the door into the entrance hall seemed to Philip to sound forth the hours in a tone which was final. Whenever he had heard that clock proclaim "FIVE" when he was in the house playing with Elaine, he had taken his cap and gone home immediately; and when, in church, he had heard the old minister who preceded Jerry Storm pronounce sonorously his text, "Now is the appointed hour," Philip had heard the Merriams' big clock sound portentously somewhere within him. The few ornaments in the room had belonged to the girls and had been left where Florence and Cora had placed them. Mrs. Merriam herself had little taste for such trivia of living as vases and bright cushions and choice bric-a-brac, and would have given Minnie Wood all of these she owned except for a deeply and silently cherished feeling in regard to her daughters.

Across the hall, and up one polished step, there was a square room known as "the small parlor." The dominating piece of furniture was the Chickering grand piano which Colonel Merriam had bought for the girls, and had shipped from Chicago, at one of those rare times when he had stepped in and which allowed of no dispute or discussion. Into this room Philip and Elaine had slipped at times, but always, on Philip's part, with a sense of daring and of trepidation. In spite of their having permission, a forbidding atmosphere seemed to linger about the small parlor. On the wall nearest the grand piano hung an oil painting, richly and deeply colored, of red and bronze and purple autumn leaves. Elaine once said, "My Auntie Cora painted that. I never saw her. She died." Elaine had several times sat down before the grand piano. Her touch on the cold keys revealed her own precision, with now and then a tiny flare-up of individuality. But in general it was as if she feared to go beyond a pretty, superficially finished correctness. Almost always she broke off before she finished a piece of music. "Go on and play the rest of it, why don't you?" Philip used to urge her. Elaine pushed back her light gold curls and got up off the piano bench—gracefully, as she did everything, but with her small face expressionless. "I don't care to."

Now Philip stood in the open doorway of the library until Mrs. Merriam called out, "Please come in, Philip."

Then he crossed the floor at once to shake hands with Mrs. Merriam, and went next to Colonel Merriam, who sat in his own big leather chair. Bradford Merriam watched this entrance with secret interest and appraisal, wondering where the boy got what was not quite the polish of a more sophisticated environment, and not quite cocky assurance, but obviously a high degree of easy self-confidence.

"Won't you sit down, Philip?" Bradford heard his mother ask with sedate gentleness.

Philip took a straight chair near the open doorway rather than one of the handsomely upholstered chairs. For all his boyish aplomb, he did not feel at home in quite the same way as in the Meserves' big sitting room. Colonel Merriam was, after all, not only Fairview's chief citizen but the employer of Philip's father. Philip's respect for Mrs. Merriam came as near being awe as his feeling for any person he had met so far in life; he recognized in her a spiritual loftiness as well as "background" and "culture." His having been invited into the library in this informal way, among the elders, showed that Philip had reached a different stage. As Elaine's playmate, he had usually spent his designated hour and a half with her outdoors in the yard and the orchard, or in the old nursery upstairs, which was now known as "the playroom." In these last two summers Mrs. Merriam had occasionally been willing to trust Philip with Bro, a stable, kindly horse; Sis, Bro's teammate, was more skittish. Philip considered that he could easily have managed the team and, had he been staying in Fairview this summer, would have proposed his doing so to Mrs. Merriam. The two young people (they were no longer children) might have driven as far as Duncan, the little nearby town which still had an old water mill; or might have stopped in Merriam's Grove

—just Philip and Elaine, without the grandmother and the mother—in that high spot overlooking the river as it flowed muddily, dragging branches, scarcely moving, and then making little eddies, under the heavy foliage of the trees. Philip felt a sudden sharpness of regret for his summer plans.

"Didn't Elaine come in?" he heard Mrs. Merriam asking.

Philip spoke up. "I think she went into the kitchen. She wanted to take in some iris blossoms."

"Expect she cut all my best iris!" Colonel Merriam growled, although the growl was something of a pretense.

"George, you know you don't care."

"Oh, I know I don't care. The child can cut anything she's a mind to."

"She knows you are here, Philip?"

"Yes, she knows, Mrs. Merriam," Philip said. He felt Professor Merriam's eyes on him curiously, and he spoke matter-of-factly. "I talked with her before I came into the house."

The Colonel observed, "Oh, she may just stay out there in the kitchen; she appears to have struck up a great friendship with Lola. Prefers Lola to any of the rest of us."

"No doubt she enjoys someone young in the house," Mrs. Merriam said.

"Young, yes, and not so stuffy as the rest of us," Bradford drawled, taking his pipe from his mouth and staring at it speculatively. Then he cocked one eye in the direction of Philip. "As I am sure is the case with Philip too.

"You still have to learn, Mother," he went on, "that Elaine never takes the straight line. You may think she will, but she doesn't. She takes the hover-about course and lights unexpectedly. I wouldn't call it the butterfly so much as the dragonfly course. That's it, the dragonfly."

"Bradford!"

"The dragonfly is beautiful, Mother. I consider it more distinctively beautiful than the butterfly. It has elegance, less flutter. My comparison isn't disparaging."

Philip sat through this exchange, looking from one to the

other, impressed by Bradford's languid ease in his manner of talking, and yet in his own mind protesting too and siding with Mrs. Merriam.

The Colonel had been sitting in some kind of deep absorption, champing his empty jaws. It was now lodged informally in Fairview annals, known to most of the old settlers at least, that George Merriam had once been a hard drinker and heavy smoker, as well as a hunter and expert fisherman; but that he had been forced to give up liquor and smoking and a few other pastimes before Lydia Bradford would consent to be his wife. He had kept his word to the letter. But it was known —and the source of much amusement—to his son that he had a little cache of dry chewing tobacco in a drawer in his office into which he often dipped when alone or with his cronies. In fact, his wife was aware of this too, but after struggling with herself had sensibly decided to overlook it.

Mrs. Merriam glanced at Philip, but was reassured by his fresh, interested young face and eyes bright and transparently clear. He was not bothered, apparently, by Bradford's irreverent sort of humor, which so distressed her.

"I really miss old Aggie out in the kitchen," Bradford now said, looking at his father, "even if she did frighten Elaine with her wild face. I thought she was the very spirit of the back part of this house."

"Poor Aggie couldn't help being so—primitive," Mrs. Merriam said.

The Colonel's somber eyes lighted, which perhaps was the result Bradford had intended. He said, "Of course she couldn't help it. Aggie had good reason to *be* primitive."

"I suppose you don't remember old Aggie, Philip?" Bradford asked.

"Oh, yes, I do," Philip replied quickly.

Who in Fairview didn't? Aggie Lucas was a historic character in a small way. She had been the sole survivor of what was known as the Settlers' Creek Massacre, a tragic event of the early days. A group of Indians had slaughtered the men and driven away the girls and women of Settlers' Creek, a log-cabin community only thirty miles from Fairview. Aggie Lucas, Fairview's "Old Aggie," had been thirteen at the time.

The three Merriams began to reminisce now about Aggie Lucas. Philip himself remembered her only as a grotesque old figure in her dark-colored shawl, with thin gray braids of hair twisted into knots above her ears, in which she had worn round gold earrings, much like those of a gypsy. Aggie used to bring ginger cookies to Philip and Elaine, which Elaine wouldn't eat because she said they were dirty—so that Philip, both from courtesy toward Aggie and from a boyish, never-appeased appetite, would eat Elaine's cookies as well as his own.

Bradford said, pulling himself up from his easy slouch, "I've always wanted to hear you tell us more about that rescue, Father. Aggie's rescue, I mean. I know what her version was. You were her noble protector. But we could never get more out of you than that you had 'picked her up'—in the literal, of course, not the figurative, sense. I wish you'd give us—and young Philip here—your own version."

The Colonel seemed pleased, although he tried to pass it off lightly. "Oh, I don't know as you'd call it rescue. Aggie made her escape herself. That was the hard part. I happened to spy her in the woods crawling down among some bushes there, and took her up on my horse—tried to cover her up in front of me with my jacket, like she was some old bundle of clothes."

"Did you meet any Indians?"

"Not so to speak met them, or I don't suppose I'd be here to tell. They didn't like having a young squaw get away. I recall seeing a band of their fellows swimming their horses across the river, but by God's own luck they didn't catch wind of Aggie and me. Zach was a mighty good horse, best horse I've ever known, and he made it straight for the cabin."

"I consider that quite as noble as Aggie's version," Mrs. Merriam said firmly, ignoring the Colonel's profanity.

"So do I, Mother. I'm completely with you. What's your opinion, Philip?"

Philip said with youthful enthusiasm, "I think it was great!"

Colonel Merriam sat imperturbably, although it was obvious that he was gratified. His son had seldom showed an interest in the early days, and his daughters—Florence, at least—had preferred to forget their existence. He was spurred on also by the shining-eyed attentiveness of John Wood's boy.

"Oh, most of the time," he said, "I was on good terms with the Indians in this section—when I wasn't obliged to fight them. I could always get along better than Paul Kruse could in the days when Paul and I were batching it. Paul was too strict in his ways, even before old Father Gilbert put the fear of hell in him—when he was quite a roisterer. Well, I expect some would have called us both roisterers."

The Colonel glanced toward his wife again, his small eyes twinkling from under those bristling white brows; but her fine features still remained unperturbed.

"The Indians weren't all so bad as white folks seem to think. Or so good, either. Not those I knew. *Hiawatha!*" The Colonel gave a snort of derision. "The fellow who wrote that should have had a bunch of hungry Indians visit his cabin and eat and drink him out of house and home! Or know what some of those women went through when they were captives. Not that the others weren't to blame, too, the Settlers' Creek folks. One of them did the first shooting. But you never hear much about that. It's all what the white folks suffered."

"I'm afraid that has been only too true," Mrs. Merriam said with sadness.

The Colonel gave her a sharp-eyed glance of appreciation. "Well, you did your part, Lyddy. You put up all those years with old Aggie. I know 'twas like living with a part-wild thing. She'd gone through too much—couldn't change back." Of course he couldn't speak before the children of all that Aggie had gone through during her "young squaw" days. His wife knew. "But you said you'd join with me to keep the poor creature, and you did it. Nursed her at the end. I don't know but, all in all, Lyddy, you were better to her than I was."

"Hear, hear!" Bradford murmured.

Philip's eyes sparkled. He felt a vivid sense of being in the very center of old Fairview life, and at the same time in touch with social and intellectual reaches beyond his own. He was proud of the connection of the Wood family with the Merriam family. There was something homely and rough about Colonel Merriam, but the same innate dignity was to be felt in the man as in his house. Philip recognized that the Colonel was an aristocrat in all his dealings, fully as much as Mrs. Merriam, and more of an autocrat than she—that is, when the Colonel chose to be one. Although he was a fierce local as well as national patriot—having had a command in the Civil War—he had gone back East for his bride and was as proud as she of the Bradford line. He was not Puritan, but had preferred a Puritan wife, accepting only a few of her precepts, scruples, and convictions—those in regard to which he had "given his word" at the start of the marriage—but standing aside from the children's upbringing except for that occasional stepping in when he thought their mother "too toplofty for any human use."

Elaine had come in as if from nowhere. All at once she was there. Her grandfather beckoned to her, but with her usual unpredictability she chose instead to draw over the footstool (one of the Bradford heirlooms; its charmingly faded woolen pansies had been embroidered years ago by some Bradford maid or matron) and to sit down at her grandmother's knee. With her clear profile, and her slender hands demurely folded, she had at this moment something of the air of a Puritan maiden herself.

Mrs. Merriam's hands, too, were held quietly in her lap. They were like her granddaughter's in being finely fashioned and slender, but were capable hands, worn by household tasks (even if the Merriams did customarily employ a hired girl, so that among women in Fairview it had more than once been said of Mrs. Merriam that "*she* has time for all that reading and studying; I haven't"). The heavy gold wedding ring on her left fourth finger, and the engagement ring above it, set with rubies and winking diamonds, represented the Colonel's handsome taste, not her own.

Philip had been too well brought up to stare. But he was sitting directly across from Mrs. Merriam and Elaine and did look at them every now and then. The resemblance between the two struck him for the first time and deeply gratified him. He saw Elaine with all the aura of the Bradford-Merriam family around her golden head. Mrs. Merriam turned, and Philip could now observe her profile against the cool light of the long window fronting on the east—her head small, as was Elaine's, but severe in its outline. Her lips made a line of severity too—and yet there was a sweetness in their expression, and a sadness modified by what seemed quiet acceptance. Her coloring had always been quiet; her hair, now gray-brown, had never shimmered with the pale gold which gave Elaine's beauty some of its enchantment; it was the patrician line, the perfect chiseling of her nose which was most like her granddaughter's. Even Florence's fair hair had been Puritan hair, straight and long.

Otherwise it would have been hard to think of any girl less like her grandmother than Elaine. Philip felt this in his new consciousness of his playmate. Mrs. Merriam was known as "capable" as well as "very intellectual," almost to the degree of being called "a manager," like Mrs. Meserve. Elaine was to Philip unique in her fastidiousness and the almost hidden quality of her emotional appeal, her person and personality at the same time clearly precise and romantically enigmatic, her quality of self-possession combined with that faraway, lost-child look which he had now and then caught in her blue eyes. Philip had wondered, of course, about Elaine's mother—whether the exquisite coloring and golden hair might be an inheritance from "that English girl" Bradford Merriam had married while at Oxford, who had died at Elaine's birth. Thinking at this moment that Elaine's just-budding beauty and look of innate aristocracy had an aspect of pathos, perhaps even of tragedy,

Philip experienced a sudden heightening of his new feeling for her. He felt himself grow hot all over. But his self-assurance stood by him. He believed that he did not give himself away.

Elaine's grandfather was looking across at her also, with his formidable scowl. But when the Colonel spoke his voice had an oddly coaxing note of gentleness.

"We see mighty little of you, young one, now that you're here, seems to me. Why don't you come over on this big hassock by your grandfather? Don't you think your old grandfather ever wants to see you?"

Elaine made no answer, except slightly to toss her pretty head.

"Well, well. We aren't much company, I dare say," Colonel Merriam grumbled, subsiding into his big chair and again champing his jaws. His son shot a whimsically troubled look at him, and then at Elaine, but made no interference.

Mrs. Merriam turned to Philip. "Your mother seems to be feeling pretty well these days," she observed.

"Oh, yes, for her," Philip answered. "You know how it is. She's wonderful, really." Friday night she had gone to the church supper and had stayed for the entertainment, had contributed one of her famous rose-flavored white cakes. But the exertion seemed not to have been too much for her.

"I know your father never lets her stay too long. He always seems to see when she is getting tired. It's remarkable how perfectly he understands her. I never cease to marvel."

"Yes, he does," Philip said reticently.

Bradford Merriam was looking at his mother and Philip with a quizzical expression. He could see his mother's pleasure in Philip's quiet, assured answer, but he did not know that Mrs. Merriam's approval of Philip Wood had been reached rather against her will; she felt that Philip had started with almost too much in his favor. Mrs. Merriam still held the belief that one ought not to be affected by good looks, Philip's any more than John's. Philip was no more to be held accountable for his fine

appearance than Dan Postel's boy for his scrawny unprepos-
sessingness. Both were equally children of God. But Mrs. Merriam was relieved to observe that Philip was, in fact, a little less
handsome than his father, although with his fresh enthusiasm
and shining eyes he was, to her, even more attractive. She had
always found John Wood "a little hard to reach," although
she had never felt that she could suggest anything of the kind
to George.

Philip went on to say that he and his father were hoping, and
trying to make sure, his mother would feel well for the week
of the high-school Commencement.

"Are you speaking of *your* Commencement, Philip?" Bradford said. "Good heavens."

"Yes, I'm going to graduate." Philip could not wholly keep
his exultation from his voice.

"Why should you be surprised, Bradford?"

"Because, Mother, I hadn't realized that Philip had advanced
so far along the great highway of education—speaking in what
I hope will be taken as a proper professorial manner. Father,
had you?"

"Don't know as I had," Colonel Merriam answered. He
looked intently at Philip from under his picturesque eyebrows,
was pleased to observe that the boy was not put out by his
scrutiny. The Colonel could make people quail but seldom
respected those who did so. "But I've come to my dodderage,
where my memory springs holes—like the mud holes in the
Upper Wahkonsa."

"What are you planning to do after the great event, Philip?"
Bradford inquired. "Of course everybody asks the same question. But I claim leniency as an instructor of the young. Besides, I'm in a mood to be trite."

Elaine all the while remained demurely silent. But now, with
the very slightest lifting of her long eyelashes and of her white
eyelids, she gave Philip a subtle glance meant only for him. He
caught it and blushed; but sitting straight in his hard chair, he
betrayed no other sign of his triumphant joy.

He replied respectfully to Bradford Merriam, "Next fall I plan to enter Willard College."

"Willard! Oh, yes, that's the little fresh-water school over in the central part of the state that used to send its glee club to Fairview. Sang surprisingly well, too, as I recall. We usually had three or four of the boys bunking here in the house. Always entertained the president, too, when he came to Fairview to raise money. Has some connection with Mother's church, I believe?" Bradford asked in his blandest drawl, his face innocent.

"Bradford, it's an excellent school, and has been from the start," Mrs. Merriam put in.

Philip could hardly have known why Mrs. Merriam had spoken so quickly, or why her own expression was somewhat troubled. Mrs. Merriam could not entirely suppress the memory that she had not wanted her own children to go to "a local college," even one to which she gave undeviating support; and she was quite aware that her son remembered this. But she held to her inner knowledge that she had come to see many things now in what she sincerely considered "a better light."

"I think it's a fine school," Philip said heartily. He was a little upset by Professor Merriam's manner of talking, although reassured by Mrs. Merriam's attitude.

Bradford was aware that he had gone a little too far with his idly ironical tongue. He was afraid that he might have dimmed young Philip's bright self-satisfaction, which was rather beguiling. He doesn't snub easily, Bradford admitted to himself. And after all, he had asked young Philip to the house, and had no grudge against him. Now it just crossed Brad's mind that possibly he was talking to his future son-in-law. *That* was a thought! Of course they were both children, especially Elaine. And yet . . . ? Bradford looked speculatively from one to the other, and at his mother too. No doubt it was a silly thought. But Brad changed his tone as he turned to Philip and asked with distinctly flattering curiosity, "And then what?"

"Well, I'm considering going East to study law." Philip spoke with his usual convincing confidence, although he added, with cheeks flushed, "I don't know yet how I'm going to get there. But I expect I'll find the way."

"I don't doubt you will," Bradford assured him—and quite sincerely.

Philip went on to speak of his financial plans with a candor which appealed to Bradford Merriam, remembering how differently he himself had thought about such matters when he was the age of Philip now. Philip said he felt sure that he could manage at Willard, where many of the students worked their own way. His parents would help all they could.

"Of course my father can't spare a great deal," he said.

He blushed then; he wondered if he seemed to be complaining about the size of his father's salary. But Colonel Merriam merely nodded his head.

Philip said that he had one job lined up at Willard which ought to pay for his board and room. He was going to live at —at— Well, he added with modesty, at the home of the college president and run the furnace and shovel snow. He smiled, showing his strong, even teeth.

"The good old American tradition?" Bradford inquired and arched his brows.

Mrs. Merriam said, "Philip will be very helpful, I have no doubt. I think President and Mrs. Ostrander are fortunate."

"Oh, I agree, Mother. But thoroughly."

Philip looked at Elaine, but she said nothing. There was no response now in the cool blue gaze of her eyes. He felt suddenly uncomfortable, wanting to explain the brightness of his future to her as he himself saw and felt it.

But Mrs. Merriam was inquiring as to his plans for this summer. "I know you usually work at the lumber yard for Mr. Meserve."

"I usually do," Philip said. And he had always liked to. But, he said, this summer he and Lyle planned to go around to towns in all this part of the state, selling the new kind of aluminum

ware. Mr. Meserve would let them take one of the horses from
out on the farm, and a kind of rattletrap buggy. "I guess you
folks remember that old buggy. It used to belong to Grandpa
Meserve."

Philip and Lyle hoped to make enough money to pay for
their tuition, and then some; the boys were both entering Willard. Lyle didn't really need the extra money, Philip added with
that same engaging openness, but he wanted to go with Philip
on the sales trip. They would work mostly through women's
clubs and organizations, giving demonstrations in church kitchens or ladies' homes. Mrs. Meserve had been writing to ladies
whom she had met at church and club conventions.

"Sounds very enterprising!" Bradford observed. "Don't you
think so, Father?"

Colonel Merriam's brief growl seemed to be one of assent.

Mrs. Merriam said commendingly, "I think it's an excellent
plan. I hope you boys will call on me. I don't see why you
shouldn't give your first demonstration here, unless my kitchen
is too old-style."

"Lola doesn't have a kettle between medium and the small
size," Elaine put in unexpectedly with her own special preciseness.

"We certainly will, Mrs. Merriam," Philip answered, his
tone suddenly joyous.

Colonel Merriam got up, hoisting himself by the arms of the
leather chair. Although he had grown white-haired and white-
browed and somewhat stiff, he had not lost his look of underlying sturdiness. He crossed over to his wife and patted her
firm shoulder before turning to go out of the room. Philip saw
Mrs. Merriam's eyes soften, and although her lips kept their
firm line, their expression changed.

Bradford saw this too. He asked, "Are you leaving us, Father?"

"Yes, I think I'll go into the office for a while. That all right,
Lyddy?"

"Certainly, George."

But Elaine cried with unexpected petulance, "*I* don't want you to go."

"*You* don't want me!" her grandfather exclaimed. He stopped to pull her long curl with bluff playfulness, but the twitch he gave it made Elaine wince slightly. "What have you got to say about it? You wouldn't even come over and sit beside your grandfather. I've known young wildcats more sociable."

Elaine curled her pretty lip. Her eyes showed their half-veiled look as she sat, with head drooping, on the ancestral footstool at her grandmother's feet. With a touch of beguiling sweetness, she said softly to her grandfather, "I *would* now."

A visible softening came over the old man's strong face, which was modeled—so Mr. Rakosi had once admiringly observed—"on se human tiger." But Colonel Merriam replied, "Now is too late. I'm going into the office."

The entire conversation had been desultory and commonplace enough. Yet to Philip it was, in some yet unexplained manner, deeply stirring. The subject of his after-college plans had been barely touched upon; they were his own secret. But the consciousness of them made him both prouder and more confident when he glanced at Elaine's golden head.

Both Bradford and Philip had risen in respect for the Colonel. But Colonel Merriam curtly motioned to his son to be seated, while he himself shook hands with Philip. His tone was very cordial. "Good evening, my boy. Glad you stopped in to see us." As he was going out of the room, he turned and with a slight jerk of his head summoned Philip out to the hall. Philip went with boyish alacrity, supposing that he would be asked to carry some small message to his father. But the Colonel, after leading him on through the front entrance hall and the narrow passage beyond, stopped with his hand on his office door, turned, and said in his usual tone of gruffness, "You might stop in at the office here one of these days after school, Philip. I'd like to have a little talk with you."

Philip answered respectfully, "Yes, sir"—while he stood wondering. He could scarcely believe what he heard the Colonel say next.

"Looks to me like you could make use of a little loan on easy terms when you get to college. You're setting yourself a pretty stiff program, although you appear to be strong, and maybe you can push it through. I hear you do well in your studies. 'Twasn't your father told me that. John doesn't open up on such things," the old gentleman said. "But they get around. Working for board and room won't hurt you, ought to be good for a husky young fellow. But you should get the full benefit of your studies if you're thinking of going into law. We don't need any more Eslick Pettimans."

The Colonel chuckled, and Philip smiled politely. Eslick Pettiman was one of Fairview's well-known citizens, comic or pathetic according to individual viewpoint. Eslick had been "intended for the law," but, due to some physical cause of which most Fairview people knew little or nothing, his mentality had not developed. Nevertheless he fancied himself as a lawyer, attended the open sessions in the Wahkonsa County courtroom, and carried papers in his old Cady hat in winter and his straw hat in summer—in his own words, "like Lincoln used to." His preternaturally awkward figure resembled a cut-down travesty of Abraham Lincoln's. Philip, his youthful heart more opened to the claims of misfortune than those of most of his friends, often stopped on the street to listen soberly to accounts of the "cases" which Eslick was about to bring into court. Philip could not echo the Colonel's chuckle, but neither could he contradict Colonel Merriam.

The Colonel concluded, "Don't answer now, my boy. Think it over, and stop in some day when you've got all your plans in mind. You two youngsters may have fun this summer, but I don't know as that enterprise is going to net you much money."

"Thank you, Colonel Merriam. I'll certainly—"

The Colonel left with an abrupt nod before Philip could finish, and went into the sanctuary of his office, where he could let his mind run on the early times and chew his tobacco.

Philip returned to the library in a state of inner elation, so that when Mrs. Merriam said to him, "Won't you take a more comfortable chair, Philip?" he sat down in the handsomest of the brocade-upholstered heirlooms. He knew that he ought to be leaving soon. Before he could bring himself to say so, however, Bradford spoke to him in a tone of genuine enthusiasm, with no cutting edge.

"You know, I think I envy you two lads on your travels this summer. I shall think of you as two Hardy characters ambling through your native prairies and woodlands in Grandfather Meserve's ancient shay filled with pots and kettles. And I confidently expect *you* to make a strong and remunerative impression upon the womenfolk in their kitchens—Mother and Lola included."

"Not any more than Lyle," Philip said loyally. "I ought to be going now," he added.

"Oh, need you leave so soon, Philip?" Mrs. Merriam said. "I've been hoping that Bradford might read to us—something you children could enjoy."

"Read!" Bradford exclaimed. It was years since his mother had made that request. As a boy he used often to read to her as she sat sewing. "What would you like to hear? Emerson?"

He couldn't refrain from that little jibe. His mother's taking up of Emerson had never been entirely convincing to Bradford even though he acknowledged that she, like young Philip, "tries to be sincere." The philosophy of the liberal-spirited Emerson was too far from stern doctrine which had ruled the house in Bradford's early boyhood. " 'I would write on the door-posts Whim,' " he once quoted to his mother, asking her if she went that far with Emerson. He hesitated, then on impulse took up *The Oxford Book of English Verse*, which he had been dipping into when Philip rang the doorbell. Bradford nearly always carried a copy in his coat pocket to help him through both short and long journeys. The thin pages opened of their own accord to "Ode on a Grecian Urn."

"Will Keats do, Mother?" His bright eyes glanced at her slightly askance.

"Whatever you select, Bradford."

Bradford hesitated again, feeling that it would have been gracious of him to turn to Milton. But she had said he was to read for "the children." He said coolly as he took up the small book and laid his pipe on the table, "Then suppose we settle for Keats. Here we have by common consent a classic. I wouldn't consider giving you children anything but a classic." After a moment's pause Bradford's clear voice sounded in the cool air of the library in the stillness of the Sunday afternoon. . . .

"She cannot fade, though thou hast not thy bliss. . . ."

When he had finished the poem, Bradford closed the gilt-edged pages. His expression was oddly remote and even stern, and Mrs. Merriam showed a faint distress. Bradford looked not at her but at Elaine and Philip, adding as if he were somehow invading dangerous territory, "Did you enjoy the poem, Elaine?"

Elaine said with her pretty preciseness, "Yes, it was very nice, Father."

"You're a splendid reader, Professor Merriam," Philip chimed in earnestly. "I never heard anybody read that well."

"Thank you, Philip! I feel overwhelmed by the commendations of you both."

"I enjoyed it too—enjoyed hearing you read again," Mrs. Merriam asserted bravely.

Bradford was silent. Then he said, "Thank you, Mother."

Philip rose, although with reluctance. "This has surely been a pleasant afternoon. I'm mighty sorry to leave, but I must now."

Mrs. Merriam said that he must take home with him some lilies-of-the-valley for his mother. Elaine, she said, might be willing to help Philip, since it was rather tedious picking those long, fine stems.

Elaine not only took the suggestion graciously but slipped out to the kitchen first to select some of the best iris for Philip to take with him also. She had never before shown any particular interest in Philip's mother, whom she thought of deprecatingly as "an invalid"—or in his father, either, although she had approved of John Wood as a handsome man.

Philip had never felt such a gratifying, and in fact flattering, sense of intimacy with the Merriams, and this, along with his inner knowledge of Colonel Merriam's offer, emboldened him —if he had needed emboldening. He felt no trepidation in speaking to Elaine's father, although he had wondered on his way to the Merriams' just how he could bring up his request.

"Professor Merriam."

Bradford had gone with Philip out to the front porch, following a cordial impulse. He turned and waited, his head lifted as if he were breathing in the outdoor scent, but his expression melancholy.

"There's something I wanted to speak to you about before I left."

"All right, Philip. In the Apostle's words, if I recall them rightly, which I probably do not, 'Press toward the mark.' "

Philip did not quite know how to take flippancy, but he tried to take a light tone too. "You forgot the 'I.' It's '*I* press toward the mark.' "

"Yes, yes. You bring it back to me, Philip. Now, shall we hear this 'something'?"

"It's about the school picnic. Our whole high school holds a half-day picnic, beginning with noon dinner, every year just after Commencement. I guess you know."

"I didn't know. Where is this revel conducted? In Father's grove?"

"Oh, no, Colonel Merriam wouldn't want a bunch of kids tearing around in there," Philip said candidly. "We hold it in

Deacon Kruse's timber lot, where we have the Sunday-school picnic." Bradford again looked much amused. "We can bring any guest we please—we seniors. I was wondering if Elaine would want to go with me."

Bradford asked with something of his father's abruptness, "Well, would she?"

"I don't know, sir. I thought maybe I'd better speak to you first and see if it would be all right for me to ask."

"Philip, your gallantry is to be thoroughly commended!" Bradford would have liked to add that there must be something in a name, Shakespeare to the contrary. "Philip Sidney" had always greatly entertained his fancy, even while it irritated him. He replied slowly and with respect.

"I think she can go, if you are on guard to see that she doesn't get tired. You remember our talk this morning. It might mean your coming home a bit earlier than you'd planned. Have you a way of doing that—granting that you want to take Elaine enough *to* do it?" Bradford added, with his quizzical look.

"Oh, yes," Philip answered confidently. "Yes, I certainly would be on guard, and I can manage bringing her home early. Lyle Meserve will have the use of a wagon and one of the lumber-yard teams, to take out a bunch of kids, and I'm pretty sure I could borrow the Meserve girls' pony."

"Then I see no reason why Elaine shouldn't go, if she herself takes kindly to your proposal. You know, that's a question with my daughter."

Thank you, Philip said, he would speak to Elaine. He went off, exuding bright confidence, turning back to exclaim with enthusiasm, "I surely enjoyed that reading. I'm going to read that poem again. That was great."

Elaine, having run out from the kitchen way with a sheaf of the iris, was already in the yard. Bradford watched her lay the sheaf carefully on the ground and then bend over the densely grown lily-of-the-valley bed which spread out in a sweeping radius of green, the thick, dark pointed leaves almost concealing the delicate sprays of bell-shaped white blossoms. Colonel

Merriam's lily-of-the-valley bed was one of the sights of Fair-view. Visitors in town were often taken past the Merriam yard for a glimpse of it in full bloom. Tommy Hardcastle had to be persuaded to mow around it and not touch it, for he considered the great flower bed "untidy." It was taken for granted that the lilies could be used for church decoration while they lasted. But Mrs. Merriam never failed to send Minnie Wood a bouquet every spring while the blossoms were at their freshest, in spite of her scruples against cut flowers. She had given Minnie a bowl of colonial glass—another of her choice heirlooms—to hold this annual bouquet. She referred to the lily-of-the-valley as "Minnie's flower."

Philip and Elaine were now kneeling at the edge of the flower bed, and Philip was talking while he picked among the thickly grown green leaves with swift expertness. Elaine did not seem to be answering, but something in her posture, with face downcast and turned slightly toward Philip, showed that she was listening. Bradford, standing near the railing of the porch, looked over at them with one of his most characteris-tically rueful expressions—at the strongly built, not quite grown-up boy, and the slim girl with her light gold hair. The long, loose, smoothly brushed curl, as Elaine stooped, hung sideways and almost brushed the lily-of-the-valley leaves. . . . The thought came to Bradford Merriam, She could do worse.

He tried to reject it, for a variety of reasons, but it stayed in his mind and seemed to have taken root there. As he turned away from the railing he frowned, conscious of mixed emo-tions. He re-entered the house abruptly.

CHAPTER

4

SUNDAY-NIGHT supper at the Merriams' had been one of Lola's excellent meals, fully expressive of the "wholesomeness" which Mrs. Merriam had attributed to her. Lola had forgone her usual Sunday-afternoon drive with the person whom she spoke of discreetly as "my friend," because, as she had told Mrs. Merriam in confidence, "Four makes too many for you, and we want to give the professor a meal to last him. He's got a lot of traveling ahead of him." It had both pleased and amused Bradford Merriam to see how the young woman, detached from her own parents and large family of brothers and sisters, was expending her affections upon her "old couple," as well as upon his own child.

His father and mother were eating better than at any time he remembered—and he could very well recall the Sunday-night suppers of old, when for his father there had been as much food as the Colonel's hearty appetite demanded, but for the children definitely plain living and high thinking. Bradford could see the long, cold, beautifully polished table in the oak-paneled dining room, set with plain white dishes, bread and butter, fresh fruit or preserves, and a tall white pitcher of milk at his mother's end of the table. All, of course, had been of the best, the white dishes of French porcelain, the bread homemade, the meat for the Colonel butchered at "the farm" (one of his farms), the milk, rich and yellow-white, from the Jersey then pastured in the back lot and milked twice daily by old Jake. It was the conscious abstemiousness, with its moral overtones, which Bradford still resented. A blackboard had stood near the table, on which the children would find written, in their mother's fine, firm hand, their "discussion theme" for the meal: "Honor," "Temperance," "Reverence," were the titles that came back to him. Bradford had been divided between disdain for his father's rudeness and admiration for his daring when the Colonel had broken into the discussion at any moment he pleased, with comments on old Jake's projects or racy anecdotes connected with his business.

But tonight had been different, almost pathetically different. Bradford was not sure whether this had been due to Lola's eager efforts to please "the professor," whom she obviously regarded with some awe, or whether his mother had really bent from her early severity; at least, she had accepted the meal with apparent pleasure and with no adverse comments. Lola had set out the polished table with some of the fine hemstitched doilies made by Minnie Wood, and had used the heavy silver, a wedding present, and the beautiful thin, faded china from the Bradford home. Tall candles in pewter sconces (also early Bradford), with their slightly unsteady glow, had a charming effect in the spring twilight in the room which Bradford had once thought of as gloomy, but which now appeared rather stately (although that word seemed to Bradford Merriam an untoward one to use in connection with anything in his native town).

Conversation too had kept much of the easy intimacy of the afternoon—marred, as Bradford now recalled with mortification, by his own irrepressible sparring with his mother. It did not make him happier to realize that he himself had started the altercation by saying of Philip Wood, in his most careless manner touched with amusement, "He seems to be a nice boy, after all!"

What did he mean by "after all"? his mother had immediately asked him, and he had replied with attempted lightness, "Nothing, Mother—merely that Minnie Wood might be a little hard to take." He might have added, "John Wood, too— and even more," but for the knowledge that it did not become him to deride John Wood, who had meant so much to his father all these years. Instead Bradford had switched. "I wouldn't have thought it possible for a boy to live down that name. Good Lord. *Philip Sidney*."

It was bad enough, his own bearing of the surname of his mother's Puritan family! But at least "Bradford" was in the line of history and tradition rather than of poetic fancy.

His mother had then remarked that she did "not know anything reprehensible about Sir Philip Sidney."

No, no, no, quite the opposite; he had given the cup of water to the dying soldier on the field of Zutphen! Bradford had felt himself forced into clumsiness as he added, "But it might well have ruined any ordinary boy to stagger under that name and try to live it down!"

"I think that Philip lives *up* to his name."

Bradford had arched his eyebrows, hearing the positive Emersonian note. But he had wanted no serious altercations tonight. He had said after a moment, merely dragging down one corner of his mobile lips, "That's the devil of it. Excuse me, Mother. Yet the lad is actually likable!"

This statement had brought his father down upon him. "Why shouldn't he be likable? Of course he's likable," the Colonel had growled, and his small eyes had held glints of the old temper.

"I agree with you, Father." Bradford had known that he was on dangerous ground. But he had not been quite able to give up his game. He had shifted, laughing a little, and saying the boy's name was "Minnie all over."

"No, Mother, I won't call Minnie sentimental. I've agreed that isn't precisely the word." He had made a gesture with his slender hands. "Highfalutin!"

Seeing his mother's lips compressed, Bradford had been aware again that he must go carefully. He had tried to turn the conversation. "Isn't her name actually Minerva? You must admit a *soupçon* of amusement there! She is so palpably—well, *Minnie*."

"Minerva was a common name in New England when I was a girl. I had a cousin Minerva Brooks. The name was not considered humorous."

"Mother, I agree. Again I quite agree. I know I'm being stupid. Suppose we drop the whole foolish topic—say that Philip Wood is an uncommonly taking lad, and let it go at that."

The Colonel had grumbled, but only briefly, and Mrs. Merriam had accepted with what seemed grateful readiness. The conversation had got back into happier lines, with Colonel Merriam—at Bradford's instigation—reminiscing, telling a story of the early times which his family had never heard before. It had concerned a long ride across the prairies which he had taken on the redoubtable horse Zach. Lola had lingered in the doorway, knowing that her plate of hot biscuits needed replenishing, but reluctant to miss a word. Bradford himself had been highly entertained, recognizing as never before his father's gift of racy narration. Even Elaine's eyes had been lifted and fixed on her grandfather. Her father had not been sure whether that blue gaze showed genuine interest, but it had almost seemed so.

Now Bradford was alone in the deepening darkness, sitting in an old cane chair on the narrow front porch and waiting to go to the office for a talk with his father which he both wanted and dreaded. He had spoken to his father just after the old gentleman had risen to leave the table. Colonel Merriam sat in a leather-upholstered chair in the dining room as well as in the library, to ease the wound in the groin which he had received during the Civil War; he considered leather more manly than soft cushioning. He still scorned a cane, but Bradford noticed that he got up with some difficulty, and that his tiger countenance, seen in the light of the candles, had taken on deeper hollows under the prominent cheekbones. Again Bradford was forced to thank Providence (if that was the proper authority!) for having brought John Wood to Fairview—even though the impeccability of John Wood, whether real or unreal, Bradford still found difficult to swallow. Was it real? Bradford had never completely decided. Yet he knew that he himself could not shove off all family responsibility, not forever. So far, he admitted, he had done pretty well.

But with the increasing evidence of age in his father, even though the Colonel was still fundamentally sound, that "forever" suddenly came close. Bradford felt it take on a different meaning. It had seemed to make necessary the talk for which he was waiting—much as he shrank from solemn, deliberate conversations. His train did not leave until close to midnight. He sat smoking—rising once to knock the ashes from his pipe over the porch railing, careful even at this moment to scatter the ashes on the ground, not over the tender young leaves of the flower bed. His father had agreed, had even been pleased, Bradford thought, by the request for a conversation, but had asked Bradford to wait a half-hour or so—"Give the old insides time to settle the good supper; the plumbing's getting out of date, don't all of it work so well!" The characteristic words, grimly humorous, spoken with a sharp eye-twinkle, made Bradford smile but brought a pang of apprehension, near and stark. . . . Footsteps went past on the sidewalk across the shady street, and then he heard the insects in the grass around the porch and in the farther reaches of the big yard.

The so-called office was at the back of the rambling house. Colonel Merriam had always liked to go over his personal accounts here at the homemade secretary of cherry wood given him years ago in lieu of some cash payment. He used also to start garden flowers from seed in wooden hot boxes in the two back windows, and to make out work schedules for old Jake. The back windows were now almost filled up with greenish-white snowball blossoms pressing against their old-fashioned panes.

There were no signs of gardening now. But the room, with its sloping floor of wide boards and its low ceiling, kept an atmosphere of pioneer days. Colonel Merriam had fitted it up according to his needs, tastes, whims, and special interests. The leather chair—another leather chair!—Bradford recognized as having been banned years ago from the library. On the couch, which was a kind of camp bed, reminiscent of army days, lay a handsome Indian blanket, a present from a local chieftain, cherished since the Colonel's log-cabin period. The colored reproductions in this room were mostly pictures of Indian battles and Indian village life. One medium-sized oil painting hung across the room from where the Colonel sat, so that he could look at it from both the chair and the couch. Bradford recognized this as the painting done by his sister Cora at their father's request: a view of the Upper Wahkonsa from the high spot in Merriam's Grove, representing George Merriam's first sight of the river when he had reined in his horse Zach and stopped under the trees. It was amateurishly painted—and why not? Codie had been only eighteen—but Bradford was surprised at the sense of atmosphere evoked: the crystal flow of the water, then a pristine stream, glimpsed through summer foliage thick almost to darkness; the solitude, awesome, primeval; and yet the patch of timber itself seeming intimate and homelike, rather than overpowering, here in the central prairie country, so largely open. To the Merriam children the Grove had meant outings and picnics, wild flowers to be enjoyed but gathered only "for some good purpose," according to their mother's precepts. Codie had never seen the Upper Wahkonsa as it was shown in her painting. She would have had to bring imagination to bear. What a tragic loss!—Codie and Flo, both of his talented sisters. Bradford would never get over it, never cease asking the ancient question, *Why?* with a feeling of bafflement and outrage, in his case never resolved. He closed his eyes for an instant.

Then again he saw the old room and its assorted treasures, all so characteristic of his father: the guns fastened above the secretary; the moose head above the door; the worn quiver of Indian arrows; Zach's bridle, used when the Colonel had first ridden into what was now Wahkonsa County; the faded flag of his regiment in the Civil War. On top of the secretary was propped a framed photograph of Lydia Bradford as a young woman, almost as elegantly slim as Elaine was now. If the Colonel had any pictures of his children, they were not in sight. Hidden in one of those drawers, Bradford surmised—pictures of the girls, that is; Bradford doubted that his father cherished one of himself.

His father had seemed too powerful and fiercely rugged ever to grow old. Bradford could not yet rise to his own perception that, physically at least, perhaps he need no longer fear his father. Age seemed wholly tragic to Bradford, almost as repugnant to him as to his daughter. Yet he felt moved by the unexpected philosophy (if it was that; possibly it was only candor) with which his father appeared to accept the realization of some degree of bodily decline. There was a composure in the face with its "tiger" modeling—as there appeared at times a softening of his wife's firm lips into a line that was almost sweetness. But Bradford remembered that both his parents had always had in them the capacity to "meet things"—something of the old pioneer fiber, which their children had lacked.

"Sit down, my boy."

"Thanks, I will for a while, Father. I don't want to keep you up too long."

"No, I'll take care of that! I take things pretty easy these days, Brad."

Colonel Merriam gave an old man's deep sigh. Yet his voice seemed to hold a note less of resignation than of a kind of contentment. He opened one of those small drawers in his secretary and took a sizable pinch from a litter of shredded tobacco, remarking, "You know, your mother don't really take it to heart any more if we menfolks use tobacco. You could light that pipe of yours in the house if you were a mind to. I'll wager she wouldn't object. I don't recommend it, though. I still use this stuff only in here."

"I know."

Bradford smiled. His father gave him another of those glances which the great eyebrows made fierce; this time, however, the look was one of humorous appreciation. The Colonel worked his jaws. He had his own teeth, was made of strong material, even though his internal machinery might now labor under some slight distress. Bradford himself was wearing a plate attached to his upper left jaw.

The Colonel said, half to himself, "Well, there's respect due Lyddy. Lots of respect due." He spoke very soberly. "Yes, and more than that."

George Merriam had some things in his background which he would not have cared to have raked up. He and Paul Kruse, when together, had not always "batched it," if the truth were told. George had offered to tell Lyddy his whole past before she married him. But she had said no, not if he said that "wrongful things" *were* past. She had accepted his assurance that they were, and she had never questioned him. And he himself, even beyond the keeping of his word, had never wanted any other woman since he had had Lydia.

He turned now and with dignified deliberation shot a small stream of tobacco juice into the spittoon, which had stood in the earliest Wahkonsa County courthouse. There was now a red sandstone building in place of the old frame structure. Whether his son had any conception of what the Colonel now looked upon as "early doings" the old man did not know, and did not want to know. Bradford did have a little but lacked the courage to presume upon his knowledge.

Bradford did not feel quite ready to open the conversation. It irked him that he was still not fully at ease with his father. He felt himself to be shifty and lightweight, even while he rather arrogantly maintained his own personality. He said at random, nodding toward the blossom-filled window, "That's quite a bush outside."

"Those guelder-rose bushes? Old Jake put in those bushes. He did a good job. Snowballs, the women call 'em," the Colonel said, audibly and contentedly champing. "The Relief Corps ladies will be after them, I expect, around Decoration Day—take all I've got. They're welcome."

"That still goes on, does it?"

"Why wouldn't it go on? The country's still here, ain't it?" Colonel Merriam growled but, like an old geyser, after a few threatening rumbles subsided. "Well," he now said, bending again toward his earthenware spittoon (a practice at which his son had always shuddered, and still did, inwardly), "better let me have it, boy, if you came with something on your mind."

Bradford kept a surface casualness which he did not feel underneath. He said with a deliberation almost like his father's, "You remember, I was remarking at supper that Philip Wood seemed . . . rather a promising boy."

He felt his father's bright gaze upon him. It had both an Indian impassiveness and an eagle-like penetration. He asked with attempted lightness, "Do you think he'll make another John Wood?"

"There is a John Wood. It's not a question of making another." Now the small eyes had a testy gleam.

Bradford tried once more. "Do you think young Philip will make a lawyer?"

"Well, Eslick Pettiman's a lawyer."

They both laughed, the Colonel with a brief chuckle, as earlier, with Philip; Bradford with the heartiness of relief. Bradford remembered how, during one of those discussions at the supper table, the Colonel used solemnly to bring in the name of Pettiman in order to relate Eslick's most recent doings to the topic of the evening. The Colonel had done this partly, of course, for the sake of hearing his wife struggle to bring dignity to the image of poor Eslick, whom the Colonel

looked upon as a frank figure of fun in a harmless way. But
Mrs. Merriam had been unwilling that the children should
view any of their elders in a comic light. Eslick, Bradford recalled, used to run regularly for the office of justice of the
peace and was always defeated. When the Colonel once said
that he expected Lyddy would like him to cast his vote for
Eslick, since she thought so highly of the fellow, Mrs. Merriam
had answered in distress, "No, George, I want nothing of the
kind." Wedding couples might come to the justice, and even
in a marriage not sanctified through the church she would not
contribute toward the ceremony's being made *humorous*. "It
ill becomes either of us to make jests of this kind." There was
a sparkle now in the Colonel's glance which suggested that he
might be thinking of the same story.

The line of Bradford's reasoning was at least becoming clear
to himself. The realization had come to him with bitterness
that John Wood had taken his place, that it was John who had
his father's confidence. He knew also, even if he could not
fully realize it, that this might be the last chance for the father
and son to have a talk together. Both were aware that there
were matters which ought to be discussed between them. Bradford had no information as to the extent of his father's property. The estate would go to his mother, in all probability, for
her lifetime. But whether to Bradford afterward, or to Elaine,
or how much of it in either or both cases, Bradford had no
idea. And might John Wood somehow enter the picture?
Greed for money was not one of Bradford Merriam's errors,
plentiful as they might be. (And they were plentiful; of this
he himself had no doubt.) He earned a sufficient salary for
himself to live pleasantly as a bachelor. But expenses for his
daughter were heavy. He wanted to give his child the best,
and more than the best. Bradford believed, nevertheless, that
John Wood deserved consideration. John had been a standby
all these years, and now was making Colonel Merriam's old age
light, or helping to do so; and John had been carrying a load
heavier in some ways than Bradford's own. Bradford would

not begrudge it if John Wood should inherit the entire business of the Merriam Company—only hoped that John knew "where he stood" better than Bradford himself did!

Yet he would never put full faith in the unassailable John. There was something in the man's eyes—or rather, there was nothing in them! Large, well shaped, open and calm as a summer day, they had still an oddity which Bradford could not define. Mother would say that is my own unrighteous mind, he thought, twisting his lips. But he could say nothing against John. Nor did he want to do so.

For a time Bradford was silent, fighting off a return of the old mixture of distaste, resentment, admiration, respect, and fear which his father could still arouse in him—he a man in his forties, cosmopolitan in experience and viewpoint, and his father a benevolent local autocrat well past eighty and with a certain wild aroma of the early days still clinging about him, for all his dignity and prestige as a leading citizen.

But again some realization of his father's age restrained Bradford. He gave up on this whole more delicate subject, and asked more or less at random once more, "How are things going?"

The Colonel brightened up, although he spoke dubiously. "Things," in his business vernacular, meant the agricultural situation as a whole; and, as Bradford seemed to remember, the prospects of farming were always referred to in a dubious tone. To Bradford this had seemed tiresome, if slightly comic; to Colonel Merriam it meant that no one could count certainly on the weather.

"Can't tell this early, of course. Still, the winter wasn't so bad in this section; we had a fair amount of snow, good March and April except for a week when it got pretty warm. I don't like a real warm early springtime. Over there in Dakota, they had a terrible winter—"

"Cold?"

"No, not near enough snow, and their early season was dry. Prospects look bad for them. Glad we're not selling any of that land. We've stuck pretty close to Wahkonsa County. But of course things can change mighty fast with a few good rains. There might still be a chance for a fair to middling crop there, though it don't look like it. They hadn't got their rain, the last time I heard. But I don't keep such close track now, except right here in our own section. John could say, very likely."

"He follows the situation, does he?" Bradford asked, trying to sound businesslike.

"Oh, John keeps his eye on just about everything," the Colonel said with satisfaction. He changed his position in the big chair and eased his bad leg. But when Bradford asked if he was getting tired he replied, "No, no, just one of those little reminders that I fought in the Civil War." He sang in a rusty growl, while with his fist he lightly pounded the chair arm:

> *"When we fit with Gen'ral Grant*
> *By gosh!"*

Bradford urged, "Go on with it!"

"No, no. That's about all the voice I can summon up." The Colonel rubbed his bearded chin humorously, chewed again at his tobacco. This was the jovial Colonel Merriam seen by his cronies, the best storyteller at the gradually dwindling meetings of the G. A. R.

As his father went on to talk, pausing now and then to locate his spittoon or to pick up another pinch of tobacco with stiff fingers, Bradford, with his essentially romantic imagination, had the sense of looking across a far-spreading prospect in summer green and blue and gold, mysteriously darkened at one spot by the deep foliage of Merriam's Grove. The name "Fairview," which he had been accustomed to speak in a tone of irony, suddenly took on meaning. He felt a kind of yearning to be able to agree with his father's profoundly affectionate statement, which until now he had regarded as a prime example of provincial complacency— "Yes, you'll not find many better places than we have right here in Wahkonsa County, don't care how much you travel, take it by and large."

Bradford now looked straight at his father and felt part of the confidence to say what he wanted to say. "Father, you know how far *I*'ve traveled. I wish—" He stopped, waiting.

He felt his father's keen eyes searching his. But he couldn't bring out all that he had wished to say. He did go on, though. "You know I can't come back, Father. But Elaine and this boy —I've been joking about Philip Wood. Elaine—I needn't tell you she's difficult. She'd make demands on anyone who married her. But I can see that it might just conceivably be a happy thing all around if she took it into her head to like this boy. You can't tell how far young Philip may be going."

Bradford felt that he had caught his father's attention. Long-pent admissions trembled on the verge of speech. But his father was not going to help him out.

The Colonel said gruffly, "Whoa. I haven't been smart enough at knowing what children have it in 'em to do to lay plans ahead. And I'm still head of the business, incidentally," he added dryly.

Bradford was silenced. He rose. "Well, Father, this has been interesting listening, but I'd better go. You'll want your sleep."

"I don't know as I want it, my boy, but it looks like sleep is going to overcome me."

The Colonel eased himself in his big shabby chair, made a last use of the spittoon. He shook his head, however, when Bradford asked if he was going upstairs. "No, I'll sleep down here tonight. The couch here is comfortable, no matter what the womenfolks say. Lola's always worrying herself about it, whenever she makes it up. 'Oh, Colonel Merriam, I'm afraid you don't get good rest here.'" The Colonel used a falsetto tone, which was certainly not the hearty Lola's. "Well, you see, then your mother can go to bed and get up when she's a mind to. We both can."

He asked how Brad would get to the train. "The hack come for you?" When Bradford said yes, he nodded. "Well, I guess they'll send it out in time. We can't ask Tommy Hardcastle to come over and hitch up old Bro any time of day or night the way we used to Jake. And Bro's getting a little stiff in the joints too, I've noticed. Sis seems to keep her girlish spirits! But she hasn't given the service Bro has. Well, they've been a good team. They won't leave the stable while I'm here in the house. And I guess your mother would feel about the same. Whatever she might feel, she'd take care of them same as she did of old Aggie. . . .

"Well, good-by, my boy. Take care of yourself."

"Good-by, Father. You do the same."

"I don't have to! Your mother does it for me." Bradford saw the mirthful sparkle from under the white eyebrows but heard contentment in the voice. "She'll look after Elaine too," the Colonel added. "You can bank on that."

Bradford was touched. "Thanks, Father!" They shook hands.

Almost the instant he had stepped out into the hall, Bradford felt his emotions veering; what he suddenly craved was to leave this house and town and section of the country and get back to New York, where he could be himself, the self that he had become. The atmosphere of the aging house weighed upon him. He would have preferred to call the hack and drive straight to the railroad station to wait there, sitting on one of the long, hard benches and reading a mystery story, if the light was not too dim. But he had one more talk remaining, this one with his mother. She had been waiting for him for some time in the library.

"Will you come in for a few minutes, Bradford?"

"Certainly, Mother. Don't you want more light?"

He snapped the switch, and the frosted wall lights came on with subdued luster.

"Yes, thank you, that will do. If you will sit down, I would like to ask you a few questions in respect to Elaine."

Bradford sat down with something like the very tentativeness of Elaine herself. Now he dreaded any approach to intimacy. He tried to hide his impatience to be gone under elaborate courtesy.

He could not deceive his mother. But certain questions were on her conscience, and she would not let her son leave until she had put them to him. After he had gone, she was prepared to assume full charge and responsibility; but while her son was in the house she would not forget, nor permit him to forget, that he was Elaine's father.

Bradford made the plunge and asked, trying to smile lightly, "What are your questions? And by the way," he added, "where is Elaine? Have you sent her to bed?"

"Do you think it's too early, Bradford? I know she's a big girl now, but—"

"No, no," Bradford answered hastily. "The earlier the better, no doubt, if you can persuade her to go. Or lure her into going. However you manage it."

"Elaine is quite obedient," his mother said in mild rebuke. "She didn't seem to mind going upstairs after Lola left."

"She seems to have a case on Lola!"

His mother asked, "You don't object, son, to having her so much with Lola?"

And when Bradford said, "Good heavens, no!" Mrs. Merriam added with a slight sigh, "It seems to be difficult for Elaine to make friends with the girls I ask here—such nice girls, the younger Meserve girls, and Claud Evans' daughter. But that may be more my fault than Elaine's," Mrs. Merriam added on reflection. "I may not make them feel at home."

"No doubt you do, Mother," Bradford protested, adding with calm dispassionateness, "We all find her rather a cool little thing. It may be partially Miss Preston's School—a matter of good manners."

"There is nothing wrong with good manners," Mrs. Merriam said firmly.

"That reminds me, Mother"—this might bring on the dreaded intimacy, but it had to be said—"I've given my august permission for Elaine to go to the school picnic—so, I believe, they call it—with young Philip Wood. Philip asked me, would you believe it—very gallant of him, becoming a knight of chivalry—before he left for home this afternoon."

His mother's expression was thoughtful. The picnic might be a little strenuous, Mrs. Merriam suggested, but they could trust Philip Wood with Elaine.

Bradford answered, with a quizzical cock of one eyebrow, "So I fear."

"You *fear?*"

"No, Mother, the remark was merely a jest. A feeble one, I grant you."

Mrs. Merriam ignored this and went on, "I can ask Philip to be a little careful."

Bradford made a movement of impatience. "I *have* asked him. I'm remiss, Mother, but not that remiss. As you say, the boy can be trusted if any boy can. And after all, he's known Elaine and they have been playmates for ten years or so."

"Yes, I know, Bradford. That's partly what makes me think —their friendship—" Mrs. Merriam now looked searchingly at Bradford, and Brad instinctively braced himself. "Philip has been—what shall I say?—the best companion Elaine has had here in Fairview. It gratifies me very much that he continues to want to be with her. He really has an excellent effect on her. But—this is where I'd like to know your own thinking and wishes—how much would we like to see this friendship—well, go further, if it should? Oh, I know they're both very young."

Bradford caught at this last and said, "They're children, infants! Surely we don't need to look so far ahead, try to penetrate what the gods may have in store for these young lives!"

Bradford realized that he was taking quite a different line in this discussion with his mother from the one he had taken with his father, or, for that matter, with himself. He smiled ironically, thinking what strange turns his fancies and his calculations *were* taking on this brief return to his home base. Was he actually now beginning to lay snares for this innocent lamb, this young roebuck? "Besides, Philip will be away most of the summer—remember?—learning his way about in the great world."

"Yes, yes, I suppose I am being unnecessarily concerned. I don't want to say anything against Elaine's and Philip's being together. Quite the contrary."

"Dr. Vinal said that she needed to get away from school and from being with a bunch of girls all the time," Bradford said. "She needs, in short, to have just what you offer here, quiet and order and freedom—freedom of a most orderly sort!"

"And this little outing, this school picnic, will not be too much for her?"

"Oh, no, I don't think so. She can't be just cooped up. And with the estimable Philip at her side, all will be well."

His mother studied her son's face, but did not press the matter further, for which Bradford was devoutly grateful. He had wanted to confide in his father, but not, in this case, in his mother. He saw the outline, still firm and spare, of his mother's shoulders in the dark silk dress she was now wearing for late Sunday afternoon and evening, and the uprightness in the carriage of her head, at the same time so like, and so unlike, that of his slender daughter.

He rose, insisting that his mother should not sit up with him. He had sent his father to bed and would send her also! Mrs. Merriam smiled at this. He would go up to his room, Bradford continued, put his things together, read a bit, say good night to his child unless she was asleep—as he hoped she would be.

Their own good-bys were spoken stiffly. Bradford kissed his mother's cheek.

"We'll look for you again, Bradford, at the end of the summer. Then perhaps you will spend a few days with us."

"Yes, Mother, I'll hope to do that." He felt that his leave-taking was graceless, and he added, "It's putting a burden on you, leaving Elaine with you. I know that, and I'm more grateful than I may sound."

But his mother said quietly, "No, it's not a burden. Why do

your father and I still keep up this big place if we can't have our grandchild here? And Elaine seems to make out well with us, even if we are so quiet here. She gains a few pounds each summer. We are pleased at that. Tommy Hardcastle is proud that his Guernseys give just as good milk, so he says, as our old Jersey did!"

This time Bradford was touched by his mother's real goodness and by the loyal inclusion of his father in her comments —not to mention Tommy Hardcastle. The Colonel was playful and coaxing with his grandchild, with gruff gentleness calling her "Goldilocks," but the burden of care was the grandmother's.

Bradford lifted his hand. *"Auf Wiedersehen!"* He left his mother, feeling at the moment more relief than anything else.

Bradford was too restless to stay in his room. He feared to waken his child on both her account and his own. But after a while, having heard his mother come up to her room, he did gently turn the knob of Elaine's door. By her own choice she slept in the old nursery. Bradford was glad that she did not occupy the bedroom of either of his sisters, although he derided himself for just that kind of superstitious feeling. The nursery was large and cool in the May night. It was still a child's room, but his mother had said to him earlier that it could be re-furnished as a young girl's room, which would make "an interesting project for Elaine."

Bradford did not leave the doorway, but he could see the outline of Elaine's figure in the white-enameled single bed which she had occupied for several summers. Even in that girl's outline there was a slenderness which reminded Bradford of his sister Florence. The pale gold hair, with its long curl, would have reminded him of someone else—if he had let it, which he did not. He did take pride in the patrician quality of his daughter's figure, was pleased to discern in her clear-cut slimness something of "the Bradford look." He was proud of the knowledge that she would be beautiful, lovelier than either of his sisters, if intellectually less "interesting"; while trying not to take into awareness a certain elusive witchery in the droop and lift of her dark-fringed eyelids.

Bradford softly closed the door and slipped back to his own room.

Soon he heard the hack, Fairview's one rentable vehicle, drive up outside. His father had obeyed him and gone to sleep. His mother, however, stepped out from her room into the dimly lighted upstairs hallway. In her neat dressing-gown she looked ladylike as ever, except that the nighttime coil of braided hair, pinned closely to her small head, showed an elastic-bound thin end of braid escaping. This touch of *déshabille* seemed somehow infinitely touching to Bradford. He set down the bag and put his arms closely around his mother; felt her head pressed against his chest. They did not speak what was in their hearts even then, but the consciousness of it was in their long embrace.

Bradford said in a strangled sort of whisper, "You should have had Philip Wood for a son."

"I don't want Philip Wood."

"No, but I want him for you."

"Bradford, please don't say such things as that."

They stood for a moment longer, Bradford struggling with his silent self-dissatisfaction, until they heard a sound at the door, a discreet knock.

"Bert must be getting uneasy," Mrs. Merriam murmured then. She drew herself away and smoothed her dressing-gown.

Bradford went to the head of the stairs, looked over the oak banister, and waved at the bulky figure just discernible in the hack. He turned hastily to his mother, "Good-by, I'll be back, send you word when."

She nodded. "Good-by, son." Then she promised softly, taking both Bradford's hands before he again picked up his bag, "I'll take care of Elaine."

Bradford could not answer. His throat was suddenly choked. The last thing he saw, before he hurried down the stairs, was his mother's eyes looking straight into his own, their expression clear-sighted, chastened, wise, above all, steadfast. In the jolting hack he sat with his own eyes closed. Later, in the swaying darkness of his lower berth, he saw fitfully the light gold shimmer of his daughter's hair, thinking, with a smile only partly satirical, as he drifted into a kind of surface sleep, of the girl to whom he had given the name of "the fair, the lovable" picking lilies-of-the-valley with a fresh-faced knight who picked with commendable industriousness and had, with just as commendable courtesy, put his boy's cap down on the thick Maytime grass.

C H A P T E R

5

PHILIP went home so uplifted and joyful that he felt he knew the actual meaning of the old phrase "walking on air." But he had time only to eat a piece of bread spread thick with butter, and to drink a glass of milk, before he went on to the Christian Endeavor meeting, gnawing an apple on the way. Lyle had stopped for him.

Philip couldn't refrain from telling Lyle, "I was over at the Merriams' this afternoon. Professor Merriam invited me."

Lyle said after a moment, "I suppose Elaine was there. She's grown a lot, hasn't she? I mean, changed quite a bit. Did you get to talk to her?"

"Yes, some. Mostly to her father, though, and Colonel Merriam. Well, all of them."

Lyle said again, after they had walked on a few more paces, "She's sure got to be pretty. I don't know, though, I always thought she was hard to talk to."

"She is at first," Philip conceded. "Not so much when she gets used to you."

"You don't think she's stuck up, then? Some of the kids do."

"Well—no, I don't think it's that so much." In the fresh evening air, under the spring foliage, again Philip could not refrain from confiding in Lyle, "Don't say anything about it yet, fellow, I don't care to have the kids hashing it over before-hand, but Elaine's going to come with me to the picnic."

"You mean our school picnic?"

Philip nodded.

"Yeah, but are her folks going to let her? They're always so particular."

"They said so. Her father said so. I asked him first."

Lyle looked Philip over. He remarked enigmatically—they had reached the steps of the church—"It's going to make some other girls feel pretty bad."

"As who?" Philip scoffed, pausing before he went up the steps.

"Oh, I don't have to name them."

The boys hurried on into the Sunday-school room, where the young people held their meeting. They were a little late; Philip was saved from trying to answer. But he knew very well whom Lyle had in mind. Gladys Cornwall and Evvie Evans were standing together, sharing a hymn book—one of the thin, green-covered Sunday-school hymn books left for the Endeavorers.

"Have you trials and tem'tations,
Su-f'ring from a load of care . . ."

Philip saw Evvie slightly nudge Gladys and saw Gladys's warm brown eyes just turned toward him for an instant when he and Lyle quietly entered and took chairs at the back of the room. Usually Philip didn't join the back-row masculine contingent (which meant that Lyle didn't either) but sat well forward. He had no fears of being called on by the leader, and he was not at the meeting for the purpose (at least, the primary purpose) of walking home with one of the girls. This one, for him, had been Gladys recently, since Gladys and Evvie were best friends, and Lyle, this last year, had been going steady with Evvie. The two girls brightened up when Lyle and Philip entered. Philip saw Gladys's round, freckled cheeks get rosy before she turned away.

The hymn itself seemed to take on new life after the two boys entered the room. Lyle immediately joined in the singing in his agreeable, although not very strong, tenor voice. Philip did not start at once, however. He cleared his throat. Howard Rechtner, standing at the front of the room, looked as if he had been rescued. Howard would not now need to dread one of those panicky silences after he had made his own halting little talk. After he had said, "I will now turn the meeting over to the rest of you and hope you will all have some thoughts to contribute," he could rely on Philip Wood not merely to "contribute" but to say something interesting enough that it would "lead others to follow." Miss Sadie Ashburton, the inevitable lingerer-on from an elder generation, droned along when she got started, putting the meeting to sleep. Philip could sound the right note. Or if the "season of prayer" lasted too long, Philip could wind it up and not sound hackneyed.

But although Philip intended to take his part, he was still preoccupied, inwardly lost in radiant dreams and lingering sensations. He was out in the late May afternoon with Elaine, picking lilies-of-the-valley, seeing the play of her delicate fingers among the cool green leaves, and feeling their clinging touch. He saw her raise her eyes when he asked her to go with him to the picnic, and the light come into their cool blue before her beautiful eyelids drooped again, slowly; a smile barely touched the corners of her pretty lips. . . .

Howard, his thin, boyish cheeks suffused with sensitive color, was plowing valiantly into his subject—"What Our Pledge Means to Me"—although, as always when he was nervous, his voice was husky and uneven. Howard Rechtner was among the few—Miss Sadie Ashburton was another—who really did "pray and read the Bible every day," according to his pledge and promise; he was listened to with respect, even though he did backtrack and stumble. Philip came to now and then—often enough to follow Howard's general line of thought. But he then fell back into blissful abstractedness. Fortunately this did not turn out to be one of those tongue-tied sessions, so that Philip did not need to "contribute" at length; although he did speak, not wanting to let Howdy down. But the parting words, which usually he felt inwardly with deep sincerity, and spoke firmly, tonight slid over him so that he scarcely knew they had been said; his lips seemed merely to be murmuring, almost like those of the back-row mumblers whose attention was fixed on slipping out ahead of the girls to be on hand for first choice.

"The Lord be with thee and keep thee, while we are absent, one from the other." The moment the meeting was over, Philip went forward to shake Howard's hand and tell him, "Swell work, kid."

Howdy said earnestly, "Gee, kid, thanks." His brown eyes were moist with effort and emotion.

Then Miss Sadie Ashburton got hold of Philip to inquire after his mother. "I missed seeing her in church this morning, but you say she was there. My, I think it's simply wonderful how Minnie attends services and keeps up the way she does! I remember her as a girl, when we all thought we were going to lose her. But of course she has your father and yew-ew"—with a glance almost coy. It would have embarrassed any other boy, but Philip was sensitive to the wistfulness in Miss Ashburton's tone, understood—as much as a boy of his age could understand—the loneliness in which she lived.

Philip was disturbed, however, because he saw that the two girls, Gladys and Evvie, were hopefully waiting near the door. Philip knew also that Gladys probably hoped that tonight he would ask if he might take her to the school picnic. The senior-class girls were all aware, of course, from talking among themselves, that Philip had asked no one so far. Lyle *had* asked Evvie. Gladys might seem to have a further claim upon Philip because he had been chosen Valedictorian of their class and she Salutatorian. They both practiced with Hank Henderson, the high-school principal, after school hours. Of course this was not an actual claim—any more than Philip's being Lyle's best friend, and Gladys, Evvie's. Yet Philip did not feel easy about it. Gladys was a swell girl, as nice as any in their class, and he did not like to disappoint her. He was quite sure as to the disappointment. But he couldn't help it—and she could not fully realize that her somewhat chunky freckled face, her medium-sized brown eyes and healthily substantial looks, and the fact that she was bright in her studies (second, in fact, to Philip) could not possibly appeal to Philip Wood "in that way." Evvie "in that way" seemed more desirable than Gladys, certainly prettier with her fuzzy blond-red hair and hazel-green eyes, her lightness and brightness, and her pretty clothes; and her family—Mr. Evans was the leading lawyer in Fairview, Colonel Merriam's attorney—was more congenial with the Wood family than the worthy but plain Cornwalls.

If Philip had not known Elaine, he might, for this one time, have asked to take Gladys to the picnic, as a kind of accolade for her virtues and attainments. But he could not even see Gladys in comparison with Elaine—the aristocratic slenderness; the beautifully carried small head with the shimmer of light gold hair falling in the long, loose curl; the perfect nose; the fringed eyelids lifted, and then his own glance into the blue coolness to depths in which excitingly dwelt something, or someone, beseeching, lost, and fair.

Philip came to again just in time to say a decently cordial good night to Sadie Ashburton and to lay his hand on Lyle's arm. Lyle was getting impatient.

"Listen, fellow, I think I'd better go right on home tonight. I've been gone all afternoon, and I expect my father wants to come to the evening service."

He didn't see how or whether Lyle asked Evvie without asking Gladys; probably he would walk home with both. Going away out to the Cornwalls'—they lived on the edge of town—would at least give Lyle an acceptable reason for having a longer walk with Evvie. All three had left, at any rate, before Philip went out into the fresh cool evening, feeling mean but relieved.

When Philip got home he found his mother upstairs, not in bed but sitting in her cane rocking chair, reading.

"Let's see what you've got."

She showed him her book, *When Knighthood Was in Flower*. Mrs. Latham and Almeda Blanchard had lent it to her. "Some scenes are a little daring, but there's nothing to object to. It has a nice background."

"Yes, you love those old castles," Philip teased her as he flipped through the book.

"I like them, and I like good love stories too. I don't care what anybody says."

Philip enjoyed the way she set that little chin in harmless defiance. By "anybody" he knew that she was referring to Mrs. Merriam, whom she loved and respected too much to contradict directly, although she herself couldn't read Emerson—was lost when she tried it, and even a little shocked.

"I'm not saying anything," Philip assured her solemnly.

"No, I know you're not, dear." Minnie put her fingers on Philip's hand. "But lots of people do seem to think reading love stories is a waste of time. What else is so much worth writing about?"

"Nothing else," Philip answered, still solemn. If anyone had a right to say that, his mother did.

Minnie was satisfied and withdrew the small, thin fingers, short and blunt-tipped. Philip, looking at them, asked suddenly where she had put the lilies-of-the-valley. She told him, in the big glass bowl in the dining room. "They're more beautiful than ever this spring. Who picked them? This great bouquet! Not Mrs. Merriam."

Philip replied, as if absent-mindedly, "No, Elaine and I did."

"Oh, of course, Elaine. I forgot for the moment. I wonder why Brad brought her early?" Minnie mused. "Did they say? How she's grown! I don't know whether you noticed. But girls do that—they shoot up all of a sudden. I was a little girl with

a round face, quite stout, you wouldn't believe it, Philip, and
then all at once one summer I was a thin, big girl."

"Not very big!" Philip smiled again with teasing tenderness.

But he saw and felt those other fingers searching among the
stems beneath the leaves; they were tapered and silken-smooth,
while on his mother's fingers the knuckles were already somewhat enlarged, so that she had to use soap to get off her plain
wedding ring and the engagement ring with the single dia-
mond. The fingers had been even thinner when the rings were
first placed upon them. But there was something about the two
—his mother and Elaine—that was alike, and that haunted him;
although his mother's face, with its wide mouth, snub nose,
black eyebrows, the round eyes with their coal-black eyelashes, was distinct and definite, while Elaine's fair face—in
spite of the pure modeling of the nose and brows and drooped
white eyelids—was all elusiveness.

Philip was glad that his mother asked him nothing about the
afternoon, except for an absent-minded "How was Bradford?"
She didn't wait to hear his reply, but at once went on to ask,
"Did you meet your father?"

Philip roused himself. "Oh, yes, I was going to tell you. I
passed him just as I got to the Schaeffers' big tree."

Minnie sighed. "I wish he hadn't had to go to the service tonight. He was so tired. He thought he had to do all that work
and studying over the books this afternoon and those columns
in the paper. Of course we wouldn't want him to take up any
other kind of work, and he wouldn't consider it, he's so loyal
—but I just wonder sometimes if Colonel Merriam doesn't
leave John too much to look after these days. Of course John
won't say so. Did you think he looked pale tonight?"

"Why, I didn't notice, Mama. I couldn't see him very well,
either, especially under that tree, and we went right on past
each other, just said hello. I said, 'Hello, Papa,' he said, 'Hello,
son.' Such was the extent of our conversation. I guess he didn't
want to be late."

"I thought he looked quite pale." Minnie's broad forehead
was puckered between the black eyebrows. "But there's to be
some kind of committee meeting after church, so of course he
went. You know how your father is."

Philip answered, "Yes." For a moment his bright visions
were troubled. He said, "Maybe I ought to stay home next
year and help out. I think Colonel Merriam might be willing
for me to do some work in the office."

He was relieved at his mother's instant, emphatic, "No, we
don't want you to do that, not either of us. Your father
wouldn't listen to it. You know that. Your education is one of
the things he works for, and I would too if I could." Philip did
not mention Colonel Merriam's offer; he felt that he wanted
to tell his father first. "No," Minnie said with another sigh,
locking her little fingers on her lap, "I'm the one who costs the
money."

"Now, you know Papa wouldn't listen to *that*."

"No," she admitted, "I know he wouldn't." Philip caught
the brightness of her gray eyes before she looked aside; they
shone with tender brilliancy from out of a setting of melancholy. "Anyway," Minnie said, "there's the old property. I did
bring us that, so I'm not all expense."

"The property and the furniture!" Philip said with a twin-
kle, knowing how little the old walnut pieces pleased his
mother's *fin de siècle* taste—particularly the homemade pieces
—but how, since they "had belonged to the folks," she
couldn't bear to part with any of them. Now and then his
father made her a present of something more to her liking,
such as the ladylike desk downstairs, and the curlicued cane
rocker in which she was now sitting.

But she said very soberly, "Well, Philip, when I think how
little we started with, John and I, in that one-story house, just
a prairie cottage, the furniture was quite an item."

"It's quite an item still," Philip said with a droll glance at the
big bed with its ornately carved headboard. His mother made
a face, which changed to a look of tenderness; she knew very

well that Philip was not going to allow her to lament that she was "a cost" or "a burden." And in fact she didn't really think that herself; they were all three too happy together. Getting up, Philip said to his mother, still with the playful air she liked, "You can read half an hour longer, although I want you to be careful of the daring parts. If Mrs. Latham read them, I suppose I'll have to say *you* can. I trust Miss Blanchard skipped them."

Minnie gave him a reproving look, but she knew that her son enjoyed her little airs of primness, which matched the plainness of her hair and the set of her small chin, yet went so quaintly with her long eyelashes and her ruffles and her out-and-out devotion to John.

"But then," Philip solemnly continued, "I'll expect you to go to bed. You know I'm boss in this house when Papa isn't around."

"Oh, *are* you?" Minnie's black eyebrows arched. She was delighted.

"Most certainly. I believe that the man should rule, like Deacon Kruse."

"That poor girl!" Minnie sighed commiseratingly. "Why wouldn't her father let her marry Russ Blachley? He was nice, even if he wasn't up to Caroline in every respect. But, Philip, who would be? Caroline Kruse is a saint."

"She has to be, to live with her father and survive. I know, Mama, I know he's good in other ways, a pillar, sound on doctrine! I'll say it before you can." Philip was the one to make a face now. "But as somebody, I don't know just who it was, said, the old Prussian lives on, if he did get converted and join our church. I pity his womenfolks, and you know you do too, Minnie Terrill Wood. The trouble is"—Philip spoke slyly, yet seriously—"there are not enough John Woods to go around."

"No, there aren't," Minnie said with deep-felt earnestness, yet with a kind of wondering satisfaction that made Philip inwardly smile.

"Well, we've got that settled. I have to leave you now. I'm

still hungry. I want another piece of Mother Dissendorfer's bread."

He kissed his mother, heard her say, "Oh, yes, dear, do get something to eat," as he turned to go out of the room. He paused to cross over and draw down the shades of the two windows facing the ravine. His mother couldn't see the tree-rimmed and bushy hollow, except on moonlight nights, but she had confided that she didn't "like to think the street stops with us."

In the kitchen Philip cut the bread and spread the butter on thick—Phoebe's light gold butter, home-churned yesterday, in the old-style up-and-down churn. Not that it was necessary to specify "old-style" in regard to anything done or owned by Phoebe and Tommy Hardcastle! After a moment of consideration, Philip added brown sugar from the small crock in the pantry. But he took the piece of bread upstairs with him; it would taste better eaten in his own room.

The air of the well-loved room embraced him. The night air coming in through the plain curtains at the open window, he loved. What if his folks had been like Boysie Wheeler's, always snooping, not willing for him to have a thought or emotion of his own? John and Minnie cared too much for each other. Philip was spared overmuch doting, although he was their only son. His mother called him by loving names, but "sweetheart" was reserved for her husband. Philip was aware of this close union of the two above him and was far from resentful; it gave him freedom. Yet he was never left out but gratifyingly included. Philip had been spared both the queenly airs and graces of his friend Will Cowie's mother, seeking to bind Will to her and get him on her side, and the dominating presence of Will's father, Austin. Lyle certainly belonged to a happy family, but he lived surrounded by sisters, while Philip was the sole heir. Philip knew his own fortune, and was grateful. He would prove that he deserved it.

He put his bread down on the table while he undressed. He liked to eat the bread after he got into bed, in spite of the bother with crumbs, or finding a sprinkle of brown sugar ground into his nice clean sheet when he got up in the morning. Fortunately, he made his own bed.

For a moment the memory of what his mother had said to him about his father returned—that John "looked quite pale." But Philip had no real fear of his father's overworking. The strength of those splendid shoulders seemed able to carry all loads. The burden of Minnie was light, although John worried about her, planned and "did" for her, was "wrapped up in her." The bearing of her frail weight acted as an incentive rather than burden. The memory of that look about the eyes, making them like the still eyes of a statue, which Philip had noticed this morning when looking at his father's face, just brushed his attention. He looked forward with pride to telling his father of Colonel Merriam's offer, thinking with inward humility that no doubt it was due more to his father than to himself. Still, the Colonel would not have made it unless he had put trust also in Philip. Philip felt entirely capable of earning his way through college, if need be; he felt confident, as he had told Professor Merriam, that a way would open for him to go to law school in the East. Again he looked through the oncoming years to the future, thinking now of all he would do for the folks. He indulged again in a dream of their visiting him at the White House. He thought of the picture of General George Washington hanging in the Merriams' oak-paneled hall, and of how he himself used to stand and silently study it when he went to play with Elaine. "Don't stand there, Philip —what makes you stand *there?*" she would protest, stepping lightly through the hall and on up the stairs to the square landing, where she stopped and leaned over the banister, looking down at him, her head a glimmer of gold and her smooth loose curls hanging over her shoulders. . . .

Philip got into bed, early as it was, and sat up, eating his homemade bread and butter and brown sugar in luxury. He thought fleetingly of Gladys—but then again of Elaine. He reached up and turned off the bare light bulb.

Not only Elaine's patrician fineness appealed to him as worthy of Philip Wood and his future eminence, nor the thrilling secret dream of her slender body. There was also the appeal of an almost hidden need, which Philip believed that only he saw. He was sure that he knew Elaine better than anyone else did, that she showed him a different side. Others of the children, particularly those in Mrs. Merriam's own church and Sunday school, had been asked over for an hour's play, and occasionally Mrs. Merriam had arranged parties for her grandchild. But Philip was "the one she took to," as old Aggie used to say. Philip smiled with some complacency at the thought of that preliminary coldness. The Meserve girls and Evvie liked to *say* they had been "invited to play with Elaine Merriam," rather than actually to play with her. "You really have *fun* there?" Ione and Doris Meserve had asked wonderingly of Philip.

The long association between the Merriam and Wood families touched Philip's vision of the future with intimate sweetness. And while he was more or less aware that Elaine's father might have other plans than for his daughter to become attached (at this moment Philip scarcely dared to go beyond "attachment") to a law student from a small town with his own way to make, Philip cherished his own inner consciousness of having as much to bring Elaine as she could give him. The name "Philip Sidney" was not without effect, after all, as Bradford Merriam had shrewdly guessed. But the effect was not of the kind seen from Bradford's half-cynical viewpoint. Philip did not consciously live up to a vision of chivalry, in spite of his avid reading of the Round Table stories of Howard Pyle in *St. Nicholas*. Yet he felt himself chosen for some form of knightliness as a kind of vocation, much as he had entered into the thought of politics—of statesmanship, rather—as a profession. Philip was deeply but silently proud of his name. And to Philip there was nothing foolish in his mother's having given him the name, nothing foolish in anything his mother did. Her indefinable charm gave all his happy world a hint of fragrance, like the springtime aroma of the crystal bowlful of lilies-of-the-valley. Her ruffles and slippers and her romantic feminine notions were endearing. She had mind as well.

Elaine was not so endearing. Perhaps she did not have so fine an intelligence as Minnie Wood's, although she possessed half-hidden, unpredictable talents. There was classical severity in her beauty, as well as romantic suggestion, something exacting and demanding, both in herself and in her ancestry, which led Philip on beyond present boundaries, made him extend himself; Philip thought of it as "something to come up to," and a mystery which could reach deep into his life.

Philip thought of Elaine again as he had seen her standing on the other side of the old-fashioned hooped-wire fence, close to him but separated, with the long stalks of the orchid-tinted iris held in her arm—upright, her slim figure as straight as her grandmother's, yet ready to flit away; her pretty lips politely smiling, but her eyes unresponsive and cold.

Philip believed, in joyous assurance not free from danger, that he was the person, perhaps the one person, who could give Elaine that gift lacking to her, in spite of her grandmother's care and her grandfather's indulgence, her father's attachment to her, which Philip had sensed beneath the nonchalant impersonality, sometimes a little cruel, which hid something painful. Philip well knew that Elaine, although correct—so that Mrs. Meserve had told Ione and Doris, "Now I want you girls to notice how Elaine acts and see if you can't imbibe some better manners yourselves"—was nevertheless "difficult," "hard to make out." Her precise prettiness held a tragic suggestion. But he had the cure. He would give her that stimulus, balm, and security in which his mother's frail physical life had survived in happiness. He knew what love was. He had lived in its light. It seemed to Philip, at this heightened moment, that the special quality of what he had known in his home—a rare, precious elixir—would be lost if bestowed upon some dependable, capable, nice girl like Gladys Cornwall, with her full, healthy lips and her warm, but not particularly pretty brown eyes; she would make a good wife and mother no matter whom she married. She could take care of herself, if need be, too. But Gladys had no such attraction, physical or visionary, for Philip Wood, no such gleam—"follow the gleam"—as Elaine with the shimmer of smoothly brushed, slightly curling golden hair.

Philip again lived through the afternoon with its beauty and its gratifying surprises. The last thing of which he was conscious, beyond his elation and his expectation, was a clear voice reading with perfect enunciation words that made beautiful music, although he was falling asleep and did not remember either the words themselves or their meaning.

PART

TWO

CHAPTER

6

M RS. MERRIAM was alone in her library. She was dusting the books. Most were in the massive bookcases behind glass doors, but Mrs. Merriam's meticulousness required that all be taken out and gone over scrupulously every short while. She reserved this task for herself. It was not among the duties carefully written out for Lola on a sheet of good tablet paper and tacked up beside the calendar in the kitchen. Little as Mrs. Merriam enjoyed housework—although she had done plenty of it in earlier years when she had had only half-wild Aggie to help her—she loved books. "A literary streak" had come down in a straight and narrow groove through generations of learned and thinking Bradfords—widening, in her own case, with the inclusion of Emerson's *Essays*, her great discovery which had led in turn to a new valuation of the Bible; but in her son's case broadened and, she feared, trivially and even harmfully diverted and diffused. But her father would have thought the same of her own appreciation of Emerson!

Some of the books Mrs. Merriam valued for family association: books with blackish covers, pages scorched or water-stained or yellowed and brittle-edged. Although their content was theological, of the kind that her own thinking and personal experience no longer permitted her to follow, they kept her in touch with the old home in Massachusetts, more than the choice pieces of chinaware and silver and furniture which she had brought to her Midwestern home.

Mrs. Merriam was opposed to the practice of stopping to read while she dusted; she used to reprove the girls for that. Florence especially would start work on a bookshelf, open an old volume of memoirs or poems, and then stand lost either in interest or in satirical amazement. Mrs. Merriam did not believe in skimming or skipping; one should be prepared to read thoroughly or not at all. Yet she permitted Elaine to take up a book, any book the child pleased, glance at a page or so, and lay it down; because she had to "lure" Elaine (a word Mrs. Merriam detested!) to any reading whatever. Nevertheless Elaine did read; for only a day or two ago Mrs. Merriam had heard her reading aloud in the small parlor, where doubtless she had thought herself quite alone and unobserved. The poem was one of Shelley's, a poet of whom Mrs. Merriam disapproved with sorrow, knowing that he was a favorite of her son's. Not only the words themselves shocked Mrs. Merriam with what she considered a lavish display of emotion and lack of high self-control, but she had heard in Elaine's correctly trained speech, her voice clear in tone and pure in enunciation as her father's (although a small voice), an inner dramatic intensity which had dismayed her. It did not belong to Bradford, but Mrs. Merriam did fear that it went back to the wife from whom in thought she shrank, yet with compassion—although such words as "unfortunate," "regrettable" were all she had ever allowed herself to use in description of her son's marriage. She still knew little of this unseen person so important in her son's past life, in the lives of all of them, nor had she pressed Bradford to tell her; she could not, unless he "came to her with it" of his own accord. Remembering with deep contrition her mistakes with her children, Mrs. Merriam could not ask for that.

But of course she wondered. She saw the golden shimmer

of Elaine's hair, the grace of her movements (which nevertheless were those of a well-bred little girl from Miss Preston's
School), and recognized that these charms did not come from
the Bradfords, still less the Merriams. Like Bradford, she perceived in Elaine some quality reminiscent of Florence. But
Florence (Mrs. Merriam had never called her daughters "Flo"
and "Codie," for she deplored nicknames and abbreviations),
although romantic and intense, had possessed too a candid
straightness that was all Bradford. The same quality was to be
seen in the earliest portraits in the old Massachusetts home-
stead. Florence's fair hair had been like Mrs. Merriam's own,
beautiful for its length and texture, but with none of that
gleam and overtone of pale gold, no alluring curls or half-
curls; Florence's eyelids lifting from the gray eyes' gaze without subtlety, although sometimes with a hint of wildness: no
elusiveness anywhere. And there was nothing at all of Cora's
sturdiness of build and emotional richness of personality in
Cora's niece, Bradford's daughter, the slim, aloof, courteously
correct, yet disturbing girl. The words Mrs. Merriam had
heard Elaine reading—

> *"O lift me from the grass!*
> *I die! I faint! I fail!—"*

had affected her most adversely; yet at the same time she had
felt herself reluctantly moved by the immediacy of the child's
vision and the almost hidden tone of drama in her clear little
voice.

Mrs. Merriam frowned in distress. She no longer thought it
right to forbid most poetry, as she had tried to do in the case
of her own children. She had been sincere in asking Bradford
to read aloud and to make his own choice. She, as well as her
husband, had seen that he had become a man, and not the kind
of man whom George and Lydia Merriam, either or both of
them, had hoped and expected their son to be. But she could
bear the consciousness of having erred greatly—she, Lydia
Bradford Merriam—and try humbly and resolutely to find "a

more excellent way," having faith in "the unsearchable riches
of God." Mrs. Merriam closed her eyes momentarily, and her
face, worn and spare, yet "older" rather than "old," took on
the look of endurance touched with sweetness which her son
had discerned without wishing to see it or to understand its
significance.

The morning sunlight through the open blinds streaked her
face and shoulders with brightness. Mrs. Merriam opened her
eyes and moved on to the next bookcase. She found herself
taking out the volume of Emerson's *Poems* which she owned
in order to have Emerson's works complete, although she had
seldom looked into it. Bradford had found amusement one day
in following his mother about and insisting that she listen to
Emerson's poem to *The Rhodora:*

> *Tell them, dear, that if eyes were made for seeing,*
> *Then Beauty is its own excuse for being.*

"That's Emerson, Mother. Do you mean to say you haven't
read it?" Bradford had felt rueful when he had seen his
mother's distress and her effort to derive something acceptable
to her conscience out of the lines. But that was one of the times
which Mrs. Merriam cherished in memory—when her son had
put his arms around her, resting his cheek against her smooth
hair, and then whimsically assuring her that she mustn't mind,
he too had never thought of Emerson as a poet. Bradford
might be right; Mrs. Merriam did not pretend to know. But
surely Emerson must have written some verse which would
be more suitable for her grandchild's present need than "O lift
me from the grass"!

The book opened of itself at one page, and Mrs. Merriam
stood much as she used to find Florence standing, her dustcloth
drooping from one lax hand.

> *Give all to love . . .*

Mrs. Merriam read the poem through twice, taking the book
nearer the light. She pondered the final lines.

> *Heartily know,*
> *When half-gods go,*
> *The gods arrive.*

"The gods." She did not quite like that term. Yet she trusted Emerson. As she stood between the long front windows, in her well-fitting morning dress, her hair now securely fastened to her small head with bone hairpins between neutral-colored side combs, Mrs. Merriam's well-defined lips quivered. Her face took on an expression of exaltation while keeping its underlying, enduring sadness. She found illumination for herself in the poem. No, she did *not* agree with Bradford. But she had gained through tragic experience too much human wisdom to persuade herself that her golden-haired granddaughter, with disconcerting ways and voice with its lilt of alien grace, would find meaning or nourishment in the angular, spare speech of the New England sage in these enigmatically stated lines. She sighed, and after retrieving her dustcloth—with a sense of sorrow as she remembered her own earlier austerities, now partly irretrievable upon this earth, at least—she carefully cleaned the volume of *Poems* and pushed it back into line with the other books.

Mrs. Merriam heard the two very different, yet harmoniously chiming voices of Lola and Elaine out in the kitchen, where Lola was preparing fresh asparagus for dinner; Tommy Hardcastle had brought in a fine big bunch. A problem came up immediately, one that had worried Mrs. Merriam during the night. She felt that Elaine was "safe" in the keeping of Lola's big-sisterly warmth. But were they themselves wronging Lola in not warning her of Elaine's nervous instability? She feared that there had been more to this problem than Bradford had confided. Bradford might seem indifferent, even neglectful; his mother often considered him so. But his pride was very sensitive in regard to this child.

There seemed to be no real need of speaking to Lola, however. She would intend to keep loyal silence, but she came of a large family, whom she often saw on their farm not far from Fairview, and her nature was open.

Yes, but ought they—or ought she, Mrs. Merriam—to inform Philip Wood? Mrs. Merriam hesitated. Perhaps the few words Bradford had said to Philip were enough. She did not want to alarm Philip and put a burden upon him, spoil his and perhaps even Elaine's enjoyment of the picnic. If Philip had promised that he would bring Elaine home early, he would do so. The doctor in the East had also said that Elaine needed to "run free." Apparently Elaine was eager to go to this picnic, although her instant acquiescence had been rather surprising. But she was always surprising!

Mrs. Merriam was more concerned in a certain sense with this grandchild than she had been with her own daughters, although she knew, and accepted, that Elaine did not truly love her, while "the girls," for all their rebelliousness (most of it *her* fault), had been devoted. But Mrs. Merriam realized now that she could not compel this child's slender little feet in a way they would not go. She felt in Elaine the alien and unforeseeable elements, so that she could not be close to the child; yet, almost more than Elaine's father, she hoped and strove for a better future for her than Mrs. Merriam's own girls had encountered. But she would not go back over old unhappy things, much as she felt her own involvement. Remembering St. Paul's increased activity after he had seen new light, she refused to brood.

She was aware that Bradford was very conscious of his daughter's patrician beauty, and, as some of her friends here in Fairview would have said, "looked high" for Elaine. That knowledge was what had surprised her in Bradford's seeming encouragement of Philip Wood last Sunday. Doubtless Bradford had had no more in mind than to give his child some normal pleasures when he had allowed Philip to take her to the high-school picnic. She would take her son at his word.

But of all the boys and young men whom she herself knew or could, in a sense, imagine, Bradford could have chosen no one more suitable in *her* eyes than Philip Wood. When she thought of Philip's boyish goodness to his ailing mother, that was almost enough in itself. And yet even Bradford with his (Mrs. Merriam feared) cynical tongue did not call Philip sentimental. There were other close ties. All in all, the future union of Philip and Elaine would be almost perfect, if Mrs. Merriam could believe it advisable on Philip's account; that side of the matter was what disturbed *her*.

Mrs. Merriam's thought turned to Philip's father. She hoped more deeply than she had ever thought it wise to say that full retirement and relinquishment of business responsibility was what her husband had decided upon. She, as well as Bradford, had seen that he was getting old, and also that he was "still himself"—the sturdy, fearless, human, robust, hard, and truth-speaking George Merriam whom she had left her home beside the Atlantic to marry, attracted by their very differences, and whom she now longed to have more often with her simply to enjoy his company while he and she were both "themselves."

But she wanted also that he should do the right thing by John Wood. She herself did not care if the sale of the Merriam Company to John might not bring them as high a financial return as would sale to some conceivable person or persons. As far as she was concerned, George could ask no more than token payment from John. John had earned that through standing by and helping George Merriam in uncomplaining loyalty all these years. He would actually in a way become their son if his boy and their granddaughter should wed, and this would mean much to George, who (though not with his wife's concurrence) looked upon Bradford as a sort of half-son: benevolently, tolerantly, even generously in some respects, but never masking the feeling that Bradford had turned out to be, to his father, a disappointment. And so too, in another way than the one of which Bradford had spoken—and she had repudiated—Lydia Merriam might just possibly have Philip Wood for a son.

And yet Mrs. Merriam dreamed of all this without in any

deeply personal sense caring for John Wood himself. He was all that she approved—but she loved him far less than she had come to love Minnie. In her largeness of spirit, she attributed her lack of any true intimacy with John to the fact of his heart's being wholly absorbed by his love for Minnie. Mrs. Merriam thought she could understand that. Minnie had a peculiar winsomeness. But to the boy, with his fresh ingenuousness, his mixture of becoming modesty and youthful self-assurance—close to bumptiousness, at times—his devotion to his parents expressed in ways that seemed completely natural and unstrained, his shining, confident eyes, Mrs. Merriam could give her whole heart.

Mrs. Merriam turned from the bookcase as her husband entered the room. Although his step sounded much as usual, and he gave no special sign, his wife knew at once that something had happened. She asked sharply, "George, what is it?"

Colonel Merriam lowered himself slowly into his chair. He did not speak. His silence itself was confirmation; otherwise he would have teased her, asking, "What makes you think anything's wrong, Lyddy? I'm all in a piece." As she looked at him, Mrs. Merriam felt a sense of premonition, which grew out of painful memories. She closed the door of the heavy bookcase, so firmly built that the glass did not shiver, and waited. Colonel Merriam had put his hands, palms down, on the arms of his chair and was clasping and unclasping the chair arms as he stared straight ahead.

Mrs. Merriam could make little of his expression. But she reproved herself. She had sensed last evening that something was amiss, although George had come to the supper table as usual and had even talked with his gruff playfulness to Elaine. However, she knew his iron control, the same with which, in his days as a woodsman and hunter, he had been able to sight a wild creature and wait motionless for precisely the right instant to shoot. After supper he had gone to his office room, remarking that Claud Evans might be over to "discuss a matter," not an infrequent happening. He had added that he might stay down in the office for the night— "So don't look for me, Lyddy." That, too, was not infrequent. Climbing the stairs was getting harder for the Colonel than he cared to acknowledge. Mrs. Merriam had not wanted to question him, he so disliked anything in the way of what he called interference. But now while he sat in his big chair, still saying nothing, her mind ranged through dread possibilities as well as going back to other tragic announcements.

She thought first of Bradford. Then of Elaine. Then that Minnie might perhaps last night have "slipped away," a thought often with her—so that she felt nothing but puzzled surprise when he blurted out in a tone that had suddenly grown savage, "John Wood is a thief."

Mrs. Merriam was unaware that her lips had turned pale as she started to make some kind of protest. "George, what did you say?"

Her husband repeated the words in almost the same tone. "What do you mean?"

The Colonel said, staring with bitter, bright eyes from under his down-drawn white eyebrows, "He's been misusing the funds in his care. I call that being a thief."

Mrs. Merriam gave a choked sound. Then she said faintly, "It can't be."

"Can't be, maybe, but it is."

Even while George spoke, and while she was still protesting, Mrs. Merriam felt that she knew that his incredible statement *could* be true—thought that in a sense she had long known it. Not, of course, that she had known anything specific, but had known, at least underneath, that in the romance which she had cherished all these years as the one ideal example of perfect harmony between man and woman she had seen upon this earth—humbling herself because in this instance her romantically inclined daughter had "seen aright"—there had all the time been some element which eluded full conviction.

Even with that, the announcement was so stunning that she

was barely able to feel relief that neither her son nor her granddaughter was involved. She looked with quick intentness to see what the discovery might have done to her husband. But he appeared not to show much change as yet, except for the brief flare-up of his old fierce temper. As he kept on sitting motionless, after having spoken, he seemed not to have lost the sense of strength and substantiality which he had always given.

Mrs. Merriam asked after a moment, still faintly, "How long have you known about this, George?"

"Since yesterday."

"You didn't speak of it."

"No, I suppose I wanted to feel sure."

"Do you feel sure now?"

Colonel Merriam answered bitterly, "Yes, I guess I'm sure now. I've heard it from John Wood himself."

Mrs. Merriam was again silent, her hand pressed against her chest, as if she were feeling and counting the reverberations from a blow.

"That's where I've come from, Claud and I—talking with John."

"Downtown?"

"No, right here in my office."

"I didn't hear you," Mrs. Merriam murmured.

"You never do hear much, do you, when both the doors are closed?"

Colonel Merriam then turned abruptly to his wife. She saw the glitter of his small eyes. She might have thought him hostile to herself—except that she knew better.

"I see that you'll have to have the whole story." Suddenly he sighed deeply. "You might as well hear it now as later."

"Yes, I want to hear it at once."

Colonel Merriam saw that his wife was sitting up very straight, her face still pale, her lips firm. He knew that look. He had had to inform her of other disasters which had come even closer home to her than this one could. He was not sure that anything could now come closer to himself—unless it was to lose Lyddy. At least he need not fear that he had a wife who would not be able to hear these tidings also, even though the knowledge cracked the bedrock of their own way of life, which had grown so comfortable and settled now that they themselves had begun to grow old. As husband and wife, throughout their long union, prosperous in so many of its aspects but infused with losses and suffering and deep variance, they had never deliberately kept things from each other; although the difference between them had made each one carry on a portion of his or her life apart from the other. He spoke plainly—the only way in which George Merriam ever did speak, except when he was teasing or jesting or letting himself go with his cronies—and with a certain curt brevity. His wife listened almost without comment, trying first of all, before she let her emotions have way, to get the content and gist of the Colonel's narrative.

The first that Colonel Merriam had known of the whole matter was when a farmer from east of town, Ben Tellyer, had stopped in to see him.

"You didn't know he was here, either, I guess, Lyddy. He came to the house office too, and Lola brought him in to see me."

The Colonel had not thought there was anything special about the call, for he had known this fellow Tellyer pretty well: Ben had bought his farm years ago from Colonel Merriam, and he'd been in the practice of looking in now and then when he came to town, to say how things were going. Colonel Merriam had always enjoyed these visits, for Ben was a nice kind of fellow, able and hard-working, never came merely to let loose one of those long, grumbling, hard-luck tales—which, like many successful men, Colonel Merriam didn't like to listen to. The Colonel preferred to have the sales he had made turn out well, and the one to Ben Tellyer had done so. Recently, in fact, Ben had bought another, smaller piece of land, intending to work both pieces. The latter he had bought through John Wood. So the Colonel had started out as usual, asking jokingly, "Well, Ben, what's on your mind this fine day?"

To his surprise, Ben didn't take him up in the same tone but said after a while, "Things aren't going so good, Colonel Merriam."

"That so? Why, what's the trouble?"

Well, Ben's wife had been sick, and now was facing an operation. But before Colonel Merriam could stop him with a brief, "Sorry to hear that," Ben had burst out about "the money," and then mumbled something about "that piece over south of me I bought last, the one Christiansen used to own."

The Colonel, a trifle huffed, said to him, "Well, that's a good piece. I should think you could raise something on that if you have need"—adding, when Ben made no reply, "We might be able to do something for you ourselves, if things happen to be tight right now at the bank; though I don't know why they should be. Have you been to the bank?"

Ben said no, he hadn't been to the bank. He didn't go on for a while then, until again he burst out, "There's something funny about that sale, Colonel."

At first the Colonel had been nonplused; but when he had got the meaning—that Ben was actually imputing some wrong dealing on the part of the Merriam Company—he had risen up from his desk. He had not been so angry in years, he confessed now, with a side glance at his wife; had scarcely been able to contain himself. She did not reply, but shook her head slightly. She knew his pride. There could not be anything "funny" about a sale made by the George Merriam Company! But Ben Tellyer had stood his ground and wouldn't let go of the matter —as dogged as the Colonel was irate—until finally he brought the accusation home to John Wood.

The Colonel stared ahead. He breathed a little hard. For a time, he said, he wasn't even willing to listen. But he'd consented finally to hear what Ben had to say; Ben was confused over something, had been his thought—probably some picayune point. But as Ben Tellyer went on to tell his story of the land transaction, the Colonel had begun to feel "funny" himself. He'd made Ben go over it from the beginning.

"This may sound complicated to you, Lyddy," he now said warningly. Colonel Merriam still made some effort to keep up the fiction of his younger days that his wife, as a woman, "didn't understand business," although well aware that her clear, exact intelligence not only followed his explanations but usually got ahead of them. "You think you want to hear it all?"

"Certainly I do. How am I to know what it's about if I don't hear it?"

"All right, but it's not a pretty story."

Mrs. Merriam retorted proudly, "I don't expect it to be pretty. Must I be told only what's pretty?"

"No, no," her husband said. "I know you can take hard tidings, Lyddy, just as well as I can. Maybe better." That was an immense concession for George! He made a gesture toward her; but his hand could not reach her, and he felt too old and stunned to get up from his chair.

Mrs. Merriam saw his intention and drew her chair closer. She pressed his hand and said, "Go on with your story."

The Colonel gave another long, deep sigh, unaware that he did so. He continued his account as briefly as he could, but left out nothing essential, for he felt the penetration of Lydia's gray eyes and knew that she could catch him up if he skipped a point.

The story was that Ben Tellyer had long had his eye on that forty, knowing it might come up for sale, since the Christiansens were moving to California, and that it was near enough to Ben's own farm so that he could work both pieces. But Ben was one of those careful fellows who didn't like to go ahead without cash pretty much in hand. He ran close to the wind at times, as farmers often had to do, since they couldn't govern the weather, but he'd kept out of any serious debt. A few months ago John Wood had said to him that there was another man interested in the forty, which the Merriam Company was to handle, so Ben had better make up his mind. Ben couldn't bear to let the land slip out of his grasp, although to buy it then meant using a fund he tried to keep aside, and which he couldn't replenish until he got his crops in at the end of the summer. But John had given him assurance that if he paid part cash down, he could borrow money on this piece on easy terms any time he wanted to. "You won't have any trouble." Those had been John's words, so Ben had kept repeating. The inference was that Ben could get the loan readily from the Merriam Company; he wouldn't need to go to the bank. Ben didn't know at that time about his wife's condition; it was just his canny way of looking into all corners before he acted. Like everybody else in these parts, he trusted John Wood, and John had every reason to take a chance on Ben Tellyer. John might have spoken to Colonel Merriam before finishing the deal, if he'd wanted to be meticulous; but as he and the Colonel had worked things out between them, John had all matters of ordinary transactions pretty much in charge. And this transaction was not out of the ordinary.

Then Ben's wife *did* get sick, and Ben had come for the loan.

The amount Ben asked for was not large, only about six hundred dollars. He had plenty of property to cover it, and the Merriam business could well stand giving such small loans to reliable people. "I'd have been glad to see Ben through personally if I'd known." But instead of saying he would talk with Colonel Merriam about it, John had stalled Ben off when Ben had brought up the subject of the loan, and in a "funny" way, so that Ben—"who, as I told you, Lyddy, is canny"—couldn't quite get the thing straight. A lot of men would have let the question ride a bit, thinking that John Wood knew what he was doing. But Ben was just the one in a hundred who wouldn't. He had come to Colonel Merriam to find out what was wrong: why John Wood, or the Merriam Company, couldn't lend him six hundred dollars immediately, on perfectly good security.

The Colonel stopped speaking and again sat clasping and unclasping the chair arms, while his wife waited. She said finally, "Go on, George, and finish it."

"Well, Lyddy, it's going to be a long time before we're finished with it. The Ben Tellyer part is only the beginning!"

Mrs. Merriam looked steadily at her husband. "Well, go on."

Colonel Merriam said that he still, after the man had left, had thought Ben Tellyer must be mixed up somehow. He had still been pretty mad at Ben. All the same, Ben Tellyer was a substantial person, one who kept his feet on the ground, not the suspicious kind, even though "careful." Colonel Merriam had gone to his downtown office, saying that he'd take over while John made a trip into the country. He often did that.

"Did John suspect how matters were?"

"Didn't seem to. But you know how John is. His face doesn't show much."

His wife nodded, while her own face revealed that she had her thoughts and reservations.

Colonel Merriam then had looked into the record books. John Wood kept all the books, had been doing that ever since he had come into the Colonel's employ. "You know I'm not tidy, Lyddy." The Colonel had looked through the book in which the sale of the forty to Ben Tellyer should have been recorded.

"Well, to come down to it, Lyddy, the account of that sale wasn't there. John Wood was keeping the whole thing under his hat. I haven't found out yet where John cashed Ben's check. Not at our bank. But you know John does a good deal of driving around. John had never mentioned it to me, either, so far as I can recollect. No, I'm positive. That was strange too."

The Colonel mused. "I suppose John thought he could get the whole amount covered long before it was needed, Ben's loan included—if Ben ever asked, which seemed unlikely. John had to get terms from Christiansen—Martin Christiansen, who was selling the forty. He thought he had the use of Ben's payment for as long as he would want it. Then it was Ben's asking

for the six hundred after all—a small amount, comparatively!
—that really toppled the business over. You can't tell what
may come up to upset any lie, smooth as it may seem," the
Colonel finished. He stared ahead glumly.

"No," Mrs. Merriam murmured with sadness.

"And then I began to find other things," the Colonel said.
"I'm not going to burden you, Lyddy, with the whole. But I
couldn't shut my eyes. I had the office to myself for more than
two hours. There was nobody there to get mad at. I guess I did
get pretty mad at Ben Tellyer for a while." Colonel Merriam
glanced sidewise at his wife. "I told him 'twas an insult for him
to accuse John Wood, and said I'd rather suspect my own son."

Mrs. Merriam saw that the Colonel's small, dark eyes, bright
as those of some aged but undaunted bird, were wet, a sight
she had not seen since— No, she had never seen it. When the
news of Florence's death had come to them, and, following it,
that of his own favorite Cora, George Merriam had been too
deeply stricken to cry. He had given the second cablegram to
his wife in silence. If he had shed tears, it had been while he
was alone. His wife now made a gesture toward him, but he
did not respond.

The Colonel continued of his own accord, after frankly
wiping his eyes and blowing his nose on a large, glossily ironed
handkerchief (which almost any Fairview person would know
had been laundered by Lavina Randolph). He then had asked
Claud Evans, his lawyer, to come to the house after supper and
to bring along from the office downtown more of the records
and papers—this book that should have had in it the note on
the Tellyer sale in particular. The Colonel hadn't wanted to
trust his own scrutiny alone.

"I hadn't wanted to take the records, so as not to make John
suspicious, or he might have skipped out."

"John Wood skip out!" Mrs. Merriam was horrified.

"If he'd misused the funds entrusted to him, Lyddy, he'd
skip out."

"Oh, no," she protested. "He wouldn't leave Minnie."

The Colonel rubbed his lips and chin, finally saying with an effort, "Well, well, he didn't skip. He's here now."

The Colonel, before leaving his place of business downtown, had climbed up the stairs to Claud's office and left him the company office key. "I left it in an envelope, didn't say what it was, but Claud understood." Claud hadn't even gone home for supper, but had got some hot cakes and coffee at that little restaurant next to the furniture store. Colonel Merriam and Claud Evans had looked through considerable material last night—"unbeknownst to all of you." More entries had been found missing. It looked as if John must have taken some of his papers home. The Colonel said that he *himself* had felt like a thief, going through John Wood's records, even if it was with his own lawyer.

"But that's the wrong view," the Colonel admitted, breathing hard, staring ahead of him. "I'm a good deal to blame. I haven't looked at John's books enough—not often enough, or hard enough. I should have done that, no matter how I felt about John. It's the George Merriam Company—my own company."

Mrs. Merriam said nothing, but her whole attitude expressed sympathy.

The Colonel shook his head. He said Claud had had no such qualms, at any rate. Claud had a lawyer's viewpoint and experience. He'd been able to spot weak points in the records. "Yes, too many weak points. Too many."

Colonel Merriam had not been able to doubt any longer. This morning, before breakfast, Claud had again come over. After his own breakfast—which, his wife now recalled, he had eaten in silence—the Colonel also had gone into the office. They'd called up John Wood—Colonel Merriam himself had done the calling—and had asked John to step in. John came over, came promptly. And he, John Wood himself, had confessed.

The stillness that followed was broken only by the Colonel's heavy breathing, the slight sound of his hands moving on the leather-covered chair arms. Mrs. Merriam waited, she herself scarcely breathing.

Finally the Colonel spoke. "I'm not going to tell you what John said to me, Lyddy, nor what I said to him. 'Twasn't much, in words. But don't ever ask me to go over it."

"No, George, I won't," Mrs. Merriam promised softly.

The Colonel straightened himself in his chair. "Well, I can tell you the facts themselves, Lyddy. I owe that to you. You'd better hear them from me."

Why had John juggled the books? It was an old story, but not one any person would ever have thought of applying to John Wood. He'd been gambling on the Chicago Stock Exchange. He had done it before, but for smaller sums. This time it was in wheat, and he was "speculating in futures," Colonel Merriam said contemptuously; for this was a kind of finance, common enough among some businessmen in the region, which was alien to the Colonel's character— "As if there aren't enough uncertainties in business without buying grain that doesn't exist with money you haven't got." John had been counting on the crop failure that had been predicted earlier for the Plains states. "But you can't *count* on crop failure, even in the Dakotas!" The Colonel showed a glint of harsh humor. The whole picture was changed all at once by the rains, which came in the nick of time. The prospects in some sections were good, after all. John was caught in a falling market. He had to cover his purchases with money he didn't have.

"I don't know how much of this you take in, Lyddy."

Mrs. Merriam compressed her lips. She had caught the essentials readily enough. She did not need to make George an answer. After all, he had told her this painful story in fuller detail than she might have anticipated.

"Claud and I found enough last night to show that this little bit of business with Ben Tellyer wasn't anything new," Colonel Merriam repeated, "even if John hadn't acknowledged it! It had been going on for years—ever since John and Minnie sold that small Terrill property and John handled the pro-

ceeds. . . . Yes. Well. 'Twas a hard thing to do, Lyddy—talk
with a lawyer, even Claud, about John Wood. I said that before, I guess, but you'll have to bear with me. Made me feel
almost like I was tattling against my own kin."

He sat with hands again clutching the chair arms, as if he
were staring back into the night hours and those bleak with
the chill of early morning, when, under his old blanket, the one
given him by his Indian friend, among the trophies he had
cherished for years—the moose head staring with its unchanging glass eyes, mute testimony to the prowess of his early man-
hood—he had been forced to readjust his whole life to the fact
that John Wood was not his support and helper, his second
son, but, in his own harsh terms, "no good." He had felt his
age to the full, as he had painfully settled to this bitter realization much as his old frame did to the bumps of the cot, which
he had long insisted was comfortable. That he had come to
readjustment showed in a certain grim hardness which his wife
recognized, and which she knew did not change—so that it
was with trepidation that she asked him (she would have
shrunk from the question except that she did not believe in
shrinking or flinching) what was going to happen now, as to
John Wood.

"That's to be seen."

Mrs. Merriam had further questions. She admitted to herself
that her chief concern wasn't about John Wood himself. She
was thinking of Minnie. But the subject of Minnie opened up
so many difficulties that it had best be skirted as long as possible. As Mrs. Merriam looked at her husband's face (not impressive except in front view, unlike her own fine profile) she
saw nevertheless a set of the white head, a thrust of the tigerish
jaw, and a stillness which she had reason to know. Fear shot
through her that he would not take Minnie into consideration;
a sense of protectiveness rose in her heart, almost as if toward
her own child. (Yet toward her own children, Florence and
Cora at any rate, in years gone by her husband had been less
severe than she herself.) She saw the small, fragile form, the

girl's waist, the large round eyes turning to look at her with a horrified appeal from out the darkened hollow sockets which betrayed Minnie's physical delicacy.

After a time Mrs. Merriam asked, "Does this affect us?"

Colonel Merriam turned his eyes upon her sternly. "How can it help affecting us?"

"I know, George. I mean our finances."

"The business is still George Merriam's. The George Merriam Company makes good on its transactions."

Mrs. Merriam nodded silently. On this they were in full agreement.

"Oh, we can stand it, I guess," the Colonel admitted, "though I don't know what it may turn out to be, all in all. 'Tisn't so much, perhaps, in actual money due, although there's more concerned than just Ben Tellyer, as I told you. More people than you and me trusted John Wood. He's been 'making investments' for years, buying lots mostly, for Mrs. Dissendorfer and folks like that. She had just about the price of a vacant lot!"

"Not Tommy and Phoebe!"

"No, they've hung on to all they owned. Good old unmitigated penuriousness has its rewards, you see, Lyddy," the Colonel said dryly.

The Colonel glanced at her with a grim humor which shocked his wife. It always pleased him that she could still be shocked. He liked to see her sitting as now, silent and stately, following one of his remarks. Even at such a time as this he could enjoy Lyddy.

"You'll have to pay this man, of course," she said after a while.

"Ben Tellyer? Certainly I'll have to pay him. Pay the lot of them, if necessary."

"His wife must have her operation. That shouldn't be delayed. I don't think I'm acquainted with her, but—"

"They go to the Methodist church," the Colonel put in slyly. "Not yours."

She replied with dignity, "That doesn't matter. And you know it doesn't, George."

"Of course I know it, Lyddy. And I'd pay Ben anyway, no matter why he needed the money, if he'd been told it was available."

Again Mrs. Merriam nodded. As to his teasing, the time was long past when that had greatly troubled her, and she had never let herself be overthrown. She thought now that she would rather see George with this grim glint of humor than see him stricken. He was not that—even though now, as the light came in more strongly through the opened shutters, she saw startling evidence of the night he had spent. Yes, he had aged. That was what she had sensed when he first came into the room. She would not yet ask how much, or how lastingly. Even now he seemed strong.

She said finally, out of her own thoughts, "But God is merciful."

This time the Colonel made no reply. He could be merciful too, when he felt the need or impulse! He had always been more tolerant of what to him were "human frailties" than had his wife. He did not know, for instance, whether his wife had any suspicion of "this other woman" in their son's life, as well as not knowing what she might have learned, or just suspected, as to his own early years. But Colonel Merriam had long ago decided that it wouldn't do for him and Lyddy to go into questions about God and religion. They were too far apart and had better remain so. He could be thankful that Lydia, on her part, was not a pesterer. The decision had in fact been mutual and lived up to scrupulously by both of them, barring a few harmless jests which the Colonel felt entitled to make.

He had an awareness now of what was in Lydia's mind, and would refer to it in his own way. He said firmly, "John will do the only thing possible, to *my* way of thinking, when he's got himself into such a situation: take the consequences. It's been his doing. No, I guess you can't rightfully blame Minnie."

Mrs. Merriam waited, her heart beating heavily, her lips stiff, as she finally whispered, "You mean, pay back?"

"With what? He's cleaned out! He *can't* pay back." The Colonel spoke scornfully.

"What, George! Stand trial?"

"Why shouldn't he?"

"Yes, but *John Wood*—"

"The laws can't be turned aside for John Wood, Lyddy. I didn't suppose you'd advocate that."

"I haven't advocated it," Mrs. Merriam murmured. "But there ought to be some way."

"What way?" George Merriam asked inexorably. He had turned his head, and his small eyes seemed to bore into her.

She said with an effort, "Friends might help."

"How are *they* going to help?"

"They might make up a sum and settle."

"Settle out of court, you mean?"

"I don't know as to that, George. I'm afraid I don't know much more about legal procedures than Eslick Pettiman. Probably not so much," Mrs. Merriam said with pitiful lightness.

The Colonel was touched. He reached out again and patted her hand with its handsome wedding and engagement rings. But he shook his head. " 'Twouldn't do. 'Twouldn't actually settle things. John Wood has lost his standing. For all I know, some folks might be fool enough to try that method, for one reason or another. For the matter of that, you and I and Williston and Claud and Ben Tellyer might agree to keep mum amongst us. You and I would make good on the quiet. But 'twould likely get out. And it wouldn't affect the fact that none of us would trust John Wood. 'Twould leave an untrustworthy man in a position of responsibility."

Lydia could not deny that. Yet some kind of protest was working within her mind.

The Colonel returned to her earlier question. "Yes, Lyddy, it affects us. I don't want you to think it means we can't eat, or will need to take in boarders, or send Lola home. But it cuts us down. It cuts down what Elaine will get some day. Oh, she'll eat, too," the Colonel added grimly. "But it cuts down her expectations. Of course, she's a pretty thing. That helps. Beginning to make eyes at the boys, too, if I'm not mistaken. I don't know for how much she can look to Bradford. But so far as what *we* give her is concerned—and that would make up the bulk of it."

Both stared ahead as if into the ruins of brightness.

"Philip," Mrs. Merriam breathed.

Yes, Philip! She ought to have thought of him before this. She remembered her visions while she was dusting the books, such a short time ago. She waited, but her husband merely said, "That's to be seen."

"He's such a fine boy, George," she urged.

"Well, and I supposed John was a fine man."

Mrs. Merriam protested the implication in silence. Instead she said faintly, after a time, "Minnie's property."

The Colonel was scornful. "There's no 'Minnie's property' any more, nor any proceeds. That seems to have been the first bit of gambling John did, with that little inheritance of Minnie's. I expect the Terrill estate shows up over there in John's house in the bathroom, and maybe in the trips Minnie took to baths and the like. He never invested it—just let Minnie think he did."

"But, George—"

"Yes, I know, Lyddy. Minnie needed things. But she didn't have to have what John couldn't pay for. If he was going in for luxuries for his wife, he should have got out into some other business and made more money—hustled for it."

"You wouldn't have wanted him to leave you!"

"*I* wouldn't, no. But John shouldn't have considered that."

"But, George, he wasn't made for hustling."

"He could have made himself hustle." The Colonel glared at his wife. Then he sobered down. His eyes lost their angry sparkle as he murmured, "Well, well, he was no more satisfied with the situation than I was. Why didn't *I* get somebody else?

Why did I hand over so much of the running to John Wood?"

"You trusted him," Mrs. Merriam pleaded.

But the Colonel would not accept exoneration. "That was the excuse. 'Twasn't good practice, though, on my part. I should have known better than to leave so much in the hands of another person, so long as I was company head. Did." Now the Colonel was again breathing heavily. He could make self-accusations, although he couldn't accept criticism from anyone else—seldom even from his wife. "It gave me time to play here at home with the old pioneer records, talk with some other old geezers, and enjoy myself." He breathed still more heavily. "No, Lyddy, I might as well admit it. John kind of made up to me for Brad. Or I was dreaming that he did."

Mrs. Merriam again thought it best not to speak. She herself could not accept her husband's flatly pessimistic view of their son; she could see that they had both erred in regard to Bradford as well as to the girls. They had kept him apart from and above those of his own age in Fairview. So many errors! But Bradford would never in any case have been the kind of son his father demanded. Things might have gone even worse if they had kept him here at home. In later years Mrs. Merriam herself had been happier because her husband had seemed to recognize this and in his own fashion to accept it. But she too had thought it a compensation of Providence (to go back to the old terms) that George "had John Wood," even though she herself had never felt—she was now admitting this in her own mind—completely easy with John.

She was entirely unsatisfied with what George had said when she had brought up the names of Minnie and Philip—particularly that of Philip. But she could see that, strong as George was, he still suffered from shock. What would it do to him? She would not look ahead. As to the money side, where they themselves were concerned she did not care much—or thought she did not. Although she, like Bradford, did not know the amount of their estate, she felt assured that it was substantial. What she said to herself was, We can stand it.

But she did feel impelled to ask further about the situation of John Wood, thinking of his wife and son. Had John nothing at all?

Maybe a little, the Colonel replied, adding with bitterness, "He may have put the house in his wife's name."

"But then surely Minnie—"

"How do you know what Minnie would do? I didn't know what John would do."

"No," Mrs. Merriam replied. Her lips trembled.

Colonel Merriam saw that. "Don't take it too hard," he said, "Lyddy. There's a lot about this business that we can't help. Every man has to answer for himself when you come down to it. That's what you believe, ain't it?"

"I believe that every man answers to God for his own soul."

"I don't understand your terms. They don't mean a thing to me. But I've lived with you a long time, and I guess we're not so far apart." He reached over again to pat her ringed hands.

As to the practical side of the situation, it did not seem to him that Lydia saw far. "Friends might help." What actually had she in mind? Was she referring to what he and she might do? Suppose he himself stood good immediately for the whole sum (as he would doubtless have to do sooner or later) and let John leave town quietly under some pretext, maybe his wife's health, and swore all concerned to secrecy? Who would credit that? The idea of keeping on John Wood and giving him another chance with the company was so abhorrent to Colonel Merriam that he would have no further mention of it. As to the question whether John Wood should stand trial, Colonel Merriam contended that there would be no standard of justice if John's friends connived together to shield him and let Dan Postel come up before the justice of the peace every time the poor old buzzard raised a little Cain on the streets after having a few drinks. He said this aloud.

"More than a few," Mrs. Merriam murmured.

"Well, made a sot of himself," the Colonel conceded. "Seems to me you ought to see that if anyone does, Lyddy. You go by principle." Then he added, with another glint of the eye, "Of course you had a religious upbringing!"

Mrs. Merriam let that statement lie. Religion was a field in which she didn't consider that George was qualified to speak, even though he was an upright man. She had long been prepared to withstand his little jibes, thinking they were made mostly in ignorance.

"Yes, George," she replied earnestly, "I do see it. Maybe as well as you do in some ways—and in the long run. But I think of more than John Wood and ourselves. I'm afraid Minnie might not be able to stand seeing John go to trial."

Finally she had not been able to keep this back. Tears came into her eyes. She tried to wipe them away unobtrusively and with dignity.

"Minnie's stood a lot already nobody ever thought she could."

"Yes, George, but you know—"

"I know I can't change the laws for Minnie Wood any more than I can for John, and I don't intend to try it. You might as well accept that, Lyddy, first as last."

In the heat of sudden temper the Colonel got up from his chair. Then at once he was repentant, although he wouldn't admit it in so many words. He said in a gentler tone, "I have to leave you now, Lyddy. I've got plenty to look after. Claud will be back."

At the door he turned. "Of course I can't tell what some others of John's friends might be prepared to do—some of the church people. Claud thinks some of them ought to be told— Henry Meserve and Austin Cowie and a few others. That young preacher. It would be pretty hard, I suppose, to have this news get out about one of their big cogs! Maybe they'd be more inclined to cover it up than I would."

Mrs. Merriam would not reply to this.

"I guess John's been a pretty big pillar. Well, well, I never held that against him," the Colonel muttered, and added, "But at this moment I've told you just about all I could. Don't know exactly how I'll proceed myself. Let the process of law take its course. I can say this much, if you're concerned about other people than John: nobody's going to suffer financially except the Merriams."

Mrs. Merriam said, "God has his own due process."

"Pshaw!"

"Wait one moment, George. I have to ask this. Does Minnie know?"

"I expect she does by this time," the Colonel growled.

"Philip?"

"That I can't answer. If he don't know, he will." The Colonel drew his formidable brows together. "You've no call to bring God into this situation, Lyddy," he said testily.

"God *is* in the situation."

The Colonel had retorts, but it was better not to make them, even to repeat "Pshaw." Instead he said mildly, "I don't like this any better than you do, Lyddy."

"My dear, I know you don't."

The Colonel briefly squeezed her hand, which she held out to him, before he left the room.

Mrs. Merriam sat on alone. The room was bright now from the sunlight of almost noon. But all had changed since an hour ago—her own familiar library. It was as if they had heard of a death. In a sense, she and George no longer had a John Wood.

That knowledge was shock enough. The thought of what this confession had meant to John Wood himself was worse. There seemed to arise before her the face of John Wood. His very handsomeness made him pitiful—that quality which Mrs. Merriam had always been inclined to deprecate. Would George ever see John again, ever talk with him in any compassionate way? She knew the hardness that lay in the core of her husband's nature, beneath the tolerance and the indulgence. Deception was the one thing he could not stand. Tears again, painful and few, squeezed out from under her closed, finely wrinkled eyelids.

There were so many other considerations which the shock of this news brought with it. No matter what George might say, or how deep her own love and respect for him, she believed that in some ways he was not in the right. He had not allowed her to quote to him, ". . . when mercy seasons justice," even though it was from Shakespeare and not from the Bible. Mrs. Merriam was not wholly satisfied with the way in which George indicated he would deal with this situation, even though she acknowledged that it was George who must handle it. She had at this moment no explicit suggestions. Still, in her heart she was convinced that there was that "more excellent way" if they could find it. It would not be simply telling John that all was forgiven and everything would go on as before. Mrs. Merriam did not want that—and she realized that it was impossible. But ought not years of work and devotion to count for something, as well as the deceit and the defaulting? Or was there to be no taking into account of motives? John had done much for the Colonel outside and beyond the work for which he was hired. Why could not George have paid John more in salary—really generously, more than the position which he had held required? George would not have agreed as to the rights of such action. But why had she herself never urged it? From the very start she had not inquired into the way George ran his business, in which he was obviously successful. He, in turn, did not interfere with her own church and other activities. At that point they had achieved a truce. Nor had he ever inquired how she spent her own money.

To go into the question of John's salary now seemed vain. But Mrs. Merriam felt restless. Like the woman who had broken the alabaster box of rare ointment (whom Lydia Merriam used to consider with some impatience), she would now "do what she could." On one point she was clear—not to leave the Woods alone, now that they were in great trouble, as she feared that her husband meant to do. It seemed providential that the two of them, she and the Colonel, had learned to take their separate ways without interference, she as a great lady, he as a strong and respected "character." This afternoon she could go over and see Minnie and be with her, help if and as she could.

But at this moment, Mrs. Merriam thought, slowly getting up from her chair, the best thing to do was to finish the task she had begun—the dusting. In such respects the old Puritan precepts still came to her aid. She was very tired. She dreaded meeting John Wood if he should be at home. But who was *she* to hold herself apart? She had failed in one of the central concerns of life, had failed as a mother to comprehend the nature and needs of her own children. Although she had come to realize that there were some mitigations, still, the realization was always there, tempering and often governing her actions. It had changed her view of people—even of God. She went on now with her dusting, not looking into her books. She put back the Emerson volumes with a sense of gratitude for all that they had helped to bring her. But at this moment, in thought she leaned less upon the beneficence of Emerson than upon the knowledge of the Apostle who himself had sinned, had seen the vision, and changed. She herself had done the same in a very minor way. But how could she bring her own experience to John or Minnie Wood? She could not bring it to her own husband and son, or to her own grandchild. It was with her, and had become part of her, nevertheless.

CHAPTER

7

THAT afternoon Mrs. Merriam went outdoors to find Tommy Hardcastle and ask him to hitch up Bro.

"You didn't want the team, Mrs. Merriam?"

Mrs. Merriam could see that Tommy disapproved of her asking him to separate "the team," as he always spoke of the two carriage horses; but she wore her great-lady air of distant dignity as she replied, "Only Bro." She did not go on to say where she intended driving, to Tommy's disgust; but he made out that it would be only a short distance—"over to see Missus Wood, likely." He tried to cull these harmless bits of information having to do with the great house (as he thought of it) to carry home to Phoebe, but would not have considered outright inquiry, such as old Jake would not have hesitated to make. To Tommy and Phoebe the Merriams, since the Colonel had become Tommy's employer, were "the family," independent as the old couple were in most respects.

Mrs. Merriam stood aside while Tommy was getting the small surrey ready. That was the carriage she liked to use, even when she was driving alone. She had some thought, also, of taking Minnie off into Merriam's Grove for an hour's respite and healing. Although she did not care to have cut flowers in the house, Mrs. Merriam took religious joy in the natural green

stillnesses of Merriam's Grove—in what to her was "the heart
of nature."

But today the world around her had taken on a different atmosphere and color: a low dark cloud had come over it. She
scarcely recognized the trees and bushes and vines of her own
back yard. Even the short, broad figure of Tommy Hardcastle
seemed strange; she was startled when he came up to her and
she looked into his very blue eyes in his ruddy old face and
saw that they were still innocent of calamity.

"The carriage is ready, Missus Merriam."

"Thank you, Tommy. How is Phoebe?" Mrs. Merriam managed to ask as she walked with Tommy toward the surrey in
the driveway leading out from the vine-grown stable. Bro
turned his head, trying to look at her with benignant brown
eyes half hidden by blinders. "I'm glad she's well."

But Mrs. Merriam found herself unable to comment further.
She accepted Tommy's hand to help her step into the surrey,
which she did rather slowly, making Tommy think, Missus is
showing her age. He was not pleased, except that this was an
observation that he might take home to Phoebe. He could also
tell Phoebe that he had an idea there was something wrong
from the way in which Missus took up the reins and the manner in which she sat there—so that there would be plenty for
the two of them to mull over while they drank their strong
tea and ate their large slices of homemade bread and cheese
for supper. Neither was a gossip in a general way; information
that Tommy brought back would go no further. Tommy had
given up going home for afternoon tea. His old legs, although
still strong, were getting more bowed, and he cared less for
walking. Phoebe had her own cup of tea at four, but it was with
the company of a neighbor who might have dropped in, or of
Malty, the large, sleek Maltese cat, grandly bewhiskered (almost like Mr. Austin Cowie!), who contributed his part by rub-
bing his head against Phoebe's shoe and looking up at her in a
mixture of melting affection and anxiety for his saucer of milk.

When Mrs. Merriam drove out into the street, that too

seemed to have changed and grown older. The trees had aged, and the Maytime brightness was darkened. Mrs. Merriam let the horse take his own pace. He needed little guidance, only a pull on the rein when they reached the corner at which they turned into the short block in which the John Wood house stood at the end. Kindly old Bro never made any trouble. Mrs. Merriam was solicitous for Sis, sympathizing with the nervous mare's little fears and eccentricities—her startled eyes when she saw a paper bag in the street, for example—but today Mrs. Merriam did not feel up to driving Sis.

She had come into the short one-way street, and saw John and Minnie's house standing in the springtime, the brightness and trimness of the flowers and bushes denying the disaster that had come upon the place, but the bushy small trees beyond the side yard at the edge of the ravine suggesting today something unexplored and threatening. Of course the ravine was not unexplored. Philip and Lyle Meserve must be familiar with nearly every inch of it. Once, however, three tramps had been seen eating their meal there, making use of the little spring for drinking water and of the stream to wash off their tin cups and plates. John Wood had climbed down the steep side of the ravine to tell them that he had no objection to their eating there and making use of the stream, but if they were going to make a fire, they must go elsewhere—over near the tracks. John hadn't wanted Minnie to be frightened.

How could "they" take away the house from Minnie? Mrs. Merriam had long appreciated the happy family life that went on in this house. It had pleased her to contribute a few of her own old treasures to the charm which even she felt, although charm was not one of the things which counted in her own personal life.

Mrs. Merriam had first started coming to see Minnie Wood because of "the girls"—as if with some thought that she might rectify her own lack of understanding of them and their artistic foibles by expending care on the fragile Minnie, for whom it had seemed to her that Florence and Cora had extravagant appreciation. Minnie had more care for romantic notions than the girls themselves. Having come to realize with such depth of silent sorrow her own austerity with her beauty-loving daughters, Mrs. Merriam had first given Minnie some of their own intimate possessions, feeling that she herself was hardly worthy of keeping these things. But she realized now, as she still sat in her surrey in front of the white house, that she had come to have a real love for Minnie herself. The successful working out of the romance which had started in her own orchard had come to be of import to her. Yet it was true that all the time she had never felt a sense of closeness to John.

She sat there a moment longer, while a breeze gently touched the colored petunias and the bush of white lilacs; a passer-by would have supposed that she was merely resting briefly before getting out of the carriage. She hoped that she could speak to Minnie out of her own experience, telling her that, if there was no escape, there was still a way out or on: "a broken and a contrite heart" God would accept. At one time Mrs. Merriam would have been sure that she could help Minnie by plain and simple speech. Now she tried humbly to empty her own mind and heart of personal considerations in order to receive the light of true guidance for Minnie's sake.

Mrs. Merriam had stepped into the hallway after giving a light tap on the screen door. Silence. Philip must be still at school. She knew that John Wood was at the downtown office with Claud Evans, going through the bulk of his accounts and papers there—so piteously neat and in apparent order. Everything John had put on paper must be looked into now! It had always been enough for George Merriam that "John has it down somewhere." Mrs. Merriam felt the almost frightening quality of the stillness. How often she had stood in the hallway, while the man of the house was away, waiting with her hand clasping the stair rail, and listening intently for a sound from Minnie before she either disturbed Minnie by a louder call, or —if there should then have been no answer—deciding whether to go upstairs and see. There was the same fear today, but with a different one added to it. The doors of the two rooms off the hallway were open. She could see Minnie's fine old walnut table in the front room with its crystal bowl of lilies-of-the-valley, most of them still fresh.

She looked up the stairs, noting the carpeting which John had put down to make the stairs warmer for Minnie in the wintertime. She felt the pain of the present situation cut into her, put one gloved hand on her breast as if from physical pain, as she had done when receiving the first news of John Wood's default. Not only did that strip of carpeting bring to mind the many things that John had done for Minnie: putting in "improvements," taking short trips and sending Minnie to resorts, buying really beautiful brooches for anniversary and birthday presents—the happiness of their precarious life together forming a sort of legend—but there was the realization that she was about to encounter the wife of the man who, in George Merriam's blunt language, was a thief. "John Wood is a thief."

This hesitation must not be drawn out. Minnie might need her. Mrs. Merriam felt quite sure that no other of the Woods' close friends, even the Meserves, had yet been informed. She was an older friend than Ellie Meserve, and more intimately involved in the catastrophe.

She called up the staircase. "Minnie?" Then, as she heard a kind of rustling sound from the bedroom, she said more loudly, "It's Lydia Merriam. May I come up, dearest?"

Mrs. Merriam seldom used endearments. Even with Elaine, it was difficult for her to use any words more intimate than "my dear." But with Minnie Wood somehow it was easy to drop formality. Ah, if she had spoken so more often to Florence and Cora, given fuller evidence of what was in her heart! Yet the girls had known that she loved them, and that her severity had been due partially to her love joined with the high standards which she herself accepted and had felt called upon to teach them. Cora, at least, had known this. Of Florence —no one could be sure. But in some manner—the mother did not know just how—they must understand now. Such a realization had been coming to her more and more clearly during the last year, without her own effort, or at least without definite seeking, much as if a new plant were making its way up through old soil which had been gaining and re-gaining richness—and coming up in the plant's own manner, not merely by reason of old teaching and immature acceptance.

"Oh, yes, come, Mrs. Merriam!" The voice was quite clear, and stronger than Mrs. Merriam had expected to hear.

"Don't get up," Mrs. Merriam hastened to say before she put her hand on the stair rail to aid herself in climbing. She found that she was very tired, almost faint from apprehension, sympathy, sorrow, longing to help.

When she saw Minnie, fear was overwhelmed by a maternal impulse only to comfort. The little figure sitting propped up on the big bed, stockinged feet looking pathetically small where Minnie had pushed back the white cashmere shawl she must earlier have put over them; the white silk shawl (Florence's!) slipping off her shoulders while she held out her thin arms; that small face with its black hair and black eyebrows, the round gray eyes brilliant and staring into hers, the large mouth sensitively quivering . . . Mrs. Merriam hurried to her, embraced her, and held her more warmly than she had held any person for a long time. The dimity curtains at the windows stirred slightly and veiled the bushy trees at the edge of the ravine while letting in green light from the freshly mown grass.

"Oh, Minnie, my dear, my poor child." Mrs. Merriam strained the slight form to her, struggling to keep her own self-possession for Minnie's sake. She whispered, "You must have courage. But I know you *have* courage. I needn't say anything like that to *you*. I'm so sorry about it all—so sorry." She stroked the smooth black parted hair, the thin little neck, and felt the pulse throb.

But when Minnie drew away from her and looked at her again, Mrs. Merriam was startled. Although tears spilled over through the black lashes of those round, brilliant eyes, the look was not one of sorrow. It was one hardly even of dismay. It was an excited look, with something almost of exaltation in it. Mrs. Merriam did not know just what to make of it, although she knew that suffering could cause a kind of exaltation—temporarily, at least.

Mrs. Merriam felt that she had little if any power to change the course of events. She had come expecting to assure Minnie of continued affection, whether or not the chance came for those deepest communications which she longed to make. She had been prepared to find Minnie not only bowed with grief and shame, but perhaps even shattered. If Lydia and George Merriam had suffered such shock over the revelation of John Wood's untrustworthiness, what must be Minnie's!

Instead, Minnie appeared strangely uplifted. As the two women talked (or rather, as Minnie talked) Mrs. Merriam gradually came to an almost unbelievable realization: that Minnie was speaking as if both she and Lydia Merriam knew, although others might not understand it, that John Wood had done no wrong. He had "made mistakes," but not committed a wrong. Minnie seemed to have taken that first loving, compassionate embrace for full concurrence—while the truth was that Mrs. Merriam saw this terrible event in such a different light that she seemed to have no words, but sat in what was close to silence, torn between a suffering affection for Minnie and a dissent so strong that she could feel her backbone stiffen in the old way, in spite of her pity.

She was able to get in a few demurs. But she doubted if Minnie heard them. At any rate, Minnie paid no attention to them. Her brilliant gaze was fixed, but on nothing palpable. Mrs. Merriam could with difficulty resist the appeal of the small fingers which clutched hers. She found herself divided between consideration of Minnie's physical state—understanding that Minnie must be at present overwrought—and that same startled surprise and shocked dissent. Minnie kept talking feverishly of John's goodness.

"*Every*-body realizes John's goodness—every person in this

town." Minnie turned to stare straight at Mrs. Merriam, who could hardly meet the overbright gaze. "I owe my *life* to him. John is utterly loyal. He has given me his life."

Mrs. Merriam was shaken. She could not deny what Minnie had said. But it was not the point at this time, for anyone except Minnie herself. Mrs. Merriam had nothing actually to propose at this moment, except the course which she now realized Minnie would refuse to hear.

She heard Philip come into the house, back from school. She felt unprepared to meet him. All she could think was that surely Philip would not react as his mother had done!

Mrs. Merriam rose to go. She was able to persuade Minnie to rest and close her eyes. Minnie was talked out for the moment. This was no time to urge any difference of opinion. The drive to Merriam's Grove was out of the question. Mrs. Merriam wanted to leave some spoken assurance of her love, but did not know how to do it without seeming to argue with Minnie. She could not wholly overcome her own restraint, to her sorrow; she would chastise herself for it later. If Minnie were temporarily stimulated, Mrs. Merriam feared that the reaction would be greater and realization more devastating.

But now Mrs. Merriam had to fall back on the usual proffers of mundane aid. Could she send over anything? Was help needed in the kitchen?

No, Philip could get supper, a very nice one.

Minnie said proudly, "Both John and Philip are good cooks."

Mrs. Merriam nodded. Her throat seemed choked as she went downstairs. She paused on the stairs to hold her handkerchief for a moment against her eyes. Then she softly and carefully blew her nose.

In the hallway she paused again, thinking, I *should* see Philip. She could not let her own distress stand in the way of doing what she could for the boy at this time.

In the shock of John's treachery (it was that, in view of George Merriam's trust) and of her fear for Minnie, she had not really thought about the son. And with Minnie taking this strange attitude, Mrs. Merriam's feelings suddenly veered all the more, in concern, toward Philip. She heard him in the kitchen; and, careful as she always was of possible intrusion, she went on through the dining room to the kitchen door. This was a time when omission might be worse than commission.

There she found Philip. He was coming into the kitchen through the other door, the back one, with a pan of fresh garden lettuce.

"Oh—Mrs. Merriam!" There was relief, first of all, in his voice. "Won't you go into the front room and take a seat? I'll just wash off my hands and be with you." Polite as ever.

"No, Philip, I don't want to interrupt your work. You're getting supper, your mother told me. I can stay only a moment, in any case. I'll sit here in this chair, may I, and you go on as if I were not here."

"Thank you," Philip answered, turning away to put the lettuce in a bowl of fresh water in the sink. Mrs. Merriam thought that she had seen his lips tremble and she had caught a look of appeal in his eyes.

As she sat waiting, she looked at the back of Philip's shoulders and neck, his nicely cut hair (like his father, he was careful about haircuts), and she bit her own lip. Philip was a large, strong boy. But the back of his neck looked pathetically young and undeveloped. Yet Mrs. Merriam knew that he was athletic. That was one reason why Colonel Merriam thought well of him.

How old was Philip? she wondered. Not more than seventeen.

Mrs. Merriam felt as if not until this moment had she been struck by the full tragic significance of what this present situation must mean to Philip. His shoulders, as he leaned over, seemed to Mrs. Merriam already bowed. She told herself firmly that she must not let her imagination run away with her. (As if she ever did!) After encountering Minnie's attitude, she would allow herself no premature understanding. But she believed she did have some conception of what it must mean to a boy to have had for a father such a man as John Wood had appeared to be all these years. Confident and shining-eyed—no wonder! She closed her own eyes momentarily. And now, to have all that confidence shaken! Some way must be found to lighten the burden now bearing down on those boyish shoulders and likely to grow heavier.

When Philip turned around, Mrs. Merriam thought at first that his fresh-colored young face looked much as it always did. But then she saw his expression, and was startled differently from the way she had been by Minnie's. For all his careful poise, Philip looked dazed, bewildered. If his youthfully curved lips did not actually tremble, they were unsteady. His eyes kept their same gray-blue color, but their shining confidence was somehow drained out of them, and they showed a kind of distracted incredulousness. Mrs. Merriam saw this expression only for an instant. Philip was obviously struggling to keep mastery of himself. But the sight struck into her heart.

This time her own emotions made it difficult for her to speak. But she felt that she must allow herself no delay. Had Philip gone to school today as usual, but carrying this fearful knowledge with him? It was knowledge he could not share with any of his schoolmates, not even Lyle Meserve. She was far from sure that she herself could speak any words now that would really help and sustain Philip. He might be too young to grasp what she could tell him. A youth such as he might find no reality in an old woman's experience. But Mrs. Merriam's maternal sympathies had already settled upon Philip, more than upon Minnie and John, if only for the uncertainty which she discerned in his attitude. And she had been inclined to think him too sure of himself! She was resolved that she would break her natural reserve and make the attempt.

"Philip—" Her voice shook slightly. It was all the more difficult to go on because she did not know how much Philip had learned of his father's situation, or who had told him; presumably John Wood himself, but Mrs. Merriam found it impossible to inquire. Long as Mrs. Merriam had known Philip, and much as she liked the boy, she had never been on terms of real informality with him, as she had with his mother.

But Philip caught the sympathy in her tone and in her face, and his eyes, to her relief, showed gratitude—and appeal. He burst out, "I hardly know what to do, Mrs. Merriam—or what to think." Again the look of bewilderment and questioning which was so alien to Philip Wood.

"I know that you don't, Philip," Mrs. Merriam answered.

"I hardly— I don't know where I am. Mrs. Merriam!" His eyes openly searched hers. "Is it true? Has my father—has he really done something wrong with the Merriam Company's funds?"

Mrs. Merriam now guessed that Philip had learned of the trouble from John Wood himself, and probably only from him. She felt the weight of the whole situation fall upon her. Philip's eyes seemed to beg her to say that somehow it was not so, that all this trouble was unreal. She could not dissimulate, and she saw Philip's intent gaze falter and drop.

"We can't judge, Philip," she said finally. "We must wait and give every opportunity . . ." But she was aware that she spoke lamely.

Philip went over to the dish cupboard. Mrs. Merriam saw that he did this so that he could wipe his eyes before he turned around and faced her again. No boy wanted to be caught crying. After a moment he unobtrusively took his handkerchief from his pocket and blew his nose.

Mrs. Merriam sat quietly in the kitchen chair. She would not force Philip to turn around, or give him any more embarrassment than she could help. But he needed to consult with someone, some older person. Jerry Storm? But Mrs. Merriam doubted whether Jerry Storm had yet been informed of John Wood's predicament.

She rose. "I must go now, I think, Philip. Bro is tied outside. He is a patient old fellow, but he shouldn't be left there too long. I have been talking with your mother."

Philip nodded miserably.

"I'll try to see her again soon. You, too."

Philip was unable to answer. He had not yet turned around, and Mrs. Merriam hesitated to go up to him. She was uncertain of what she could say to him, because she herself did not know her husband's further plans. But she could not leave him without a few words which might be sustaining—or so she hoped.

"Philip, I want to tell you that if you feel *I* can be helpful in any way—" Unconsciously she had stressed the *I*, as if she were telling him that he might not find the help he wanted in anyone closer to him than herself. She tried to soften that implication as she went on. "In *any* way, my dear. If your mother should need me—or if you should—I want you to call. Don't hesitate."

Again Philip nodded. Mrs. Merriam heard his muffled "Thank you." Because she was a woman of wealth, and always had been—at least had had what she termed "a sufficiency"— it did not occur to her at this minute to ask whether the Woods might be short of ready funds. She would gladly have supplied them. She felt sure that more should be said, but was conscious of Minnie upstairs, even fearful that John Wood might come home before she could leave. Whatever she might say to Philip could be said more freely in her own house.

"That's all I'll say now. But you know that I mean it. You can call or come to see me at *any* time."

She was about to leave the room, but Philip turned suddenly. His eyes no longer showed tears, but the lashes were wet.

"Mrs. Merriam. I ought to tell you. I was to come in to see Colonel Merriam."

"When, Philip?"

"Well—soon. He didn't set a particular day. I guess I can tell you, he offered me a loan for college next year. But of course that's all out now." His look was bleak.

Mrs. Merriam stood silent in dismay. Her husband was a just and truthful man, and would do what he had promised, if he had made a definite promise. But there were many considerations now involved, and no one could yet say just what they might prove to be. There was George Merriam himself: his character, honest but harsh, and crotchety in streaks. His position as the town's leading citizen had allowed him to indulge in a degree of crotchetiness. But Mrs. Merriam did not want to counsel Philip to shirk his interview.

She said finally, "I hadn't heard about that. Not as yet. The Colonel keeps these matters largely to himself. But I think you should not give up the idea of seeing him—but not do so just now. After a while."

Philip went on in an unsteady voice, "I don't know as I ought to—think about college at all. I guess I'm up in the air."

"Shall we talk about that later too?"

"Yes, thanks," he answered, his voice faint but relieved.

Go on to college all the same, was what Mrs. Merriam wanted to advise Philip. But she did not feel justified in telling him that—not yet. She did not know how much actual need of him his parents might have. She thought of what her husband's attitude might be, even toward Philip as John Wood's son. She was not sure of Elaine. The child was not moved by trouble, but froze up and drew back from it.

It seemed in answer to these thoughts that Philip gave her an appealing look and said, "Then there's one other thing, Mrs. Merriam. I was going to take Elaine to the school picnic. But now I don't know—I think I shouldn't."

Philip had come up to Mrs. Merriam, and she knew that one thing, anyway, had been accomplished. The boy placed reliance on her. He would communicate with her. She instantly realized what the answer should be to this question. "Would you like me to tell Elaine for you?" she asked gently.

Philip replied, so low she could scarcely hear him, "If you would."

"Yes, I will. I think, too, that it might be better if I should speak to her. Of course you don't know just what to look forward to at present. Not that there is any personal reason why you shouldn't take Elaine—not in the least. But it's thoughtful of you, Philip, and I can understand how you feel about it. Good-by, my dear, for the present."

Mrs. Merriam hurried out of the house to which she had often gone in her stately way, drawn by the charm she had felt there. She could not blame Minnie now, but neither could she understand her. Philip, at the moment, seemed closer to her than Minnie. She felt that Minnie had rejected her because she had not been able to look at John's action exactly as Minnie required. Her sight was dimmed with unaccustomed tears. Mrs. Merriam untied Bro and put her foot on the carriage step, wishing that she had Tommy Hardcastle to help her. She was a New Englander to the bone, after all these years lived in inland country, and she seldom desired help. Feeling old and spent, she seated herself and took up the reins. At this moment she could be glad of only one thing—that she had taken Bro and left Sis at home. She could trust old Bro to go back to his stable and teammate of his own accord—if, now, any living creature could be fully trusted.

She thought, We have felt only the first shock, all of us.

CHAPTER 8

PHILIP had been excused from school early so that he could be present at a meeting to be held in the front room of the Wood house.

The news of John Wood's default had by this time gone beyond the first few to know of it. At Mrs. Merriam's insistence —with which Claud Evans agreed—it had been given in strict confidence to the minister and trustees of the Congregational church. Austin Cowie and Claud Evans had not spoken of it even to their womenfolk. But Henry Meserve had felt that his wife, Ellie, was as much concerned with it as he was; and Ellie had felt that "the girls"—which meant the two older girls, Mae and Vera—should be informed. Henry and Ellie Meserve had gone to see John and Minnie the night before the meeting, as reluctant as Colonel Merriam had been at first to believe in the possibility of such news until they heard it from John's own lips. Then they had been confused by the attitude of Minnie in particular, at her interpretation of the matter as John's "being in difficulties." But later, as they walked home in the cool nighttime, under the great sky and the stars, the truth of the situation had come to them too forcibly for denial.

One reason why Ellie Meserve had wanted to "bring the girls into this" was that she had felt strongly that, no matter how John had erred, help was needed at the Wood house. Vera had gone over soon after breakfast to take care of the housework; Mae, who had music lessons to give, had gone early in the afternoon to wash the dinner dishes. Philip heard her light footsteps in the kitchen when he entered the house, but he had not wanted to encounter even Mae. Mr. Meserve had agreed last night that Philip should be present at this afternoon's meeting.

Philip went first to his room. It still seemed to him—in spite of Mrs. Merriam's confirmation—that this disaster could not have happened. And if it had happened, something would come along to make it right! His father had been the one to tell him, as Mrs. Merriam had surmised, and Philip took some small satisfaction in that. His father had told him at the first possible moment, on returning from Colonel Merriam's office. He had asked Philip to come into the front room, where he also found his mother sitting next to the desk in which John Wood kept his books and papers. Philip immediately knew that something had happened, but was puzzled as to its meaning. His father's face was pale and set; his mother, sitting close to his father, seemed strangely excited. His father had spoken briefly.

"Son, we are in some difficulty financially. I made use of funds which I did not have in hand at the moment. Your mother and I think you should know this from us, rather than from others. My connection with the Merriam Company is severed."

Philip could recall every one of those words. They were scored into his memory forever. But he had not been entirely sure of their meaning—their whole meaning—and something in the attitude of his parents had forbidden him to ask. He had looked at his mother. She had even smiled, as if nothing were really wrong. Philip had thought about the words ever since. They had come between him and his textbooks at school. Even now—though a terrible dismay was upon him—they had not become real.

Time had passed inexorably. The church people would soon ·

be here. Philip moved as in a daze. He looked into his parents'
room, feeling himself awkward in his sense of confusion and
solemn crisis. His mother was sitting in her cane chair, and his
father standing at the dresser. Indentations in the beautifully
laundered, fringed white bedspread showed that John and Minnie had been sitting on the bed together.

"Come on in, Philip dear. Sit down."

Minnie's quick smile included Philip in the small family
group. But his father did not turn from the dresser at which he
was meticulously brushing his hair. Philip felt himself an in-
truder. He sat down on a stiff chair. He had always been a
third. But he had never resented his parents' absorption in each
other—had never been made to feel himself any less the loved
son, but more so, as the factor making their own love complete.
Philip was too young to understand that John did not meet his
son's eyes because of his own uncertainty and loss of status; in
Minnie's brilliant eyes John's status seemed even raised!

But it was undeniable that in this trouble John and Minnie
had drawn together. They did not purposely exclude Philip.
His mother definitely included him, as her smile of a moment
ago had shown. As to his father, Philip was unsure. His father
had not asked him how *he* regarded this situation in which all
three were now living. But father and son, for all their feeling
for each other (and John Wood had been, in a sense, the cor-
nerstone of Philip's life) had never been on entirely intimate
terms. But who was on intimate terms with John Wood, unless
his wife? Even she had known little of his business affairs.
Henry Meserve, John's long-time friend and associate, his co-
deacon in the Congregational church, had gone away last night
realizing that he had never known John. Colonel Merriam had
been acquainted with him in only one capacity. Although a
man so pleasant to meet, John had always been without small
talk; perhaps his impressively good looks had spoken for him.

But Philip had never lacked the sense of being both loved
and approved by both his parents. He had taken for granted
their pride in him, aspiring—and intending—to live up to it

and to increase it. Yet now, ever since his father had told him of this still incredible occurrence—"made use of funds which I did not have in hand . . . connection with the Merriam Company . . . severed"—a blank wall had seemed to stand between John and Philip. Even with Minnie, although she had been loving, the old closeness had been lacking. Philip—so he now realized—was not her first consideration.

Philip wanted to talk with his parents about the coming meeting. But because he was a third, it seemed he could not. He could make little out of their attitude now. He saw his mother's face more worn, perhaps, the bright gray eyes deeper sunk into sockets marked with brown and plum color. Yet she seemed somehow uplifted and showing the strength of her constitution (on which old Dr. Bushnell had always insisted) beneath the impairment of ill health. His father's face, when Philip saw it in profile, was even more like that of a statue than when Philip had caught that odd aspect of it, with the sad droop of the eyelid, last Sunday morning.

John turned full-face. Minnie looked up at him, smiling, and putting out her little hand, which John clasped. This was the first time Philip had looked straight at his father for some days. He could do so now because John was unaware, lost and upborne by Minnie's support. Philip might have expected some great change. But John Wood showed even less the impact of the disaster now upon them than did Minnie. His face had taken on a not unbecoming pallor, that was all. The regularity of his features had a changelessness in itself. His eyes alone, which he could not govern, told what must be the truth of his condition. For the first time, Philip discerned a slight misalignment. (Mr. Rakosi's keen photographer's eye had noted this some time ago, and he had puzzled over it.) But it was so very slight that Philip was not certain he was not imagining it. Only last Sunday Philip had seen those large blue eyes as showing the visible effect of long, silent endurance, wholly brave. There had been more cause than Philip had known for that ordeal of endurance.

Men's footsteps sounded on the front walk and on the porch. Philip's heart began to pound. Startled, he looked at his mother. His father had again turned to the dresser, but Philip could not have looked at him. His mother's expression, he was astonished to see, was one of bright relief.

"There they are!" she whispered, and gave a little sigh. Now she actually turned to Philip. "This is the sort of time, son, when the Spirit gives one strength! And faith!"

Philip again felt confused. The religious look in his mother's face, which had often inspired him, puzzled him. What did it mean in this connection? Faith in what this meeting would do for his father, for the family? His mother seemed to have no doubt that the meeting here of the men of the church meant relief. These men might be thought of as constituting a close inner circle of the church, inside all official circles. The pastor was the only one who could be regarded as definitely official, and he was a friend of the Woods. All were friends. They would not want John Wood, who was one of their own number, to suffer. Something surely would be done to restore the world as it had been! The matter might be "hushed up" (a phrase which Philip had often heard in regard to bad situations, and at which he now clutched with a shamed hope, for he had never expected to think of such a phrase as applying to his own family). In spite of his questions and puzzlement, his spirits rose. His mother's confidence might be well placed. His father's mistakes might not be irretrievable. "Funds I did not have in hand at the moment," John Wood had said. The connection with the Merriam Company, to be sure, had been "severed." But Colonel Merriam's quick temper was well known. The Colonel's hasty action might explain what Mrs. Merriam had said to Philip, and the sadness of her face and tone. The whole matter would be fixed up. Then Philip himself could step back into the bright springtime, the opening world, and regain the place that was his by rights. He had not yet lost that place among his largely unknowing schoolmates and teachers.

Need he lose it? Need they ever know? In some manner his friendship with Elaine could be magically retrieved. Mrs. Merriam could achieve that. Surely that other clear world was the reality, not this one of fogs and bewilderment.

Mae called from the stairs, "Mr. Wood."

John waited a moment to adjust his necktie with scrupulous care; then, going to Minnie, he gave her a long, silent embrace. Glancing at Philip, he said approvingly in a low voice, "Yes, you stay here with Mama"—as if he thought that was what Philip was intending to do.

His footsteps sounded even and unhurried from the stairs; if they were heavier than usual, the carpet muffled the sound.

Philip was left standing near his mother's chair. He felt himself on the balance line between great hopefulness and awful dismay. He stood without moving, yet with inner uncertainty, as his mother took his hand and held it against her cheek. He thought of Elaine's fine-textured cheek, which he had never yet touched except in childish play. Minnie held Philip's hand as if he were completely at one with herself and John. Philip felt his old protective emotion toward his mother, yet the position was a constraint to him, and he became more and more uncomfortable.

"I want to go downstairs, Mama. You know we said last night that I was to be at this meeting. Mr. Meserve said so."

Philip pulled away his hand, aware that his mother did not approve of his intention. He went out of the room blindly. Halfway down the stairs he paused, hearing voices, silence, voices again. The door into the front room was closed. Philip was abashed at the thought of breaking into this gathering of elders. But he must be there. He had to know more about everything than he did now. He resolutely opened the door.

There was a brief pause. Then, to his relief, he was welcomed. Mr. Meserve said, "Come in, Philip."

A look of sharp pain flashed into John Wood's eyes when his son appeared in the doorway. Then he turned away before the others noticed it.

Philip's first feeling was that his mother was right. He had seen these same men here in this room many times before, and always as friends and co-workers: Henry Meserve, Austin Cowie, Claud Evans, Jerry Storm, who had just slipped in from the dining room, where he had been talking with Mae before she left. One might almost have thought this an ordinary meeting of trustees to consider church finances.

But the expressions on the well-known faces were not those of every day. Austin Cowie's large, strongly modeled face with the old-style muttonchop whiskers making him look older than need be ("Why *does* he wear those whiskers? I shouldn't think 'she'd let him. . . . 'She' admires anything that Austin does!"), was solemn, even shocked. The lawyer, Claud Evans, with his shrewd light eyes, showed a sober sense of the occasion but little more. But Henry Meserve's face, small, neat, colorless, with scrub mustache, looked somehow ravaged. Jerry Storm had regained color since he heard the story first and since his drive back from the country in the open air—he had been called out to visit an old woman who was bedridden—and he was too young for lines of anxiety to seem more than temporary, but his thin face revealed openly that he was suffering. He had taken an inconspicuous seat near the closed door into the dining room. He greeted Philip with a quick smile but then turned his eyes away. And the look of suffering seemed deeper.

Philip's hopefulness sank. The atmosphere which prevailed in this room taught him all over again that, although these men might come as friends, the disaster was real. At the same time, he looked to friends to change it. They could not let disaster go on being real for John and Minnie Wood—and it could not possibly be real for himself, for Philip Sidney Wood. It was totally incongruous.

The talk so far had been desultory. There was a sense of paralyzing awkwardness of which all had become aware. It affected even Austin Cowie. Philip looked down at his own hands, which were trembling, the fingertips cold, seeming to

refute the hopefulness to which he still clung. He understood
what this embarrassment meant. These men were accustomed
to working with John Wood in worthy undertakings, respect-
ing him, looking up to him, if anything, sharing the belief that
they could "always count on John." How was it possible to suspect him of dishonesty? To break open the subject would
amount to that, unless John himself spoke first.

John Wood's self-containment and fine appearance seemed
to make everything more difficult. Philip felt within himself
an unformulated appeal which he was not able to make to his
father—and he was not sure that he wanted to make it.

Henry Meserve was probably the person (outside John's
own family) who was closest to John Wood, but a man
of much reticence and shyness. Austin Cowie was not ordinarily troubled by such qualities. He, Henry, and Charles Williston of the bank (not here today, since he was a Methodist)
knew themselves to be Fairview's leading financiers of this era,
following after Colonel Merriam, now more than half retired.
Austin sometimes took on a look of great seriousness when he
had to listen to what he regarded as inordinate praise of John
Wood, such as that John "was not a money-maker." Austin,
devoted to the church as an organization, and, according to his
measure, sincerely religious, was particularly aroused by the
implication that being a "money-maker" in some way came
into conflict with being a genuine church member, and did not
think it to John's credit that he should all these years have
been willing to hold a subordinate position—"ride along on old
George Merriam's coattails." His providing Minnie with her
special needs and with some added comforts, Austin had often
thought, must take hard scrounging somewhere. Still, Austin
had always considered that John might be more astute than
people supposed: he might well have an understanding with
Colonel Merriam regarding disposal of the Colonel's business
interests. Brad would inherit the estate from the old people,
aside from the business, no doubt, and the Colonel's holdings
in land were, of course, considerable; but, according to Austin's

view, Brad had let a good thing slip in giving up the business for teaching, in New York City or anywhere else. But now today's revelation showed that Austin had been more right than he wanted to be, where John Wood was concerned. *This* was how John had obtained those comforts; Austin was dumfounded.

Claud Evans knew John Wood less well than did the others. Colonel Merriam had never leaned heavily on a lawyer, had consulted Claud only when necessary, and only during these very last years since Samuel Ranney, the pioneer lawyer (on whom, as well as on Lincoln, Eslick Pettiman had tried to model himself), had died. But, as a lawyer, Claud was well informed as to the possible peccadilloes and missteps of all men. He had never considered it wise for Colonel Merriam to leave so much in his assistant's hands. But try to tell the old man anything! It would have been like trying to argue old King Lear out of his notions of abdication. Nevertheless, Claud shrank from having to encounter such a man as John Wood with the detailed knowledge he himself now possessed. He had seen how deeply the old man was affected, even though the Colonel's hard streak had reasserted itself. Claud sat with tired eyes averted, holding his glasses in his hand.

A horse and buggy were heard to drive up outside. The men all looked up.

"Must be Deacon Kruse," Austin Cowie said.

"You sent word to him, did you, Austin?" Henry Meserve asked.

"Yes, I thought we should have him in on this matter," Austin answered ponderously, not looking at John.

"How did you reach him? He hasn't put in a phone, has he?"

At another time all would have smiled at this rhetorical question. As it was, Austin replied, "I sent word by Lockie Burrows. He was in town." But Austin added, "No, but I hope some day to put in a phone out there. Caroline needs it if the Deacon thinks he doesn't."

An expressive half-smile went around the group, in which

even John Wood joined. They all knew that Deacon Kruse
was not going to put in any "convenience" merely for his
daughter's sake. Miss Almeda Blanchard had once put the matter at its mildest by saying that the deacon was "not a ladies'
man." He had kept the old European conception of woman's
place in the household, although with rigid piety. Some of the
church ladies said they did not want to see Deacon Kruse's fine
farm buildings because the money had gone into them which
should have gone into medical aids and comforts for his invalid
wife, who had been long a-dying. He would treat Caroline the
same. Caroline had loved her mother. Nevertheless, now that
she was the only remaining daughter on the farm, she and her
father were seen to be deeply attached. Caroline, of course,
must have driven her father in today.

John Wood said punctiliously, "You may be able to help Miss
Kruse, Philip."

Philip had already sprung up. Caroline Kruse had aided
her father to step out of the well-kept, old-fashioned buggy before Philip went outside; but she was glad to have Philip tie
the horse to the hitching ring in the cement block while she
went beside her father slowly up the front walk, ready to as-
sist again, although well aware she must not offer. Deacon
Kruse had "failed" only during the past winter, and he was not
yet willing to make the admission. Caroline's care had to be
unobtrusive. The deacon gave Philip no more than a nod as he
labored on, but Caroline looked back and smiled with her
usual sweetness. Not that Deacon Kruse intended to be surly,
but he was preoccupied with what lay before him and with the
exhausting difficulty of his progress. Philip felt his eyes blurred
with moisture as he finished fastening the big old white horse
to the iron ring, thinking how it had always been considered
an honor to have Deacon Kruse and Miss Caroline stop in for
a cup of coffee when they were in town.

When Philip entered the house again, Caroline, on orders,
was on her way upstairs "to find Minnie." The men got to
their feet when Deacon Kruse came into the room. John

Wood's face suddenly flushed all over. After that, although the flush receded, a bright color remained stationary on his smooth cheeks, making him handsomer than ever—almost startlingly so.

The whole atmosphere changed. A different kind of tension came into it: a full sense of this being not merely a secular gathering of friends and associates but a meeting of the "representative" men of the church come together to consider the errancy of one of their members—one of themselves. Deacon Kruse now dominated the group, not because he demanded to sit at the head, for there was a kind of simplicity in the old man which was above the pettiness of rank. The same quality went far, in the minds of the other men in the church—and even with some of the women who had loved the dead wife—toward redeeming his attitude toward his womenfolk. "That's what he believes." In the prayer meeting (to which he would drive, in earlier days, through five miles of snow or mud) the deacon used to pray for the women of the church, deploring their frivolous ways—fortified by passages from the letters of the Apostle Paul. (Gertrude Schilling, of all people, had once risen to say tremulously that Saint Paul had many other admonitions which applied to both men and women—and anyway, Saint Paul had written that he "did not have this from the Lord!")

Jerry Storm had not been in Fairview when Deacon Paul Kruse was still active in the church. He had thought of the other men now present in the Woods' front room as "the leading men." But suddenly, in his trouble that came from his shattering loss of esteem for the man he would have spoken of as his "strongest member," it had occurred to the young minister that he would not have thought of addressing John Wood or Henry Meserve as "Deacon"—not even if John Wood were . . . what people had thought him. But Deacon Kruse was a "pillar" in the old Biblical sense. With him the term "Deacon" had almost superseded that of "Mister." Jerry fixed on the old deacon a look of acute questioning.

The deacon, as he sat in the straight chair he had chosen,

refusing the rocker which Austin Cowie had solicitously offered, seemed someone out of another age among these middle-
aged townsmen and the youthful pastor. Even now that he had
become infirm, he had not lost a rock-ribbed quality. His
hands, with their weathered skin stretched between enlarged
joints, showed him to be an old farmer; but there was still a
commanding look about him which must have come from his
little-known early years in Germany—and which was strangely
tempered by inner devoutness. His blue, burning eyes held
both martial authority and the deep piety of his religious sincerity. His white beard, the tip of which reached beyond the
top button of his black coat (he often tucked this tip inside his
waistcoat before asking the blessing at a meal, a familiar sight
at Fairview church suppers) gave him an Old Testament air,
even though his name was Paul.

The young minister knew little of Deacon Kruse's background. But the townsmen were familiar with that phase of it
which was now passing into the annals of Wahkonsa County
early history. They esteemed the old man both as a pioneer and
as a tower of strength of the church. Now that he had grown
old and they no longer need fear his domination, the esteem
was taking on a glow of affection. In a way, the deacon was
more influential than he had been a few years ago.

Paul Kruse had been one of the first white men to settle in
what was now Merriam Township; along with Colonel Merriam he was one of its oldest inhabitants. The two men, once
sharing the same one-room log cabin, had both been fierce
hunters and hard drinkers. "I could tell a few tales," some other
early settlers occasionally hinted. Both had changed since those
early times, but in different ways: George Merriam through
his marriage, his ambition to become a stalwart citizen and help
develop this region; and Paul Kruse through religion. Like the
great Apostle, Paul Kruse had local and churchly fame as a man
who had experienced a genuine conversion. He had told the
story many times, with sonorous but simple impressiveness, in
the days when he had been able to get in to the weekly prayer

meeting. Henry Meserve had heard the story from his own father, Abel Meserve, who had been present on the very occasion: a gathering in Lew Stokes's barn when Isaac Phelps, a home missionary sent out by New England Congregationalists, had preached—a man said to have been as dauntless as Paul Kruse (Isaac Phelps was fifty-six when he made his journey into what were then "the wilds") but with a spirit which had worked powerfully upon the lonely, unsatisfied young man. Whatever might have been Paul Kruse's past (he had "got into some kind of trouble back there in the Old Country"), with him the old religious terms had been immediate and real; he had been "convicted of sin" and had "found his Savior." His conversion had lasted and had altered all his ways; he had taken up land and settled to farming; the "Deacon Kruse place," with its white-painted buildings and the well-managed wood lot in which grew oaks, black walnuts, and hickory trees, where the Sunday-school picnics and latterly the high-school picnics had been held, had become—like the Merriam house and lot in town—a local landmark. Of the deacon's family, only Caroline was left. But the Congregational Church, which he had entered by way of Isaac Phelps, had become central in his life.

Deacon Kruse straightened his aged body in the stiff-backed chair and let loose a long, rumbling sigh. It was obvious that he was not pleased to have Philip present; even though Philip was male, and an only son, he did not belong among the elders. The young people in the church had dreaded Deacon Kruse more than they had looked up to him; until his decline in strength he had felt a personal responsibility for keeping them in line. He knew also what the church had meant to him and wanted it to hold the same place in their lives. (Vera Meserve had complained bitterly to her father, "If he keeps coming to the Endeavor meetings, I'll quit. He *prays* for us— yes, Papa, he stood right up in front of everybody and prayed in so many words for Curly Meems and Boysie Wheeler. I know they cut up and fool around, but to pray right out loud for them—!") But in the burning of those blue eyes—in the days when Paul Kruse and John Wood in their capacity as deacons had passed the silver goblets at the Communion service —there had been an innocence of exaltation which had affected even the younger ones. Philip felt its influence now. Since the deacon had entered, the room held a sense of solemnity.

Deacon Kruse said, in his voice which kept a German accent and was still deep although it had grown hollow in tone, "Reverend Shtor-r-rm, vill you lead us first in pray-yer?"

The deacon bowed his head and put his large, well-formed, aged, work-worn hand over his eyes. The other heads were also bowed. Philip blinked his wet eyelashes. In the silent room the young minister's voice now sounded with a tone of intensely pleading, extremely humble, devoutness. "Our Father . . ."

Philip could not listen further. The two words brought a sense of revulsion. He was again conscious, as he had been last night, that his life's foundations were shaken. But at the same time he felt welling up in him a sense of passionate protectiveness toward his father. He swallowed painfully—was occupied with keeping control of himself, resolved not to break down before these older men, but tortured with confusion.

". . . Help us in our thoughts and decisions. We ask it in Thy name. Amen." The last word was barely whispered.

The heads were raised. There was a sound of throats being cleared. Henry Meserve had averted his face and reached for his handkerchief; Philip heard the familiar little checked, sniffy sound of Mr. Meserve blowing his nose—Philip and Lyle had often imitated it behind Mr. Meserve's back. Philip bit his lip and looked away. It hurt to hear all familiar sounds on this day when the world about him had become unfamiliar. John Wood, however, stared straight ahead with immobile endurance. Only the bright color on his cheeks showed that he was suffering. His eyes were again apparently empty; they might have been sightless.

Austin Cowie had been affected, like the others. But he now began, "Well, I think we should feel prepared—"

Deacon Kruse broke in, "Vait." The old man again spoke with an authority which brought silence. The deacon had slowly opened his eyes following the prayer and now turned their blue gaze upon John Wood.

"John,"—he said "Yon," and the sound was somehow more impressive—"is this thing true?"

The silence now was breathless. John Wood was again staring straight ahead, but a glare had come into his large eyes; he licked his lips under his full brown mustache. Philip could hardly stand it. He wanted to cross the room and stand by his father, but at the same time he wanted to know where the truth really lay. He shrank back, waiting.

Claud Evans started to speak, but Deacon Kruse stopped him, saying, "We should hear from John's own lips."

They waited. The brown carved clock on its shelf (a Terrill heirloom) audibly ticked. "Yes, I—used the funds," John Wood said in a low voice. He put his hand over his eyes once more. He added after a short time, "I believed I could return them."

Claud Evans made an impatient movement. As a lawyer, he had heard such statements too many times. People all "expected to put back the money"—unless they were out-and-out rascals, which he did not suppose John Wood was (although he did not know just how to describe John). He felt sick enough about this sorry business. Although he himself was less shocked than the others, having "seen too much," he had been aware of what the discovery had done not only to Colonel Merriam last night, but to Henry Meserve also; he would not have supposed Henry had so much feeling in him.

Deacon Kruse started to speak again, but Austin Cowie interrupted firmly, though with respect. "Pardon me, Deacon, but don't you think that now we should let John go on and tell us this story in his own way?"

"*Ja, ja,*" the deacon muttered. He sat back, again closing his eyes, perhaps in fatigue—or it may have been in prayer, for his lips could be seen to move slightly through the glisten of white beard. Philip felt a sense of passionate antagonism toward the old man, on his father's account. But he was glad to have that blue gaze covered, for there was something in it which he himself feared to meet. He could scarcely bear to hear his father tell this fateful story. And yet it was for this that Philip himself had been waiting.

John Wood had command of himself. Although his voice seemed strangely toneless, he spoke now without hesitation. It struck Claud Evans that he seemed to be reciting a narrative learned and rehearsed to himself many times. To Henry Meserve, too, it seemed that John must have long known that such a moment as this was coming. Pity worked in Henry; yet he was conscious that his deepest and most sincere friendship had been struck in its most vital part, for it had been based on esteem and admiration. What affected Henry most of all, so that his trimly featured face was gray with suffering, was the realization that throughout these years of close association between himself and John Wood and their two families—their boys intimate friends, so that it was almost as natural for Henry to see Philip in his house as one of his own five children; his wife telephoning "to see how Minnie was," if "Minnie wanted anything from downtown"; Vera and Mae running over with their embroidery or fancy sewing "to see what Minnie said"; most of all, these last two years since Deacon Kruse's retirement, when Henry and John had passed the silver goblets with the grape juice that Ellie had made, while his own daughter Mae played the organ softly—during all this time, John Wood had been deceiving the people who trusted him and never giving the thing away. That was somehow the worst—*never giving it away*. Henry had not thought of himself as more than ordinarily decent—he tried to deal honestly in business and still bring up an expensive family—but he had looked to John Wood as above him in character.

Austin Cowie, on the other hand, took it for granted that

John should have put a good front on what he was doing. John's success and aplomb together made the one element in the case for which Austin still kept a spark of respect—although that well-sustained success had crashed now.

To Claud Evans, the one among those present the least affected personally, the framework of John Wood's confession now being given was, as he had expected, embarrassingly familiar. Claud had to listen for the details, however; some of these were new and, even to him, surprising. He was only too conscious that he might be brought into the case legally, might even be called upon to prosecute John.

To Philip each of these details which his father now recited came like a nail pounded in by a stunning hammer blow, one after another.

John Wood's course of defraudment had started when he had taken the money from the sale of the Terrill property to buy shares in the Chicago grain market. From that point on John had continued to speculate, winning and losing, winning a little more than losing, using only his own funds at first (or Minnie's) until finally, either from the pressure of the market or from the elation of good fortune, he had begun dipping into the Merriam Company funds during those years when the Colonel had (by his own confession to Claud Evans) "left most of the actual management of the business to John."

Why had he done it—speculated, then finally "embezzled," to use a word that had not yet been said aloud? Henry Meserve, figuring rapidly in his head, had tried to connect the details of John Wood's recital with what he knew or could surmise about John's needs and expenditures during these years. Henry was pretty sure that his friend's first entering the market came about the time John had made the improvements on his house. John also had a mortgage to pay off at that time, Henry believed. And John had sent Minnie away "to a warmer climate" during several of those winters. People had wondered, then and at other times, how John could do it. Henry had told his wife, Ellie, that he "supposed John was able," even though Henry had heard that Colonel Merriam was not paying John a very good salary, especially in those earlier years. The Terrill inheritance, though it was not large (hadn't there been some encumbrance on it?), had presumably been the answer to John's expenditures around that time. Yet John had begun gambling just then! It was not clear to Henry, or probably to anyone else, just why John had started on such a path at that time.

That a man so hardheaded as George Merriam should have been so lax about overseeing his own business had amazed Claud Evans—or would have done so if the practice of law in a county-seat town had allowed him to feel amazement at any human inconsistency. The Colonel's explanation had been that "John was the only one I would ever have trusted that way." (Inadequate, but Claud had supposed that unspoken family feelings were bound up in the brief statement.) Claud could see that these other men, associated with John in the church, might well have felt the same; although Austin, that old fox, might have had some sly reservations. And by the way, how well Austin could keep his own countenance with respect to some things which would not look well at all if exposed to this same company! Claud was secretly amused. It seemed to him also that there was a vein of simplicity in George Merriam as in Deacon Kruse—perhaps in all men who were in some degree first-rate—a quality that Claud admired, but would not himself, as he thought, have been able to afford. The community had taken for granted that John Wood possessed this quality too, almost above all other men. Perhaps in some odd, almost perverse way he did, Claud thought, and glanced at that sculptured face. As for the boy's face, Claud could not even look at that.

To Deacon Kruse, few words were more self-damning than those contained in the term "playing the Chicago stock market." He himself knew the temptation, even the possibility, and the fact of his resistance to it; for he was a man who liked large transactions. To him, however, it was a simple axiom that every convinced Christian knew the wickedness of gambling in any form. He had opened his eyes again when he heard the word "market" and had turned their formidable blue blaze upon John Wood.

John faltered in his recital when he came to the part about the speculation, the change in the weather, and the drop in the market. "That was entirely unexpected," he said, and finished lamely, "Well, that's about the way it is."

There was a long silence. No one seemed to know just where to take hold of the case, now that it was out in the open before them. Claud might have known, but he did not feel it incumbent upon himself to elicit more than the main facts. The men now had those.

Henry Meserve was still trying to come to some estimate of how much money was involved. The shock of John Wood's defection had to be met, whatever the sum of money concerned. Yet he and the other men here ought to know what sum it came to, approximately. It would make a difference if, after all, the losses to people other than Colonel Merriam should turn out to be not so very great. For John Wood's sake, Henry could not help but wish that the whole sum would be small. Yet he couldn't ask John himself to try to state a figure —if John were able to do so. His face showed pain as he turned to Claud Evans.

"Claud, have you any idea how much this is likely to come to—I mean, in losses to other people?"

Claud screwed up one side of his mouth. He seemed to be hesitating, either because he did not want to be on record at this time or because he actually did not know the answer. Finally he said, openly enough, "We've taken only a superficial look at the books so far. I really could not say—would not want to say. Some people are going to lose some money," he brought out. "Unless, that is, it's made up to them."

Everyone looked at John Wood then, and the color on his face deepened, even though his expression did not change. His eyes seemed not to take in the implications of Claud Evans' last remark.

Henry Meserve, studying thoughtfully, now said to John Wood, "John, how does this leave your personal—estate?" He spoke not unkindly, and yet with earnest interest in the answer.

John Wood looked directly at Henry and said with unwonted flatness, "I'm cleaned out."

There was another of those stunned intervals.

"That was a bad thing to get started on, John," Austin Cowie muttered finally. "Speculating in the market, I mean." In his own mind, Austin added, And in dealings you know little about. Austin himself, as a financier of the community, accustomed to sizing men up, would have known at once that John Wood had in him little of the really astute manipulator. Those large blue eyes showed it. Austin's own green-gray eyes looked straight at people, but with a candor that was only seeming; the hooded upper lids with their drooping lines from the outer eye corners told a different story.

"I know that, Austin," John Wood said in a low tone. He had kept such firm control of himself that he seemed frozen; but for the first time he now showed a personal emotion as he added, "I had—special needs."

"Minnie" was in the mind of almost every person in the room. However the older men might regard John's half-admission, Philip felt a passionate return of love and loyalty toward his father. He knew, better than anyone, what was involved. And he saw his father as a noble gentleman in not having named his wife as in any way the cause of his reaching out for money. Those handsome features were not altogether false. His father's protectiveness, manly fortitude, loving care were before Philip. The boy could not now keep tears from coming into his eyes; a few spilled over and ran unchecked down his cheeks before he reached up and smeared them off almost fiercely while he was fumbling in a pocket for his handkerchief.

A degree of sympathy showed on most of the faces. Jerry

Storm bit his lip and looked down at his thin, strong young hand, which he clenched and unclenched. Henry Meserve, his face sad, shifted his position.

Deacon Kruse gave another long, rumbling sigh. He had seemed to have sunk back into his own memories; his bearded mouth was stern, but the expression of his fine old face was sad, while he kept shaking his head and smoothing his beard with his fingers. Now again he brought his attention back to the matter in question, fixed his blue gaze, and asked John Wood sternly, "Haf you thought of how this affects the church, Brother Wood?"

"I hope it doesn't affect the church," John said quickly. "Only myself."

"*Ja*, but it cannot be only yourself, John," the deacon said mournfully, shaking his head.

"No," Austin Cowie put in, "there's going to be a lot of feeling about this, I'm afraid—not only in our church but in the other four. You stand for a good deal in the eyes of many people here in the community, John. We have to recognize that as a factor in the situation—a pretty big factor."

John Wood stared down at his clean, well-made, well-kept hands and was silent. Deacon Kruse turned toward him and reminded him, "You are a deacon of the church of Jesus Christ. You bear the name of the Apostle John, whom our Lord loved."

The aged voice sounded with sepulchral authority. It opened up a further dimension in the thinking of all. A spasm of pain distorted John Wood's features. Philip got up and slipped into a chair near his father. The men were so absorbed they did not notice.

Austin Cowie finally said, in a placating tone, though subdued, "Well, we must think of what's best to do. We can't turn events backward. We'll have to deal with them as they are, and go on." He turned. "Won't you give us your thoughts on the matter, Reverend Storm?"

Jerry Storm had said nothing after offering his intensely

earnest prayer. Now he shook his head numbly. "I—I have nothing to say at this point." He felt wretched. He shot a pleading look at John, but John's face was again immobile. Henry Meserve too sat in silence, looking down, tugging his mustache.

Austin made another effort to bring the discussion down to literal fact. The defection of a man like John Wood hit them all hard, but they could put the best face on it that seemed possible. We can do *that* much, he thought—and might be said to know from personal experience.

Austin had supposed that "some such plan" (as he put it himself; he did not like to state the matter more explicitly) was what had brought this particular group together. He began to be sorry that he had gone to such pains to notify Deacon Kruse. We younger men, he thought, might have been able to act in a more practical manner. He was highly disgusted with their pastor, who ought to take charge of the situation, keep the ball rolling. Why, he's no good at all! Austin turned to the lawyer. How did Colonel Merriam feel about the matter? "You can tell us that much, I should think, without transgressing legal ethics."

Claud Evans said cautiously, weighing his words, "I can't speak for the Colonel, of course." He kept his face dead-pan but inwardly felt an ironic amusement. As if anybody else ever could speak for George Merriam! "But I think I can say this much: as far as the Merriam Company is involved, the Colonel will not be inclined to let its credit suffer."

A look of relief showed momentarily in Austin's eyes. But then he said bluntly, "Will he prosecute?"

Claud gave a shrug of his shoulders but said nothing more.

"Well, friends," Austin went on, "we have to get this thing straight while we're all here together. We're busy men. I don't enjoy asking such questions. But if the Colonel prosecutes, I don't know that there's anything much *we* can do. I think Claud should ascertain something in regard to the Colonel's intentions in the matter—at least, as soon as you can, Claud— and bring the matter again to us, or to some of us." There was

still no response, even from Claud Evans. Austin finished desperately, beating down his irritation, "At least, that's as I see
things now. Later, some of us may have a better light. Maybe
someone does now. If so, speak up, Brother."

Henry Meserve took his hand from his mustache and said in
a low tone, "What's John going to do?"

The eyes of all were turned toward John Wood. But he
made no reply. Philip felt that portentous beating of his own
heart—a fear, and at the same time a painful hope.

Austin Cowie asked hastily, feeling that they must get beyond this silent deadlock, "Can we have a prominent member
standing trial? Can we meet it as a church? Permit it to take
place? Or can the situation be met in some other way? That's
what I'm trying to get at. I know we all have sympathy for
John, although he has—got off the straight and narrow path,
one may say. But I'm thinking now of the best interests of the
church."

"*Ja, ja,*" Deacon Kruse muttered. The tone of his words
brought the same sense of intense discomfort as his earlier
speech, although this time he scarcely lifted his eyes.

Before anyone else could speak, the hall door opened and
Minnie Wood was standing in the doorway. The men were
startled. They had not heard the patter of Minnie's feet in her
soft house slippers on the carpeted stairs—not even Philip.
They rose—all but Deacon Kruse: it was difficult for the deacon to get up from his chair without aid, however, so that his
intentions might not be disrespectful. Caroline Kruse had followed Minnie, but she was still on the stairway, lacking the
boldness to enter a gathering of men. The men's faces showed
their consternation.

"Now, Minnie—" Henry Meserve said, expostulating. But he
did not know how to go on. He could only wish that he had
brought Ellie, who might have managed Minnie and kept her
upstairs. Caroline Kruse was too gentle.

Jerry Storm went over to Minnie in impulsive sympathy,
holding out his hand. But she passed him and crossed straight

to John. Her little feet were almost noiseless on this carpet too, which was of extra thickness to keep out the winter cold; but the starched skirt of her pale blue dress faintly rustled. Minnie Wood's intensely feminine daintiness, her individuality which made such a strong impression on some people and alienated others, was in that thin rustle of dimity. She paid no attention to Philip, either, but clasped John's neck. He had sat down again, and his fine shoulders were bowed. Minnie put her cheek against his thick brown hair. A murmur of expostulation seemed to run through the room—a sound of reluctant pity for Minnie, her thin arms reaching out from the lace-trimmed sleeves, the great gray eyes ringed with black lashes staring straight, it seemed, at them all from under the strongly marked eyebrows.

She spoke in the same clear voice in which earlier Philip had heard her call downstairs to his father. "You can't put John in jail."

Austin said to her, in the tone which he used toward his own wife, one of majestic indulgence, "Minnie, we didn't speak of putting John in jail."

"Yes, you did. I heard you say 'stand trial.' It means the same thing."

"No, no. Minnie, look here, you should not have—"

Minnie interrupted furiously. "Don't tell me I 'shouldn't'! I don't care if I listen at the door or what I do."

Her gray-green eyes held fiery sparkles. But her little neck worked painfully. Her voice grew husky and faint as she went on. "You let John tell that whole long story, and never once mention my name, and you all of you know as well as I do that every dollar he took was for me."

There was intense embarrassment.

She said with defiant emphasis, "Every dollar that he borrowed. You can put me in jail, but you can't put John there."

"Nobody's going to put you in jail, Minnie," Austin said soothingly.

"Yes they are. If they do John. Aren't they, Philip?"

She turned pitifully to Philip for confirmation. His mouth worked, but he could not speak.

Minnie said again to them all in accusing tones, "It was his unselfishness. You talk about punishing John for his unselfishness."

The men caught Minnie's meaning, and perhaps in their hearts came close—for a moment—to agreeing. They were in varying degrees sympathetic, even Claud Evans, who feared the peculiar logic of women. The words Minnie had just spoken brought before Henry Meserve what, as a friend, he knew of the difficulties and triumphs of the Wood family. Although Henry loved Ellie, valued her as a good wife and wouldn't have exchanged her for any other, he felt there was something between John and Minnie that was more than his philosophy encompassed, and that set them apart from ordinary couples. Jerry Storm sat again with hand pressed against his eyes, his fingers taut as if he would have sprung to Minnie's defense—yet something restrained him. Only the old deacon was certain of himself. But for the moment his voice was silent.

Now in the attempts of the others—Austin particularly—at reassurance, they may have allowed themselves to imply that they would give more help than they fully intended, or than was possible, if Colonel Merriam *should* prosecute. Minnie seemed to take it for granted that they would offer a loan which would carry John through, and that they would see the whole matter kept quiet. Surely they could manage this among them!

"We can pay back. Can't we, Philip?" she pleaded again—while again Philip did not know what to say.

The older men felt sorry for the boy—almost as sorry as for Minnie, who after all might be said to be in some degree implicated in John's "error."

"John's always been the one you could fall back on. You know how *all* of you have turned things over to him that you didn't want to do yourselves. This church would hardly be here . . ." She sobbed.

The men recognized, half guiltily, that there was indeed much truth in what she said.

But Deacon Kruse was sitting with his eyes again opened and blazing with that strangely impressive commingling of burning indictment and devout simplicity. He put his large, work-worn hands on his knees and spoke in a tone of slow, hard-won, convinced, and experienced rectitude. "Vat a man sows, that shall he also r-r-reap."

While those words were still vibrating in the close air of the Woods' front room, the old man turned his awe-inspiring gaze on Minnie Wood and declaimed, in the same tone of complete authority, oblivious in the fierce purity of conscience to her physical fragility or her personal suffering, "Minnie, here is no place for you." Then, pointing at her his large, shaky forefinger, in his hollow voice he quoted, " 'Let the vimmen keep silent in the churches.' So Scripture tells us. You should let Caroline go with you back upstairs."

Philip put his arm silently around his mother. Although he too had been appalled at her sudden appearance in the front room, it had been for her own sake. He was choked with indignation at the old deacon—but at the same time uneasy, dissatisfied. The other men were both displeased and embarrassed. The young minister made a restless movement. Even Austin Cowie, himself known as something of a domestic autocrat (although an indulgent one) said, trying once more to placate, "Deacon, we should not be too harsh."

The others murmured assent. Philip could now see Caroline hovering outside the door, which Minnie had left open into the hall. Her face was drawn with distress, and her large, beautiful eyes had tears. She wanted Minnie to come with her, but even now hesitated to join the forbidden masculine gathering.

Jerry Storm found his voice, although it sounded strained and unsteady. "We can quote many sayings from Saint Paul, not all of equal value. In any case, Deacon, I hardly feel that this is pertinent here."

That brought the blaze of the old blue eyes upon Jerry, even though, from his background in the Old Country, Deacon Kruse held the position of pastor in high veneration. Yet the pastor himself could not put aside the word of God. Deacon Kruse pointed at Jerry his accusing forefinger, while his words came slowly. " 'But I suffer not a vooman to teach . . . !' "

Minnie said tremulously, "I don't want to teach. But I can't let John take all the blame for this—mistake. He's a noble man, and you all know it. *I* know it." She searched blindly for her handkerchief, and Philip quickly gave her his, which had a beautifully made small darn in one corner.

Deacon Kruse was wrought up, however, and the men who knew him were aware that they would have to hear him out. No compunction for an individual was going to stop him. Besides, the men could not entirely refute him; might not agree with him, but felt themselves confused and half ashamed in comparison with his utter conviction. He had lived by his beliefs. Looking sternly at John Wood, Deacon Kruse said, "I know of vat I speak."

He now began to tell something of his own life story: his earlier erring days, filled with "vildness," his conversion, his giving his heart to his Savior—then of turning from the "vildness" to a better life, making his farm from raw prairie and timber land, doing most of the work himself. He had earned all he had ever got with his own labors, had gone without rather than play fast and loose; he had learned long ago "what was there the outcome." As he spoke, the German rhythm and pronunciation of his speech became stronger, again making all that he said more oddly impressive.

"My wife got sick, *ja*, I wanted also that she should have things, but better she die than live on the fruits of deceits and lying—*ja*, better too for *her* soul."

The men were affected. But they remembered the questions about the death of Mrs. Kruse. People disagreed as to what she had died of. But there had been considerable talk of "the lack of proper attention" and talk of "not in time." Other people said, "It wouldn't have helped," for she had been worn out.

As for Philip, he had only one memory of Mrs. Kruse that remained clear. When he was a small boy, before he had started school, he had driven out to the Kruse farm with Mrs. Merriam and his mother to "pay a last call." Philip had been too young to stay in the bedroom, where he might disturb the sick woman. Caroline had taken him into the parlor, which seemed a mixture of ruralness, homeyness, ultra-cleanliness, and awesome dignity. She had given him a cold, smooth, brown-speckled sea shell to play with. But he had got up to stare at the two crossed pistols fastened above the bookcase, not aware that they had seen use in the old days in Germany. Philip's father, Mr. Meserve, and most of the other men Philip knew (except Colonel Merriam) fished but did not shoot, and Philip looked on any kind of firearms as of use only in wars and to guard the house against burglars. Wars, and the rumors of wars, were not about in the thriving young inland town, except in regard to the past. Once during that half-hour at the Kruse farm, Philip's mother had come to the parlor to tell him that Mrs. Kruse wanted to speak to him. Philip was to stand just in the bedroom doorway and "tell Mrs. Kruse good day." He had kept the memory of that brief glimpse of a spectral figure in a large, high bed; with long braids of hair and eyes large and dark like Caroline's, but piteously and submissively tragic.

All this while, in the Wood parlor, Philip had kept his arm around his mother, feeling the thinness of her small body, with his father's bowed, strong shoulders close to him, listening without wanting to hear. From his own boyish insignificance and helplessness, Philip glared at Deacon Kruse. Yet Philip too, against his will, was impressed.

Minnie, who had been listening to Deacon Kruse with a wide and scornful look in her eyes, now took the floor almost imperiously. "I want you to know this," she told the room. "Doctor Bushnell himself said of me, 'Your life could be saved only by a miracle. And John Wood performed that miracle.' That is what you are trying to pass off here as if it were nothing!"

This was her final shot. No one, not even Deacon Kruse, had an answer. Yet what she had said did not settle anything, either.

Obviously it would be useless, as the other men now recognized, to get anything in the way of a decision this afternoon. They had had poor John Wood's straight confession, and perhaps that was all they could expect. Some of them—Austin and Henry (not Claud Evans, since he was too much involved legally)—would get together themselves with one or two others, perhaps Mr. Rechtner and Mr. Hungerford, and discuss the situation in a down-to-earth way. Later they could call in John Wood. It would be done out of the hearing of "poor little Minnie Wood." The young pastor also seemed to be too much affected emotionally to be useful in any such intimate taking counsel together. He was not a businessman. Austin thought with disappointment that this was where the young man's inexperience showed. A young pastor appealed to the young people, helped to "keep" them; that was why Austin, as chairman of the Selection Committee, had wanted to call the Reverend Storm. But the young man was of little value in such a situation as now confronted the church.

And certainly they would not bring in Deacon Kruse another time! Yet there was enough substance in that "counsel" which Deacon Kruse had been giving them to make all of them, even Claud Evans and Austin Cowie, uncomfortable; to leave the knowledge, still unformulated and unspoken, that there could be no "cover up."

None of the older men had thought much as yet about Philip, except that they pitied him.

They started to leave, saying, "John, we'll talk this over again soon. I don't think we're any of us quite ready this afternoon." They gave the effect of slinking away, although the original fault was not theirs.

John Wood slightly nodded. He had not moved when Deacon Kruse had begun to speak. His face was again expression-

less, except for the bright color on his cheeks. He had not returned Minnie's caresses, but she was still beside him, with one
arm around his neck and the fingers of the other hand tightly
clasping Philip's.

Philip had at first intended to stay close to his mother and
father. But at the last moment he hurried outdoors to untie the
Kruses' big white horse while Caroline, with patient care,
aided her father to climb into the high old buggy. When Philip
made a move toward helping her, she shook her head; then, lest
the boy should misunderstand, gave him one of her singularly
sweet smiles and an expressive glance from her dark eyes. She
would have spoken, but refrained because of her father, who
was now almost too exhausted to sit upright. They drove away
in silence.

As Philip went slowly up the front walk to his house—which
stood so incredibly looking just as always, cheerful and fresh
—he thought again with aching sympathy of his own parents,
of the unwearied strength and patience his father had showed
time after time—always, when Minnie was ill, undertaking the
chief nursing. "Minnie would rather have me," was what he
said. Philip felt himself in almost unbearable confusion. "Papa,"
he whispered to himself.

Jerry Storm had stayed behind the others and was trying
once more with pained awkwardness to give some comfort to
Minnie. She still refused to look at him, however, and he really
did not know what to say. He turned reluctantly to go. He
glanced longingly toward the closed door into the dining
room; but Mae, as he was aware, had left some time ago.

Although the meeting had ended so inconclusively, with no
course of action recommended, the outcome seemed to have
been apparent in a general feeling that John Wood should not
only make full confession but show his intention to make good
his "mistake" in so far as possible. Philip, returning from outside, could sense this in the very air of the room in which Deacon Kruse had so recently spoken.

Minnie, her head lifted, was saying to Jerry Storm, "You want John to stand trial like a criminal. Yes, you do. I can see that you do."

Jerry made a deprecating gesture with his hand but was unable at the moment to deny this. He stayed only a moment more.

When Jerry had left, Minnie turned her face to Philip—the face partly that of a child, yet also a woman's face molded by years of physical suffering transcended and lighted by the exultant gratitude of her love. "You understand. *You* wouldn't go with those men and allow your father to stand trial, would you, Philip?"

Philip answered, shaken, feeling himself both with his parents and yet so strangely and newly apart from them, "Mama, I don't know."

CHAPTER

9

J ERRY STORM woke up after a night that had been at first
tense and troubled, though later on he had fallen soundly
asleep.

He heard at first the chirping and chatter of birds in the
maple tree outside his window. He felt the comfort of his large
brass bed, the smoothness of the sheets and softness of the pillows; felt and saw the pretty pieced quilt over him. At first he
had not known enough to take off the big white bedspread at
night, but he had learned, and he saw it now lying properly
folded in the rocking chair. From downstairs came the smell
of coffee. He looked at the table which his two landladies, Mrs.
Latham and Miss Blanchard, had given him for use as a desk,
the calendar from the Meserve Lumber Yard hanging above it,
the swivel chair which had belonged to Mr. Latham but had
been brought down from the attic for Jerry's use, the bookshelf. All these things seemed to take on a special preciousness
in Jerry's mind; but the feeling was precarious, and beneath it
lay deep trouble.

This was one of Fairview's older houses, comfortable and
peaceful, with large well-established trees in the yard. To
Jerry Storm it had at first seemed luxurious and had then become a haven of comfort. Mrs. Latham and Miss Blanchard

were neither rich nor poor, but, having this house with four
bedrooms, and needing only two for themselves, they had offered to take in the young unmarried minister. They had
given him what used to be the guest room, or "spare room,"
since the other unused bedroom was small. He had by now got
used to this comfortable room facing north and east. It was a
better room than he had ever known. The sisters were more
concerned than most people of the period as to springs and
mattresses, and to Jerry his seemed almost *too* good for him.
He had been afraid to move around at first. But now he had
learned the orderly ways of the house. The sisters had been
most good to him. He had been so happy here that he had tried
earnestly to fit into their fixed, sedate, industrious yet leisurely
routine.

He turned over. He heard the pad of footsteps coming
slowly up the stairs, and knew that Pug would in a moment be
grunting and whining outside his door, wanting to be let in
while Jerry was dressing.

With that small, accustomed sound, Jerry all at once knew
clearly the trouble that on first waking he had felt dimly. The
meeting of the inner circle at John Wood's house yesterday
came back to him, with all its dismay. Worst, of course, was
the fact of John Wood's having proved untrustworthy—the
man in his congregation whom, above all, the young minister
had relied on. Then he felt the attitude of Mrs. Wood, whom
he had idealized, believing he had never known a woman like
her. But he was young, self-centered in spite of his calling, and
he suffered most from his own burning realization of not having come up to the needs of the situation.

The meeting yesterday had been bad enough. But Jerry
realized that worse lay ahead of him. He could not think into
the matter at this moment, for he must get up at once and not
keep the two ladies waiting for breakfast.

Pug was now giving short howls. Jerry got out of bed
quickly and let Pug into the room. The low-slung, overfed,
ancient, ugly small dog came in waddling and, worn out by

his climb up the stairs, lay down, grunting, on the round braided rug in front of the dresser. The old dog was so affectionate that Jerry's return friendliness was no pretense. Pug was a town character. Nobody seemed able to say how old he was, only that they couldn't remember when he hadn't lived with Mrs. Latham and Miss Blanchard. The two sisters had confessed to Jerry ("Reverend Jerry," as they had decided to call him) that Pug made "something of a problem" in regard to their attendance at the mid-week prayer meeting. The dog was so lonely without them that his howling disturbed the neighbors. They had tried taking Pug with them to the meetings, but had to stop because he "joined in the singing." Jerry had learned that this meant that Pug had lifted his head and howled during every hymn. The sisters said anxiously that the only solution seemed to be that they take turns attending the meeting; and Jerry's eager, instant assurance that this was quite acceptable had been the first thing to make them feel genuine affection toward the young man.

Jerry dressed as quickly as he could, and still appear neat. He combed his sandy hair, with the rampant cowlick, before the more than ample mirror. But he felt this morning how easily he had come to accept this pleasant living and to look upon this room as his home. The precariousness of his tenancy again came upon him. He saw in the mirror that his face showed his tension. He realized that Mrs. Latham and Miss Blanchard had not yet learned about the Wood case. They were not gossipers, and the news passing around the town was often slow in reaching them. They would be too much concerned if Jerry admitted to having spent a poor night, so that he felt that he must carry off his trouble before them.

"Come on, Pug. We'll go downstairs now."

The old dog began to struggle to his feet. Jerry bent down and put Pug on his shoulder. He had a feeling of relief that Pug did not know, and would not have to know.

The dining room was just below his own room and, through two long windows, got the morning sunlight. This room also had at first seemed to Jerry terrifyingly stately, with its large sideboard and crowded china closet, and the heavy table with the smoothly ironed, always fresh-looking table cloth. Now Jerry was used to the dining room too, and to the satisfaction of the well-cooked meals. Mrs. Latham was waiting for him before she sat down at the table's head. Jerry did not know enough of the amenities to draw out her chair for her, but she was too kind to hold this against him. She and her sister had both talked over what must have been his early hard times, always commiseratingly. "Poor boy."

"Sister," Mrs. Latham explained, "is in the kitchen tending the pancakes. So we won't wait for her, Reverend Jerry. If you will ask the blessing, Sister will hear it too."

Both Mrs. Latham and Jerry bowed their heads. Jerry had never found it hard to say grace in this house before. He had been truly thankful! But this morning he felt difficulty in beginning, and because of the innocence of the two ladies could not speak out his trouble. He felt that his voice was strained and his "Amen" abrupt. Mrs. Latham's softly puckered face seemed unchanged, however. Jerry was relieved that Miss Blanchard was not in the room because, though gentle, her eyes were sharper.

Mrs. Latham put a paper down beside her chair for Pug, who also liked pancakes, and it had been gratifying to her and her sister that Jerry too fed the dog bits. In fact, it had so far been gratifying in every way to have the young minister with them. He had been quite satisfied with the invariable breakfasts of pancakes, coffee, and stewed prunes. Mrs. Latham had explained that Mr. Latham had "wanted his pancakes every morning; would not call it breakfast unless there were pancakes"; and after his passing, she and Sister had kept on in the same way. The thin, hard-muscled young man, who had lived at times on a very low-cost diet as he had worked his way through the seminary, had seemed to enjoy with relish—if not with discrimination—all the foods that the two sisters put on the table.

They had grown fond of assuring people that the young minister made "no trouble whatever" and when they needed a man's work in the way of hammering or knife-sharpening, he was always ready to help out. He insisted that he enjoyed mowing the grass in the early summer mornings. Miss Blanchard had once slyly threatened to "tell a certain young lady what a good husband Reverend Jerry would make."

Now Miss Blanchard, somewhat smaller and thinner than her sister, but otherwise looking much like her, came in from the kitchen with a platter of piping-hot pancakes delicately and lacily crisp around the edges.

"I think the pancakes came out well this morning," she said as she took her place at the foot of the table.

The meal followed its accustomed course. Miss Blanchard looked after the pancakes. Mrs. Latham poured the excellent coffee into the thin Haviland cups. Having the minister eat with them gave the two ladies an excuse to use their Haviland daily, as they preferred—although Jerry Storm had never seen Haviland china before he came to their house. Because of the necessity of eating the pancakes while they were hot, the custom had developed of eating the stewed prunes at the end instead of the beginning of the meal. This too had been perfectly agreeable to Jerry. It might be the correct way, for all he knew.

At first this morning Jerry had thought that he could not force down a mouthful. But when he made himself start he found—almost to his chagrin—that his appetite was as good as always. It must be, or the two sisters would have worried about him. The time would come soon enough, he feared, when the ladies would learn the secret he was hiding. It was very difficult for Jerry to "put a good face on things." His outspoken earnestness was one of his notable qualities. But he had great endurance, and this took him through the meal. Even when Miss Blanchard said cheerily, "Well, what's happened lately? Anything?"—Jerry was able to smile and make no answer.

Yet the whole meal had an air of unreality about it. When

the impulse came to ask to be excused from the table, Jerry was able instead to stoop and put a piece of pancake on Pug's paper. He knew that his hostesses had gone through trouble, even though they seemed so serenely contented. Mrs. Latham had lost her husband, and her son at about the age of eleven. Mae Meserve had told Jerry that Miss Almeda's fiancé had died of typhoid fever. If they could be tranquil, he, the minister, should be able to maintain calm. But he was glad when the meal ended, said at once that he had some work to do, and went upstairs.

After he had left the dining room, the two sisters looked at each other. Jerry's concealment had not been so complete as he had thought. They conversed in low voices.

"Doesn't he seem troubled?" Miss Blanchard asked.

"I'm afraid he does. You weren't in the room, Sister, but he said grace as if something were the matter."

"Do you suppose it's Mae? I wonder if he's worried about his chances with Mae."

"I presume that may be it."

"Well, *I* think Mae likes him. Her father may be hard to approach. Henry is hard to talk to."

"Well, Sister, until he tells us, we won't know. He's something of a worrier, you know. He takes things to heart. At any rate, he made a good breakfast."

"Yes, but he was troubled in a different way from ordinary worry," Miss Blanchard insisted.

In his room, Jerry automatically combed his hair again and put things straight on his dresser. One or the other of the sisters would make up his bed—he did not know which, only that the bed got made.

Now his trouble and confusion flooded back upon him. He thought of last Sunday and of the Sunday-school lesson he had given his boys—Lyle's defense of "pleasant places," and Philip's standing out for the discipline of trouble. Philip could have had in his mind no such disaster as had since opened up before him! His own inadequacy again tore at the young min-

ister. As pastor, he would be delinquent in his duty if he did
not take hold of the situation, as yesterday he had failed to do.
He knew that he must see and talk with John Wood. But again
he shrank, feeling himself to be a young man, inexperienced
in dealing with personal situations, and feeling a kind of horror at the thought of himself confronting the older man who
had so helped to make up the joy and seeming security of his
position here in Fairview. He said to himself, in agony, "O
Lord, be merciful to me, a sinner!"

Deeply as he felt the words, they seemed not to help him to
regard John Wood as a sinner. He felt the need of some sort of
consultation before he went ahead. Yesterday's meeting had
been too inconclusive. Mrs. Wood's defense of her husband
had shaken him. Mrs. Merriam was the person who seemed to
Jerry Storm to have the most wisdom of any person in his congregation. But the Merriams were so deeply involved in the
John Wood case that he realized he could not go to her. He did
not care for the kind of counsel which Austin Cowie would
probably give; he did not want expediency. Indeed, the
thought of Austin Cowie sitting in judgment troubled him in
itself. He knew very well what Deacon Kruse thought. The
deacon's words and prayers had brought up the strength of the
religious rigidity from which Jerry thought that he had es-
caped, and to which he could not return.

The Meserves were the people to whom his thoughts went.
Henry Meserve was also his deacon, so that it would be proper
to consult with him. But would Henry have anything much
to suggest? As the two sisters had said, Henry was hard to talk
to. Nevertheless, Jerry Storm remembered, with a faint
thought of comfort, that Henry had seemed as much disturbed
yesterday as himself. Mrs. Meserve talked easily, but she was
so active that she was not a good listener. There were the two
older girls. Jerry had to assure himself that he was not turning
to the Meserves merely for a sight of Mae. Mae might well be
giving a music lesson. The thought of that seemed to absolve
him. Yesterday the Meserves had shown their continued kind-

ness to the Woods. Jerry knew that Vera had been there in the morning, and that Mae had come in to get the dinner. It did not seem to him that he could talk with people who were not in some way demonstrating the gospel of love which had come as a new revelation to him in the seminary. Yet in what way could it be all-sufficient and meet the issue now confronting them all?

Without stopping to speak to Mrs. Latham and Miss Blanchard, who were both in the kitchen—and Pug too—Jerry left the house and walked as quickly as he could straight to the Meserves.

The big green-painted frame house, with its porches and swells, was in many ways of all the pleasant houses in this pleasant place the most pleasant. It was newer than Mrs. Latham's house, and the trees in the yard were not so tall. But the yard occupied more than one lot, so that children could gather and play there. Above all, it was the house where Mae lived.

As he pressed the bell, Jerry thought how hasty he was. Henry Meserve would doubtless be at the lumberyard at this hour of the morning, where it would be too risky to talk with him confidentially—if such a thing were possible anyway, without Henry's womenfolk at hand to help out. But Jerry had committed himself now.

Mrs. Meserve came to the door. She was always as cordial as she had time to be, but this morning she greeted Jerry with enthusiasm.

"Just the man! I'm so glad you came over. Come in."

As she took Jerry into the large, not too tidy parlor, she was explaining that Henry was still upstairs in bed. He had telephoned his helper at the lumberyard that he would not be in this morning—something almost unknown!

"We're all upset. I've never known Henry to be so upset. But sit down anyway, and I'll tell him you're here. I think he'll want to come down. The girls are in the house somewhere. They've been discussing what's best to do. Yes, this is our

chance to talk things over and come to a little better understanding, with Henry and Mae and Vera all at home, and the
children at school."

Jerry sat down in the comfortable, standardly furnished parlor, and Mrs. Meserve went upstairs to call Henry. Jerry's eyes
went to the piano. The large grand piano, bought for Mae and
according to her instructions, stood in full light, so that Mae's
pupils could see what they were doing. The piano bench,
which held music, was vacant; but Jerry pictured Mae's figure
there, as he had so often seen it, with the head lifted and then
bowing in the intense passages of the music. It was still a miracle to Jerry that Mae's small fingers could work so fast and
easily and stretch so far. It was Mae's declared intention to
"teach him to love music," and he was beginning to do so.

The two older girls came in together from another room.
Vera was crisp, fresh, with style, always delightful to see, but
she did not have Mae's soft loveliness. Jerry saw again, with a
pain he had not yet analyzed, Mae's charming daintiness; her
curling brown-gold hair and brown eyes; her small, capable
hands.

The girls both greeted him as "Jerry." They wouldn't have
wanted to see any other person this morning, but, like their
mother, they were glad to see *him*. Jerry felt the sweetness of
that—of the realization that he had come to feel at home in
this large, easy-going house. Mae said that she had canceled her
music lessons; she did not feel well.

Vera said, "None of us here feels well. I expect Jerry
doesn't, either. How can we? It's as if the ground had been
taken out from under our feet."

Mae said softly, "I'm so terribly sorry for them."

Vera replied more sharply, "We all are. But that doesn't solve
the problem."

Mae murmured that she was not sure what "the problem"
was.

Vera retorted even more sharply, "That doesn't keep it from
being there. There are people who have suffered more from

it than we have—financially, at any rate. We don't know what we would say in their place."

Jerry's sympathy was with Mae, but he felt the truth of Vera's statement. Mrs. Meserve came downstairs at that moment, announcing, "Henry will be down."

All sat in tense silence until Henry Meserve came into the room. He was wearing his slippers and house jacket, and that, in the conventional Henry Meserve, seemed to point up the shattering effect of yesterday's meeting at the Woods'. At the same time, it made Jerry Storm more of an intimate member of the Meserve family circle. Henry showed his distress more obviously than young Jerry Storm. His face was ashen. But he said briefly, "Glad you came over."

This morning the Wood case seemed to show a dozen fresh aspects that ought to be discussed.

Henry said, "It will be out in no time. Probably is now."

Mae confessed softly, "Dad, I went ahead and told Lyle last night. I know the secret won't be kept long—no secret is in Fairview. Maybe I should have spoken first to you, but I knew how done up you were feeling last night. I thought it would be too hard for Philip at school today if some of the other boys had got wind of this, but not Lyle. Will Cowie might, for instance. And then Philip would have no one on whom to depend."

Her mother exclaimed, "You told Lyle!"

"Yes, I did."

Her father said mildly, "I think you did right, Mae. I can hardly bring myself to speak of the whole matter, even to the children; although of course they'll have to know. It may not mean so much to Ione and Doris."

Mrs. Meserve had been mulling over Mae's words. "Philip! Yes, that poor boy. We've been thinking of Minnie, but we shall have to think of Philip too."

Vera said with earnest confidence, "Jerry can talk with him."

Jerry muttered, "Yes." But he himself felt little confidence.

They all seemed at sea these first few minutes. Mrs. Meserve was indomitable in all practical matters, but in one such as this she seemed to have little to suggest.

Vera assumed the captaincy, to the relief of all. "One thing we know is coming up before us," she said firmly. "Whether Mr. Wood is to act as superintendent this coming Sunday."

"But surely he will withdraw of his own accord," Mae said.

"We don't know whether he will or not, especially since we've heard how Minnie acted yesterday. You can't take anything or anyone for granted."

"Neither of them had had time to think it over," Mae pleaded.

"That makes it all the more necessary for those of us who are John and Minnie's friends to have some definite thoughts in mind."

It gave Jerry a sense of relief that the Meserves seemed still to regard themselves as John Wood's friends.

Vera went on, however, "I think we have to make *sure* about next Sunday. There could be an awful row, and there needn't be. Jerry is the one to make sure."

Jerry knew well that Vera was right—while he hoped, with Mae, that the suggestion of withdrawal would come first from John Wood. He managed to say now that a man in John Wood's position neither should, nor should expect to, act as an official of the church—not until he had cleared himself.

Vera asked inexorably, "How can he clear himself when he's already admitted his guilt? If Minnie doesn't regard what he's been doing as guilt, that doesn't change things. He's been dishonest."

They all agreed then: if John himself did not speak first, Jerry as pastor must tell him that it would be better, for himself and for everybody, that he should not take his usual place next Sunday.

But who would step in as Sunday-school superintendent at this late date?

Vera again spoke crisply. "I will. People are used to having me pop up almost anywhere. The children will think less of it. If I can take charge of Primary, I can of the Sunday school. Almeda Blanchard can take Primary. I don't mind asking her."

"Miss Blanchard doesn't know about the trouble at the Woods', nor Mrs. Latham."

"No, but they'll hear about it. I think you should tell them, Jerry, if you don't mind my saying so."

"I don't want to tell anybody until I've talked with Mr. and Mrs. Wood."

"Well, that's all right. You *should* do that. But better your telling Mrs. Latham and Almeda than some busybody."

Jerry agreed. He knew, also, that he could not hide his deeply troubled state from the two sisters during many more meals. He felt with gratitude the efficiency of Vera, but it was Mae who had his heart; although he hoped—and really supposed—he did not show where his feelings lay. Mae seemed to regard both John and Minnie in the light of invalids to whom she must be tender and helpful. She was going over this noon to get their dinner, as she had done yesterday, was going to take part of the roast now in the Meserve oven, and one of Vera's lemon pies. This was with her family's sanction. But it was she who had thought of Philip. Jerry was ashamed that he himself had not called to see Philip last night. He knew that he was too much governed by his veneration for John and Minnie Wood. He had not yet been able to adjust to a new conception of them. Jerry tried to keep his eyes from Mae, unaware that Vera's keen eyes were seeing with amusement his self-consciousness and penetrating the meaning of his hands held stiffly and his heated skin.

What would be Colonel Merriam's attitude toward the case? The group discussed this point for a short time. To Jerry's relief, the Meserves were doubtful whether Colonel Merriam would bring the case into court.

Mae said, "Mrs. Merriam would be against that. She's such a friend of Minnie's."

Henry Meserve answered, "Mrs. Merriam has nothing to say in the Colonel's business."

But Henry agreed that Colonel Merriam might not prosecute, unless forced to do it by others involved. However, he was not easily forced. "He has too much pride to want the Merriam Company to be involved in any public legal battles. He's more likely to settle all accounts himself. That's my guess, anyway."

Mae's face brightened. "Well, then, Dad, he may let John Wood go on."

Jerry Storm's face unconsciously reflected Mae's hopeful look. He put in, "Some of the men, I think, would like to bring that about if they could. I know Austin Cowie, for one, would like to see if the losses people have suffered could not be made up privately, and the whole matter kept from becoming public. I don't know," he finished lamely, looking at Henry Meserve. He really had no confidence in such a scheme, but, like Mae, could not keep from clutching at straws. There ought to be *some* way to return everything to normal.

Henry Meserve was frowning, but before he could reply Vera broke in. "It *would* be Austin Cowie!" she said bitingly. "He knows how to keep the lid on things. On his own little doings, for instance, which wouldn't look pretty if people knew about them. What he gets away with!"

"Vera, I think that's off the subject," Mrs. Meserve said in reproof. "And besides, it's mostly rumors." She looked worriedly toward Jerry.

"Rumors nothing!" said Vera. "You know very well *I* don't think so—and don't hush me up just because Jerry is here. He's a man! He doesn't need to be coddled."

She turned directly toward the young minister. "I don't go around telling these things, but this is a time when we ought to be frank. Mama and Papa, and Mae too, know what I'm talking about, and maybe you do—what people say, or whisper rather, that Austin Cowie 'has someone in Chicago.' Of course, he only goes there on business!" She mimicked Mrs. Cowie's reverent tone. " 'Austin has gone to Chicago on business.' But I met him there once right on the street with that woman he has 'business' with! He turned all colors."

"Vera, that's enough on that!" Henry Meserve said firmly. "It won't help us here."

Vera subsided, but not before saying, "Well, Jerry might as well know things about other people as well as about John Wood."

"The question was whether John Wood could go on, under any circumstances," Mr. Meserve said. "We shouldn't get away from that. And the fact is, he can't. Who would trust John in money matters? I wouldn't myself." A spasm of pain contracted his mouth.

"But what are they to do, Dad? The Woods."

"I don't know," Henry muttered, leaning his forehead on his hand. "Go away somewhere and start over."

"But Minnie—!"

Henry waved his hand. He could not think further now. He himself did not see how it was to be done, since John was cleaned out financially; and he was tortured by the realization that he himself could help little. A hundred dollars, maybe. He would have been willing to help John, even now. But although Henry had a good business, and good income, he had an expensive family and must think of them first. Was not that what John, in his different circumstances, had been doing? Yes, but John had been doing it by defrauding others and betraying his trust. That was what shook Henry Meserve, who had thought of John Wood as superior to himself. Besides, his own astuteness sadly told him that Minnie's needs could not be the sole cause of John Wood's playing the market. John must have in him a streak of the gambler. None of them knew what lay in John's past.

There was a suggestion that Colonel Merriam might help John Wood to leave town and get into some other business. At this, however, Henry Meserve shook his head. Colonel

Merriam was upright himself, but no more forgiving than Deacon Kruse—less so. Henry happened to know that the Colonel had not helped Brad with a dollar since he had learned of "that marriage, whatever it was." He had taken Brad back, but only so far. He might well intend to do something for the little girl.

"But, Henry," Mrs. Meserve said excitedly, "that isn't showing mercy."

Henry retorted, "When did Colonel Merriam ever pretend to show mercy? He's been a kind man in many ways, but always on his own terms. He's built up what he has by good hard dealing. But he isn't sneaky; he keeps his given word."

Vera said with indignation, "I think he ought to have turned over the business to John Wood or else kept closer hold on it these last years."

Her mother said, "I suppose that's what we all think."

But her father answered, "Well, that wouldn't have helped, Vera. John, by his own word, started this double dealing a long time ago. Every man must take the responsibility for his own acts. That's what I don't understand about John. It seems to me he acts in two ways at once and doesn't put them together."

But they might have gone on discussing this situation forever, as Mrs. Meserve said, and still got nowhere.

Jerry Storm himself, realizing now that an interview with the Woods was before him, was in a fever to go on with it. The others agreed, only suggesting that he telephone from their house to find out whether John was at home. John himself answered. He agreed to see his young pastor.

The two girls went to the door with Jerry. He had one pressure from Mae's hand, one glance, full of troubled sweetness but of reassurance, from her brown eyes. He left the house, thankful for a family so loyal and dependable as the Meserves. Yet he could not wholly depend upon them, or upon any one person. It was true that John Wood had taken the ground out from under all their feet. The freshness of the spring air, and the open look of this pleasant town on the prairies, had become treacherous to him. He was glad that he did not have to pass the church. He could not even find certainty in a small circle of "the faithful" and "the saved," as his grandfather and father had found it—or had thought to find it. He was unsure now even about Mae; or rather, about his future relations with Mae. She had brought home to him that he must talk with Philip as well as with Philip's parents. Unconsciously he had thought of the three of them—John, Minnie, and Philip—as almost one. But Philip seemed to Jerry, at this moment, at the edge of the problem. Jerry was absorbed now in the almost insuperable difficulty of speaking to the changed John Wood—and the changed Minnie—to any vital purpose. He tried to put off all other decisions, even emotions, until he had seen them and heard what they might say. He felt far more keenly than when he had first come to Fairview the rawness of his inexperience. And beyond that, he had been troubled all night and morning by the memory of Deacon Kruse's burning blue eyes and the deacon's harsh words, some of which Jerry could not gainsay.

Jerry Storm waited, after pressing the bell beside the front door of the John Wood house. He could not escape the memory of the many times he had stood here, just as he was standing now, but with a very different kind of anticipation. Fortunately, John Wood came to the door almost immediately. His manner was apparently calmer than Jerry's. Like Henry Meserve, Jerry felt all the more dismay at such calmness. It made him realize more clearly that he had never known the man upon whom he had most counted in his church. Then whom did he know?

John led him into the front room.

To add to Jerry's distress, there sat Minnie Wood. Jerry was not like the old deacon, and could not order her upstairs. He sensed at once that she was subtly different from when he had called upon her before. There was a tautness, almost a defiance in her attitude. She did not rise from her chair, and, though she nodded in reply to the young pastor's greeting, she did not hold out her frail hand. Jerry was left standing, until John Wood pulled up a chair for him.

This was the most difficult interview Jerry Storm had ever been forced to carry on. Even the day when he told his father and grandfather that he intended to go to a seminary which, in their view, was one of the dwelling places of Satan, had not been so painful to him, because he had felt sure of himself and of his own needs and intentions. Now he was unsure. He was aware that as pastor he should take the lead. He should ask that question which must trouble all the people in his congregation: "Do you have faith? Did you believe in what you were doing and saying?" He should pray.

But he did not know how or where to start. He was conscious of his youth; not pleasingly conscious, as with Mrs. Latham and Miss Blanchard, but agonizingly so.

He realized how he had always looked up to John and Minnie Wood. They were the same people in outward appearance; this front room, with its mixture of commonplace and good old pieces of furniture, was the same; there was even a fresh bouquet of lilacs on the small round table. Above this table hung the framed, enlarged photograph of Minnie Terrill at fifteen. Most enlarged photographs of that period were ghastly. But this one, with its delicate tints, held the charm which Minnie seemed to impart to all things connected with her. Not only was the young face delightful in itself, but its quality was enhanced by the pathetic contrast between the rounded cheeks and the eyes purely gray and bright, their sockets not yet sunken or darkened, and the ailing middle-aged woman of the present. Yet it was this present woman, in her paradox of strength and weakness, who was the more distinctive. It was she, even more than the pretty young girl, who had led Mrs. Merriam—no aesthete—to say that lilies-of-the-valley were "Minnie's flower."

Jerry knew, in his own heart, that he had not come here as an enemy or an accuser. He was eager to help if the way would but open. But he also knew that he must speak of John Wood's relation to the church—specifically to the Sunday school. He feared that his suggestion that Vera Meserve was prepared to act as a substitute superintendent would cause him to be regarded as an enemy. He could see that in Minnie's bright, round, wide-open eyes, and in her closed lips—as if she knew his errand already.

Neither of the Woods helped him to open the conversation. There went through his mind many things which, as their pastor, he might do, and desperately wanted to do. He had often prayed briefly but fervently when he had called upon Minnie Wood, and she had been responsive, even inspiring. He prayed silently now, but it seemed to him that he could not utter a word aloud. Suddenly he found himself doing so. The words welled up and forced themselves to be spoken.

"Dear God and Father, help all of us. Help both these dear friends. Help me. Amen."

There was silence—no outward sign that the Woods had received the prayer in any manner. But Jerry Storm himself felt a relief.

"Mr. Wood, I want to say first of all that I know you are in great trouble. I don't want to add to it in any way." He felt Minnie staring at him, but he continued. "I don't intend to go over what was said here yesterday."

He looked at the Woods for help, but got none. They were apparently going to put all the burden of the talk on him. And even though he understood, in a sense, the peculiar part that Minnie Wood played in this case, he did believe that John Wood should feel contrition for having betrayed the trust of so many people. Jerry could not go back on that belief. Yet John's handsome face, when Jerry looked somewhat pleadingly at it now, seemed to reveal even less of his inner feelings than it had yesterday. Jerry Storm, less shrewdly observant than Mr. Rakosi, did not observe that very slight mis-alignment of the eyes, now accentuated.

Yet if John and Minnie Wood could speak out to anyone,

would it not be to their pastor and friend? Many times Jerry
Storm and John Wood had gone over church matters together.
The young minister had confided to John some of his own
problems. But he had done so, of course, because of his strong
respect for and reliance upon his senior deacon. That was what
was lacking today in his attitude—that unquestioning respect.
He no longer looked up to John Wood. Yet it seemed to him
that Minnie demanded that he should still do so.

He felt the two of them as completely together and closed
against any third person. But if he could not show or feel the
old respect, the young man could not show authority, either.
He could only hope that they would open their minds to him
and of their own accord express concern in some manner; he
did not ask for or want emotional groveling.

His heart was full of what might be said to them. He wanted
to speak of the Apostle Paul—not as Deacon Kruse had spoken,
but of the man who had committed the sin of persecution, far
worse than John Wood's "error," and who had acknowledged
it, always been conscious of it, but had gone on, and in his own
person had "overcome evil with good." Yet Jerry could not
break through the glassy barrier which stood between him and
the Woods. He could even admire Minnie Wood's complete
loyalty to her husband. He still felt the indefinable appeal of
her slight frame and her big eyes in their darkened sockets.
There was still something "spiritual" about her, Jerry felt, but
it was being entirely concentrated upon John. She scarcely
knew that other people were alive.

Jerry began in a pleading tone. "You realize, don't you, Mr.
Wood, how the church is being affected in this—unfortunate
situation?" No response. He stumbled ahead. "You are our
senior deacon, and the head of our Sunday school. Our young
people must be affected."

Minnie said in the clear, hard tone which had come into her
voice yesterday, "Are you trying to tell us that we ought to
stay out of the church?"

"No, no," Jerry pleaded. (The words came to his mind, but

he could not utter them: "We have all sinned and fallen short
of the glory of God.") He now spoke directly to John Wood.
"You must have thought about these things yourself?"

This time he received an answer, although a reserved and
reluctant one. "I am quite ready to withdraw from any positions I may hold."

"We will neither of us attend the services next Sunday,"
Minnie said with dignity.

"I am sorry for that. But"—Jerry spoke with gathering firm-
ness—"it is best that Mr. Wood should not act as superintendent next Sunday. Don't you feel that too?"

"Yes, I feel it," John Wood murmured. He bowed his head
slightly now and put his hand over his eyes.

Jerry said earnestly, "I hope you both realize how little I
have wanted to say this. There is no man I have more . . ."
He could not continue. "I want to be a friend to both of you,
but I feel that you won't let me."

Minnie seemed to take charge. "You are too young to understand. You do not know what it is to have been dead and
brought back to life by one person's devotion."

"I know that I am young," Jerry answered humbly. "I do
know—have always felt—how wonderful your marriage has
been. It has been an inspiration." He stopped and swallowed.
"But I *am* the ordained pastor of the Fairview Congregational
Church, whether I deserve to be or not. Perhaps I do not. I
have the same duty to all my church people as to you."

Minnie said, "He who is not for us is against us."

"Oh, no! You are not making the right use of those words.
And they are not true of me in this case."

But Jerry could not assure Minnie of the one thing which
she seemed to require of him: that he did not consider John
Wood culpable. He wanted to tell her how painfully Henry
Meserve had been hit by this blow. Henry had also trusted and
looked up to John Wood. But Jerry sensed that at the present
stage of things any such statement could only lead to contention. He thought, How difficult it is to make anything clear!

See how the very words of the New Testament can be turned to a wrong meaning!

Jerry rose. There was no value in his staying longer. He said awkwardly, and without confidence, "Please let me know if you—if I can be of help in any way."

Minnie looked scornful.

Jerry made his own way out of the house. He was trembling with emotion, baffled compassion, personal chagrin. But at least he had accomplished his mission. John Wood had not asked who was to take his place on the next Sunday morning, and Jerry had not been forced to mention the Meserves. Otherwise, in Minnie's present frame of mind, she might have refused to let Mae come in this noon to put their dinner on the table—his tender-hearted, uncondemning Mae.

As Jerry was going down the walk, he thought of Philip. He might have said to the parents, "I hope, at any rate, that Philip will be in our class next Sunday. We need him." In some way, Jerry would have to reach Philip. Where did Philip stand in relation to all this?

Jerry thought back, but he could not tell from Philip's behavior yesterday. Philip himself did not know. Jerry felt a rush of warm sympathy for the boy, almost of fellow feeling for his youth and for the disaster which had fallen on him. Jerry was not certain what he would say to Philip, but surely it would be possible to get through somehow to the son, as it seemed he could not to the parents.

As he left the house, it came to Jerry, with wonder, that that character who seemed to belong to fiction—"a man of mystery"—he himself had just encountered in the person of one of his closest associates in church and community. This person might always be controversial. Fairview people might never know what to make of John Wood.

CHAPTER

IO

JERRY STORM went early to the church on this Sunday, well ahead of the time for the opening of the Sunday school. Tommy Hardcastle was there ahead of him, putting the Sunday-school hymnals in their proper places.

"Good morning, Mr. Hardcastle."

"Good morning, sir." At once Tommy shook his head. "This is a sad thing, Reverend Storm."

Jerry did not pretend to mistake Tommy's reference. "Yes," he replied, "a very sad thing."

"Phoebe and I could not believe it."

"Many people feel that way, no doubt."

"Colonel Merriam, however, sir, could not be mistaken."

"I'm afraid not."

"Yes," Tommy repeated, and again shook his white head. "A sad thing. That's what Phoebe said. She said, 'I think it's all so sad.'"

Jerry Storm could do no more than nod his head. Tommy Hardcastle's more than moderate words were part of what the minister himself felt. It seemed to him that he could see Phoebe Hardcastle, in her old-fashioned neatness, sitting in her big wooden rocking chair, holding the Maltese cat, shaking her head, and hear her speaking these words in her slow, deep

voice. Jerry had always delighted to hear her. She spoke lacon-
ically, yet with a strain of Old Country poetry.

Jerry was relieved that Tommy had not been more con-
demnatory. If the church members would all be that temper-
ate! Jerry quailed when he thought of Mrs. Caddie Rathbun.
But Tommy's reference showed that the John Wood situation
was widely known. This Sunday would have to be faced. John
and Minnie would not be present at the church service. Philip
might just possibly be in Jerry's Sunday-school class. Lyle
Meserve had said that he was going to bring Philip.

The young minister felt the disheartening contrast between
this Sunday and last. First of all, this was a gloomy morning.
Tommy, with his great concern for economy, and his English
accustomedness to chill, had not built a fire in the furnace. Perhaps the day did not actually call for that. But the varnished
pews felt cold and forbidding to the touch.

Jerry suggested, "Mr. Hardcastle, you might make just a
temporary fire in the basement before it's time to ring the
bell."

Tommy said cautiously, "It would require some of the kindling."

"Yes, but we might have just enough to take the chill off before the children come."

Tommy obediently went down to the basement on his
bowed legs. He did not argue with the minister any more than
with Colonel Merriam.

The Meserve girls had brought over some of their own lilacs
yesterday evening; but these too looked chilly, not living, like
the wildflowers on the platform a week ago. Jerry had only a
few minutes alone. Then the room began to fill. In spite of the
unpromising weather, there were almost as many children as
usual. The Adult Bible Class, taught by Mr. Hungerford since
Mrs. Merriam had resigned as leader, was larger than on most
Sundays. Jerry could not avoid the unhappy thought that its
size might be partly due to curiosity concerning how the
Sunday-school exercises were to be carried on, and whether

John Wood was to be present. But Jerry told himself that this
was better than having people stay away.

People soon learned how the exercises were to be managed.
On the very dot of the hour Mae took her place at the piano
and Vera hers in the superintendent's chair. The adults in the
rear pews craned their necks to see what was happening in regard to the Primary Department. They leaned back, satisfied,
when they saw Miss Almeda Blanchard sit down among the
smallest pupils. Jerry could not hear Mrs. Rathbun breathe,
"So that's how!"

The minister went to one of the front pews.

He felt his gratitude toward Mae and Vera. Vera had told
Jerry that she would take hold of things, without explanation,
and would follow the usual order, except that she would not
give an opening talk, and would not offer the prayer. Jerry
would help wherever necessary.

Vera tapped the bell on the table beside her with decision.

"The Sunday school will please come to order. We will first
unite in singing Hymn Number Seventy-eight."

At the sound of her unshaken, well-carrying voice, Jerry
Storm breathed more easily. His eyes dimmed as he saw Mae's
small hands raised above the piano keys, and then striking the
opening chord:

"Rescue the perishing. . ."

Vera had not instructed the school to stand, but the pupils
and teachers were well enough trained to do so anyway. The
school joined moderately, if not "heartily," in the singing.
Almeda Blanchard urged on her little ones to sing in their
quavering and off-key voices. And yet there was a lifelessness
about the whole service. Mae played almost by rote. She was
wearing, this Sunday, a plain sailor-type hat; there were no
flowers to bob gaily. She had chosen this old hymn of gospel
type, but it was being sung—it seemed—with little sense of
meaning. Vera, in spite of her competence and self-possession,

could not possibly take the place of John Wood. Her slight girl's figure was not truly a substitute for his large and handsome presence. Her voice, in comparison with John's, seemed small and thin, especially when she read the Golden Text.

"And he said unto David, Thou art more righteous than I: for thou hast rewarded me good, whereas I have rewarded thee evil."

The words seemed singularly ill chosen for this day; but Vera, Jerry, and Mae, talking together, had decided that it would be ostentatious to change the text given in the Lesson Quarterly. And how very hard it would have been to select a text which would not have seemed inappropriate—or, even worse, too appropriate! In Vera's reading, the words received no emphasis. She would have preferred not to call for the repetition in chorus by the Sunday school. But that too would have been ostentatious, and might well have caused comment. Vera had said, "I don't want to give Caddie Rathbun or anybody else a handle to get hold of to criticize." Therefore the voices repeated in a loud drone after her, "'. . . Thou are more righteous than I: for thou hast rewarded me good, whereas I have rewarded thee evil.'"

Another hymn was sung. Then Vera said, "Our pastor will lead us in a few words of prayer."

Jerry Storm rose and faced the Sunday school. He bowed his head and, after a short pause, said, "Let us unite this morning in repeating together the Lord's Prayer."

His voice trembled slightly at the sentence, "Forgive us our debts as we forgive our debtors." But he went through with it, and in that phrase, at least, his personal earnestness came out, so that he did not know whether some of the older voices had abstained from the saying of those words.

He was relieved when Vera again took over, and announced briefly, "We will now all go to our separate classes."

Before Jerry left for his own, he inconspicuously pressed Vera's hand. He felt it warm and perspiring—that hand ordinarily of such even temperature and so dry. She was going through an ordeal, after all. He looked at Mae, but could not reach her.

He went up the aisle to his own class of boys. The lesson, in line with the Golden Text, dealt with the Old Testament story of the young David sparing the life of his enemy, King Saul, found asleep in the cave. To Jerry it offered no such problems as the story of Job. Now his chief concern was as to whether Philip would be found sitting in one of those two rows reserved for the class. At first, Jerry thought not. But at the last minute, just before the class started, Philip entered with Lyle Meserve. Lyle had persuaded Philip to come, Jerry did not know how.

The class today was not the usual class. Though Philip was present, he said almost nothing. There was no real liveliness in the discussion of the others. Lyle would go no further than to say that "he guessed David did the right thing." Jerry saw with pain that Will Cowie kept obviously apart from Philip and had not greeted him, and that two or three of the other boys followed Will's lead. Lyle Meserve sat close beside Philip. After the lesson, the two slipped out. Jerry made no move to keep them. He knew, from his own emotions, how devastating it would be for Philip to see someone else in his father's place, even Vera Meserve. But he wished that he might have had a chance to shake hands with Philip. That might have served as a demonstration to the boys who were giving Philip the cold shoulder. He wondered whether Will Cowie was acting in accordance with his father's present view, or spontaneously. Jerry sensed, however, that Philip's self-control was precarious —as his own was. It was just as well to take little notice of him, particularly since Philip had promised Jerry that he would come to see him when he could.

Now followed the church service. It was difficult for Jerry Storm to carry it on at all. He felt alone and conspicuous in his chair behind the pulpit. That chair with its leather upholstering seemed too ostentatious for him. Mae, he knew, was at the little pipe organ; but that was out of his sight, as were the members of the choir. Jerry was facing his congregation. The young minister felt great anxiety as to who was present, who had stayed away. The congregation appeared much as usual. He looked down with a sense of familiarity upon the bright black butterfly on Mrs. Sayles's bonnet. Mr. Sayles, beside her, already had his hand cupped to his ear. Mae was playing her prelude. The Cowies were present, the Meserves, the Rechtners, Mrs. Latham and Miss Blanchard—almost all the standbys. Tommy and Phoebe Hardcastle sat as always in the back.

Jerry's vision just flicked across the face of Mrs. Rathbun. He had never feared her, but he felt that he did now. He knew that she was particularly sarcastic toward Minnie Wood—jealous of Mrs. Wood, the minister feared, besides being critically unbelieving where Minnie's "delicacy" was concerned. Yet Mrs. Rathbun was here; she must be faced, and in good spirit; she was as much a member of this church as motherly Mrs. Latham.

Jerry felt a touch of gladness to see that Mrs. Merriam had come into her accustomed pew. He was relieved, however, that Deacon Kruse had not driven in—although he missed Caroline's sweet, dark, deeply attentive gaze. It troubled him more that he did not see Miss Gertrude Schilling, who, as people put it, "never missed a Sunday."

The most conspicuous absences, of course, were those of John, Minnie, and Philip Wood. Nobody had taken their places near the rear of the room. The vacancy in the pew was glaring. Instead of Philip, Howard Rechtner had agreed to act as usher, although he was agonizingly shy. Vera Meserve had said confidently, however, that "she knew she could get Howard." His great conscientiousness alone would keep him from refusing. His sensitive skin flushed deeply when he bumped into a pew while showing some members to their seats. Will Cowie, however, on the other side of the room, put a kind of dash into his ushering which was far more unpleasant to the young pastor than the bashfulness of Howard Rechtner.

But it was useless counting faces. It only added to the young man's nervous sense of the occasion. His uneasiness found relief when his gaze rested upon the spare, upright figure of Mrs. Merriam. The expression on her fine features seemed always to hold a controlled sadness, lightened by the gaze of her clear eyes. Her expression was not motherly, like that of Mrs. Latham's large, soft-featured countenance; but the young man felt in it a more comprehensive wisdom, as well as courage. He realized that it must have taken individual courage for Mrs. Merriam to come to the service today without bringing Minnie Wood, and certainly not with the encouragement of Colonel Merriam.

Jerry scarcely knew what the first hymn was. He had left the selection to Mae, although usually he felt a delicious intimacy in talking over the Sunday's music with her, outlining to her briefly the sermon he intended to give, and helping her look through the hymn book for appropriate hymns. Through Mae, he had learned to appreciate better hymns.

Today he directed his sermon to Mrs. Merriam, thankful that Mrs. Rathbun sat on the other side of the room. But he felt that his preaching was wooden, and his spoken prayer stumbling and unworthy.

Yet the service continued almost as usual. Jerry Storm felt the character of this church, so well organized, and with such efficient members, that it might be said to run itself. He did not want to change it. But what need did it have of him, a young man who—it now appeared—had little beyond scarcely tapped energy? A man of wisdom and experience, and of fatherly concern, was needed today at this pulpit. The service might not seem out of the ordinary, on the surface, but all the same the church had received a blow which could eventually prove shattering.

At the noon hour much the usual group gathered around the table in Mrs. Dissendorfer's upstairs dining room.

Mr. Rakosi came in just after the others were seated. But,

although he gave his customary sprightly greeting, the first thing which his keen eyes noted was that no places had been set for the three members of the Wood family. He had not expected the Woods to come. But he glanced sharply at Charlotte as she entered with his dinner plate and poured his coffee. The girl's plump face was flushed and set. Mr. Rakosi looked inquiringly at Miss Janeway, who was seated next to him; she slightly shook her head.

"Don't refer to any of the Woods," she whispered to him as he stooped to pick up the fragrantly scented handkerchief which she had dropped between their two chairs. She could say no more but turned her gaze significantly toward Charlotte.

Mr. Rakosi nodded. He understood; he had already learned that Mrs. Dissendorfer was one of the people who had asked John Wood to invest her tiny funds. There was probably more general indignation regarding Mrs. Dissendorfer's minute defraudment than about that of any other person. Fairview respected her for her hard work as a widow (or to all intents and purposes a widow) in building up this good little home business and in raising her four children.

Today Charlotte's glumness seemed to affect all in the dining room. To fill the gap, Mr. Rakosi at once began talking in frivolous strain, purposely letting his accent be funnier than usual. Eleanor Janeway followed his lead, although not all did. Miss Gale was prim. Mr. Rakosi felt himself *en rapport* with Eleanor Janeway in keeping the conversation going, so that no one would have an opportunity to mention the Woods. Mr. Spear started to do so. Looking around, he said innocently, "I don't seem to see the Woods today."

But Eleanor Janeway said at once, "They don't always come, you know."

And Mr. Rakosi immediately followed her. "Well, I see se spring is not always so pair-fect here in Fairview."

"Is it perfect anywhere?" Eleanor retorted. "I suppose in Hungary."

"Ah!" he sighed. "In Hungary! In Budapest! Ah, se Blue Danube, which is not blue!"

"Ah! the Upper Wahkonsa, which is dirty brown!"

Both were talking drivel and aware of it. Miss Gale's pretty face looked more and more closed and disapproving. Mr. Rakosi had an impulse to protect the Woods, felt sympathy for them. Yet, after all, the fall of John Wood gave him a kind of gloomy satisfaction, confirming his ingrained belief that no family life could be so faultless as that of the Woods had seemed. In anything that aspired to reach beyond the ordinary there was always a flaw. He had said that to Eleanor Janeway, who had enthusiastically disagreed with him. He had hoped she was right. But now, sadly, he thought she must agree. The really surprising element in the situation was that John Wood's fault should turn out to be in the financial, not the sexual, line. Yet those eyes—did not their set suggest that very kind of falsity, while the mouth was perfect?

At any rate, the hard silence of Charlotte and her younger brother, who helped her to pour water and remove dishes, made the meal a strain, even though the food was well cooked. Only the coffee was not good. Mrs. Dissendorfer was noted for her coffee. Mr. Babson had to put his full attention on eating, because of his new false teeth. But Mrs. Babson made a face when she sipped her coffee. If she had a remark to make on it, however, Mr. Rakosi and Miss Janeway saw to it that she got no chance. Finally she did manage to give her cup to Charlotte.

"Something seems to have gone wrong with this first cup," she said. "Maybe your ma's got better in the kitchen."

Charlotte took the cup ungraciously. Usually she was anxious to please.

"I wonder what's the matter here," Mrs. Babson muttered.

Miss Janeway said gaily, "Everybody has to have off days."

"Yes, I guess that's so."

There was a certain triumph for Mr. Rakosi and Miss Janeway both, in carrying through the conversation at the dining table without its degenerating into gossip. Some of the people present knew of the Wood situation; some didn't.

Yet even Mr. Rakosi was not satisfied. He wanted to discuss the Wood case with a person of generous instincts—in fact, with Eleanor Janeway. He did not walk home with Eleanor, however. She said that she had letters to write.

"I too have work," Mr. Rakosi said.

He went home to the wooden building on Main Street in which he lived and worked. His photograph business had prospered in Fairview. He himself had been so warmly accepted, and in fact had cut such a dash in the town, that up to now he had never thought of the little place as solitary. His bedroom, with the framed photographs of relatives and friends in Hungary, had been a bachelor's refuge. But today he went instead into his gallery room, lighted by a skylight, and looked over some proofs that he had recently made. One was of a group picture which he had taken of the high-school senior class. In the pale glow from the skylight he examined the proof and saw that it had come out well. In the very center of the group stood the Valedictorian, Philip Wood. Next to him a girl stood, Gladys Cornwall, the Salutatorian. But although wholesome-looking, with her strongly built neck and shoulders, her sturdy legs, she was not pretty, according to Mr. Rakosi's standards, and he spent little time studying her. Philip Wood was outstanding. Mr. Rakosi observed particularly the youth's confident bearing, which had always somewhat amused him, although he admired it. The bright eyes seemed to look straight at the photographer. Innocence seemed to be written on the good-looking face.

Sadness invaded the Hungarian photographer. He wondered, as he often had—was this boy's goodness genuine, after all? Trained in observing people, Mr. Rakosi realized again that he had never completely believed in the seemingly flawless virtue of John Wood. He had never precisely disbelieved in it. John Wood's blue eyes had always seemed to him impenetrable. But he had had the impression that in a photograph they would have come out expressionless and a trifle odd. The eyes of Philip, on the other hand, were direct and shining. Mr. Rakosi felt now that he wanted to believe in Philip, that the boy's genuineness actually meant something to him; it had added to his satisfaction in the prairie town in which, for purely commercial reasons, he had set up his photograph business. He had heard from another passenger on the westbound train that Fairview was a "nice town and doesn't have any good photographer now." On an impulse, Mr. Rakosi had got off at Fairview. Since his start here, his business—partly, he knew, because of his popularity with the girls and women —had done extraordinarily well. But he also knew himself to be a good photographer. He had grown, against his expectation, to like the ways of the town so much that he had been coming more and more to the conviction that he would like to settle here.

But, as the son of an old civilization, he knew—as it seemed to him that these people did not know, at least in this flourishing era—what actual evil and actual hardship were. Here they supposed they had little worse obvious sin to deal with than the drinking sprees of Dan Postel! Mr. Rakosi was sure that there were other sins that might be dug up in the town. But all Europeans knew more of evil and accepted it as inevitable. The general friendliness and lack of suspicion of the people of Fairview had been exhilarating to the young stranger from a foreign country, even though he had been inclined to deride it. Now he realized that he wanted to feel himself in a new land. Unconsciously Philip Wood had come to stand for this new land. To some degree the whole Wood family had seemed symbolic. Minnie he had always—to the disagreement, and sometimes the indignation, of his young women friends— looked upon as a variant of the species of *femme fatale*. The variation lay in the obvious fact that she was entirely devoted to one man only, and he her husband.

"What's so surprising about that?" Eleanor Janeway had asked him. Minnie owed devotion to John Wood. And anyway, who wouldn't admire John Wood?

Yes, yes, all doubtless true. But Mr. Rakosi had wondered to what extent Minnie was proving herself a mother.

Eleanor had cried indignantly, "Philip simply adores her!"

"Sat is not my question."

"Well, I don't know what it is, then. Philip Wood is just as nice at school as he is at home. You can't say Mrs. Wood hasn't been a successful mother."

"No, no, I say nothing. But I do not make it out."

"Pooh!"

At any rate, in the pallid light of the somewhat chilly gallery room on this sunless day, it seemed to the young photographer that his first fling of joyousness in the openness and newness of the town had received a let-down. Fairview could never be the same again. Old evils were cropping up. The defection of almost any other citizen might have been taken lightly.

Mr. Rakosi brooded. He wished that he had insisted upon taking photographs of the separate members of the Wood family. He felt that he had a kind of intuition that enabled him to know when he was getting a significant photograph. He thought of this particularly in the case of Minnie Wood. Now his chance of having come to know her through his own talent had faded. And in the case of John Wood—how *would* those eyes have showed?

He sat on for a while, reviewing the events of the day. The different attitudes at dinner of Miss Janeway and of Miss Gale had decided one thing for him: Eleanor Janeway was the one of the two whom he would want to marry, if he married either. He was not content with his renewed, and apparently justified, cynicism. Miss Gale's disapproving lips only added to it. Eleanor Janeway's warm, enthusiastic personality might be its antidote. The two girls were equally pretty, in their different ways. Whether Eleanor wanted to write letters or not, he would go to the house where she roomed. He could not let the Wood case stand where it was at the moment. He must have a confidential talk with Eleanor Janeway. She, any more than he, was not directly involved, except that Philip Wood was one of her students. She was candid, filled with the zest of living, but Mr. Rakosi had never found malice in her. Although a schoolteacher (so Mr. Rakosi put it to himself), she was womanly. He felt that she would stand up for Philip, and that he wanted to hear her do so. Her tall, full figure, her wavy brown hair and hazel eyes, her instinct for dress, her pleasant degree of worldliness, combined with her warm interest in her high-school pupils—all appealed to him. He considered her too pretty, in a not unusual way, to offer an interesting subject for photography. But this prettiness appealed to him all the more when he seriously thought of her as a wife. He could offer her no such promise of single-minded devotion as John Wood's to Minnie. But Eleanor herself neither needed that nor called it out.

Oddly enough—"as things went in this world"—the Wood case seemed to have made up Mr. Rakosi's mind for him. It seemed to him that he had a right to be a citizen of Fairview, to carry on a business there, and to try to build up a family life which would not differ too much from what he had known in Hungary and yet would have an added freshness and unexpectedness. A woman such as Eleanor Janeway might be tolerant of his mistakes and excursions—and might have the charm to hold him! To his astonishment, he found that he wanted to be held. But he did not want to aspire to any kind of union "above his head," as it now appeared to him that the Woods' had been—and as, for all his cynicism, he wished that it had proved to be in full reality. He was now down again on the ordinary plane of "human nature," and yet of human nature as fresh, free, and valiant as he saw it in Miss Janeway.

In the afternoon, Jerry Storm was in his room, presumably studying and getting a little rest before going to the meeting of his young people and after that conducting the evening service. He heard a ring at the doorbell, and then heard Mrs. Latham welcome someone. He thought, but could not be sure, that the visitor was Philip Wood. There was a special mother-liness in the tone of Mrs. Latham's voice. Jerry knew that she had always thought that Philip Wood "reminded" her of the son who had died, and that if Blanchard Latham had lived to be the age that Philip was now, he would be very much like Philip.

She called up the stairs, "You have a visitor, Reverend Jerry." Mrs. Latham's kind heart, since Jerry had broken the news of John Wood's defection to her and Miss Blanchard, had been chiefly filled with warmth toward Philip.

Jerry went out at once to the head of the stairs, and Philip Wood, as he expected, was coming up them.

"Come in, Philip. No, you're not interrupting me in anything of importance. Come on into my room."

Jerry closed the door. Philip's coming helped to assuage his own nervous restlessness, and yet it presented him with problems which he had not found how to solve. But he was truly glad that the boy had sought him out.

He saw at once the distress in Philip's eyes. His own questions in relation to John Wood became small in his mind as compared to the boy's.

"Sit down, Philip." He drew up a comfortable chair, and himself sat down in the swivel chair at his work table.

"Maybe I shouldn't have come this afternoon, Mr. Storm."

"Yes, you should. It's exactly what you should have done."

"But I felt as if I had to talk to somebody. I mean, somebody older than Lyle."

Philip did not know how young Jerry Storm felt! But at least Jerry *was* older than Lyle Meserve, had gone through some hardships, and was Philip's pastor. He said, "This is the place for you to have come. We can talk as freely as we want to. Mrs. Latham and Miss Blanchard are used to my having people in here."

"Mrs. Latham was nice when she opened the door."

It was touching that Philip should remark on any person's in Fairview being "nice" to him. "She thinks a great deal of you, Philip."

Philip glanced around the room with the large brass bed, the study table and bookshelves. His gaze stopped at the photograph of Jerry Storm's mother, which was fastened above the table. Hers was a small face, very gentle and subdued in expression, and had a rustic air. Philip seemed to be studying the photograph. But now he plunged at once into his subject.

"Mr. Storm, I don't know what to do."

"In what way, Philip?"

"I guess you know. You were at our house at that meeting. Mr. Storm, do you think the church ought to—help my father through this? Do you think it ought to protect my father?"

"Those are hard questions, Philip."

"I know they are," Philip said miserably. "Mr. Storm, did you think Deacon Kruse was right that day?"

"I certainly didn't agree with the way he spoke to your mother, Philip. She had as much right as the rest of us to be present and to speak out."

"I know she did," Philip answered eagerly.

"But otherwise . . . This question is very hard for me to answer. I feel that I am not too clear myself on all this, Philip. I do appreciate all the years of service your father has given the church. I leaned on him. But—"

"That makes it all the worse, doesn't it?" Philip asked outright, raising his dismayed gaze to Jerry's.

Jerry could not in truth deny that statement. And, as he looked at Philip, it seemed to Jerry that Philip had taken and accepted this view. He was grateful for the boy's candor even though saddened at not being able to say what would be comforting to him.

Philip went off on another tack. "Is that a picture of your mother, Mr. Storm?"

"Yes, it is, Philip. Taken some years ago."

"How would she have felt if your father had—done something wrong, not honest?"

"I can't say, Philip. My mother never had much chance to express herself. She was always busy, and my father and grandfather were stern men—more like Deacon Kruse."

"Would she have stood by your father?" Philip persisted.

"Yes, I'm sure she would have done that, in her own way."

Philip suddenly began to fight back sobs. He tried to speak through them, while he wiped his nose and wiped off the tears with one of those beautifully laundered handkerchiefs which seemed somehow representative of the life of the Wood family. Jerry put his arm around the boy's shoulder.

Jerry Storm found himself no longer in any sense envious of Philip's upbringing. He had sometimes compared it with his own to his own disadvantage, as he thought of his arguments with his father and grandfather, their harsh denunciations and bitter predictions concerning his future, while his mother worked silently in the kitchen at her ironing or baking, showing Jerry her sympathy only in the gentleness of her tone and in her good-night kiss. The men of the family had never brought her in on any theological arguments—nor would she have asked for it, for she was humble in mind and spirit. It came to Jerry now that some touch of her tenderness, combined with qualities which she did not possess, had drawn him to Mae. Mae's attraction for him was not only physical, not only because of her being such a bright, charming, talented person, a kind of woman new to him; it was because she was womanly also, and tender-hearted. But he could not think of Mae now, or let her attraction for him distract him.

"Mr. Storm, I don't feel as if I know my mother and father any more. It isn't only what my father has done. They almost hold away from me. I want to be loyal to them, but how can I? My mother didn't feel I was being loyal when I went to Sunday school with Lyle this morning!"

Jerry sat back in his chair. "Well, Philip, you did nothing wrong in coming. On the contrary."

"I'm not sure any more whether my folks really care for me."

"Yes, they do, Philip," Jerry said earnestly. "Of course they do. You know they're exceptionally close together, especially just now."

"Yes, but I thought they cared for me, for myself!"

Jerry was silent. He knew all too well what it was to be misunderstood by a parent.

Philip went on, "Mr. Storm, you don't know *how* good my father is to my mother!" Philip raised his head with a puzzled, yet half-proud expression.

"I can't know as well as you do, Philip. But maybe we should look at it this way: your mother knows, and is trying to repay him—anyway, trying to show him her love."

"Yes, yes!" Philip said, almost impatiently. "But isn't there a doing right?"

"Yes, that's it, Philip. There is," Jerry said firmly.

"It wasn't because I didn't care for my father that I went to the class this morning."

"Of course not!"

"Sometimes, though, I don't love him. I'm even against *her*. I didn't suppose I could ever be against my mother—or either of them." Philip sobbed.

Jerry wanted to meet this confession with more than platitudes. He had known rebellion against his elders, and it was not all gone yet. He felt it cropping up in dismaying, unexpected ways. Somehow he must tell Philip, however, that such feelings, if held in a personal way, would poison his own life.

"Philip, you know as well as I do some of the answer to that. It isn't your parents you differ with—only certain things about them. We've taken this kind of subject up in our Sunday-school class, and you've always been the best thinker there."

Philip said, "Maybe I never knew what I was talking about.

If my father"—he sobbed again—"if my father didn't act out what he said he believed all these years, I don't know what difference the whole thing makes."

Jerry was stopped. Philip had spoken so exactly his own sense of shock and division. The right words were there somewhere—he still believed that—but he could not immediately find them.

Philip said in a low voice, looking down, "I don't know whether I'll ever go to church again."

Some inspiration then came to the young minister. He assured Philip that he need not decide that now. Only, Philip must act on his own convictions, not those of others, even his parents.

"I had to break with my father and grandfather to follow what I believed was the right course. I couldn't see religion in the way they did, and especially—I see that now—because of the way they lorded it over my mother. I felt I had to get away from them. But it meant leaving my mother there at home without me."

Philip seemed to be considering this. But then he said abruptly, "Mr. Storm, do you think my father ought to stand trial?"

"I don't honestly know, Philip. Colonel Merriam and the others—will have to decide that. I hope not, for your mother's sake. But I wouldn't be truthful with you, Philip, if I didn't say I believe it will be best—for all of us—not to pass over this awful business as if it were not there."

Philip said, his lips trembling, "Mrs. Merriam thinks that."

"I didn't know that. I haven't talked with Mrs. Merriam. I think of how James in his Epistle speaks of 'a double-minded man.' I apply that term to myself just as much as to your father and to others," Jerry added.

Jerry repented the words the instant after he had spoken them. They had been in his mind all these last few days. But, to his relief, he saw a clearing of confusion in Philip's eyes. A moment later, the boy burst out, "But I don't see how *my fa-*

ther could have been double-dealing. I don't take it in, Mr. Storm. I just don't."

"None of us do, Philip," Jerry murmured.

"But where does that leave me? I'm the son of my parents."

The young man felt that there was too much here to deal with, but he pressed on. "You have to stand on your own feet, Philip. You have to find your own faith and make your own decisions. All of us do. Ultimately we do."

The boy nodded. Jerry saw him draw a deep breath. After a while Philip said that he must leave.

Jerry went downstairs with him to open the door for him, so that not even Mrs. Latham need see his tear-stained face.

Jerry's own distress came back upon him as he returned to his room. It did not seem to him that he could preach another sermon this evening. His only relief lay in thinking of—Mae. If only he had the right to her presence and help. "Mae," he whispered as he restlessly sat at his desk, then lay down on his bed, after carefully taking off his shoes.

He tried to find the all-loving Father. He had been more and more assured of the presence of this Father, rather than the stern and wrathful God of his childhood, since he had been living in Fairview. He had not lost his faith. He felt that it existed, if he could grasp it. But all the answer of which he seemed to be conscious at this moment was the sense of the darkening of late afternoon outside his windows, and a movement in the foliage of the elms and maples.

CHAPTER

II

THE Fairview high school was a brick building, completed only two years ago. Large, bright windows looked out across a level schoolyard in which tender new grass was beginning to grow. There was little planting around the building as yet, and the trees along the curbing were still small. In the Assembly Room the green-tinted walls were staring-clean, and the woodwork light and shining with varnish. Above the rostrum hung pictures of three United States presidents: Washington, Lincoln, Theodore Roosevelt; and above the Roosevelt picture, the middle one, the red and white stripes and white stars on blue background of the national flag. The whole had an air of newness and youth.

Eleanor Janeway had charge of the Assembly Room during this last hour of the afternoon session. She too was young, only a year out of college. She might not have been able to keep order, especially during this restless period, except for the students' personal liking for her, their admiration for her warmth and flowering good looks, and her social popularity in Fairview, which was considerably enhanced by interesting attentions from the exotically dashing Mr. Rakosi. Her hazel glance went to the clock on the wall opposite the rostrum, then to Philip Wood, sitting among the seniors in the row next to the east windows.

She kept herself from looking directly at Philip, for fear of embarrassment to him. But although his eyes seemed fixed upon his book, she felt, even in the sidewise glance she gave him, the tension and uncertainty in his attitude. Anton Rakosi had been talking with her about Philip only the evening before, exaggerating his doubts about the boy.

"We are all sinners."

"I know we are all sinners! But you have no grounds for doubting Philip!" Eleanor had retorted energetically.

Mr. Rakosi had replied that it would have been better if more people had had doubts of John Wood.

"I know people might have got hurt less," Eleanor had said, "but who wants to go around doubting everybody?"

"Is se question one of 'want'?"

"It is so far as I am concerned."

Their discussion had ended in a curious way: with Eleanor standing up for Philip Wood and Mr. Rakosi for Minnie Wood He had praised in flowery terms Minnie's complete adherence to her husband, and had said it was the way all women should act under any circumstances. At the same time, a cynical strain had run through his comments, even his praises, which Eleanor had felt she must counter vigorously. All women, according to Mr. Rakosi, should meet any domestic situation just as Minnie seemed to be doing, although of course her attitude was not right, all false—yet at the same time ordinary rules of conduct and judgment should be suspended where Minnie was concerned. This was because of Minnie's elusive quality and her charm. In Europe (Mr. Rakosi had rolled the word on his tongue) Minnie would have had more male callers than a pious young preacher doing his pastoral duty!

"*You* haven't called on her," Eleanor had said pointedly.

"No," he had answered softly, "but I have had others to call on, who do not give seir whole beings to a husband." Eleanor had breathed quickly and flushed, while she had felt the meaningful pressure of his hand. "Maybe I hope sey will some day. One of sem."

That was further than he had ever gone before in the way of a declaration to Eleanor. But there he had stopped. He had returned to the contention that no trustworthy man could be so handsome as John Wood! The moral imperfection of John Wood was now plain to all Fairview. Eleanor could not make any substantial objection to that; but when Mr. Rakosi had hinted that no boy could be so good as Philip she had fired up. Of course, this was no more than Mr. Rakosi had said, more or less playfully, at other times. Once, indeed, he had stated flatly, "Sere is no such boy."

Fairview seemed to have divided on the question of the Woods. Minnie had always come in for her share of criticism, as well as of devotion. Now John Wood was being generally condemned, and Minnie with him, even though some friends were personally loyal. But some people were now saying they did not "know what to think of Philip." To Eleanor, this seemed peculiarly unjust.

"Why?" she demanded.

"He's egotistical."

Eleanor, seething inwardly, had said, "No! no! There's a difference between egotism and confidence."

Mr. Rakosi, while admitting that Eleanor's viewpoint was defensible, and seeming to want her to prove her case, had nevertheless been unwilling to state that he shared it. She was "a young soul," he had told her.

Thus their Sunday night time together, though more intimate than any that had passed between them, had—in Eleanor's belief—not come to anything, and had even left her unsure that she desired that it should. So far as physical attraction went, she knew that she desired it, or was just on the thrilling edge of desiring it. But a husband's attitude toward women, and toward his wife in particular, counted strongly with this warm-hearted, unspoiled girl. At one point Anton had hinted that it might have been well if he had tried to see how far Minnie's devotion to John went. "I would despise you then," Eleanor had flung at him, "simply despise you." There was something about Mr. Rakosi's attitude toward the Wood family which she could not accept. He had praised Eleanor in her wrath, which had made her cheeks flame and her hazel eyes shoot sparks. But she had been less flattered than she would have expected.

The whole business was now a tangle. Her emotions seemed to have centered upon Philip. If somehow Philip could prove that there *was* "such a boy," she would have made her point with Anton Rakosi. From that point on, "almost anything" could follow. She could brave out the almost certain reluctance of her father—a prosperous businessman in a middle-sized town—that his daughter should marry "a foreigner." Eleanor did not lack dash and courage, but she did have to feel enthusiastic conviction. She had felt attracted to other men besides Mr. Rakosi.

Anton Rakosi had often expressed amusement because of her enthusiasm for her senior class. Well, why not? Eleanor had retorted. She had named some of them over: Philip Wood, Lyle Meserve, Will Cowie, Mort Hungerford, Gladys Cornwall, Evvie Evans. She had acknowledged that she could not include Boysie Wheeler among these elite. But he was "a pretty good kid," especially when he was with the others. His foolish upbringing hadn't been his fault. *Was* there a finer set of young people anywhere?

Eleanor had believed thoroughly that there was not. But her case had rested first of all on Philip Wood. It still did. She did not know just what the students were now thinking and saying about Philip, but she was aware that he no longer held the position of unrivaled young monarch. It had seemed to her that some of the boys and girls passed Philip by, although they were careful not to make this so obvious that any of their teachers could charge them with it. The only one of them of whom Miss Janeway felt completely sure was Lyle Meserve. He was obviously standing by his friend. Her liking for this nice but rather colorless boy had risen accordingly. She sensed a stubborn protectiveness in his attitude toward Philip.

In this final period of the afternoon Miss Janeway had often let her thoughts drift, dreaming about her students and picturing their future lives—mostly in terms of matrimony. She had wondered what kind of girl Philip would eventually marry, and had considered that no girl now in the high school was quite a match for him. Gladys Cornwall was so very nice and capable, sturdy and intelligent, that Miss Janeway had felt like a traitor to her in not mentally wedding her to Philip. But if Philip went out into the world, he could have almost any girl, one would think. Mr. Rakosi himself had said as much. Lyle and Evvie, on the other hand, made a perfect match—well, "a promising one," Miss Janeway amended, conscious in spite of herself of overdoing the ideal.

She did not have to remind Philip. Even before the time for him to leave the Assembly Room she saw him thrust his textbook into his desk. She smiled at him and slightly nodded. He tried to smile in return, but the smile was painful. Miss Janeway was disturbed by the brief glimpse of misery in his usually clear, bright eyes. She told herself that Hank Henderson, at least, had not lost confidence in Philip and would have the right thing to say.

Philip started to walk through the clean, rather chilly front corridor to the principal's office. He was accustomed to feel an easy sense of proprietorship toward the high-school building. Ordinarily he would not have been above enjoying the slight feeling of superiority in his "being excused early," taking a leisurely drink at the drinking fountain, greeting anyone he happened to meet—teacher, student, janitor—with a pleasant comradely feeling. Philip had not been aware of a touch of lordliness in his usual manner of meeting a person in the high-school building, simply felt assurance that the other person would also be pleased at the encounter.

This afternoon someone was at the drinking fountain ahead

of him—a girl. He had recognized the plump figure, but had
not even said the name in his own mind, when the girl turned
around. She was Charlotte Dissendorfer. Catching at his self-
control, Philip had started to nod to her as usual, but she stared
him straight in the face with hard, prominent china-blue eyes,
then turned her back and walked on through the corridor. This
was the first time that Philip had received the cut direct. He
felt almost sick. But he realized that he could not resent her
action; for although he himself had done nothing to injure
Charlotte, his father had. He felt himself all at once a stranger
in this familiar place.

His leaving the Assembly Room early had done him no
good, for he found the principal's office vacant. It might have
given him relief to talk at once to Hank Henderson. But now
he was left with time to consider not only the hurt that Charlotte had just dealt him, but other hurts as well. The principal's desk, with the typewriter and untidy papers which Philip
had liked because they had meant "Hank," now gave him pain
to see. The empty chair, left carelessly askew behind the desk,
made the pain worse.

The meeting with Charlotte brought back other recent en-
counters. Last Saturday, when Philip and Lyle had been coming home with the wheelbarrow and kindling from the lumber
yard, they had seen, at the end of the block, Miss Gertrude
Schilling. They were favorites of hers, among the many favorites throughout her years of teaching. But instead of coming
on down the street, Miss Schilling had turned abruptly and
obviously, so it seemed. She had gone fairly scurrying in another direction.

Philip could not restrain himself from saying, "See that?"
Lyle had replied, apparently unmoved, "Who cares?"
Philip had not been able to acknowledge, "I do," or even to
say, "That was meant for me." But the action had wounded
him deeply, and unexpectedly, for he had always counted on
Miss Gertrude Schilling as a friend.

He could not know Miss Schilling's reasons, or that he personally need not have taken her abrupt turn-away to heart. She had thought she was unobserved. But her idealization of John and Minnie Wood had been so intense, and had meant so much to her—experiencing vicariously and unselfishly, through their union, "love like that of the Brownings"—that she had not been able to bear meeting their son. John Wood had been her chief reliance in arguments with her father. She had gone so far as to see in John Wood's character, and his devotion to Minnie, what religion could do for a man, how it could sustain him. "*Ja*," her father had muttered, drawing on his pipe, "John Wood is well enough. But he does not think. He gets his living by working for Colonel Merriam, and the Colonel is not a religious man." Now Gertrude's main image, in the personal, human sense, had failed her. Her father's scornful accusation that she too "did not think" would have to be met in another way, perhaps abstractly, theoretically, and Gertrude had little gift for abstract argument. She had dealt with people, with boys and girls. Perhaps her father's arguments could not be met at all. Gertrude would not stop going to church, but how could it mean the same to her? With the fall of John Wood, romance seemed to have gone from her life, leaving bleakness. She was a person who needed hero worship. Some day not too far distant she would have to retire from teaching. She feared that even now she was less alert; her pupils tended to run over her.

She had gone on downtown by another street to buy Saturday supplies. But she had not wanted to pass her father's shop, for she knew that he would be able—temporarily, at least—to triumph over her by saying in sarcastic tones that he, although "an infidel," had always done good, reliable work on the shoes of the people of Fairview, and had never overcharged. "I haf been honest." When Miss Schilling got home, she had opened her Bible and read Paul's first letter to the Corinthians. But even the grandeur of those immortal words of the thirteenth chapter had seemed blurred and stained. She had prayed, "Let me go deeper." Gertrude was sure even now that there existed a "deeper." Her faith in the ideal of love, then, had not been wholly wrong, even if she could exalt John and Minnie Wood no longer. Now, she had not the slightest conception that, by turning at the corner to avoid meeting Philip, she had given one of her beloved pupils his first individual wound from the outside in his almost unbearable situation—would have been dismayed if she had known.

As he sat waiting in the principal's office, Philip dwelt again on the Sunday-school class which he had attended so reluctantly. He felt more deeply now the way in which Will and two or three others in the class had avoided him. Yet, in this case too, Philip did not understand how his being just a little ahead of Will Cowie in every field—studies, athletics, school popularity, the church, as the chosen playmate of the Merriams' granddaughter—had ground upon Will for years. As Austin Cowie's son, Will might have expected to be first and foremost. At this moment, Philip forgot Howdy Rechtner's smile, and even forgot Lyle's dogged loyalty. He sank into depths of personal gloom he had not known existed.

Silence. Footsteps somewhere in the building. The wall clock ticked. Philip glanced toward the window, saw Eslick Pettiman go by in his longish coat and summertime hard straw hat fastened to his coat with a black elastic, carrying (as he often did when not wearing his "plug" hat) his lawyer's black satchel, which he dropped on the sidewalk. Some papers spilled out. Eslick stopped and fumbled for the papers, and for just a moment Philip watched him with his old sense of compassionate amusement and even stifled an impulse to run out and help the "poor fellow."

Philip had always been willing to stop and talk with Eslick, when Lyle had wanted to hurry him on and had said with harsh boyish contempt, "He's nuts." Philip thought of one of the many stories about Eslick which the town enjoyed. Austin Cowie—no less—had met Eslick on a snowy morning and, wanting to be affable, had remarked, "I see it snowed last night." Eslick had retorted with scorn, "Any fool would know that." Philip remembered this well-circulated story, but now he did not enjoy it. He saw Eslick go on, awkwardly hugging the satchel, and he felt a sickened awareness of what was damaged in poor Eslick. Philip could no longer think of himself as handing out cordial and generous greetings to such a "poor soul" from a consciousness of abundance. How little his general good will had cost him! But now he was also a pariah, down on the level of Eslick Pettiman and the little blotchy-faced, mean Dell Postel. Philip had not really supposed that he himself was proud. He was unconscious of his attitude of bright-eyed confidence, which to some people whom he had regarded as friends had seemed self-conceit; or that Will Cowie, Boysie Wheeler, and others were taking it out on him now.

But Philip did have pride. It was raw and smarting. Again he lost sight of Lyle, Howard, Miss Janeway, Mrs. Latham, of the marked friendship toward him of the whole Meserve family. He almost forgot how Mrs. Merriam had stopped to speak to him at home. He did not feel at this moment that he had gained much from his outpouring to Jerry Storm—was more ashamed of it than appreciative of the young pastor's support. It seemed to him at this low moment that his father and mother were right, and that he could never go inside the Congregational church of Fairview again. He had lost that too. He was conscious of Lyle's silent determination to keep him in things. But at this instant the only way seemed to be to crush down all other, more individual feelings and to join with his parents, a tight little triumvirate against the world.

Philip's gloomy reverie was broken by the sound of the principal's footsteps outside in the hall. They could be recognized because Hank Henderson took such long steps. The students had no particular grievance against Mr. Compton, the superintendent of schools, but neither did they have enthusiasm for him. His chief contribution (and a not inconsiderable one) had been in getting the new high school built. Their principal, whom they called "Hank" behind his back and frequently to his face, held the positions both of principal and of basketball coach, and taught classes in American history and public speaking. He was very popular—"the students' friend."

Philip and Gladys Cornwall had both looked forward to this after-hours period of practice and consultation with Hank, saying they "got so much out of it." Hank was less a critic than a listener whose acute attentiveness lifted them. He had said, when asked to approve Philip's plan for his Commencement Valedictory, "Well, that's quite a topic you've got there, boy, but, by golly, it's a mighty good one. Some of these ideas ought to raise the roof." Hank had kept hands off, except for giving some help in the matter of emphasis and delivery—and there was not much that he could teach Philip there. Today was to be the last of the sessions in the principal's office; beginning tomorrow, a room was to be taken in the basement, so that Philip and Gladys could gauge the carrying power of their voices, which they kept subdued here in the office. Hank might then be a sterner critic. But Philip already had poise, a good voice, a pleasing manner, natural and earnest and bright, and—still more gratifying—he had ideas. Hank Henderson agreed with Eleanor Janeway that Philip Wood was something of a wonder. It was only when you saw his parents, the home he came out of, that you could understand and accept his superiority. The best thing about him, both the teachers had agreed, was that he had never showed himself a prig. Both Hank and Miss Janeway had agreed with Miss Gertrude Schilling in foreseeing a fine future for Philip.

Philip had never before dreaded the sound of Hank Henderson's footsteps. They had broken one form of tension just now, but created another. Philip was determined that he would not cry and make a baby of himself, as he felt that he had done yesterday with the Reverend Jerry Storm. Yet he must get out what he had resolved he would say.

Hank came into the room and said, "Hey, Philip, I hope I haven't kept you waiting."

He shut the door behind him with emphasis. Hank seemed troubled. The heavy lines in his still youthful face were deeper than ever. His long, cadaverous, likable face twisted itself into various odd expressions, some of which meant little. In a later era, he might well have been a character actor in motion pictures. But today Philip felt that the troubled expression did have meaning.

Hank settled his long, ungainly form in the chair pushed back from the desk.

"Well, Philip, have you had any new thoughts? I don't think your oration really requires changes. We're pretty well set so far as the oration goes. If you do want to make changes, this is our time for going over them. I want to get downstairs in the big room and hear you kids let out your voices."

Philip could not wait longer. He blurted, "Hank, I don't think I can give the Valedictory."

This was what he had finally decided.

Hank looked keenly at Philip. He tried at first to jest. "This is a fine announcement for a fellow to hear just after he's been called into a classroom to help the teacher keep order! I was, into the Latin room. Miss Carrigan—" Hank shook his head.

But he realized that he could not pass Philip's announcement off so easily. The natural drollery which had carried him through many crises would not work in this one. He would have to meet Philip directly, although he thought to himself, I'd rather be licked.

"I guess you'd better tell me why you said that, Phil. You know you don't have to mind speaking out to me." When silence followed, Hank added, "I expect I have some idea why you *think* you ought to say that. But let's hear your own reason!"

"I can't go into it all," Philip muttered, with eyes downcast.

After another short silence: "Well, let's pass over the part that really doesn't involve you, Philip. Let's just concentrate on your own personal reasons."

Philip began to try to explain. He could not stand up on the platform and face the big audience of Fairview people; and his oration itself had "gone back on him"; and finally he blurted out, "I don't represent the class any more."

Hank screwed up his mouth, tapped first on the desk and then on his teeth with a pencil, got himself into a still more awkward position. He finally asked, "Is this your own idea? Or have you some reason to think the students don't want you to represent them?"

Philip answered almost inaudibly that yes, he had.

"Well, boy, that may be true of a few, but I don't believe it's true of the majority."

Philip miserably answered nothing.

"They elected you," Hank reminded him.

"I know they did, but—" There was no need to finish that sentence.

Hank decided that he must probe a little. "Have you any reason to think your parents don't want you to give the Valedictory?"

Philip looked startled. He had not discussed the Valedictory with his parents. When he thought of this now, he had an idea that, unlike his going to Sunday school, they might want him to go on with the Valedictory, as if dropping it would be a sort of public admission of his father's guilt. But he did not know. He shook his head indefinitely.

"This is chiefly your own feeling, then?"

"No, Mr. Henderson, I don't think it's all my own feeling."

Hank sat and considered, doing various eccentric things with his pencil and small objects on his desk. His mind was clearing and coming to a conviction: that Philip must not drop out.

"Philip, I can imagine how getting up in front must be pretty difficult for you. But it's your job, given you by free choice; you've done nothing to forfeit it. *Not a thing.*" Hank emphasized that last sentence in a tone meant to startle. "I'm

going to tell you this. I'm going to grab right hold and advise
you. If you drop out, it will be harder for you to go ahead all
your life."

"I don't know that there is anything to go ahead with,"
Philip muttered.

"Of course there is! Everything!"

Philip shook his head, but he was listening.

"Philip, I want you to let your pride work in the opposite
way, and make you stand right up before these people who
may not all have shown a good spirit toward you, and prove
that you're not afraid. You have no reason in yourself to be
afraid. You aren't on trial before anyone! I wish you could
know what a scarecrow I was when I first went in for Public
Speaking in college. I could hear snickers when I stood on any
platform. I don't think even the professor was much pleased
about having to take me on. But I wanted to learn public speaking, and to teach, and I somehow got myself through the
course."

Hank saw that Philip was moved, if not convinced, while
Hank himself was truly convinced of the counsel he was giving. He could not see this promising boy start out with what
he believed to be a retreat, and an unnecessary one.

Hank suddenly made up his mind to play his last card—perhaps an unfair play. But no, he felt that he was justified.

"You can pull out, of course, if you're determined upon it,
Philip. But I want you to understand that you'll be letting me
down."

Now he had succeeded in startling Philip. He plunged
ahead. "You were the seniors' choice, and my own personal
choice, if I could have spoken of that. I would have done the
best I knew how with any student chosen, but I could put my
heart into it with you. I don't think you realize the after-school
hours I've put into this work with you and Gladys, until
I know I'm going to be mighty proud of you both. Now
Commencement is almost here, and you tell me you're going

to walk out on me! Put yourself in my position. Who'd take your place?"

"Lyle," Philip finally said.

"Won't do! Lyle's a swell kid, but he's no speaker—and, well, he's just not up to it!"

"Will Cowie gets good marks."

"Nonsense!" Hank spoke almost vehemently. "He's had good enough marks, but yours have been consistently higher. There would be utterly no sense in your abdicating in favor of Will Cowie."

Hank had reason for his irritation which he did not intend to divulge to Philip. Mr. Compton had recently ventured this same suggestion concerning Will Cowie; Hank had, as he thought of it, gone to bat for Philip. Hank had, in fact, gone through what he thought of as "a session" with his superintendent on this very matter. Mr. Compton was an able administrator and not, on the whole, a difficult man under whom to work. The one fault which Hank had found with him was a tendency to stand well with all sides, and particularly with his school board (of whom Austin Cowie was a member), and to let nothing "cause controversy." He had feared, no doubt with some cause, that for Philip Wood to take such a prominent part in the coming Commencement exercises would "cause controversy, especially in some quarters." Hank had maintained that Philip was the boy for the place, deserved it, and "could be ruined" by a change at this time; and had finally said that he could not undertake to train another student at this late date. He had vouched for Philip.

"Of course, I don't claim to know the high-school seniors personally as well as you do, Mr. Henderson. In my position, I can't. I don't entirely like the idea of Philip Wood, under present circumstances, coming forward as Valedictorian. But I'll take your word for it. We may run into some trouble."

Hank had left the superintendent's office in the nearby elementary-school building, disturbed but triumphant, and sure of his case. Now he had to deal with Philip himself!

"Well, what about it, Philip?"

Philip raised his troubled face. "I will if I can," he brought out. "I'll let you know tomorrow, Mr. Henderson."

Hank saw that this was the best answer he could get.

Then the door softly opened, and Gladys Cornwall stood hesitantly in the doorway. It was not unusual for her to come before Philip had finished, and to enter on tiptoe and sit down and wait; she had learned the last few sentences of Philip's oration by heart. Neither the principal nor Philip had been disturbed by her quiet entrance. But they could not tell today how much she might have heard. Her round, flushed face betrayed that she had caught something of the conversation.

Hank tried to say easily, "Hello, Gladys, I guess it is your time."

"Yes, it is, Mr. Henderson, just about."

Philip said that he was ready to go. He shook Hank's big, bony hand, his handshake a further promise that he would consider all the principal had said. But he could not even yet feel himself to be decided.

When he went out of the office, Gladys followed him. She *had* heard, after all—couldn't have helped hearing. She faced Philip and looked straight at him with her honest dark brown eyes.

"Philip, if you won't be Valedictorian, I won't be Salutatorian. There won't be any orations."

Then she went straight back into the principal's office and closed the door.

Philip had been left gasping at her directness. He did not think at the time of the magnanimity of her statement, since he had not asked her to go with him to the school picnic and had asked somebody else, somebody outside the class. Moreover, on the Sunday evening which now seemed long ago to him, he had left her to go home ignominiously from the Christian Endeavor meeting with Evvie and Lyle. He had never shown Gladys any but the most lordly, casual favors.

But as he walked away, her straight-out announcement warmed his forlorn heart in this troubled moment. Indeed, it had made more impact upon him than he knew, and would remain with him and return to him again and again in the years ahead.

CHAPTER

12

JERRY STORM had been left unsatisfied by his talk with Philip Wood. *I fell down*, he kept telling himself afterward. He had been made aware, too, that Philip had suffered more acutely during the Sunday-school hour than Jerry had then realized. Was there something the young minister had left undone?

The congregation at the evening service had been meager for the Fairview of this period, and again it had seemed that the dominating figure was that of Austin Cowie. Jerry Storm had not believed that Austin Cowie had the qualifications for a deacon in any sense of the term which Jerry could accept. Now he was sure of that. What Vera had said about the trips to Chicago had turned him from reluctantly admitted distant possibility to conviction. Vera's words had been sinking into Jerry's mind ever since he had heard them, adding to the torturing complexity of the whole problem. There was no certainty that Austin would be suggested for taking John Wood's place temporarily, but there seemed every likelihood. If so, then the only honest thing to do was for the pastor to talk with Austin. If Austin himself would refuse!—but how unlikely also that Austin *would* refuse. Would Jerry himself have strength and stamina to stand up against Austin, a far more

237

formidable opponent than John, and ask—perhaps even de-
mand—him to clear himself of this question, before he accepted
an office which meant what that of deacon should mean? Jerry
felt chilly, even in the sunshine, still more inadequate, unprepared, inferior. But—Jerry's thought ran—Austin Cowie,
whether or not he refused, would be no more fit to act as
deacon than John Wood; less so, in a way, because John
Wood's love for his wife was real, in and by itself, and his
feeling toward the church in and by itself might well be genuine. The trouble was that feelings could not exist merely in
and by themselves but stood in relation and in proportion to
one another. Everything was interrelated.

Austin Cowie did not have the kind of trust and respect
which had been given John Wood, but he was more firmly
entrenched in the town and in the church organization. The
church counted on him financially. His trips to Chicago were
his own affair; anything amiss with them was not out in the
open as John Wood's default now was, and they cost nobody
other than Austin himself any money. Jerry was by no means
sure that, if he tangled with Austin Cowie, he would have the
church with him. It might be that even Henry Meserve would
say, "The situation ought not to be stirred up further."
Henry and Austin had business connections; all these men did,
except perhaps Mr. Rechtner, who seemed to be entirely on his
own.

I may have to leave after all, Jerry thought, with a sense of
piercing pain, so that he could not bear to look around him. If
not immediately, then the Annual Meeting, when every member had a voice, might go against him. Austin Cowie did not
give up easily! The pastor thought, If I myself could name a
deacon, it would be Mrs. Merriam. By her spiritual and intellectual gifts, her dignity and her charity, she was naturally
qualified for the position. But although women were appointed
as deaconesses, their chief duty at this period was to set the
Communion table. It was not until some years later, even in
this comparatively liberal-spirited denomination, that women

were occasionally named as trustees; and then it was against the prejudice of just such men as Austin Cowie.

I'm simply not up to things! Jerry said to himself in despair. Who is good enough to sit in judgment on other people? he asked agonizingly. Mrs. Merriam, perhaps—who for the most part refused. Now almost every person in the church—this church he had considered so well run, almost "a sinecure"— appeared fallible and unreliable. Love itself could be treacherous, as the John Wood case proved. There seemed to be no firm ground anywhere, no person to whom he could turn.

Mae? It was to her that all Jerry's thoughts and struggles returned. Mae Meserve. He said over her name. He had been a little afraid of Mae's prettiness, talent, and prosperity—even her attractiveness, dreading lest he might allow himself to be carried away. When they had looked over the hymn books together, at times he could scarcely read the words. He did not know, of course, that Vera teased Mae about her timid suitor, asking, "Has he ever shaken hands?"

All the same, Jerry had aspired, and been proud that he was aspiring. Now he doubted his ability to fulfill such aspirations.

Jerry thought that Philip could consult *him*, if he had any counsel to give. But whom could *he* consult? Mrs. Merriam was out of range by the nature of the John Wood case, in which her husband was involved. Mrs. Latham and Miss Blanchard were kindhearted and loving, but they did not have Mrs. Merriam's far outlook.

Jerry was forced to the realization that he would have to put his case to Mae herself. He might seem brash in doing so, for they were not engaged—or not explicitly so. Having reached his resolution, Jerry with characteristic impatience could not wait. He went at once to telephone to Mae and asked when she could see him, speaking in low tones, even though Mrs. Latham was in the kitchen and Miss Blanchard out shopping. Mae answered in her gracious voice, unchanged, that the music lesson which she was now giving would be over in half an hour.

"Can you see me then?"

"Yes, of course, Jerry."

He was uplifted, and then cast down, by that simple, natural "Jerry," which yet—or so he imagined—seemed to have a new intimacy in its tone.

Jerry changed to his better suit and to a clean shirt. He usually let down a little on Mondays. But he did not remember to shine his old everyday shoes. To have put on his Sunday shoes on Monday would have seemed ostentatious. At the dresser he nervously tried to part his unruly hair. The cowlick in front was unamenable to the comb, and he was reduced, as usual, to giving his sandy hair as good a brushing as possible. His own thin, freckled face looked youthfully haggard to him. His light, intense eyes were slightly red-rimmed from lack of sleep. Mae certainly must have had handsomer suitors—with far more to offer her in the way of money, too! Anson Royce, a prosperous widower in town, who sometimes took Mae driving in his Stanley Steamer—a conveyance beyond Jerry's dreams of ever owning—would like to marry Mae, if reports were true. Jerry thought he saw his grandfather in his own features, which caused him revulsion, along with a renewed, if reluctant, respect for that hard, convinced old man.

As he went along the now familiar street to the Meserve house, under a sky of alternating dark spring clouds and spring sunlight, Jerry Storm prayed; he prayed for truth and courage. His problem now stood before him in abstract terms of love and truth. But concretely it turned in the relationship between himself and Mae.

He pushed the bell. He was relieved that Mae herself came to the door. Her blooming face, with tender lips and charming brown eyes, seemed unchanged. She did not reveal anxiety, if she felt it. But she did take Jerry directly into the parlor, where her grand piano stood, the exercise book which she had been using still open upon the rack. During weekday mornings and early afternoons, this room was given over to Mae for her lessons and practice. Here Mae and Jerry could have assurance of privacy—or as much assurance as this big, active household,

characterized by much running in and out, could afford. So
Mae did understand that Jerry's errand had a serious purpose.

Mae herself was lovely in her light blue dress. Her brown-
gold hair, brushed back from her forehead in a low pompa-
dour, was knotted with artful carelessness on her pretty neck.
Mae's hair had a natural soft curl—to Vera's disgruntled envy.
"Well, *you* have curly hair," Vera would always charge Mae, if
Mae uttered any kind of complaint. The pressure of Mae's soft-
skinned hand was always unexpectedly firm. To Jerry's distracted vision her charm was more apparent than he had ever
seen or felt it. He took more note than he had usually done of
those details which marked her as the daughter of a well-to-do
family. Mae wore no rings, because they got in the way of her
piano playing; but everything which Jerry perceived seemed
perfect: the gold beads which she wore around her throat; the
flawless fit of her simply made summer dress and the fineness of
the material; especially her small, trim black pumps with Cuban
heels, appropriately plain for morning wear. Jerry looked
down then, and saw his own dusty, shabby shoes. He supposed
no minister in Fairview ought to go out on the street in such
shoes. He could have bought a new pair—his very modest salary seemed munificent to him—but he had bought books instead.

Now he sensed in Mae too a nervousness which, although
not so apparent as his own, was thoroughly unusual. Mae began talking at once, almost as if she were Vera. Mae's role was
usually that of appreciative, sympathetic listener. She took it
for granted that Jerry had come to talk with her only about
the Wood case. There was a slight breathlessness in her voice.

"Mother and Vera and I scarcely know what to do. We don't
think Minnie's fit to do housework and stand up under what
simply *must* be a blow, no matter how she carries it off. I know
that some people are holding away, but we can't any of us bear
to do that. Matters are bad enough, just of themselves. And
we've all of us been friends too long. Vera and I have been trying to take turns going over to John's and Minnie's to get din-

ner on the table. It's not hard. We do so much cooking here in this house, and there are four of us girls besides Mother to do it. We can just as well take a few things over there. We know Minnie hasn't wanted to see Mother or Dad ever since the meeting that afternoon. I think, too, that John just can't look Dad in the face. And the thought of talking with John nearly kills Dad. But Vera and I weren't in on that meeting. This morning, though, when Vera went over with a meat casserole and a dish of floating island, and was going to offer to make beds, Minnie wouldn't ask her to come in. Honestly! I suppose she had heard somehow of Vera's taking charge of the Sunday school, and thought that was directed against John. Now I don't know whether she'll want me either, and I can't bear to intrude."

Jerry tried to keep his mind on what Mae was saying, although he was doubling and undoubling his hands on his knees and could feel perspiration warm on his forehead around the roots of his hair. Mae rushed ahead.

"Oh, poor *Minnie*. You know we were all of us afraid she would go to pieces physically. But it seems—so far, at least— to have had just the opposite effect! *I* say she's risen to the occasion. But Mother says she's proud and stubborn, and won't admit the truth before her eyes. Her eyes are so bright, though! It hurts to look at them. You have to wonder how long this strength can last. Right now, the only outside person she'll have in the house is Mrs. Randolph. Mother says it's because Mrs. Randolph still makes a pet of her, and says 'Miss Minnie' and 'Mistuh John' the way she always has. I like Mrs. Randolph for being so loyal. Dad says John probably has nothing to pay her with, either. But I think our family has been loyal too. Lyle says some of the high-school kids are pretty cool to Philip. Even Evvie Evans tries to argue it out with Lyle—except that he clamps his mouth shut and won't argue. He's a lot like Dad. I suppose Evvie's attitude comes from the fact that her father may have to prosecute John. That must be why she feels the way she does, because Evvie is such a *nice* girl. And then Evvie claims that Philip thinks too much of himself, because it seems he passes up Gladys Cornwall. Evvie says, 'He's after Elaine Merriam.'

"Oh, a lot of all this seems so petty! But Jerry, how will it all come out? We can't talk about it any more to Dad."

Mae's hurried speech seemed to have run out. She now sat silent, waiting, and looking at Jerry. Her fingers were clasped in her lap. Jerry thought she was looking at his shabby shoes, just as his eyes seemed to be fixed upon her circlet of gold beads.

The truth of the matter was that both had become conscious that their undefined delight in being together had reached another stage. Each was trembling a little. Some sounds came from the back part of the house, where Vera must be at work, perhaps in the kitchen. Jerry's face was now pale under his freckles.

Jerry did not pretend to answer Mae's outpouring. With his thin, strong hands pressing his knees, and his eyes burningly bright, he went straight to the point with startling suddenness.

"Mae, I don't think I belong here in Fairview."

Now all Mae's color left her face also. "Jerry, how can you say that!" she protested. "The church called you, and *every*body has liked you."

He mumbled, looking down, "Yes, but I'm not ready for it. I don't know how to handle it. It's too big a job for me."

"Do you mean the Wood case? Or are you talking about the church?"

"Both."

"Why, Jerry, I don't see how you can say such things," Mae said in a pleading voice. "You're so much needed. The whole church is in trouble."

"I haven't dealt with the trouble, though. That's it. I went to Mr. and Mrs. Wood, and I didn't really know what to say to them. What I did say didn't make the slightest impression."

"Well, Vera and I haven't made any impression, either."

"I know, but—you girls are personal friends, and if I'm any

good I ought to have something to give beyond friendliness. I
ought—I don't know just how to put it. The pastor ought to be
able to throw some true light on this situation."

"You *are* able to!" Mae indignantly assured him.

He shook his head. "No, I'm not. I'm all mixed up about it
myself. I don't know what to say, even to Philip. I think the
truth simply is, I haven't had enough experience." Jerry's voice
sank almost to a whisper. "The church here shouldn't have
called me. Or anyway, I shouldn't have accepted."

"I don't think that's so at all! I heard some of the other candi-
dates, too."

"I don't mean just preaching. Though I expect some of my
sermons have been pretty fatuous, too."

"They *haven't*."

Jerry started to look at Mae. But he dared not. And he could
not accept her protest, even though it gave a moment's balm.
He stumbled along, even though his voice was hoarse. He did
not realize that it was also pleading.

"You don't know, Mae, in what a different kind of life I was
brought up. I went against it. But now I don't know how much
there may have been in it—I mean, in my father's and grandfather's way of looking at things. I don't know much of anything, even if I have gone through the seminary. I guess that's
the truth of it."

"Everybody will stand behind you, Jerry. Just about everybody," Mae added truthfully. She thought of the Austin
Cowies, Mrs. Rathbun, perhaps a few others. But there always
were "a few others," no matter who the minister might be.

"Anyway," Mae said in a low voice, her eyes averted, "you
know *our* family will."

"Yes, I know that," Jerry whispered gratefully. But he still
would not look at Mae. He broke out, "I have to find out for
myself."

"Find out what, Jerry?"

"Well—the worst. The worst there is in people."

After a moment's silence, Mae whispered, "What does that mean?"

"I guess it means I've got to go somewhere to test myself out." He breathed heavily again.

"Isn't *this* a test, Jerry? With the Woods?"

"Not the kind I mean."

"What kind do you mean?" Mae again whispered.

"I don't know exactly," he confessed miserably, yet with resolution. "But I guess it signifies going off alone somewhere —in the slums, maybe, or maybe in the coal mines—and finding out if the kind of faith I have can stand up against the hardest kind of living. I want to get right down to bedrock."

"And I suppose this isn't!" Mae said after a while, looking through tears at the ample, comfortable room, at her mother's flourishing great fern and her own beloved grand piano.

Jerry said hoarsely, staring down at his hands, "The worst thing to me is that I can't ask you to go with me."

Mae made a little movement. She asked softly, "Why can't you?"

"Well—all this here"—he gestured—"and your musical talent, and—I couldn't put you through what I'd put myself through." He did not add something else that he felt: that he mistrusted his own sense of need for Mae herself. It seemed to him a weakness.

"That's an awfully hard judgment on me, Jerry."

"No, it isn't! It's a judgment on myself. I'm the one who needs the seasoning."

"I must need it too, if you think I have to have things just the way I've always had them."

"No, Mae," Jerry protested wretchedly. "No, I didn't mean that."

Mae loosened her tightly clasped fingers. Some of the color came back into her cheeks. She said, softly again, "Maybe I *would* go with you. I expect I could play an organ or something in what you call the slums."

This was almost an offer, as both were aware—Mae breathlessly aware. But Jerry swung away from it. "This case of John and Minnie Wood," he said, "has shown me up as—as a novice."

"You wouldn't be taking an invalid. I'm not an invalid," Mae proudly persisted.

"I know you aren't. I know that. But . . ." Jerry began then to tell Mae of his mother's subjection to the harsh rule and heavy work of their somewhat isolated rural household.

"She wasn't an invalid. But she was gentle and tenderhearted, something like you, and she couldn't bear controversy. She had to do things the way my father and grandfather said. *She* had no say—any more than Miss Caroline Kruse. Probably not even so much. She was kept even more in the background."

Jerry acknowledged that he himself would not treat a wife in this same manner. But he miserably insisted that the conditons of life he sought would be "no way for Mae to live." They would be too harsh. He realized that to the full, had thought it all out, and he couldn't subject her to any such ordeal as had formed vaguely in his mind.

"I care too much for you," he managed to say.

He was not sure, without having tried himself out, that he might not fall into as bad an error as that of John Wood.

"That isn't sensible, Jerry."

"Maybe not. But it's the way I feel."

Mae—sitting now with eyes downcast, pretty hands more tightly clasped again in her lap—was coming at last to realize that fundamentally the decision did not lie with her. The knowledge was hard to take. She was "a popular girl," and her pride was hurt. All she could think of for a few moments was that Jerry did not want to take her with him. She would be a deterrent.

But perhaps, with all her best will, that was true. At least, it might be true at this time. She was as young and untried as Jerry, but she had never dreamed that she might not get her testing through the kind of life which she had known, and which she loved. It had seemed to her a thing of real worth to play better music in her own church, and to start her pupils out with a genuine understanding of what music was and could mean. She tried to give them simplified versions of what was good and lasting music before letting them try out the best, for which few of them were ready. She felt now a painful drop of spirits when she realized how little her joy and faith in music, which was part of religion to her, really meant to Jerry. He had known almost nothing of it in his childhood, had small aptitude for it himself; and what he had gained had been through her. Perhaps it had even meant to him Mae herself. Mae had known very quickly that her young pastor was charmed by her, but had not made too much of it at first, since men and boys always found her charming.

Yes, but she had more in her than prettiness and charm! More even than talent. She knew that herself, and would not let herself stop with being personally aggrieved. She had something to prove, as well as Jerry.

Her great power of sympathetic understanding went out to Jerry. Perhaps it always had, since the first Sunday when he had appeared, a tense, youthful, awkward figure in the pulpit. His inner intensity had been something new to Mae, still had the same power of appeal. She wanted to make Jerry know that she believed in him. But how could she get the words out when he had not asked for them? Jerry, in his single-track simplicity, was unaware that he had given Mae any cause for humiliation. No doubt he supposed that he was honoring her, in treating her like a delicate flower that would easily wilt unless constantly tended and cultivated in its sheltered habitat! Yes, but somehow—Mae did not yet know how—she must open Jerry's eyes to her real feelings.

At this moment Vera knocked somewhat tentatively at the door. Mae said almost automatically, "Come in, Vee."

Vera came, but stopped inside the doorway. Her keen, bright face showed astonishment. She had been prepared to find them together, but not sitting in mute misery which was instantly apparent to her by no means unsophisticated eyes. She actually stuttered.

"I—I thought you were through talking. I thought maybe— Excuse *me*."

She would have withdrawn at once; the two sisters scrupulously kept out of each other's private affairs. But neither Mae nor Jerry would permit Vera to leave. Her entrance gave them both a reprieve.

"It was only that I thought Mae might have been telling you about the Woods, and I couldn't keep out of it. That's me, you know. But I didn't intend to break in on—anything."

Vera was highly conscious of Mae's unaccustomed pallor. Then her brown eyes—a lighter brown than Mae's, almost amber—scrutinized Jerry. In some manner, she didn't know just how, he had been upsetting Mae. Yet he was crazy over Mae. What was the matter with the man? Vera's expression became tentatively hostile.

However, she had broken in on the two of them now, whatever might be between them; and they had asked her to come into the room, so she did. But she sat stiffly on her chair until Mae said softly, "Jerry thinks he ought to leave here."

"Leave this *church*?" Vera demanded.

Mae answered miserably, "Yes."

"What next!" Vera exclaimed. She sat back in her chair and drew a deep breath. Then she added, "But you don't mean leave right now, Jerry?"

Jerry did not reply, and Vera became excited. "Why, you simply can't go now! I don't know what this is all about between you two, and I'm not going to be nosy and try to find out. But I don't see how you can *dream* of leaving our church at such a time as this."

Jerry mumbled something about not being "adequate."

"Who is adequate?" Vera retorted. "I wasn't adequate last Sunday morning, but I went ahead and did the best I could under the circumstances. Now I seem to be paying for it by having Minnie Wood practically refuse to let me into her house."

Vera went on, having got started. "I don't care what you plan to do, Jerry Storm, in the future. *I* plan something myself. I plan to go to Chicago and get into some kind of business. But I won't leave right now, I can tell you, when things are all in a mess, and Dad's about broken-hearted as it is."

Jerry looked miserable but said nothing. Vera had no pity on him.

"No, what you do in the future is up to you. But I'd like to tell you straight that I think your business right now is to stay with your congregation. For you to leave for any reason short of absolute necessity—if you needed an operation, or were dying or something—would be just the same as a captain deserting his ship and leaving the mates to take over. What would you think, I'd like to know, if Tommy Hardcastle didn't show up to get the building ready for next Sunday? He works for Colonel Merriam, and I expect he hasn't the best feeling in the world toward John Wood."

Vera's eyes snapped. Her fair, freckled skin was reddened. She made it clear that it was the Fairview church, not Jerry Storm and what she called his "personal qualms," in which she was interested.

"I'm not meddling between you and Mae. You don't have to be afraid of that." But what she wanted to tell Jeremiah Storm right to his face was that he couldn't duck out from under until this John Wood case had come to some kind of settlement. "And anyway, John and Minnie Wood aren't the only members of the church."

Mae was pleading, "Please, Vera."

" 'Please' what? I'm not going to do any 'pleasing'; I just want you both to know that I think Jerry Storm would be the worst vacuum living if he skipped out on us right now. He can wait to hand in his resignation, if that's what he's got on his mind, until we have the Annual Meeting. Not that I know of anybody who's asking for it—right now, anyway," Vera added pointedly.

The church "couldn't stand another explosion now," she said. Later, Jerry could do whatever he had in his head. But he could take his time and do it in the regular manner. Her tone was scathing.

"Vera."

"Oh, all right, I don't want to stay longer, anyway. I'll get dinner here at the house, since I'm not welcome at Minnie's. *We* have some feelings, too, in this house, if we don't make a parade of them."

Jerry sat deeply abashed under this tirade; Mae, further distressed. Vera went sweeping out in her best grand manner, with a rattling of starched skirts and tap of heels.

Mae murmured, "Vera has a temper, you know, like Mother."

"I deserved it, though." Jerry had a wondering look.

They were both silent. Then Jerry rose to leave.

Mae went up to Jerry and put her hand on his arm, although she made no move to come closer. Decision was in her face, but that was all that he could read there. Her eyes were averted.

"Jerry, I want you to feel free, so far as I'm concerned, to do whatever you think you must. I don't want you to think about me."

"I do, though," Jerry muttered, his vision clouding, his heart beating so that he thought Mae must hear it.

"Perhaps you are right that I could not live up to the course you want to take. Maybe you ought to try it out alone—at first, that is. But no matter what Vee said, I can understand it. I think I can." Mae spoke humbly. She glanced again at her piano.

Jerry stared at her. "But Vera was partly right about me. I see that. I'm acting like an impatient fool. I can't just run out. What Vera said about Tommy Hardcastle—I don't know; that struck me."

He was studying Mae's face now, as she had his, but with far less penetration. "I can't say now what I'd like to say to you, Mae—dear."

Mae stood in silence. Her face flushed again.

Jerry pleaded, looking away, "I don't know whether you could stand it to go over the hymns with me. If we're going to keep on for now—"

"Yes," Mae answered practically. "We'll have to do that. Not at this moment, probably; it's too close to dinnertime. But you might come in this evening. Don't be afraid of Vera," she added. "Her temper will all have run out by then. She'll probably make sea foam for you!"

"Oh, I'm not worried about that!" Jerry said with relief.

Mae followed him into the hallway. He stood looking at her, too *gauche* and ashamed of himself to kiss her even now— more afraid of her than he had ever been, and afraid of himself. For the moment he had reverted to his rustic youth.

They stood there mutely, Jerry's face screwed up and averted from Mae's. He seemed unable to leave and unable to say anything more. He started blindly toward the front door, put his hand on the knob—but somehow, also blindly, he turned and found Mae moving toward him. Silently they were together, in the familiar hallway where they had so often said good-by to each other in a delicious restraint—the ample stairway leading to the rooms above, Lyle's old cap on the newel post where he had tossed it.

This was not restraint; it was an avowal of their love and their physical attraction for each other, and both Jerry and Mae knew it. Neither was ignorant of the manifestations of physical love, though both had been scrupulous, during the years of their growing up, in refraining from giving their own. Jerry knew very well the common ways of experimenting with sex, in the rather crude code of the rural community in which he had lived as a boy, where it was the custom for parents to retire upstairs when the young folks were entertaining themselves in the parlor below, and let nature more or less take its course. Jerry had been touchy and stand-offish in those painful, hazardous years. He felt that he was unattractive—although he was not so—and he also, quite early, considered his life reserved, somehow, for more than personal ends.

As for Mae, she was quite accustomed to being a charming object to men and boys of a wide range of type and age, but she had never yielded her favors to any of them beyond a brief embrace and kiss. She was as adept as Vera, and even more graceful than Vera, in subtle ways of diverting and discouraging the attentions which she so readily drew to her. Somehow, with some not particularly attractive boys who found hope in her kindness, she managed to prevent serious involvement without hurting their pride. Now both Mae and Jerry had everything to give each other, and this they knew.

"Mae, I can't stand to hurt you in any way! I don't mean to, I don't want to."

"I know you don't, Jerry. Anyway, you've been hurting yourself more than me. Why are you so hard on yourself, Jerry?"

"I don't know. I think I don't know *anything*, Mae!"

But something was released in Jerry's tense feelings, some obstacle removed—he hardly understood what or how, at this moment, except that Mae's love was concerned in it. New worlds opened up to him.

This is so completely natural, was what Jerry thought, in so far as he thought anything. He held Mae's fragrant, fresh, womanly warmth pressed against him, more real and more miraculous than in any of his wonderful yet half-frightened imaginings. Of course, of course! they could both have said. Their discussion of only a few minutes past, with all its painful attempts at wisdom, had become irrelevant.

They were conscious of standing close to the front door. Before long the younger Meserves would be coming home from school, breaking in upon them more ruthlessly than Vera had.

Mae pushed Jerry away from her. She was looking at him

with glowing confidence, and yet with decision in her brown eyes. He stood still while she put her hands on his shoulders, holding him away while she whispered, "You don't know what I can do! I can do more than you think. I can wait."

"We don't have to wait."

"Right now we do," Mae said, still in a whisper.

She kept Jerry pushed away until he was outside and she had closed the door.

Jerry went down the four porch steps in dazed amazement. The light outdoors seemed extraordinarily bright (the sky actually had cleared) and he felt as if he had come out of a dark, murky cellar, where he had been stumbling and groping, afraid of every step and every shadow. Yet all the shadows, all the problems were still here! Why did they seem dissipated?

Jerry felt only that he was once more part of the springtime and of the town—of the lawns and the trees, the rose bushes with their first crop of rosebuds, the children coming home from school. His joy in the town returned in a flood, but it was changed. It no longer half an illusion but held a reality such as he had never before known. He felt all reality heightened. He belonged not only to the little town, but to life.

He suddenly saw his idea of leaving Fairview as a half-primitive, half-romantic notion, a leftover from the restrictions, the lonely struggles, the poverty of his earlier life—his bare, unheated room at home; the silent meals at which he inwardly rebelled at his grandfather's unchanging, sonorously spoken prayer; his shame and stifled anger as the men sat at the table, shoveling in food, while his mother waited on them. She got the leavings. He thought of the days at the seminary when he had got up before dawn, in the winter months, to work for two hours in the packing room of a wholesale house—kneeling first on the cold board floor beside his narrow, thinly padded cot, for prayers which he muttered with a harsh effort to break through the dense, doped sleepiness. Hardships were what he *had* met; why did he think he had to meet more of them? He didn't want all hardship for other people; why should he for himself? He felt an amazed gratitude toward Mae, who had softly and insistently held him back from returning to the world of his past.

Bodily pleasure, comfort, joy could be tests too. They were tests. God might have had a hand in putting them into this pleasant little town—in which there was so much that was not good, after all. With his quick mind and his truly devout nature, Jerry suddenly felt, in a flash, that this was so, and his sense of gratitude to Mae was mixed and swallowed up in awed gratefulness to God. God worked in His mysterious way, through what circumstances, using whose hands besides His own!—including those of dear and wonderful Mae. His love. He resolved to deserve this happiness, which surely had come to him undeserved, almost unsought, by sheer grace.

Jerry no longer thought of John and Minnie Wood; or rather, their dilemma, as it returned to him on the way home, no longer overpowered him. His own joy, so warm, human, yet "reaching to the skies," absorbed him. And—amazingly —it had been brought out by the dubious circumstances of the Wood case.

He could feel a sympathy for John and Minnie such as he had not known before. It was not lost in fears and anxieties. He was sure that, however the case came out, he would be able to stand by them personally. Wherever they and Philip went, whatever they did, his real love would go with all of them.

But the future of the church here in Fairview? Jerry's unconsciously rapid pace suddenly slackened. Yes, it was here that he still had to meet the worst part of the Wood case. He was walking on air now, but he saw, clearly enough, that he would be coming down to earth, perhaps with a thud, before all the after-effects of John Wood's situation were cleared up. All Jerry knew now was that he would and could face up to the question of the senior deacon; and in that decision he felt new strength and maturity in himself. Is this the way one grows up? Jerry asked himself—by not running away? The image of Austin Cowie, large as it was, had lost much of its formidableness in Jerry's mind. "He has his reward," were the words which occurred to Jerry—and there was even a twist of humor in his lips. He saw the figure which Austin made in a new light, with its poor, limited objectives, so dependent on appearances and reputation—and those so flimsy. He had no desire to strip and tear down Austin Cowie! At the same time, he would not let Austin's views control his own. Jerry's pace quickened again as he neared the Latham home.

The sisters had another of their good meals waiting for him and were just about to sit down to the table. "Well, we have to eat, don't we?" Mrs. Latham had said mildly to Almeda.

After the Reverend Jerry had said grace—holding in check this time his exultance rather than his despair—Mrs. Latham added with beneficent approval, "I think you got a nice piece of steak, Sister. Eat all you can of it, Reverend Jerry. I'd like to see you put on a little weight while Sister and I are cooking for you."

Both ladies sat sedately through the meal, scarcely gave each other a significant look. But as soon as Jerry had gone up to his room Miss Blanchard whispered, "Mae must have accepted him."

"Of course. That sticks out all over him."

"He probably thinks we haven't the slightest inkling. As if the whole church wasn't in on it!"

"Well—poor boy."

C H A P T E R

13

PHILIP WOOD'S life, through which he had moved
with unconscious princely ease, now seemed to him to
raise up one ordeal after another. For the first time Philip, without the loving backing of his parents, was having to make decisions. Having promised Hank Henderson that he would go
on with the Valedictory "somehow," now he could have no
peace until he had also fulfilled his promise of stopping in to
see Colonel Merriam.

Philip walked on past the blossoming semi-wilderness of the
Merriams' big yard, but he tried not to see it.

Mrs. Merriam, when he had called her, had suggested that
he knock at the back door, as people usually did when they
came to talk with the Colonel at his home office. Lola would
let him in. Mrs. Merriam had thought it would be "the wiser
course" for Philip to speak to the Colonel without earlier notice or preparation, even on her part.

The back porch of the Merriam house was shady with vines,
like the front porch. Philip did not question Mrs. Merriam's ad-
vice. Nevertheless, thinking of that past Sunday when Bradford Merriam had invited him to call, Philip had a feeling of
humiliation when he knocked at the back door. Lola answered
quickly.

"Yes, Missus said you were coming about this time."

Lola spoke with a certain breathlessness, but apparently anything that "Missus" said was right. Before leading Philip to
Colonel Merriam's office door, Lola stopped and looked around
her, and told him in that same low, breathless voice, "*She* said
to tell you that you weren't to leave this same way, but go out
through the passage and the front hall. *She* wants to see you."

Philip tried to gather his self-control as he followed Lola to
the Colonel's office. He was not going to offer any apologies
for his father—he was sure of that much—nor act as if he believed that any were needed. That far pride could still carry
him.

Lola had evidently been given instructions of the precise,
far-looking kind that Mrs. Merriam could give; for she knocked
quietly on the office door, looked in, and said, "Colonel Merriam, Mrs. Merriam says Philip has something to say to you."

Then she ushered Philip into the room before the Colonel
had a chance to answer. She discreetly closed the door.

Philip had been in this room only a few times; his father had
always worked in the downtown office. He was confusedly
aware of its special old-fashioned quality, which ordinarily
would have interested him. But he could not take in the maps,
the moose head, the Indian relics, the reproductions and Cora's
painting, the snowballs pressing against the small panes of the
two back windows. He had to meet the gaze of the powerful
old man, the old gentleman whom his father had betrayed.
Colonel Merriam's small bright eyes bored into him from under the remarkable eyebrows. Philip felt how formidable that
unwinking gaze could be. The Colonel might order him out.
But he was here and was going to speak.

"Colonel Merriam, you said I was to come to your office to
have a talk with you. I felt I ought to come, even though I
know you can't give me any loan now." He said this with only
the slightest hint of faltering.

The Colonel scowled. "I've never gone back on my word
yet, young man. I don't intend to begin now."

"Yes, sir. But I don't believe— What I have to say is, I can't go away to college next year."

Silence. Then the Colonel said, "Well, I suppose that's for the best, under the circumstances."

Philip said doggedly, "I want to thank you for the offer, anyway."

Colonel Merriam nodded. It was plain that he readily accepted Philip's withdrawal. He seemed to consider the interview over, but Philip was not yet ready to leave. In his daydreams he had had big visions of some day paying all his father's debts and redeeming the credit of the Wood family. But in the presence of this impervious old man, he felt his own temerity in broaching the subject.

He made the attempt, though, saying huskily, "Sometime I'd like to try to pay—"

The Colonel cut him off. "You don't have anything to pay with."

"I know I haven't now, but—"

"I can pay any debts of my firm," said Colonel Merriam roughly. "You don't come into it."

"Well—good-by, sir." Philip managed to say.

Blinded by tears, which he did not want Colonel Merriam to see, he turned and went out of the door and into the passageway which led into the ample dignity of the paneled front hall.

He stopped in the passageway to wipe his eyes and blow his nose. He had left the Colonel, baffled and both angry and humiliated. The Colonel had allowed him no shred of pride to cling to. Yet the Colonel's own rectitude was unassailable. After all, the deep wrong had been committed by John Wood. There was no getting around that. Philip did not try. But his realization of what his father's own interview must have been with this terrible old man—as fierce now, it seemed, as in the old days of hunting and fighting, of leading his men in the tangled territory of the Civil War at the murky battle of Shiloh —made Philip feel weak, so that he leaned against the wall. No wonder that his father had kept silence! John Wood had not been the same man since—perhaps never would be. It was plain now why only Minnie's devotion upheld his self-respect.

The Colonel might have given one sign that Philip had at least been trying to carry out a former promise, that it was not easy to give up the thought of college, that . . . But the knowledge of his father's betrayal of the Colonel's trust cut too deep. Philip felt that he had run up against an ancient, solidly established stone wall, and in his untried youthfulness had knocked against it with flimsy strength. But the hardness of the Colonel's attitude was the most that he had the right to resent. His bruises might not be due to his own fault, but they were bruises he had been willing to take as his own.

The kitchen door was open, and Philip heard voices: Lola's hearty voice from the pantry, and another smaller, cooler voice nearer by. Philip stopped. He saw Elaine, sitting, as he had often seen her sit, in a little low rocking chair by the kitchen window, a chair which Elaine virtually appropriated as her own. Elaine was such a grown-up girl this summer that Philip scarcely expected to see her in the kitchen, her favorite haunt as a child. Yet why had he stopped, except on the chance of seeing Elaine? He looked at her, taking in the graceful ease of her slight girlish figure as she rocked in the little chair.

Did she see him? He was sure that she did, for she had turned her face toward him as he stopped at the door.

But then she only looked at, or past, him with a completely frozen, blank stare of blue eyes. She even went on talking to Lola as if he were not there.

"Elaine," he started to say in a choked undertone, but loud enough for her to hear. He made a little gesture toward her, unconsciously supplicating. The stare did not change. Lola was talking now—fortunately Lola was not even aware of his being there—and Elaine's pretty features remained as immobile as those of a doll. Philip stood a moment longer; he really did not know how long he stood, but it was only a moment; and then he turned away. This was not the familiar hostility, which he had always ignored. It was far more daunting. No rejection he had met since his father's action had broken on the town had hurt as this did; none ever could.

Mrs. Merriam stepped from the library, where she must have been waiting for Philip. He did not know what she had in mind to say to him, and, if left to himself, he would have gone straight out the front door. He scarcely understood that Mrs. Merriam was making this visit as easy for him as she could. Her voice was always quiet, precise, and sedate—no more so now than at any time.

"Will you follow me upstairs, Philip? I think we'll go into my sewing room. There is nobody else upstairs, and nobody ever disturbs me in the sewing room unless there is need. The little room is my business quarters, just as the office room is the Colonel's."

Mrs. Merriam smiled at Philip, and Philip accepted the smile gratefully. He followed her up the oaken stairs, past the square landing from which Elaine liked to look down, fitting his steps to Mrs. Merriam's. She seemed entirely undisturbed, made no particular effort to step more softly than usual. This gave Philip confidence. It gave him the feeling that this house was as much Mrs. Merriam's as it was the Colonel's. Mrs. Merriam was probably the one person whom Colonel Merriam had never been able to outface, cajole, or overawe.

The sewing room at the farther end of the upstairs hallway— her "business quarters"—expressed the austerity which was her inheritance; it contained a couch, two plain chairs, the closed sewing machine, and a small bookshelf on the wall, which seemed to have in it now only a faded album of the type which girls used to have (Philip's mother had one, but much more artistically bound) and a copy of the Bible. The room's one window, with a sheer white curtain, perfectly plain, looked out on the grassy cross street which led virtually nowhere—it ended in the fenced green pasture which Colonel Merriam now rented to Tommy Hardcastle for the use of Tommy's two Guernsey cows.

Mrs. Merriam said, "Sit down, Philip. First, I want to ask how your mother is."

"She's all right, Mrs. Merriam. She seems almost better than —well, than lots of times." Philip could hear that his voice was husky. But if Mrs. Merriam heard it, she gave no sign.

"I'm glad. Does she have help?"

"Yes, ma'am. Mrs. Randolph is coming in every day now for a while."

Mrs. Merriam knitted her brows slightly and said, as if to herself, "I wonder how Lavina manages her other work."

"I don't know."

"No, of course you don't know."

But Mrs. Merriam was doing some rapid calculation. Mrs. Randolph—or rather, Jason, her little boy—was due to come after the Merriam laundry tonight with his small wagon. Mrs. Merriam determined to wait and see—at any rate, not to disturb Philip. If necessary, Lola would do the washing this one week, and Mrs. Merriam herself could help with the ironing. Elaine knew nothing about such activities, except in the way of changing her own clothing often and keeping herself immaculate.

Then Mrs. Merriam started out with straightforward directness. "You had your interview with the Colonel."

"Yes, ma'am, I did. I mean, I told him I couldn't accept his offer."

"That was all that was required of you."

Philip was grateful that Mrs. Merriam did not question further. She probably had little doubt as to how Colonel Merriam had received him. But of course she would not suggest any criticism of her husband. She turned to another subject which she knew must be troubling him, though she could hardly have known how much it did just now. Her voice was gentler.

"I spoke to Elaine, Philip, as you requested. I told her that you would not be able to take her to the school picnic as you had wished to do. I did not say much to her, but I gave her to understand that the reasons for this were beyond your control."

Philip dropped his eyes. In Mrs. Merriam's opinion, Philip had a right to know something of how his old playmate regarded him. All of them, even Elaine's father, had made much of the boy only two Sundays ago. Mrs. Merriam did not intend to speak in detail. She herself had been taken aback by the apparent coldness with which Elaine had received her information, asking nothing about Philip, although she had been given to understand that Philip was in trouble; with no expression at all, so far as her grandmother could make out, except for a faint sarcasm—or was it fatalism?—which had shown on her lips. Mrs. Merriam's own bafflement where her granddaughter's attitude was concerned inclined her also to speak more openly to Philip than she had been accustomed to doing. She was closer to Philip, it seemed to her, than to Elaine. She wondered now, Is the boy crying?

"Philip." She spoke firmly, although with some difficulty through her restraint. "I would like to speak to you just a little further in regard to Elaine. I have never been able, I'm afraid, to come to any real intimacy with my grandchild. I regard that as chiefly my fault. But it is why I really have nothing more to tell you as to how far she actually understood your situation. I have told her something about it—a little. I know you will understand that I had to do this, and that it was better that Elaine should learn it from me. I would not, I think, exaggerate. I cannot say that I am sure as to just what Elaine took in, or may possibly have learned before I spoke to her—or what her attitude is, what she hopes for in life. But, as I told you, that is my fault. I have not been able to give the child what she needs."

The miserable look of Philip's face, the unaccustomed droop of his straight shoulders, drew Mrs. Merriam on. "You know, Philip—Elaine has not been able to lead what I should describe as a normal girl's life, like that of Ione Meserve, for example, and Doris, such lively, healthy girls. I won't particularize. I know that you are at least partly aware of her—handicaps. There are elements in Elaine's ancestry, as well as in her situation, which incline her to be high-strung. My own daughter—your mother's friend—was high-strung. I don't know how much you may have heard of my daughter Florence's history —something, no doubt. My girls— But I will not go into that. That was largely my fault too. Cora was a warm-hearted, generous-spirited girl. I know that she guarded and helped Florence all she could while the two girls were in Europe. I think Florence's death killed her. Yes."

Mrs. Merriam stopped. She closed her eyes. She did not know just what had led her to reopen these old wounds. And with this young boy! But Philip was silent. He had looked up again and was listening with the deepest interest. The oddly matched couple—the boy of seventeen and the elderly woman —were together in a communion of suffering.

Mrs. Merriam murmured, "I suppose that I am a high-strung person myself. But physically I have always been strong. Much stronger than my daughter Florence. *Very* much stronger than Elaine.

"I am taking you into my confidence, Philip," she went on. "I have never known Elaine to be on such easy and friendly terms with any other person as with you. Lately I have wondered if— But we will let that go. I would consider that your continuing friendship—or even closer association—would be entirely favorable to Elaine. But close association would require a great deal from you. It might require your whole life, and even then—I cannot express confidence that you could make such an association a happy one. I am not speaking against my granddaughter, Philip. But I need not tell you that. *Cer*-tainly not against you. It is only that I cannot remain silent on a matter of such importance to you. To all of us."

Philip's first instinct was to feel protective toward Elaine, to think, as he always had, that if he could take her fully into his care he could somehow overcome the oddities and difficulties in her make-up. He could draw out something wonderful in Elaine which she herself, perhaps, did not know was there, under that strange, cold manner of hers. But then he realized that this quick, confident feeling was no longer one to which he had any right. And, in his misery, he realized the honor of receiving Mrs. Merriam's confidence—more than had been given to any person in Fairview outside her own family, more even than had been given to his mother. Perhaps she had been carried further than she had first intended, but he knew she meant all that she had said. He realized too that, in comparison, Elaine's father had been flattering him, perhaps playing with him, making use of him, by the attitude of unexpected cordiality; and that Philip himself had let Bradford Merriam's assumption of intimacy go to his head. The torturing bewilderment which Elaine's stare had given Philip remained. The Colonel's gruffness still hurt. But he felt a reverent gratitude to Mrs. Merriam.

Mrs. Merriam sat up straight. "Well, let that be. There are other matters I want to take up with you also, now that we have the opportunity."

Of course she could not say how "your father's situation" would be resolved. But she could assure Philip as to this vital question: "Colonel Merriam will not prosecute."

Philip's heart gave a great throb. Again his hands began to tremble. Mrs. Merriam was aware of this, but thought it best to go on in her kind but dignified manner.

The Colonel would pay all the debts incurred which he regarded as in any way connected with his business. He preferred to do so. Philip need not suffer anxiety on that score. The Merriams did not have— "We do not have"—anything deserving the name of a great fortune. The Colonel's money had been made locally. But their funds and resources could stand the strain. Mrs. Merriam could not promise, but it was her own personal opinion that if John Wood's creditors were satisfied, and if the Colonel himself did not bring the case into court—"and I have reason to believe that he will not"—the others involved would be less likely to do so.

"All court action is expensive, and very few, except Colonel Merriam, would have the means. It is expensive in other ways too—in terms of human emotion. I cannot be absolutely certain, but I hope and trust, Philip, that it will not be attempted."

Mrs. Merriam added that preferably Philip should not speak of this matter as yet to his father and mother. "That should be left, I believe, to Mr. Evans, who has the Colonel's legal interests in charge." But she had wanted Philip to know.

Mrs. Merriam did not refer directly to Philip, but her expression and the tone of her voice showed that she realized how heavily this situation bore upon him. She did not know what his father's present financial status was.

Philip thought that his father did not *have* a financial status.

"No, my dear. And I am obliged to add that I think what I have indicated is as far as the Colonel is prepared to go. It is a considerable distance."

Philip murmured, looking down at his hands, "I know it is."

"Not bringing court action will spare your mother particularly. But I realize that non-prosecution, even if other creditors concur, will not solve all your difficulties."

Philip mutely assented.

Mrs. Merriam continued in a very gentle tone, "Philip, I wish you would tell me if you are short of ready cash in your household. I was too stupid to think of that when I was at your home."

Philip was startled. He himself had not even thought of such a thing. The household had seemed to run much as before.

"You must not be allowed to be short. There are several of your friends whom you may count on to see to that. I am convinced that this is true. But you yourself have still to reach your graduation. You must reach it. Your high-school diploma and the excellent grades you have received will be of future help to you. And I trust that you can go further, even if there should be some little delay."

Philip told her that he had promised his principal that he would go through with his Valedictory oration—"if I can."

Mrs. Merriam said in her sedate tone, "That is quite right. And you will."

But she then said somewhat tentatively that she wondered if Philip had considered—if his parents had considered—what course they might take providing there was no court action.

Philip answered, still looking down, "The folks don't talk much to me."

Mrs. Merriam did not want to bring more anxieties upon Philip. But she did believe that he should be prepared for whatever action was necessary. So she asked, "What do *you* think?"

Philip answered almost inaudibly that he supposed his family must leave Fairview. It was a terrible admission, one that he had not made openly until this moment. He hoped that Mrs. Merriam would disagree. But instead she remarked, "Under all the circumstances, that course might be best. It might offer more. Although I don't want to dictate. But if that should be the case, you will need funds, won't you?"

Mrs. Merriam rose. "Well, you will need funds in any case. Please excuse me a moment, Philip."

She walked, calm and unhurried, into another room. She returned shortly with an envelope in her hand—no, two envelopes.

She said earnestly, "Philip, I am trusting that you will not refuse these small gifts. I should tell you, perhaps, that I have funds of my own—a family inheritance—which are quite separate from my husband's affairs. I can use these funds exactly as I choose. My son has a good position. He does not need them. If you *should* leave Fairview, I would feel very much distressed if you were to go away penniless. It would be quite unnecessary. You will require something for a journey—if you make one—and for a new start in unfamiliar surroundings. And I don't want your mother to suffer beyond her strength. It has been my thought that you might go to some climate which might be beneficial to her. In that case, you would have a journey of some distance before you. Of course, that is merely a thought."

Mrs. Merriam pressed one of the envelopes upon Philip. He took it in his lax hand and was able to do no more than sit staring at it.

Mrs. Merriam said softly, "It represents an old woman's choice, who has committed many grave errors in her life, of a different nature from those of your parents but essentially as serious. She cannot retrieve many of them. But she can do this much—*wants* to do it. She has everything in a material way that she can need, so this little contribution need not be regarded as in any way a sacrifice. I prefer that you do not open the envelope just now, Philip. But please take it with you. You will be hurting me if you refuse."

Philip silently accepted the envelope—closed his fingers upon it. Mrs. Merriam then gave him the other.

"This may give a little help toward present expenses, so that you need not feel financially pressed before your graduation and before you have had time to get straightened round. Yes, you must accept this too."

"I can't, Mrs. Merriam," Philip protested. "There isn't anything I can do in return—ever, probably. I know Colonel Merriam thinks that."

Mrs. Merriam passed over the final remark. But she hesitated. "Yes, there is, Philip."

She turned to her desk, severely neat, and took out of one of the drawers a wrapped package. Philip accepted it wonderingly.

"You can read every week from St. Paul's Epistles. They may not help you now, but in time they will mean something. They will show you that a man can rise out of error which he can never undo. The Epistles *can* do that, whether you accept every sentence or not. I am by no means asking you to accept every sentence. I can speak out of long experience. That is the only value we older people have to give, it may be, and some of us have paid dearly for it. Philip, I am not going to preach. I don't consider that I have the right to do so. This is merely a gift from me to you, a graduation present."

Philip tried to say, "Thanks."

"We will now return downstairs." Mrs. Merriam, standing up, was again somewhat the great lady. "Remember, you can always call on me." She suddenly stopped and gave Philip a singularly sweet, yet penetrating, look. "I say 'always.' I speak foolishly. I am an old woman, and of course that 'always' does not mean very much. Let me say something of more worth. Philip, it is God, your Heavenly Father, whom you can always call on, and can trust as you can no mortal person. It is He who can give you all that you need or can ask for, although it may be in some manner unexpected."

The light in Mrs. Merriam's face seemed to hold in it a secret that Philip was searching for, yet could not take. His own deep questioning, which had been struggling these nightmarish days for expression, seemed exposed.

"But, Mrs. Merriam!" he appealed. His voice shook. "How can I call on God as my Father? I thought He was, but now—everything I am and come from seems far from God."

Mrs. Merriam said with firm assurance, "Philip, every person, every soul, stands alone before God, regardless of past history or events. Nothing can stand between you and God."

She added, "My only wish is not to stand in His way, but somehow to be His instrument, knowing myself to be a feeble one."

She stepped forward—both were standing—and he felt the brief pressure of her lips on his forehead, "Always remember I have full confidence in you, Philip. Nothing has changed that. You are yourself. You have duties to your father and mother. But you are yourself."

Philip half blindly followed Mrs. Merriam's spare, dignified figure down the handsome stairway and went out the front door of the old house which had meant to him both stateliness and romance. The two envelopes, unopened, were in one of his pockets, and the wrapped package in the other. He might be leaving this house forever, with all that the fine old place symbolized. But for the time being, his pride and shame, his emotional torment, were assuaged; and although it seemed to him he could not bear to remember the flavorsome old office —and even now could not look at the flower bed surrounding the trunk and roots of the great tree—he need never forget the plain, small sewing room.

He did not glance over the white wire fence to catch sight of Elaine, if she might now be roaming about in the big yard, pulling down lilac sprays to smell of them, or standing and looking at the sky through branches already thick with young leaves.

Mrs. Merriam returned to the library. She was too tired at this moment to see her husband or her granddaughter. She could only wait, with closed eyes and hands lax, until Lola called her to supper.

A talk with her husband would be particularly difficult. Seldom as Mrs. Merriam had "interfered" in the business of the George Merriam Company, she had done so recently to this extent: she had tried to persuade her husband not to take the Wood case into court; and when he had seemed obdurate— saying that John Wood must not be "pampered"—she had used personal means which were foreign to her, but which she had realized might be the only ones at present to move him.

"George, I understand how you feel, and I realize that John's conduct in view of your trust in him has been shameful. I don't condone it. But there are other considerations too. There is Minnie—and I am thinking even more of young Philip. In any case, Philip will have a heavy burden to carry. At any rate, George, we would gain nothing financially. You yourself said that John had nothing except the house and the furniture, which are really Minnie's."

"The house isn't hers—except as John was smart enough to put it in her name."

"I don't think that was his reason for doing so at the time—'smartness.'"

"What was it, then?"

"I don't know, of course. Perhaps protection for Minnie in case something should happen to John."

"Hmph! Pshaw! Great—"

"That will do, George Merriam."

"All right, Lyddy. All right."

"Prosecution," Mrs. Merriam had continued firmly, "would be pure retaliation in this case. I ask you not to prosecute for my sake."

Such a plea was so astounding from Lydia that George Merriam had not refused her. She had said what she had to say and had refrained from any sternly uttered quotation such as she might once have made. These quotations had always riled George Merriam, particularly when they were Scriptural. Lydia's request had upset him with an unexpected impressiveness.

Lydia had sat quietly waiting; and when her husband had given a growl which had indicated assent, she had rewarded him only with a dignified "Thank you, my dear."

But now that her point had been gained—far more easily than she had been prepared for—and now that her talk with Philip Wood was over, Mrs. Merriam felt spent. She was able, however, to go into the dining room when Lola struck the gong in the hall (a gong brought from China by one of Mrs. Merriam's seafaring ancestors). The meal was eaten almost in silence. Even Lola was subdued. Colonel Merriam was merely taciturn and grim, making none of the jesting comments which pleased and flustered Lola. Elaine was as quiet as her grandparents. Her small, pretty face told nothing.

Mrs. Merriam saw that her husband was even more drained of energy than herself. As they rose to leave the table, she said to him, "I hope you have no work tonight, George."

He gave a short sound of exasperation. "I have plenty of work, but I don't know as I can get far with it tonight. I may look over a few papers, so that Claud can have them tomorrow morning."

"George—" She spoke in a lowered tone, so that neither Elaine nor Lola would hear. "Are you going to see John Wood again?"

"No, I'm never going to see him again. That's my last word on the subject, Lyddy. He can run, now that you've got him off."

Mrs. Merriam said nothing more, but went back to the library. She felt traitorous because she had spoken so intimately to a person outside the family about her granddaughter. She wanted to make it up to Elaine, but was conscious of being unsure how to do so. Fortunately, Elaine drifted into the library soon after her.

On a sudden impulse Mrs. Merriam said, "Elaine, I wish that you would read to me. I am tired tonight. And you read so well."

To her surprise, Elaine did not refuse. Sitting down in her beautiful old brocaded Bradford chair, Mrs. Merriam suggested that Elaine herself should choose their reading matter.

"I don't know what to choose," the girl said petulantly.

"Anything that you like, my dear."

"*You* won't like it."

"You don't know that. What do you like?" she asked, a little concerned.

"I like Lola's book."

"I'm afraid I don't know what 'Lola's book' may be."

"Oh, it's about a duchess, and a gardener, and—some other people," Elaine answered carelessly.

"Indeed," was Mrs. Merriam's only comment, calmly spoken.

Elaine scrutinized her grandmother's face. She started to go out to the kitchen to get "Lola's book"—but at the last minute, she whirled, ran lightly up the stairs to the old nursery, and came down with a book of her own.

"What is that, dear?"

"It's called *Golden Treasury*. We read it at school. I like it all the same, though. It's poems."

This was said rather inquiringly. Mrs. Merriam, however, looked acquiescent. Elaine seemed satisfied.

"Well, I rather like this one. It's called 'Daffodils.' "

Elaine's voice sounded small, clear, pure, but without emotional extravagance—a Bradford voice. Mrs. Merriam noted with satisfaction the fine enunciation. *That* much the school had done for her.

> *"I wandered lonely as a cloud*
> *That floats on high o'er vales and hills . . ."*

"Did you like it?" Elaine asked airily, when she had finished, aware that her choice had been discreet, yet inwardly and secretly pleased with the "wandering lonely." That was what she herself did through her grandfather's orchard and big overgrown yard.

"Yes, very much, dear. You read it beautifully."

"Then I'll read some more."

It was apparent that Elaine was gratified, and Mrs. Merriam was thankful. The child was in one of her docile, ladylike moods. Mrs. Merriam let her go on without interference—how often she had interfered with Florence and Cora!

Even as she listened, or half listened, her thoughts returned almost inevitably to the Woods. She was glad she had spoken so openly to Philip. Although it was true, as she had told Philip, that she did not know what might be Elaine's dreams for her own future, and although she was still disturbed because the child seemed to have dropped her old playmate, the words which came to Mrs. Merriam were: It would never do. And this for more reasons even than she had told Philip—her son Bradford's pride, for example, which would hardly accept the son of John Wood, now, for a son-in-law. What *was* in store for the girl? Mrs. Merriam sighed. Alas, there were questions, many questions, which an old woman could little afford to ask, to say nothing of answer, and this was among them.

She heard Elaine's final words:

"*And answer, echoes, answer, dying, dying, dying.*"

Elaine closed the book. With sweet obedience she acquiesced in her grandmother's suggestion that she should now go to bed. She stipulated that she say good night to Lola first—to Lola and Harm, they were both in the kitchen. Yes, she might tell them good night. Mrs. Merriam approved of the calls of the good-looking young carpenter Harm on Lola. A kiss just touched Mrs. Merriam's smoothly brushed hair.

Mrs. Merriam sat on in her Bradford chair of old mahogany. She listened to the ticking of the grandfather's clock. For the first time, that measured sound seemed to her—as it had to Philip—to carry remorselessness. But it could mark off only the minutes and hours of this earthly life. Mrs. Merriam, unlike her ancestors, felt no certainty as to what lay beyond; but her spirit said, Something.

No man has seen God.

The clock was deeply a part of her daily intimate life, fraught with associations, and its ticking was acceptable.

Mrs. Merriam hoped that her husband would come into the library. But she would refrain from disturbing him. She was risking offense to him by giving some of her own money to Philip Wood. But it *was* her own money, and George had always considered it so. He had made no comment on her use of it for "benevolences" generally, keeping that one of his promises as he did others. The chunk of money which would go for payment of John Wood's defaults and the re-establishment of the good name of the George Merriam Company would be paid out from the Colonel's own resources. Estimates as to how much Colonel Merriam was "worth" were, of course, highly varied in Fairview. Probably only Claud Evans had anything like precise knowledge. But Mrs. Merriam, with a slight sigh, thought that it would be unwise to question George closely, unless—as she hoped but scarcely expected—

George brought the matter up himself. Lydia Merriam had
the income from thirty thousand dollars—still, at that time, a
good and sufficient estate. She would gladly give George all
that she owned, even though to discontinue her "benevolences" would be a wrench. But, knowing George as she had
finally come to know him, Lydia realized that such an offer
might be taken as an affront. She understood the value of the
promise which she had recently won from him by means
which she considered beneath her, perhaps—although not
sorry that she had used them. Once throughout these many
years, it was not unfitting that she, as George Merriam's wife,
should make a plea on personal grounds.

She heard George's footsteps in the hall. The perception of
his having aged was now much accentuated. The footsteps
were those of an old man.

"Well, Lyddy." The Colonel gave a deep sigh. "Still up, are
you?"

"Yes. Would you prefer to go to bed directly, George?"

"No, I want to sit here in my chair a while. There's nobody
coming in, is there? No committee, or whatever?"

"I don't have many committee meetings these days,
George."

"Hmph! Well, that's something. Has Elaine gone upstairs?"
he asked abruptly. "I don't feel like coping with that young-
ster tonight."

"Yes, Elaine has gone to her room. She was in a very good
mood tonight, dear. Nobody will come to the house, to my
knowledge."

"I'm too tuckered to talk with anybody now, except you. I
don't want to hear this business rehashed."

Colonel Merriam had sunk into his great leather chair and
closed his eyes. He opened them to say, "Lyddy, I think I
ought to let you know more clearly how our finances stand."

Much as she had wanted to hear this very thing, anxiety
made Mrs. Merriam say, "Can't you let the matter go for tonight, George, since you are tired?"

"No," he answered grimly. "I can't let anything go."

Then he gave, unconsciously, his long, deep sigh.

"Who else is there I can speak to?" he demanded. "Claud. He knows what he has to know, as my lawyer. But he don't know quite everything!" the Colonel added with satisfaction.

His wife said nothing.

"First of all," Colonel Merriam said, straightening in his chair and frowning with his great eyebrows. "I intend to let the business go. I can't take in anybody in John's place, and I can't manage all the work myself any more. The heart's gone out of it for me."

"Just how do you mean, you will let the business go?"

"Pay liabilities and close the doors."

"But don't you intend to sell the business, George? To realize something from it?"

"Claud can dispose of what's left—if there's anything left. Have you any objection?" The Colonel's small eyes stared piercingly at her.

"No, George," Mrs. Merriam answered tranquilly. "None. I would much prefer having you here at home with me."

He grunted. "Well, I've been at home plenty. That's part of the trouble."

"You haven't been much with me. But, George, won't the sale bring in some profit?"

"I don't know. The time may have passed for selling out with profit. I can sell the downtown building. I own the whole building, besides the office upstairs. That will find a buyer easy enough. I expect there's a number of people waiting for me to sell out or die. No, I don't know as the sale of the business itself will attract customers."

"But the good will—"

"I don't suppose there is any good will. How can there be?"

Mrs. Merriam protested indignantly. "There will be if the Merriam Company pays all that's now owing."

The Colonel grumbled, sinking back, "I don't know as to that. I can't see anything of it at present."

"George, I feel certain that there will."

"How do you come to know, Lyddy? You've never been in business."

"No, but I *do* know your standing in Wahkonsa County. It goes back years before John Wood ever came into your employ."

"Hmph! Some of it may not be too much to my credit—before you came on the scene." The Colonel added, as if to take off from the handsomeness of this admission, "Maybe your church people will say I brought this business upon myself by being an unbeliever. Your young preacher will probably come in and give me a pious talking-to."

"He'll do nothing of the kind. Mr. Storm isn't like that in any way."

"All right, all right," the Colonel muttered with something of the old sardonic glint in his eyes as his mind went back to the supper-table "discussions," and the texts which used to stare at him from the outhouse wall—all years ago, and he certainly felt no blame in his unregenerate old heart toward Lyddy. He conceded, "I expect this young man has plenty troubles of his own. He won't bother with an old dyed-in-the-wool sinner like me."

Mrs. Merriam retorted with great dignity, "You are not a sinner."

"Yes, I am, Lyddy, and always will be."

"I have been a sinner too."

Mrs. Merriam saw the frown that crossed her husband's brow, and she knew he understood her reference.

"But you've changed more than I have."

"I have only tried, George. And in some ways *you* have changed."

"Don't know what the ways are."

Mrs. Merriam sensed that her husband was thinking of Cora. The loss of Cora was a wound which had never healed. It "kept bothering him," like the bullet wound in the groin. But with stern justice, he did not hold his wife responsible: Cora's death from pneumonia might have occurred anywhere, at home as well as in Germany.

He shifted in his chair. "Well, let's not you and me go back into past history. We could blame ourselves forever for this and for that. We have enough on our hands right now. I want you to know roughly what we do have, Lyddy, on the side of resources."

"Are you comfortable in that chair, George?" Mrs. Merriam asked suddenly.

"As comfortable as I can be anywhere."

Colonel Merriam straightened up again. His temper flared unexpectedly. "I've given my promise not to prosecute John Wood. But I'm going to take no steps to prevent him from adding what he can. That's in order, and he won't get out of it."

Mrs. Merriam waited tensely.

"The house is mortgaged already, Claud informs me. We won't get anything out of *that*, unless maybe we take over the mortgage and resell. Of course, technically, it does belong to Minnie. He has some personal belongings, furniture and the like."

"But those things are Minnie's!" Mrs. Merriam cried. "They came to her from the Terrills."

"I can't help it. John has to help where he can—which means precious little."

"Some of their furniture is good," Mrs. Merriam protested.

"It might bring in a little—put out at auction."

"At auction!" Mrs. Merriam exclaimed in horror. "We couldn't let Minnie Terrill go through an auction of her furniture."

"She can do it as well as anybody else," the Colonel stubbornly reiterated.

"No, George, she can't."

"None of us can, when it comes to our own things."

"I could sell everything I possess, if you needed that."

"So can Minnie Terrill sell all she owns for John."

"But it seems so useless, if her furniture will bring so little."

"It will bring something."

Mrs. Merriam closed her lips firmly. She could not agree with George, and his decision seemed petty, but she could not ask another favor on personal grounds. She calculated rapidly. She thought that she could get together a few of the old friends to bid for Minnie's choicest possessions. . . . Mrs. Latham and Almeda Blanchard—Almeda could do it, or Ellie Meserve. Other names went through her mind. Her own presence at such a sale would lead to more talk. But she might bid through some other person—Vera Meserve, for example. Vera was dauntless and in a favorable position. She had taste, even though she herself wanted all her belongings to be strictly contemporary. Mrs. Merriam could not keep the pieces here in her own house, but the Meserves had room. Mrs. Merriam saw in imagination—with a sensation of tears pressing against her closed eyelids—the pretty dishes, the handmade tablecloths, the lacy pieces which spoke eloquently of Minnie. Surely Minnie could keep *those?* She could keep the cherished small expensive things which had belonged to Florence and Cora. Yes, the best of the furniture and keepsakes could be stored in the Meserve loft, or barn, and shipped if and when the Wood family left Fairview—probably forever.

George was now recounting their own various assets readily turnable into cash. There were really a good many of them. Mrs. Merriam had not thought that George possessed so much. He owned land throughout the township and county. Farm lands brought in less in those days, of course, than now; Iowa land was viewed more as an investment for the future, showing confidence in the region, except for farms being worked by their owners. Some of George Merriam's lands were attached to the Merriam Company. Some represented his own personal investment. Prices were variable. But just at the present time they were fairly good.

At last Colonel Merriam mentioned, with obvious difficulty, "The Grove."

"George, you don't mean Merriam's Grove?"

"What other do I own?"

"But not that. That is to be your gift to the community."

"Oh, I expect the city might put up funds for it, or the bank might, and it wouldn't be changed too much. It might be broken up into lots, though, if the town continues to expand, as I've always looked for."

"No." Mrs. Merriam was very decided. "The Grove is not to be sold. You have preserved it in its native state all these many years, and it will be of great value to the community in times to come. No. I will not agree to such a sale. I have something of my own—far more than poor Minnie Wood does! I would rather mortgage this house and grounds."

"You'll have to live in this house, Lyddy, after I'm gone."

"I don't want you to say that, George."

"I have to say it. I'm an old man."

His words were true. The sturdiness of aspect which he had kept even after the first blow of discovering that John Wood had failed him had deteriorated since then. Of course they were both "along in years." But Mrs. Merriam had looked forward to a period of companionship when the Colonel had wholly given over business affairs to John, and when they two could enjoy each other's company. She had loved George Merriam with passion. But they had never "believed alike." There had been some stormy times, in which they had contended with each other on equal terms. Now it seemed that the few months last winter when they had finally come to a full admission and adjustment of their wide differences (although they had always believed in each other) would constitute the best period of that enjoyment. Lydia Merriam would be taking care of an aged man. But compared to the loss of George—to the loss of his integrity—what would it matter if she had to live in a mortgaged house? Or even if part of the beautiful big yard were to be sold? Of course, any marked change in the Merriams' way of living would involve loss to Tommy and Phoebe Hardcastle.

There were ramifications of the John Wood case, so it

seemed, in all directions. Mrs. Merriam could not go into them all. There was only one aspect which she must bring up to George before they finished their discussion tonight.

"George, you *will* see John Wood again?"

"What for? I said I wouldn't."

"You will have to speak to him about some of these things. Find out from *him* what he can pay, if anything. You can't let him go away without at least seeing him, even if that should be hard for you both."

"Claud can see him," the Colonel stubbornly reiterated.

"That's not the same as if you saw him yourself. You tell me you left too much to John Wood. Don't do the same with Claud Evans."

The Colonel would not now reply, but Mrs. Merriam felt assured that he knew she was right. But he was exhausted. She could not press the subject at present. She could not say, "Forgive John as much as you can." It might be that George *had* forgiven John to the extent of his powers.

The Colonel finally said, pressing his hand against his eyes wearily, "I don't know as to the child. It might be best for Brad if *he* were to lay aside for her. No doubt you will leave her your own money—although that's *your* business. Lyddy, you're to leave it to the girl, mind, not give it to her. You won't come to want while you have your inheritance. I can feel assured as to that much."

"George, we won't any of us come to want. You know that. You're seeing things at their blackest this evening."

"Well, they are black. John Wood is a black-hearted scoundrel."

"No, he is not. He thought he acted out of love."

"What kind of love?" George demanded cynically.

"Not the best, I think," Mrs. Merriam said, after a pause. "Truth and love go together. George, I think we shouldn't talk any more tonight."

Tragically unlike himself, George was obedient to his wife's suggestion. He even waited for her to help him out of his

chair. He said pathetically—but the pathos entered her heart
—"Lyddy, I don't want to sleep in the office tonight. I want to
be with you."

"Yes, George, I want you to be."

As they slowly climbed the oak stairway, he leaning on the
balustrade, she just behind him—he had always courteously
let her go up the stairs ahead of him—Mrs. Merriam appreciated and took into herself the understanding that George's
dependence upon her was to be, after all, that "crown of life,"
her compensation.

CHAPTER

14

PHILIP WOOD was in his room. He was dressing for his graduation, which was to take place that night. The sky outside his window had just reached the stage of twilight.

He heard his parents moving about in their room across the hall. They were going to the Commencement program. Philip had not been sure that they would make this decision. He himself was not going to the Opera House with them, but with Lyle, who would come past for him. It was necessary for Philip to be at the Opera House early.

John Wood had not intended to go to the program. But Minnie had said indignantly, "Certainly we're going to hear our son speak and see him get his diploma. I can't go without you, John. You know that." John had said, "Perhaps Philip would prefer not to have us there." She had replied, "Now, my love, you know that's foolish. Besides I want to go, and I want you to take me. You wouldn't compel me to go alone." That had won John's consent. John had gone outside the house no more than was necessary. All the time which he could spare from conferring and going over records with Claud Evans he had spent close to Minnie. It was almost as if the two had changed places: she had now become the sustaining force. Almost miraculously—it seemed to Philip—she had kept her bright countenance, and, more than that, had held to her fiction of John's "mistake."

Philip was touched that his parents should be coming to the Opera House tonight. But their presence in the audience was going to make his ordeal harder for him. The oration to which he had looked forward with confident anticipation had become another ordeal, the most difficult so far.

Philip put on his becoming good suit and the gray and red silk necktie which the younger Meserves had given him for a graduation present. He did not have new shoes, but he had learned from his meticulous father to keep shoes in good condition; tonight he had given his best pair, still not badly worn, a special polish.

As he knotted the necktie, leaning toward the mirror, it struck Philip that he had received few graduation gifts. Lyle, by comparison, had a stack of them. Philip could count the people who had sent him presents. From the Meserves he had received not only this necktie, which no doubt Vera and Mae had picked out—Vera with her flair for knowing what was becoming—but from Mr. Meserve a crisp ten-dollar bill; from Jerry Storm, a book, *Natural Law in the Spiritual World*, by Henry Drummond, a book of which Philip had never heard; three fine handkerchiefs, one each from Mrs. Latham and Miss Blanchard, and one from Mrs. Randolph; and, to his astonishment, another necktie from Mr. and Mrs. Sayles "for being such a good usher." There were, of course, the package and the two envelopes from Mrs. Merriam—none of which Philip had yet opened. He had told his parents that they must not buy anything for him—the nice suit had been their gift—and they had acquiesced because there was nothing else for them to do. Philip had not a single gift from a relative. His mother had been the Terrills' only child.

As to his father's relatives, Philip had known almost nothing of them and had seldom wondered about them except in the most casual way. "Family" simply meant his father and mother and himself. Of his father's early life before John Wood had come to Fairview, Philip knew little more than that the old family home had been in New Jersey, and that his father's parents had both died while John was still a very young man—perhaps no older, or not even so old, as Philip himself was now. Somewhere in the background there had been an "Aunt Margaret" and an "Uncle Rufe." But letters had long since ceased coming from either of them; they must have died when Philip was a small child. If there were cousins, John, apparently, had not kept in touch with them. Philip had not thought of the matter in this way before; but it seemed to him now that John Wood must always have been a rather solitary person. There might be something in his past, or in his ancestry, which would help to explain "what had happened." But Philip was not going to inquire into that. Not now. It came to Philip with a shock that, for all his father's fine presence and pleasant manner, his high standing in the church and community, there was a quality in John Wood that was inscrutable. Philip himself had felt this in his father; but—like so many others—he had taken his father on trust. He knew that he had his father's love, and had not asked for closer personal intimacy. (For the matter of that, Lyle was not intimate with *his* father.) Only to his wife, Minnie, out of the whole world, had John Wood fully opened his heart. Even she had not known some of the secrets John was keeping to himself. As Jerry Storm had thought, John Wood was essentially, and might always remain, "a man of mystery."

Philip stared into the mirror as if he did not know his own face. It looked almost as usual—not quite. His fresh cheeks were somewhat pale. His shining eyes had a serious look, even somewhat strained. He had given his light brown hair a careful brushing. It was nice hair, growing becomingly, thick and strong.

Philip had no fear about the oration itself. Public speaking had always come easily to him—some said, too easily. He did not fear now that he would not get through his Valedictory. His torment would consist in standing up, facing a crowd of his townspeople, most of whom would know about his father's situation, some of whom—Philip could not say how many— would be definitely hostile. A few, or even more than a few, might be against his representing his class as Valedictorian.

He was not able to pray, as he used to do so glibly—so it now seemed to him. He had a natural ambition to vindicate himself by a marvelous speech tonight; but the ambition to make his parents proud of him was strangely numbed, so that he felt himself bereft. He found himself holding on to Mrs. Merriam's words, repeating in his mind, "I have full confidence in you, Philip."

He heard Lyle's voice from the foot of the stairs.

Calling out hastily to his parents, "I guess I have to go now, see you later," Philip went swiftly downstairs and, with Lyle, outdoors into a fresh, cool, not-quite-rainy evening.

The back part of the Opera House, behind the scenes, was drafty, plain, unromantic. There was one actual dressing-room, in which Hank Henderson was giving tonight's performers a few last-minute instructions and encouragements.

Philip found the others there: Hank, with Evvie Evans, Gladys Cornwall, and Will Cowie. It had been the decision of the class to make this program what Hank called "short and meaty"—not to drag it out in the effort to give every senior member a part. The class had no really good musicians, but it did have exceptionally good speakers. There were to be two recitations and two orations, that was all. Evvie and Will were to present the recitations: Evvie, Whittier's ballad "Amy Wentworth"; and Will, two short poems, the first by Longfellow, the second Milton's sonnet "On His Blindness."

Philip was cordially received into the chilly room with its cheerless cement floor and long dressing-table board beneath two mirrors. Hank set the tone. "Ah, here's our Valedictorian! Good."

But Evvie and even Will were friendly also, although Will had something of a patronizing air. Gladys was quiet, but her

kindness showed in her eyes. All four, as performers and repre-
sentatives of their class, were now in the same boat together.
More was required of them than of others, but they had been
picked out as having more to give. Evvie was shivering with
nervousness which was half delightful.

"Hank, you have to promise me *faithfully* to prompt me
instantly if I should forget!"

"Yes, sure. I have a copy of 'Amy' right with me. But you
won't forget. You don't really mind speaking, pretty as you
look tonight. You want everybody to get a good look at that
beautiful dress. None of you is going to forget. I want Will to
remember to make a short pause, until the house is quiet again,
before he gives his second poem. Remember, Will, you know
the words, but the audience doesn't. Not many of them do,
anyway," Hank added with a humorous twist of his lips.

"If only we didn't have to sit up there on the stage in front
of everybody the whole time!" Evvie exclaimed. She gave another slight shiver.

"Oh, that won't be so bad. The seniors will all be there together. You can prop each other up, if need be. But there'll be
no need," Hank said again reassuringly. His eyes twinkled.
"And you know, Evvie, you rascal, that you'll be enjoying
yourself."

"*You'll* give the signals for us to get up and go forward on
the stage."

"Sure, sure. I'll be there, ready to dash out and grasp any
fainting form. But I expect to see no fainting form. Why, you
people are all veterans."

Hank went over the order of performance again: Evvie,
Gladys, Will, Philip.

Some old smears of paint had been left on the walls of the
dressing-room, a few old showbills. In spite of its tawdriness
and chill, the room had an atmosphere of excitement. Philip
saw how the other three performers had taken on the air of
strangeness which seems to go with any public appearance.
Evvie was lighter, brighter, and more dignified than her usual

self. But Gladys was even more changed. She had eaten supper at the Evans home; afterward Mrs. Evans and Evvie had fastened her graduation dress for her and combed her hair. Philip, like most boys, did not know just what Mrs. Evans and Evvie had done to it, but the plain black hair looked softer—pulled out some way, he thought, and made to frame her face becomingly. Gladys's white dress had been made by a good dressmaker instead of by herself or her mother, as her school clothes were made. Evvie's sheer white dress was enticingly, femininely pretty, with finely lace-edged ruffles. But Gladys's dress, too, which had only tucks for trimming, showed her sturdy figure to a new advantage. Both the girls wore roses—Evvie's bouquet pink-gold, and Gladys's single rose a deep red. Will Cowie was completely new as to suit, shoes, blue necktie, white shirt, and high, shining collar. He was uncomfortable, but his round face with short nose and high eyebrows did not show it; he seemed a symbol of assurance. He did not recite as well as Evvie; but since his father, as chairman of the school board, was to give out the diplomas, and since Will had received higher grades than Evvie, it had been thought well to give him a place of equal prominence on the program. He wore a white carnation in his buttonhole.

Gladys cried out in sudden protest, "Philip doesn't have any flower!"

Philip said, "I forgot about that."

"But you ought to have one. Oughtn't he, Hank? Evvie, you could give him one of the smaller ones of your roses."

"No—no, I don't need a flower."

Gladys insisted. "Yes, you do. You'll look funny, the only one of us four without. I can't give you mine, because I have just this one big rose. But Evvie, you have that whole little bouquet, and one of yours is so pale it's almost white. Then Philip's flower would correspond to Will's."

"Evvie doesn't want to spoil her bouquet," Philip protested.

But, to his surprise, Evvie agreed with Gladys, and after very carefully pulling out and detaching the pale rose from among the pink-gold ones, she graciously said, "There. Now let me fasten it on for you, through your buttonhole, and pin it underneath, so that it will be just right."

Philip submitted with thanks, although the touch of Evvie's light, deft fingers brought back with pain the memory of Elaine's even smoother, lighter hand.

"There now, Glad, don't you think that looks nice? I do know how to fasten flowers and bows and things like that," Evvie observed with complacency—more complacency because she perceived that Will Cowie was fully alive to her attractions tonight. Too late, however. She was going home with Lyle and had no intention of changing—preferred Lyle to "that know-it-all Will Cowie." Lyle had just as much to be set up about! Let Will ask Gladys. He would if he had any sense, but Evvie doubted that he had.

"Come on, now, little ones, come along," Hank was saying. "What you don't know now, you won't learn. But you know your parts."

Hank had given no instructions to Philip, merely a friendly slap on the shoulder as the five left the dressing-room. Philip had not cared to look into either of the battered old mirrors. He was aware that this night did not mean to him what it did to the others. All he seemed to feel was numbness.

The members of the senior class were gathered in the wings at the near side, ready to march out onto the stage when, following the overture, the processional march began—both played by a willing if rather feeble combined high-school band and orchestra, the march set to the music of the high-school song, which in turn was a local variation of "Far Above Cayuga's Waters" (here they were "Wahkonsa's Waters," since they could scarcely be "Upper Wahkonsa's Waters"). The class members lined up in alphabetical order, which meant that Philip, as a W, came at the end of the line. Ahead of him was Boysie Wheeler, certainly no aid in facing what lay ahead. Lyle and Gladys seemed far away. But Hank Henderson's gaunt, encouraging face, fixed in one of its usual expressions of meaningless agony, while the eyes remained bright and kind, was not far from him—just beyond him, as Hank remained in the wings. Hank's ungainly form stood out in front of one of the topply scenes which helped to make up the wings, in sight of the class but out of sight of the audience.

The school song started, and the seniors moved out in order upon the stage. At a signal from Hank, all sat down on the straight chairs at the back of the stage—all nineteen.

This was the senior class of which both teachers and community had been particularly proud, the most promising group so far to be graduated. The members had seemed unusually congenial too, until these last days when the John Wood matter had thrown unexpected shadows.

Mr. Compton, the superintendent, gave the welcome to the audience. His little talk went smoothly, after long practice in this sort of thing, repeating, in slightly different phraseology, what he had said last year. It was the turn of Mr. Conningbear, the Baptist minister, to offer the Invocation.

Philip scarcely heard either Invocation or welcoming remarks. While the superintendent spoke, he looked out over the audience, not wanting to do so but unable to help himself, seeing the Meserve family, Mrs. Latham and Miss Blanchard with Jerry Storm—Jerry with his serious face unusually radiant. Philip saw Miss Janeway, wearing what in Fairview in that period would be called a "party dress," sitting beside Mr. Rakosi, who was very spruce in fancy waistcoat, with his black hair brushed into a shining crest and the ends of his black mustache curled upward. He saw Tommy and Phoebe Hardcastle, Tommy in a rather long black coat which must have been cherished for many years, and Phoebe extremely neat in black silk. He saw Eslick Pettiman, hatless, wearing an expression of dignity which was slightly comic, one could not say just why. He saw the Dissendorfer family but quickly shifted his gaze. He saw Gladys's plain, substantial parents, looking proud tonight, and with good reason. Mrs. Caddie Rathbun—Philip's eyes took in, before he could pull his gaze away, her well-made

face, with aquiline nose, and mouth which could utter words
both cutting and malicious and had doubtless been speaking
such words about the Wood family. Philip was touched when
Howard Rechtner, acting as an usher from the junior class,
bashful but competent, led Mr. and Mrs. Sayles to seats in the
very front row. Philip need not dread to meet their kind old
eyes. . . . No Mrs. Merriam, it seemed. No Elaine. Philip was
first cast down, then glad, in a way, because he had not wanted
to speak empty-sounding words to them tonight; earlier he
had pictured himself as shining before them, perhaps as so
wonderful that Elaine's coldness would be miraculously
changed. He did not know, of course, that Mrs. Merriam had
intended to come, largely because of Philip, but had yielded
to her husband's very unusual request: "Lyddy, I'd rather
you'd be in the house here this evening. I don't feel just right."
. . . Philip saw his old teacher, Miss Schilling, far at one side
of the Opera House, her head bowed most of the time, although once he caught her looking at him with a strange expression of distress on her great-featured face. Philip was puzzled at this expression but relieved that Miss Schilling was here.
He felt nothing antagonistic to him in her look, though he still
did not at all understand the complex reasons back of her behavior, or realize her shyness.

Philip saw his father and mother. They had found places at
the rear of the house, on the left-hand side. Only a few seats
beyond them was Mrs. Randolph, who seldom appeared at
public gatherings; tonight it was out of compliment to the
Woods. Philip saw that his father appeared impassive, but that
his mother held her small head high. A sense of sickness went
through Philip. Again he wanted to make a great impression
for their sakes. He had the feeling that he would be able to
speak the words of his oration well enough, but that the words
had lost significance.

Mr. Compton announced the speakers. Hank Henderson
would stay in the wings on the unlikely chance that prompting
might be needed. There were to be no "solo numbers" or "in-

strumental numbers," but the two recitations were to constitute the entertainment, the two orations the heavy fare.

"Evangeline Evans will now recite for us." Mr. Compton
paused and adjusted his eyeglasses, studied the program. "Her
recitation with which she favors us will be 'Amy Wentworth,'
by the New England poet, John Greenleaf Whittier. Evangeline Evans."

Light, pretty, lacy, ruffly, self-conscious but now in high
command of herself, Evvie stepped forward in her white kid
pumps. Lyle's eyes were lowered. Mrs. Evans, in the audience,
was particularly occupied with making sure that Evvie's slip
did not show, although she could have done nothing in the
way of remedy if it had. Evvie had chosen the poem with
Miss Janeway's agreement and Hank's somewhat quizzical
consent. She had said that she knew the poem was long, but
she wanted to give only the last part. There was nothing she
cared about in the first part, anyway; it was "too deep." But
she simply *loved* the second part. Evvie's voice was not pure
and precise, as that of Elaine, nor was it ever disturbingly over-
intense, but she spoke with verve and relish, and with romantic
dash:

> *"Her fingers shame the ivory keys*
> *They dance so light along;*
> *The bloom upon her parted lips*
> *Is sweeter than the song."*

Evvie put herself, of course, into the role of the faithful,
aristocratic Amy. There was little reason, other than the dramatic, why she should regard herself as Amy Wentworth. She
was well born enough, but not particularly so. Her parents
would have no objection—would, in fact, be highly pleased—
if Evvie were to marry Lyle Meserve. Yet the audience sat in
stillness, affected by her reading. Jerry Storm bent his head,
and his face colored. He did not dare to glance toward Mae.
Philip Wood was in that boyish state of groping confusion in
which the words seemed to reach him as a personal message;

and although Evvie's comprehension was girlish, with no depth
beyond the atmosphere of romance which appealed to her
and suited her talent, when she spoke the last stanza Philip
strained his hands together.

> *"O rank is good, and gold is fair,*
> *And high and low mate ill;*
> *But love has never known a law*
> *Beyond its own sweet will."*

Philip's heart gave a leap of hope, and then he sank into
deeper depression. The applause was a noise in his ears. He did
not see Evvie's demure little bow before she returned to her
chair, her cheeks very pink, uplifted by her success, anything
but cast down by sitting in the public gaze.

Philip was scarcely ready to attend to Mr. Compton's
blandly praising introduction of Gladys Cornwall as Salutatorian "by choice of her classmates and by reason of the excellent record she has made in the four years of her course at
Fairview High School. Gladys Cornwall."

Even when Gladys stood where Evvie had recently been
standing—solid, with feet firmly planted, her voice stronger
and deeper-toned than Evvie's, although less sweet—even
then, it took Philip some time to realize, She's never given her
oration so well as this. He was glad. He wanted Gladys to suc-
ceed. He no longer felt a sense of princely condescension toward Gladys Cornwall. He remembered her brown eyes
raised, their straightforward look into his, and her plain statement, "If you won't be Valedictorian, I won't be Salutatorian."
She had meant it. But Philip knew, rather than felt, that he was
grateful. He knew also that what she was saying now was firm,
well reasoned, convincing, not showy; although he could not
take in her words.

After the two girls had done so well, Will Cowie could not
let the class down. No, nor himself. He had been given careful,
intelligent criticism by Miss Janeway and Hank Henderson
and was thoroughly sure of himself. The lowering of Philip

Wood's standing had undoubtedly raised Will's own. Philip had always stood in the way of Will's being the leader which he, Will, felt cut out to be. His voice seemed somewhat toneless after that of Gladys, and he lacked Evvie's personal attractiveness and her native dramatic ability. But he spoke well—no denying that, even though Lyle Meserve did sit staring at his back with thorough skepticism. Again the words of the poem came to Philip with the acuteness of personal application:

"I shot an arrow into the air . . ."

Will began with proper emphasis and clarity; even—it seemed to the boring gaze of Lyle Meserve—with considerable relish.

. . . the song, from begining to end
I found again in the heart of a friend.

Will took his bow happily, unconscious that Lyle was staring him down and thinking, Little skunk, you.

Will waited until the house was again still, as Hank had recommended, before he started out on Milton's great sonnet, which he delivered in exactly the same tone and manner as he had the Longfellow verses. But the massive lines themselves created their own impressive stateliness—since Will was remembering also to speak slowly. Lyle still stared with mute belligerency. But Philip forgot for the moment that Will Cowie, no longer friendly to him, was the person speaking, and listened as if his life hung upon this utterance.

"When I consider how my light is spent,
Ere half my days, in this dark world and wide . . ."

Will Cowie to be reciting these lines! Philip could not have spoken them. The audience did not care quite so much for this sonnet as for the Longfellow poem. Still, the sonnet was familiar to a few of them. It was worthy. It was by Milton. It deserved, and received, respectful applause.

Philip's own turn was now at hand. He had the same sense of meaninglessness and of competence as earlier.

Mr. Compton's introduction was brief; had it come a year
ago it might well have been fulsome.

"Philip Wood has attained the highest grades of any member of the graduating class during his four years in Fairview
High School. The class has therefore chosen Philip as its Valedictorian. The subject of his oration is"—Mr. Compton consulted the program—" 'The Parliament of Man.' Philip Wood."

Philip caught one sight of Hank's face, concentrated into
an expression of intense encouragement. His feet took him re-
liably to the center of the stage. He felt none of that buoyant
eagerness which had always made speaking a joy. He stood
waiting a second, not because of Hank's instructions, but unable to open his lips. He could sense a special kind of attention
throughout the audience. But he tried to look at nobody there
—least of all at his father and mother. He did see Mr. Sayles
lean forward and cup an ear with his shaky right hand. Somehow that small familiar action restored some of Philip's assurance. Mrs. Merriam's words repeated themselves in his mind:
"I have full confidence in you." Philip was able to speak, and
to do so with little difficulty. His many practices and his own
natural fluency and ability carried him through. He was fortunately unaware that his well-built boyish figure had about
it a drooping quality, although, as usual, he stood up straight.
He *could* look at Mae and Vera. They were almost his own
older sisters. Mae's brown eyes, even more glowing than usual,
and Vera's lighter, sharper eyes were raised. Philip could look
at Miss Janeway too, and let himself be conscious of the brilliantly interested, sparkling gaze of Mr. Rakosi. He could be
glad that Mrs. Randolph had come, and had even—he saw now
—brought Jason.

The words of Philip's oration were now speaking themselves
with ease. But the idea back of them, which Hank Henderson
had considered original, was cold to Philip. He was not "in"
what he was saying, as Evvie had been, and Gladys. He had
tried to present a conception of government nourished—although Philip did not realize it—by his whole background in

family, church, school, and community; based upon Tennyson's well-known lines—his mother had often asked him to
read aloud to her from the poems of Tennyson—foreseeing a
union of peoples. His oration was youthful, limited in experience, over-optimistic, yet in truth ahead of his time—so that
years later a new Valedictorian, looking through the handwrit-
ten and then typewritten copies of earlier Valedictories preserved in the high-school library, would come upon this
particular one in the discouraging, dusty stack, and be excited
by his discovery: "Why, this fellow was really going somewhere."

At the present moment Philip was concerned almost altogether with getting through creditably; with not too much
disappointing Hank and Lyle and Miss Janeway and Gladys;
with rising above his own personal wretchedness.

He closed with the full quotation, not even conscious that
he spoke it well:

"Till the war-drum throbb'd no longer, and the battle-flags
     were furl'd
In the Parliament of man, the Federation of the world."

Tennyson's words, by the time the later Valedictorian came
to read them, were an old story, a "pious platitude," long out
of vogue. "Old Tennyson," an English poet laureate with long
hair and a beard, had written romantically unreal poems and
become naturally tiresome through familiarity. Now this poet
suddenly appeared to the young future Valedictorian as pro-
phetic, "not so simple," and the boy was led to look up and
read through both the poems of "Locksley Hall." They were
not bad poems at all, he found. He said to one of his friends,
"That old guy had something on the ball."

Philip's oration, to himself sounding wooden and flat, was
followed by applause, faint at first in some quarters, almost
over-vigorous in others, and finally strong throughout the entire audience. He could not know that the very diffidence in
his carriage, the subtle addition of unconscious pathos, the

faintly crestfallen look, the lack of the old shining-eyed full confidence, had actually served to make the applause generous. His true friends were proud of him for "not backing out," as Vera Meserve described his appearance on the Commencement program; and the emotions of others who didn't "see how he could have the nerve" had been touched. Mrs. Caddie Rathbun had looked at him briefly with sympathy, perhaps regretting—who knows?—some words too easily spoken by her cutting tongue, and had willingly applauded. The young Dissendorfers, perhaps affected by the attitude of others around them, had clapped once or twice. Hank Henderson's mobile face, seen just inside the wings, had beamed congratulations.

Nevertheless, Philip himself knew that he had not risen to his best. He had passed this particular ordeal and now must meet others, always others. He did not want to look down and across at his father and mother now, for fear that they might be disappointed in him. But at least, he thought, they had not been forced to see their son broken down and obviously suffering.

The high-school band-orchestra played again while a table was being brought in and placed at one side of the stage, the side farthest from Philip. The rolled diplomas, tied with white satin ribbons, were arranged upon the table. A chair was placed for the chairman of the school board. Hank Henderson with his long legs had raced noiselessly across the stage, behind the backdrop, and now suddenly appeared beside the table to hand the diplomas to Mr. Austin Cowie. Another chair was placed for Mr. Compton. Austin Cowie, wearing frock coat, dark trousers, wing collar—his Sunday regalia—with great solemnity climbed the three steps to the stage and was met by Mr. Compton.

Mr. Compton spoke. He had no need to introduce to the citizens of Fairview their eminent fellow citizen Mr. Austin Cowie—"nor need I remind you, the respected head of the Fairview school system."

Mr. Compton retreated, and Austin Cowie, his full cheeks cleanly shaven between the familiar muttonchop whiskers, spoke his own little piece: his pleasure in presenting this fine young graduating class of our splendid high school—"among whom happens to be my own son, but he has already spoken to you"—his pleasure in presenting to these young people their well-earned diplomas. . . . Something about "it is with joy and sadness"—and, of course, about their "going out from us now into the great world." If he had any realization that he carried an unacceptable secret, his pompous complacency did not show it.

Again Philip was squeezing his hands together. He felt himself to be sitting like a deaf mute. The words spoken, with Austin's own flourish although in commonplace terms, hurt him sharply. As the last in line, he would have to walk across the width of the stage. "The last"—it seemed to Philip, in bitterness, that "the last" was now his proper place. He had no happy feeling, as he might otherwise have had, that the acceptance of his diploma was the evening's culminating event.

Hank Henderson was to give the diplomas to Mr. Cowie, and each graduate, having received his or her beribboned cylinder, was to go down those three steps and take a place in the right-hand row reserved for the seniors.

After an impressive pause, during which the class members sat confronting the audience, the boys in new suits and uncomfortable collars, the girls in white dresses, the final ceremony began. Hank nimbly—and, for him, gracefully—handed Mr. Cowie the rolls, one by one, and Austin read out each name in sonorous slowness. His ponderousness was not out of place in his present position. His wife—fat, overdressed, but comely—was proud of him, and, of course, extremely proud of her son Will. Although she had strongly believed that Will, not Philip Wood, should have been given the Valedictory oration—particularly under present circumstances—she was mollified by Will's successfully carried-out recitation.

Not until he heard the reading of the first name on the list

—"Clarabelle Mabelline Anderson," who was a small, wispy, and far from prominent classmate—did Philip reach a full sense of what was happening. This would be his last meeting with the class which had meant so much to him, in the midst of which he had moved as a natural leader. He would not go to the school picnic in Deacon Kruse's woods. All Lyle's urging could not persuade him. The picnic had become a blank to him now that he was not to take Elaine Merriam—worse than that: that he was not to think of ever taking Elaine anywhere.

Philip began almost to wish that the giving-out of the diplomas could be prolonged. He was glad for Austin Cowie's portentous deliberation, which was driving Vera Meserve crazy. After he had got through the anguish of crossing the stage and receiving his own diploma from the plump hand of Mr. Cowie, worse would be waiting for him. . . . But what? He did not yet know. He only knew that everything in his life was going to be changed, he did not know how.

Philip felt his family going somewhere, far away. This was his last night at the Fairview Opera House, in which he had watched other graduation programs, watched and taken part in Memorial Day programs (in which Colonel George Merriam in his G. A. R. uniform, fading gradually but still a good fit, had been the leading figure on the stage), had been fired by an evening's "impersonation" of *A Singular Life* by Elizabeth Stuart Phelps, which had been one of his mother's favorite novels along with *The Gates Ajar*—a vision of heaven—by the same author. ("Nonsense!" according to Mrs. Merriam. "Minnie, what comfort can you find in such palpable nonsense?") Most clearly remembered of all was the home-talent operetta of some years ago, in which Mae Meserve had played the charming heroine, and which had contained within it a short "Cinderella" play for children, with Evvie as Cinderella and Philip himself as Prince Charming—the one time when Lyle had been jealous and had refused to speak to Philip for nearly a week. Here Philip had listened to lecturers, to some with eagerness, to some with adolescent coldness, thinking ar-

rogantly, I could do better than that myself. Always he had
felt pride that Fairview should have such a capacious and frequently used opera house. . . . All this Philip took in with
poignant vision, for the last time. He had expected to leave
Fairview, but not as he might now be leaving. It was incredible
to him that he should no longer be an active, happily, successfully functioning part of the community of Fairview.

All this time he had been listening acutely to the rolling out
of the names, his heart seeming to throb when certain names
were reached.

"Gladys Martha Cornwall."

With a sense of remorse Philip saw that sturdy figure, was
glad again of the applause that greeted the name.

"William Trent Cowie."

Momentarily Philip shifted his gaze.

"Evangeline Evans."

The light figure stepping daintily forward, infusing a sauci-
ness even into acceptance of the diploma from the portly Austin Cowie—Lyle's girl.

"Mortimer James Hungerford."

Mort—not exactly estranged, but no longer close to Philip.

"Lyle Hibbard Meserve."

With the reading of that name Philip felt a pang of loss, a
flaring-up of silent gratitude that made his eyes water. He
blinked and watched the slight figure, handsome tonight in the
new blue suit; and his gratitude, spreading within him, diffused
a sense of sweetness which lessened his tension and enabled
him to sit quietly, waiting. Wherever he went, he would never
forget Lyle. No friend would ever take Lyle's place.

Nearly all the chairs were now empty.

"Rodney Philander Wheeler."

So that was Boysie's full name! Boysie stepped forward with
solemn dignity. But there was always something funny. This
time it was Boysie's coat, in some manner getting caught on
his chair, so that Boysie had to turn around to find the trouble
and to yank the coat loose. In the expectant hush he was heard

to mutter, "Doggone." Audible giggles broke out. But the applause was more generous because of them.

Now came the final, fatal moment. Philip should have gloried in it. But his feet and hands were heavy.

"Philip Sidney Wood."

He walked across the lonely stage, did not glance at Hank, saw only Austin Cowie's small, cold eyes. The applause was again somewhat scattered, until Mr. Rakosi leaned forward and with flashing gallantry led a kind of "Bravo!" clapping— Eleanor Janeway striking her hands together, careless of her long white kid gloves. Others joined in, as if glad for the cue that some special reaction was called for. Philip went down the three steps from the stage to the noise almost of acclaim.

Commencement was over for the senior class, having been carried through with the genuineness, the good taste and talent, the lack of showiness which had always characterized these seniors (Boysie's mishap merely a small note of fun), and which made Miss Janeway, breathless from her vigorous clapping, take out the fragrant handkerchief tucked into one of her gloves and openly wipe her brimming hazel eyes. Mr. Rakosi patted her wrist. This exhibition of feminine sensibility he highly approved.

One act more remained—for the Methodist minister, a strikingly white-haired elderly man with kindly countenance, to climb the three steps, walk to the center of the stage, lift his hands, and pronounce the Benediction: not a speech, as had happened last year with another minister, but a true benediction.

"May the Lord bless you and keep you. May the Lord make his face to shine upon you and be gracious unto you. May the Lord lift up the light of His countenance upon you and give you peace. Amen."

Now it was fortunate that Philip's seat was at the end of the front row. He was able to slip out of the side door—the fire exit—before anyone could stop him and congratulate him.

The audience was milling around, people stopping to speak to the graduates and to each other. But John and Minnie Wood had left among the very first. Philip had a vague plan of catching up with them. His place was with them, no matter how his father's case might turn out. He was still their only son.

Who would walk home with Gladys? Philip owed something to Gladys. But his escort now would be a detriment to her. And he did not want to speak to anyone tonight, even though he could honestly have congratulated Gladys. She had her father and mother, if no one of her classmates asked to "see her home."

Philip felt the moist, cool freshness of this evening at the beginning of June. He was not a stranger as he walked through town past the well-known store buildings, but even now Fairview was not his home. He had a home nowhere.

He saw ahead of him his own parents, walking along slowly, turning at the corner which led into their street, their short block of houses. Minnie's slight figure in the spring coat was leaning on John's; he was again physically upholding her. Philip recognized the little shawl tied over her head. It was one of those which had come from the "effects" of Florence Merriam: of slightly crinkled silk of a very pale blue color, which Florence had picked up somewhere abroad. The delicate shawl was only one among the innumerable things, material and otherwise, which bound together the Woods and the Merriams.

Philip could easily have overtaken his parents, but instead he stayed behind them, feeling a kind of shyness, a mingling of devotion and estrangement. They had gone into the house before he himself entered the familiar front door. Philip had paused a moment on the porch to look across the yard in which he and his father had worked, often together, in companionable silence, or close to silence; and had looked over toward the dark rim of trees along the edge of the ravine.

In the front room, his mother was sitting in the rocking chair and his father on the couch. Minnie was undoing the knot of the scarf beneath her little chin. She was the kind of woman to whom a scarf was becoming, giving her at once the look of a little old-fashioned New England dame and a touch of the exotic.

Suddenly the couple appeared to Philip in a solitude far more tragic than his own. Philip thought of his long talk with Mrs. Merriam, of how much she had confided in him, and he felt entrusted with responsibilities which were being withheld, now, from his parents. For all the impassiveness and endurance of his father's attitude as he sat on the couch, there was an effect, somehow, of a broken spring in his whole person. Philip realized that with a feeling of chill. Oh, John could work— could do physical labor, would dig the proverbial ditches if it was necessary for Minnie's sake. But he was not the same man. His parents seemed to Philip to be living in a world of their own, a dream world, while he had stepped out of the dream into actuality. His father had showed suffering, but had not openly accepted responsibility.

As soon as Minnie saw Philip she ran to him. She put her arms around him and her head against his shoulder. Philip felt that she was again his mother.

"Oh, you were so good! You were splendid!"

"I didn't think so. I got through it," Philip said.

"Oh, no! You were the best one. You always are. You vindicated yourself, and us too!" Minnie looked up with large, intense eyes; then her face took on a tragic expression and she began to cry.

"Don't cry, Mama. *Don't.*" But even as he held her, Philip felt that her praise and her tears both were for something quite different from the things which concerned him.

Minnie controlled herself. She could not let herself cry while John sat on the couch, stricken, his handsome face now clay-colored, his hand again covering his eyes. Minnie almost instantly realized John's suffering. She went to sit beside him and forced his hand away from his eyes. For an instant Philip saw agony in those usually unreadable blue eyes. John did not offer his hand to his son, but Philip understood that it was because he could not; that with his son, who had recently been proclaiming noble hopes for the future of all mankind— deeply held, too, and partly the outcome of what John himself had apparently been teaching through example—John Wood was bitterly ashamed. Even John's interview with Colonel Merriam had not cut into him with such pain.

At that moment the telephone rang in the hall. Philip turned swiftly to answer it.

Jerry Storm was calling. "Philip, I couldn't catch you after the program. You disappeared like magic!"

Jerry's voice had an unexpected exuberance, almost gaiety, in it, which was very far from any emotion Philip felt. "Well, I wanted to tell you how fine your oration was, Philip! Mrs. Latham and Miss Blanchard agree. And other people."

"Oh, thanks, Mr. Storm! I didn't think I spoke very well. It seemed to me I was just rattling it off."

"I know that feeling, but the speaker isn't always the best judge. I took in all you said, and I'm going to think about it. Philip!" Jerry added.

"Yes, Mr. Storm?"

"I want to say something more. I just want to say how much we're all counting on you—in more ways than you can realize."

Philip felt the seriousness behind Jerry's words. He did not understand just what Jerry Storm meant. But he was grateful, and those tears which kept bothering him came to his eyes as he answered, "Thanks a whole lot, Mr. Storm."

Back in the front room, Philip told his parents that Reverend Storm had called and said he liked the oration.

"Well, I should think so!" Minnie exclaimed.

But now Minnie was suddenly very tired. "John, I wish you would carry me upstairs this evening." She laid her smooth black head against John's arm in an exaggeration of fatigue. John responded at once. He took off her light coat for her, leaving Philip to hang it in the hall closet, and picked Minnie up in arms that had lost none of their splendid strength.

Both John and Philip avoided contact with each other. Philip said only, "I'll lock up, Papa. You won't need to come back downstairs."

Philip heard with relief the climbing of the stairs, the closing of the bedroom door. He took his time about the small household chores, intending that his father and mother should have gone to bed before he himself went to his room.

He was enwrapped in the nighttime quiet of the house at the end of this street. The front room breathed of the personalities of his mother and father.

Then a thought brushed and bruised his mind like a thorn, stirred by some words one of the boys had let drop (it was Mort Hungerford, of all people): "Post, are you going to have an auction at your place?"

Philip had turned the question aside. "Haven't heard of any!"

Mort had mumbled something about, "Well, my mother wanted to know."

Auction? Were people talking about an auction? Mrs. Merriam, who had been so careful to prepare him for all eventualities, who had raised the question of a trial for John Wood, had not mentioned the possibility of an auction. Philip had tried to dismiss it from his mind, but the thorn had left its scratch and hurt again. Philip had sounded out Lyle. Lyle claimed to know nothing, and yet something in Lyle's manner—Lyle never could disguise his thoughts very well, in spite of being taciturn—made Philip think that he might have heard some rumor, too, that "the Woods will have to hold an auction at their place."

The idea seemed unreal. But for the first time Philip thought it might be true. All these familiar objects—perhaps even now they no longer belonged to the Wood family.

Philip usually took the room's furnishings for granted, but now he really saw them: his mother's silk scarf on the couch where she had tossed it; the secretary desk-and-bookcase at which his father had spent many hours, silently absorbed; his mother's small desk with the framed photograph of his father upon it, and one of himself in a natty sailor outfit, taken when he was five. She had wanted to dress him in Fauntleroy costume, but he had rebelled, and his father had upheld him, saying, "No, that wouldn't suit a big boy like Philip." Beside the desk hung the mysteriously meaningful photograph of Florence and Cora Merriam. All these pictures had been taken before Mr. Rakosi had come to Fairview, when old Mr. Jerell was still running the photograph gallery, so that the four faces, even his own, seemed to look at Philip out of the past.

Of course the pictures wouldn't be worth anything, would they? But Philip had a ghostly feeling, as if already the furnishings were removed from the room.

He shook off the feeling and went through the dining room into the kitchen. It was spotlessly clean but breathed a certain staleness of leftover cooking smells. The faucet dripped a little. Philip thought automatically, I must look at that tomorrow. Pain touched him, but he would not stop now to ask what it meant. Why had he talked about locking up? Few people in Fairview locked their doors at night. But Philip, for no reason of which he was conscious, closed the back door and turned the key fitting loosely in its lock. He had had just a glimpse, through the porch screen, of the morning-glory blossoms furled in the nighttime. Philip locked the front door also. Its key turned with a strange sound, slightly grating. Philip stood for a moment, staring at nothing. Finally he climbed the carpeted stairs.

Philip was once more in his own room. Rain had begun to fall gently upon the roof; and for an instant he felt his old happy security—but only for an instant.

Even this room was no longer his. Philip was aware of that before he knew why. He could not look at the photograph of the first grade on the steps of Old Central, or that of the summer baseball team which would soon be playing on the vacant lot near the fair grounds in the last of the June sunlight and the early twilight.

The room was even so a refuge. But from whom? From his own father and mother.

Philip stared at the few graduation presents set out on his table. The belief that "under other circumstances" there might well have been many ought to make him cherish these few all the more. In a way, he did—not the presents themselves so much as the loyalty of those who had given them; most of all, perhaps, the necktie sent him by way of the post office by Mr. and Mrs. Sayles, because it was unexpected. He did not care much for its ornate pattern, but that made no difference at all in his feeling of thanks. Yes, "in other circumstances" there would doubtless have been some token, of the kind which his mother called "comical," from Phoebe and Tommy Hardcastle, with whom Philip was a favorite. Even before he started going to school, he had gone to their trigly kept house with two shining pails of different sizes, one for milk and one for cream, and had waited in the kitchen, warmed by the cookstove, hearing the sober ticking of the old black-framed clock from England, while Phoebe filled the pails with thrifty exactitude. There might have been a card, at least, from his old teacher, Miss Schilling (Philip was still puzzled by her strange manner); and probably a thin book of verse, more suitable for a pious elderly person than for a boy of seventeen, from Miss Sadie Ashburton.

Why let himself be hurt by such omissions, or by the meagerness of the outlay upon his study table? Philip had never been touchy on such matters. But there had never been the need. Approbation and praise had come to him in abundant flow, "naturally," he would have thought, if he had thought about it at all.

Philip clenched his fists in self-scorn. What baby stuff! He was not going to sink into self-pity for the boy who had always received the most valentines, the most Christmas presents, the most of nearly all things which showed popularity and high standing among his schoolmates and fellow citizens. This boy had no inherent right to expect more than Dell Postel. He would have to harden himself to that knowledge. His father had done more vital injury to the community than Dan Postel ever had.

There was one more gift at which Philip had not yet looked. He had been reserving it, he himself scarcely knew why. The moment had come now. Philip went quietly to the table and got out from the drawer, which nobody but himself ever opened, the wrapped package which Mrs. Merriam had given him. He carefully undid the wrappings.

Philip had known from the shape and size of the package that it must contain a book. But he had thought— What had he thought? That it would be "something intellectual," some collection of essays or lectures. Not this! He held in his hands a very old Bible with slightly frayed black covers. He thumbed through the pages, seeing the old-fashioned printing with long *s*'s. He felt a deep disappointment and thrust the book back into the drawer.

How could Mrs. Merriam have supposed he would want *that?* There were plenty of Bibles around the house. Philip had his own, with name printed in gold letters on the knobbled cover—PHILIP SIDNEY WOOD. He had received it from the heads of the Sunday school, and it had been presented to him by his father, because for a year he had been neither absent nor tardy.

Those babyish tears came into his eyes again. It seemed to him that Mrs. Merriam had not understood him after all. Her quoting verses to him and asking a promise from him he had taken in good spirit. But did she think he needed to read the Bible more, perhaps to have it impressed on him further that his father had done wrong?

A kind of revulsion came over him, not only against the musty old Bible that Mrs. Merriam wanted to give him, but against all the religious training and churchgoing that he had experienced all his life. What did it mean? It had meant little—

or so it seemed to Philip now—to his father, and even less, in a way, to his mother. And what did it mean to other church people? Mr. Cowie, for example? Old Colonel Merriam, who scorned the church, seemed now, to the puzzled boy, the most truthful and decent man around.

Philip almost looked forward to their going away and starting over somewhere else. There he would not get caught in a lot of churchgoing but would be free to live his own life. He wanted to study out things for himself. He might even take a room apart from the folks.

He thought, Is there really a God? He had sometimes had mysterious feelings of the existence of a "Divine Being." But were these not childish fancies? He had no proof. As for Mrs. Merriam, her kindness had no doubt been well meant, but it seemed to him now only that of any motherly elderly woman, such as Mrs. Latham or Miss Blanchard.

But then he realized that he was unjust to Mrs. Merriam, particularly since he had not even opened the envelopes she had given him. He was sure that one, at least, contained some money. The other? Probably a message of some sort. For some curious reason Philip had left the envelopes sealed, not mentioning them to his parents. He hardly wanted to open them now. But he had to do so sometime.

The envelope marked "For Current Expenses" he opened first. It contained bills—crisp bills of ten-dollar denomination. Philip began counting them, half unbelieving. There were twenty of them: two hundred dollars. His eyes blurred. He felt that he had wronged Mrs. Merriam. This was a very large sum of money to Philip Wood, and the thought that Mrs. Merriam had entrusted it to him made him feel unworthy and at the same time proud.

After what seemed a long lapse of time, he took up the second envelope, marked only "Philip." He actually had to blink his eyes, hastily and half angrily, before he could see what was in it. The "message" was a cashier's check on the

First National Bank of Fairview, made out to "Philip S. Wood" and signed by Burdette Williston. It was for two thousand, five hundred dollars.

This piece of paper at first seemed entirely unreal. As he re-read it he was convinced that it was a mistake. He could feel himself trembling—with astonishment, incredulity, he did not know what. He whispered, "God!" The magnitude of this amount of money was out of relation to anything Philip knew; it did not belong in his own experience. Mrs. Merriam had done something of this incredible kind—and yet it was she and Colonel Merriam who would have to suffer most for his father's action. He whispered again, "God," before he put the two envelopes back in the drawer with shaking hands.

Ought he to take such gifts? He had already taken them. He could not go back to the Merriam house.

He began to move about automatically, getting ready for bed. He took off the coat of his gray suit and hung it carefully in the closet, as he had been taught to do. Then he stood for a space of time which was unmeasured and unnoticed. He was still trembling. Mrs. Merriam had had the draft made out to him—to "Philip S. Wood." She had given this sum to him with "full confidence." He did not know very much about the management of money. He and his mother had always been in awe of his father's ability there! Philip had received some small wages for helping Mr. Meserve in the lumber yard. But now he had this sum to handle. It had come to him, and not to his father and mother. He was afraid. And yet, what it might mean to his family! He could not take in the whole meaning at once.

Philip stopped and turned back suddenly to the drawer into which he had dropped the book, the old Bible, that Mrs. Merriam had given him. He was curious about it now.

It had a different aspect to him as he picked it up, not because it was a Bible but because he now sensed that it had some meaning he had missed before. He saw in a flash that it

was a family treasure of Mrs. Merriam's. On the mottled fly-
leaf he read what he had not noticed earlier, a signature and
date in elaborate, faded old handwriting:

Elijah Hale Bradford, D. D. 1837.

Beneath this name was a second signature, written with
clarity which resembled that of the earlier one, but freshly
penned, the handwriting both classic and characteristic:

To Philip Sidney Wood
From his friend Lydia Bradford Merriam.

And then in the same handwriting two verses carefully copied:

*"God is a Spirit: and they that worship him must worship him
in spirit and in truth." John 4:24.*

"God is love." 1 John, 4:8.

Philip, who had been a model Sunday-school scholar, took in
little of the familiar verses at this moment. Perhaps they were
too familiar. But now he felt more of what the gift of the book
meant, as coming from Mrs. Merriam. It would have been
passed on from generation to generation in the Bradford family, carrying its flavor of the ancestral past. But to whom would
it go in the Bradford family as now constituted? The two
daughters were dead. Bradford? Elaine? From Mrs. Merriam's
painful and careful words to him, Philip knew that she no
longer rested hopes on her son or her son's daughter as carrying on the things she valued. And he himself no longer thought
of courting or marrying Elaine. But, in giving him this family
heirloom, Mrs. Merriam seemed to be saying that she trusted
him, Philip Wood, to understand and cherish the things she
cherished.

In a sense—especially when he considered the other gifts—
she picked Philip as her heir. He realized that he had somehow expected to be the Merriams' heir!—but in no such way
as had come about.

Philip heard a sound from across the hall—his father's step in the other bedroom—and came back to the actuality of the present. He felt too young, too inexperienced, for the responsibilities that were gathering about him. Suddenly he saw in inward vision the furnishings of his parents' bedroom and thought again, with a more vivid flash, of that word "auction."

Philip had seen auctions of family goods, all of the family's possessions standing out nakedly in the yard. He saw his own few things that were about him here—his rather battered chiffonier, the table with the bookshelves he had made in his manual-training course. He had studied and done his homework at this table all through his school years. He looked at the little walnut bed with its handwoven coverlet. He saw all these things standing in the green grass of the side lawn. He had loved his room, and it would hurt him to have all his furniture put up for sale. But he could stand that. It was the furniture of the other bedroom that he could see now, being stared at and commented on. He could imagine the caustic remarks of Mrs. Rathbun, the bawdy comments of some of the boys as they looked over the big walnut bed. People would say how large the bed was, and what an old-timer. It was the bed in which he himself had been conceived and born—"as by a miracle," his mother had often said—into a bright world. Perhaps someone would lift the cane rocker to test its condition. Surely his mother's personal treasures would not have to be displayed and taken from her—the beautiful old glass bowl which Mrs. Merriam had given her, and the set of water pitcher and dozen tumblers of rose color faintly frosted with white, which had been a wedding present from the Adult Bible Class? The scene was almost too awful to think about. Could his mother survive it at all?

Philip was certain of this much: his mother and father would not be exposed to the auction if it came. He himself would have to be there. Lyle would stay with him. But he would be essentially alone. He could not count upon anybody but himself.

Well, did he expect to go through life without suffering? He had spoken glibly in his Sunday-school class about the need for it. Other people suffer, he told himself hardily. Why shouldn't I? Standing by his own bed, he bent and struck the mattress with his fist. If he had got through his Valedictory in front of an audience of people, he could get through the auction—even though the house furnishings, once so handsome and satisfying, now seemed plain old stuff which nobody would care to buy except the people who were looking for something for nothing.

There was no use in dwelling upon the scene. He would go through with it when the time came, and probably worse ones. The strain of fierceness which had made him knock the ball farther than anyone else on the team, steal bases, and dare homers, never allow any of the fellows to twit him because he helped his mother at home, would come to his aid, whether or not there would be other help. Yet it was poor help, in a way, held no conclusive answers.

Philip suddenly felt very tired. He could not settle everything tonight. He finished undressing, turned out the light, got into bed.

Still the images passed before him: the blank stare of Charlotte Dissendorfer's china-doll eyes; Austin Cowie's hooded cold eyes as he held out Philip's diploma; the sensation of his giving his Valedictory address, which it seemed he could not even hear. He did hear Jerry Storm's voice, happy over the telephone: "I'm going to think about it. . . . counting on you —in more ways than you can realize!" He saw the broken-spring look of his father's posture.

There loomed before him the talk that he would have to have with his father, soon, to plan the future ahead of them all. Philip felt a paralyzing embarrassment. He again saw his father carrying his mother upstairs, and it seemed to him that it was he, now, who had to carry them both.

Yet somehow he felt the beginning of a strength in himself that was of a different kind from his old easy exuberance. It was steadier, more wary. He inwardly braced himself, as he had felt his mother do physically time and again. Even if he went to a new place, to make a new start, something of his life here in Fairview would go with him. Gladys Cornwall, Lyle, Jerry Storm, Hank, Mrs. Merriam—all of them, in different ways, had stood by him and proved their friendship for him. He felt the meanness of fair-weather friendship, and in a way he was embarrassed for Mort and for Will Cowie.

"God is love." "God is a Spirit." "Spirit and truth." What had Mrs. Merriam meant by writing down those verses? How is God "love"?—or "spirit" or "truth," either? Is this how God "tests" or "tries" people (as he used to say so easily in Sunday school)—in just such actual situations as Philip was trying to live and breathe in now?

He was using the word "God" again, which he had not meant to do. But he felt no more the prickly sensation he used to feel sometimes as a little boy.

Dimly Philip seemed to catch meanings that had never come to him before—or snatches of meanings. Could he "love" his parents in some such sense as he now glimpsed—because they were his parents, and were people? They must come first now, in any case—before he could think of a Gladys Cornwall, or an Elaine, or any other "new love" of his own. His love for John and Minnie was the "old love" which at present claimed him. Philip partially understood that it was turning into compassion.

He lay and stared into almost darkness. He had thought first of Gladys Cornwall, and *then* of Elaine. He was not in love with Gladys. Was he still in love with Elaine? Where Elaine's image had so long been secretly cherished, there was now what people must mean when they speak of "an aching void." Philip thought he would never know more of that slight body, exquisitely made, fine-grained, white with faint pink—the wild glint of blue eyes. He would not find and bring home the lost child.

Philip had joyfully believed in his inmost mind—not open

even to Lyle—that the name "Philip Sidney" exactly suited
him. He had never read Sir Philip Sidney's sonnets—nor had
his mother. Both Minnie and Philip knew only that Sir Philip
had given his cup of water to his dying enemy—the occasion
about which Bradford Merriam had jested in his manner. Philip
had secretly, confidently believed that he himself would have
done just that. In the same way, he had supposed he could rescue Elaine. With sorrow he had to leave her in that half-illusory
world out of which he had stepped.

The cool night air of June came in through the open window, redolent and freighted with the odors of growing things
in Fairview, which was no longer Philip's home—the "nice
town" in the wide, rolling countryside smelling of deep, rich,
plowed earth and young green corn; the muddy river flow-
ing through Merriam's Grove under the bent boughs and
heavy foliage of virgin timber. Rain was again falling inter-
mittently.

Confusion instead of clear confidence. But the boy had
strength. The ground may have been, as one of the Meserves
had said, "cut from under his feet," but there was still, somewhere underneath, a foundation.

Philip's last image was that of a long, dark tunnel, at the far
end of which there seemed to be light; although he could not
give a name to the light, and did not know what its meaning
was, or why it should be there.